M000205933

Time Management

a novel

S.W. Clemens

From Scott Clemens

To Scott Ashcraft

Copyright © 2015 Scott W. Clemens

Fezziwig Publishing Co.

All rights reserved. No part of this book may be reproduced or transmitted in any form or by any means, electronic or mechanical, including photocopying, recording, or by an information storage and retrieval system, without permission in writing from the author.

This is a work of fiction. Any resemblance it bears to reality is entirely coincidental.

ISBN 978-0-9966123-5-7

Also by S.W. Clemens

With Artistic License

For my children, Jonathan, Colin and Elaine, who fill my days with joy and gratitude

"The creation of the world did not take place once and for all time, but takes place every day." — Samuel Beckett

"We all have our time machines. Those that take us back are memories. And those that carry us forward are dreams." – H.G. Wells

Forethought

Each day a whole world passes away, largely unappreciated, numbly relegated to obligation, commerce and routine. One day seems as unremarkable as the next. It's only through the inexorable accretion of days, weeks, months and years, that we come to appreciate with heartbreaking clarity how incredibly unique and precious each lost day has been. — SWC

Prologue

Virginia Porter awoke to the cell phone looping a jaunty marimba tune on the nightstand.

"I didn't wake you, did I?"

It was her daughter Rosalynn (Rosie), and her voice was chipper, so she knew it couldn't be bad news. "It's all right; I should be up by now anyway." The clock by the bed read 8:31 a.m. Virginia scrunched the pillow behind her head and glanced to the empty side of the bed. Her husband awoke each morning at 6:00, rain or shine, summer or winter, happily adhering to a self-imposed schedule that hadn't varied in 40 years. "Why are you calling so early?"

"I was thinking about taking you out to lunch. I have to be down the peninsula for a meeting with our broker at 10:00. I was hoping we could meet at the Stanford Shopping Center."

The center was a high-end mall and Virginia quickly rooted through her memory of restaurants there while calculating the cost. "Can we go someplace cheaper?"

"It'll be my treat," Rosie said. Unlike her brother Jeffrey, she never worried about the cost, because she'd never *had* to worry. She'd married an attorney 11 years her senior (her first marriage, his second). In the beginning they'd lived in San Bruno, and as his practice had grown they'd moved north, first to the City, then to Marin County.

"I don't feel comfortable in those places."

"There's a Greek restaurant in downtown Palo Alto — Gyros — casual, not too expensive."

"That sounds good."

"11:30?"

"Fine, I'll see you soon. Love you."

Virginia rolled out of bed and padded across the creaking floorboards to the bathroom. It would be good to get out of the old house. In many ways she felt as though she were living alone; her husband of 44 years had never been much of a conversationalist. There was a nervous industriousness about him that had not flagged in all the years they'd been together. He was always out in the orchards, or fixing some equipment in the barn, or reading farm journals. And lately he'd been taking unannounced "walks," disappearing for three our four hours at a stretch.

She showered and dressed and went downstairs for breakfast. Randall had made a pot of coffee. She poured herself a cup and added half-and-half and sugar (her daughter had lately been touting the health benefits of agave syrup, but Virginia had never taken advice from her daughter whose passions seemed to change with the seasons).

As a concession to her doctor, who insisted that she lower her cholesterol, she made an omelette with egg whites and low fat mozzarella. Randall had left a coffee cup, a plate of half-eaten toast and the morning paper on the table. That he left his mess for her to clean up struck her as a mark of disrespect, yet her sense of order would not allow her to just leave it be, and she grumbled to herself as she rinsed his plate and cup and put them into the dishwasher, as annoyed with herself for not being able to let it go, as with him for leaving the mess in the first place.

She checked her watch. It was 10:35. She would have to leave no later than 11:00 if she were to meet Rosie by 11:30. So she went to the back door and called toward the barn for her husband. No answer. She walked down the hall to the front porch where she surveyed their property, looking for signs of movement. Ahead of her the land sloped down to the creek and the vineyard on the other side, which spread out to the edge of a housing development built on land they'd once owned. Beyond the houses loomed the dark eastern flanks of the Santa Cruz Mountains. She looked to her left, to the south orchard and again called her husband's name. No answer. She stepped off the porch and headed around back toward the barn, thinking that he may have gone off on an errand. But his truck was parked next to her car in front of the barn. She searched the barn, even going so far as to climb the ladder to the loft. She called out once again, feeling foolish now, and a bit miffed. This wasn't the first time he'd wandered off; he'd been making a habit of it lately. It angered her, because it was inconsiderate. It worried her, because it was out of character, and that could signal a couple of scary possibilities — a brain tumor, or early onset Alzheimer's.

Back in the house she was beginning to feel a whisper of trepidation. He wasn't so very old, but when a man reached his mid-sixties, there was always the gruesome possibility he could have had a stroke or a heart attack, or he might have taken a bad fall somewhere and was unconscious. And what then? The thought gave rise to competing emotions — fear, as she contemplated how truly lonely her life would be without him, and annoyance that he stubbornly refused to carry a cell phone.

She took a quick look into each room, noting with dismay her husband's profligate use of electricity. Lights were burning in the office, in the half-bath under the stairs, in the hall and in the dining room, which she now dutifully turned off. In the kitchen she turned off the light over the stove and unplugged the coffee pot, a potential fire hazard if left on all day. She opened the door to the root cellar and peered down the stairs. Another light illuminated the shelves of canned goods below. *Ca-ching, ca-ching!* she thought. *No wonder our electric bill is so high.* "Randall?" she called out one last time. But she could see he wasn't there and flipped off the light switch.

Then she wrote a note and left it under the saltshaker on the kitchen table. It was a note her husband was never to read.

PART ONE

Something Missing

Chapter 1
Jeffrey's Problems Exposed

All of Jeffrey's problems could be summed up in two words: Time Management. There was never enough time to do all he needed to do, let alone wanted to do. If he was deficient — as a son, brother, husband, father, employee, neighbor, friend, citizen, human being — it could all be laid at the feet of poor time management.

Usually he was too busy to think about it, and when he did it was with a real sense of frustration and desperation. No solutions presented themselves. The years tumbled by one after the other, and like Sisyphus he didn't seem to be getting any further ahead. Sometimes he just wanted to scream.

At the moment this thought occurred to him he was in an airplane at 37,000 feet, hurtling through the sky at something like one mile every seven seconds, on his way home to San Francisco. From this height the horizon curved, the sky above turned a deep cobalt blue, the outside air was 60 degrees below zero and too thin to breathe. Jeff was too frazzled to be aware of any of it. *They pack us in like frigging sardines,* he thought, flexing his ankles.

Since 9/11, seven years ago this very day, travel had become more inconvenient than ever, with limits on what you could pack and carry on board, and far fewer flights, which resulted in over-booking, over-crowding, and longer delays at the baggage carousel. Or worse — lost luggage, lost time. If the terrorists had accomplished nothing more, he mused, they had spawned the huge bureaucracy of Homeland Security and stolen time from every passenger who was forced to shuffle through interminable security checks. Millions of hours. Billions of hours.

These days he traveled light, cramming all he could into his carry-on luggage. It saved time — 45 minutes, give or take 15 — which was not insignificant at the end of a trip. He always took the window seat so he could turn his attention away from his seat-mate; he dreaded conversing with fellow passengers, as there never seemed to be a polite way to end the conversation and get on with his work. He had spent enough flights listening to people blather on about nothing. This particular idiot was wearing a Rolex. *What kind of fool would knowingly spend thousands of dollars for outdated technology?* he wondered. After all, a Rolex was just a watch. His own $40 Casio could tell time in two time zones, could work underwater to a depth of 50 meters, had a stop watch, an alarm function, a count down timer, a nightlight, and could store up to 15 phone numbers. That was a timepiece you could count on.

Jeffrey Porter was...what shall we say? — any number of adjectives would suffice. However, the usual convention is to insert a man's profession here (doctor, lawyer, teacher, accountant), as if that is his defining characteristic. But honestly, by the age of 43 Jeff found himself (through a series of missteps and blunders, through necessity and pragmatic compromise, by roads taken and abandoned) a jack-of-all-trades. Since earning a degree in Visual Communication he'd been a dishwasher, short-order cook, clerk, bookbinder, winery "cellar rat," photo-journalist, commercial photographer, travel writer, graphic artist, ad salesman, wine critic, and editor. He had never aspired to anything but photo-journalism; the rest just sort of happened, the way things do.

His current occupation was Managing Editor of *Gourmet Traveler*, and if his profession were to provide him with a last name (as presumably "Porter" had provided his ancestor with the family name) he might have been Jeff Wordsmith, Jeff Wineman, Jeff Imagemaker, Jeff Bookbinder, or Jeff Journeyman.

He was on his way home from back-to-back press trips to Grenada and Jamaica. He'd spent the last three days in Jamaica touring the restaurants of posh resorts and floating down a river on a bamboo raft, preceded by three days in Grenada, the Spice Island of the Caribbean, where he'd visited spice plantations, a rum distillery and an artisan chocolate manufacturer. He had seen flying fish and a remarkable double rainbow arching over Port St. George's. It had been a good trip filled with new experiences and abundant material to fill the pages of the magazine.

As Managing Editor he usually delegated all press trips to freelancers, as his editorial duties left him too little time to indulge in wanderlust: he was too busy coordinating with his publisher, with writers, photographers, advertisers and advertising reps, the graphic artist, copy editor, copy writer, editorial assistant, printer and newsstand distributor. But this last month his publisher had announced that they had a "cash flow problem" and could not afford to pay the freelance writer and photographer who had been assigned. The press trips, around which advertising had already been sold, could not be postponed, so it fell upon Jeff to both take the photographs and write the articles, in addition to his usual duties.

Over the years he had worked for three other magazines with "cash flow problems," and each time the magazine had gone under owing him a boatload of money that he would never see. Nonetheless, the unstable and capricious nature of publishing had led to his acquiring many of the skills that now made him so valuable, if underpaid. Depending on who was on vacation and who had recently been fired or had quit, he was often called on to fill other roles. Such "assignments of necessity" had never made him much money, but they had expanded his talents and had landed him, for better or for worse, in his current position. And now there were more "cash flow problems."

He knew better than to expect a sympathetic ear from anyone; fresh off a luxury tour of the Caribbean it would have seemed petty. It was, as his wife was quick to point out, a "First World problem." In any event there was no use complaining about it — most of his friends and family would gladly have traded places with him. What they didn't understand was that the trips were never relaxing, his other work backed up when he was gone, and upon his return he was under an urgent deadline to turn his impressions into a stellar article that would make both his employer and his hosts happy. And at the end of the year it didn't put enough money in the bank to justify the hours.

It gnawed at him that his salary was grossly inadequate to support his family, despite the hours he spent working. Carolyn had always made more money, even on her meager high school teacher's salary, and in the early days when Abby and Jake were toddlers his income had been barely enough to pay for daycare. As it was, they had never put away enough to buy a house. It was all they could do to make payments on a small, two bedroom, two-bath condo in Foster City, on landfill at the edge of San Francisco Bay. At first the kids had slept in a bunk bed, but now that they were older (14 and 11), Jeff had divided their room with a floor to ceiling bookcase, and hung curtains to give a modicum of privacy, though the room still had just one door.

On this return trip he'd spent the day, as he spent far too many days now, both anxious and annoyed. The small turbo-prop from Jamaica had been hot (some problem with the air conditioning), and they'd flown a weaving path around thunderheads, through periods of such intense turbulence that the lady across the aisle had heaved her cookies. She got most of it in the barf bag, but had sprayed the rest across of the back of the facing seat, and the smell kept re-circulating throughout the cabin making a number of passengers queasy and grumpy.

By the time they arrived in Miami, twenty minutes behind schedule, he'd had to sprint to make his connecting flight. Hot and sweaty from his run, he'd strapped himself into his seat with a pervasive sense of being harried and anxious, and nervously picked up the in-flight magazine. Nothing new — he'd already read it in the other direction. For a man with too much to do and not enough time to do it, this was a sardonic moment — he could do nothing until they were in the air, as electronic devices were prohibited until they reached cruising altitude. And he was parched.

Half an hour into the flight the snack and beverage service began (he had a small bottle of Chardonnay with his pretzels). That was followed by the movie (a vapid romantic comedy), and then the meal service, such as it was (service had gone downhill post 9/11, another present from mid-eastern malcontents).

A gin-and-tonic lolled him into a dream-like reverie as the flat-topped bluffs of Monument Valley passed by below. The man next to him leaned over to look out the window.

"Can you imagine," the man asked rhetorically, "crossing that desert in a horse-drawn wagon?"

"Hmm, not really," Jeff replied, hoping that was enough to satisfy his seat-mate without inviting further conversation. He fished in his coat pocket and brought out his newest acquisition — an Apple iPhone. Carolyn had gone ballistic when he'd brought it home. It wasn't just the initial cost, but the additional monthly data fee that annoyed her. But he'd patiently explained how he needed it for his work (the fact that he'd gotten along just fine without it for the preceding 43 years notwithstanding). But it really was a marvelous gadget. He plugged in his earphones and listened to Bill Evans and Stan Getz while he set about sorting through the photographs he'd taken on the trip. He had better cameras, but the iPhone gave him 2 megapixel images, and that was overkill for a print magazine. He'd learned his craft in college using a 35mm Nikon, and for a decade he'd traveled with a camera bag filled with heavy lenses, filters, film canisters, flash and tripod. Now he could carry all he needed in his pocket — no cost for film or developing, no need to bracket exposures.

The new technology allowed him to do so much more. Though whether that was a blessing or a curse was debatable, for now that he could do so much more, so much more was now expected of him. Such amazing leaps had been made in software, not to mention the internet, that it was now possible for one person to do what it had taken a dozen people to do just a decade earlier. Film developers, photo retouchers, color separators, layout artists and typesetters had all gone the way of the Dodo. It could all be done digitally: If forced to, he could resize, filter and touch-up photographs, receive and edit articles, check facts, layout the copy and give the final approval to the printer in Kentucky all by himself. He hoped it wouldn't come to that.

But now *Gourmet Traveler* was having "cash flow problems," a clear warning signal, and he couldn't help but worry. If he were to lose his job once again, they would fall further behind. The bills were relentless: car, mortgage, condo fees, utilities, food, clothing, medical insurance, entertainment, saving for college. Worrying about bills was a burden that sucked the joy out of life. When he was young and daydreaming about a future as a National Geographic photographer, bills had never entered the equation. That, he supposed, was why it was called day *dreaming* — reality conveniently stepped aside. But the future had a way of becoming the present, and in the present the demands of the moment weighed on his mind. Somewhere along the way he had left the insouciance of youth behind.

He knew he should be happier, particularly when he compared his lot with others he came across in his travels, those limited by health or education, people who could barely afford a pair of shoes, yet many of them seemed perfectly content, if not happy. He remembered a little girl of perhaps four, standing in a clean white dress beside her stick hut in a Yucatan jungle, smiling and waving as their bus bounced and juddered down the narrow dirt track stirring up a cloud of dust. He'd turned to take a photo, too late, but the image was burned into his memory.

Similarly, on Grenada he'd met an unfortunate old woman who seemed, if not happy, at least content with her lot in life. The six visiting journalists had been driven up a winding dirt road, surrounded by dense vegetation, to the Dougalston spice plantation. They'd been escorted into a long, low, grey wood building that had been weathering in the jungle since before the American Revolution. It was a dim room without electricity, lit by an open door and four windows. The warped and dusty floorboards creaked with each step. The guide led them to a table laid out with raw spices: a cinnamon branch, balls of nutmeg, mace, cloves and allspice. As the guide spoke, Jeff looked around the room for a photograph. Sunlight filtered through a cloudy window, lighting a wooden table piled with mace, the spice derived from the lacy red covering of the nutmeg shell. An elderly black woman sat on a worn bench before the table, carefully sorting mace into three piles. Her cotton print dress hung so limply that it must have seen two hundred washings. Her moist eyes were red with irritation. She hummed a tune softly. Jeff disengaged himself from the group and sat beside her on the bench, watching her deft fingers sort bits of mace from the main pile into the three smaller piles.

"Hi, I'm Jeff Porter."

"Where are you from, Mr. Porter?" she asked in reedy old voice, never looking up, nor pausing from her work.

"California, San Francisco."

"My daughter lives in Miami."

"What are the three piles?"

"Mace. I sort them: Bad, good enough and best."

"How can you tell the difference?"

"Honey, after 50 years I just know." Her fingers nimbly pushed the curled, dried mace from a watermelon-sized mound to three smaller mounds, one small piece at a time. "I got job security; you can't teach a machine to do this."

"Would you mind if I took your picture?"

"What anybody want with a pi'ture o' me for?"

"It's for a story on spice."

She shrugged. "Suit yourself."

He took a few shots of her hands, then of the piles of mace, then a few portraits. She just kept working and humming.

He said, "I'll need a name for the caption."

"Delta Duprey," she said and spelled it for him.

Jeff wrote the name in his pocket notebook. "It must be hard on your eyes," he observed.

"It's harder now, since I broke my glasses. Can't afford new ones."

"Try these." Jeff handed her his reading glasses (they were just simple magnifiers he'd bought at the drugstore for $10), wondering why her employer didn't think to give her a new pair. She put them on.

"That's much better. My daughter is going to send me new ones," she said, pausing to hand the glasses back.

"Keep them; I've got an extra pair in my luggage."

She nodded her head, put the glasses back on, and went back to work with a Mona Lisa smile on her face.

One of the journalists called from the doorway. "Jeff, we're all in the van. Let's go!"

"Thanks for the photos," Jeff said.

"Thank *you* for the glasses," Delta Duprey said.

How could he complain when he compared his lot in life to the Delta Dupreys of the world? He was fortunate on so many levels; yet even as he reminded himself of all that he had to be grateful for, he couldn't deny the niggling thought that his own wife worked harder than she should have to, that he had achieved less than he should have, that he was a lesser man than he should be.

It all came down to time and how he spent it. If he had more time he could find a better job. If he had more time he could be a more attentive father, a more loving husband, a more helpful son. If he had more time he would get in shape, learn to play the piano, put together the photo essay he'd been planning for at least 15 years. If he had more time...

Jeff was 43 and not getting any younger.

Chapter 2
A Nasty Surprise

Flying east to west Jeff gained three hours, which would bring him into San Francisco at 1 PM. He figured he'd have about two and a half hours before Carolyn and Abby and Jake all came home from their respective schools, time he'd use to go over the day's emails — queries from freelancers, missives from PR firms hoping to coax editorial space for their clients. And there would be snail mail. Carolyn would've already done a preliminary sort, weeding out any mail that might have been of interest to her, but he knew it would still take time to sort through the bills and business correspondence before tossing unread pamphlets, credit card come-ons, charitable requests and mail-order catalogues into the recycling bin. If he had time, he would download, resize and touch-up the photos he'd taken on the trip.

Then it would be time to cook dinner for his family (Carolyn only cooked on rare occasions), followed by his post trip routine of laundry and deciding what to do with the brochures and press materials foisted on him by his erstwhile hosts. It was usually while he was cooking or unpacking that Carolyn would fill him in on the minor crises that had occurred during his absence. And there were always crises. A week was not a long time to be gone, yet on previous trips the washer had broken down, the power company had threatened to turn off the electricity, one or another of them had been ill or injured, the car battery had died. There was always something.

The condo in Foster City was just ten minutes south of the airport, built on landfill at the edge of the bay. Each condo had a boat slip, though few owners actually kept a boat, as flat-bottomed skiffs and kayaks were the only boats capable of navigating the canals at low tide.

He knew something was wrong as soon as he pulled the Silver Subaru into the driveway and punched the button to raise the garage door. As it rolled back on its hinges, he saw Carolyn's white Honda Civic. She was supposed to be teaching a high school History class. Either she or one of the kids was sick, he surmised, or maybe she'd lost her job. She was in the doorway by the time he shut off the engine, a grim look on her face that did nothing to reassure him. Worst-case scenarios raced through his mind. "What is it?" he prodded, thinking *just give it to me quick.*

"I didn't want to leave a note...your mother...," she began, and in that split second Jeff could see his mother in a hospital bed, hooked up to a monitor. "Your mother's been frantic; your father's disappeared."

Jeff's mind reeled back from the hospital room and tried to make sense of the last sentence. "What? What does that mean — disappeared?"

"He went missing Monday. She left a message here Tuesday morning, but by then I'd already left for school, so I couldn't do anything until that night, and it didn't seem worthwhile to call you to cut short your trip when you'd be home in a day and a half anyway."

"I don't understand. So what does that mean? Did they have an argument or something?" A man didn't just pick up and leave a 44-year marriage without kicking up a little dust on his way out the door.

He knew his mother had been suspicious that something was wrong, ever since she'd taken him aside at his father's birthday party in August, but he hadn't taken it seriously. "I think you should know," she'd confided, "that your father has been acting strangely these past couple of months. He's become distant, and he's taken to disappearing for hours at a time; he won't say where he's been, just says he's been out walking."

If it were anyone else, Jeff might have suspected another woman was involved, but at 66-years-old Randall Porter was shaped like a pear, and as wrinkled as a desiccated apple. Who would want him?

"I'm worried he may be showing signs of dementia or something," his mother had gone on. "He seems preoccupied. And when he's not out walking, he's down in the root cellar tinkering with one thing or another for hours on end; I barely see the man. I wish you'd talk to him and find out what he's up to."

Jeff had rolled his eyes at the thought. Though he loved his father, he had to admit that theirs had been an adversarial relationship ever since high school. Randall valued tradition as much as Jeff valued innovation. Randall hated change as much as Jeff found change invigorating. From Jeff's point of view, his father was judgmental. From Randall's point of view, his son lacked the courage to take a moral stance. "Ask Rosie; he'll *talk* to her," Jeff had said, referring to his sister, whose eccentricities had never seemed to bother his father.

"Rosie can't draw him out the way you can."

Nonetheless, he'd found nothing amiss when he attempted to sound out his father who took umbrage at the questioning. "Are you really interested, or has your mother put you up to this?"

"She's worried. She thinks you've been acting strange."

"I think *she's* losing it," the elder Porter had countered with more than a little annoyance.

"The walks..."

"Oh for God's sakes — she's got a bee in her bonnet. I don't know what her problem is; I walk for my health. What's wrong with that? I swear — if anyone's acting strange around here, it's her."

Had all that been dissembling? Was his father hiding something? Had he wandered off in a haze of dementia? Or had his mother driven him from the house with her incessant worrying?

Carolyn took Jeff in her arms. He felt stiff. "It'll be okay," she whispered in his ear.

He buried his face in her shoulder-length auburn hair and breathed the comforting scent of her. "I know; he'll show up. If nothing else, we can track him by his credit card trail."

"That's just it; that's why the police are concerned — he didn't take his car or his wallet; he didn't take any clothes or suitcases as far as anyone can tell. He just vanished. They're treating it as a missing-person case. Your mother's been out of her mind, as you can imagine. Your sister's been holding down the fort; she needs your help."

She pulled back and looked into his eyes, trying to see how he was taking the news. After 20 years she knew him almost as well as she knew herself, but they'd never experienced a loss before. *A death*, she thought, for though she would never come right out and say it, she thought it probable that Randall was dead. She was relieved to see worry instead of fear, a calculating mind instead of trembling emotion. They needed to stay focused on what they could do to help.

Jeff called Rosie's cell phone. She wasn't encouraging. "It's about time," she answered curtly. "I've been staying with her during the day, but I have to get back to my kids. Her doctor has her on anti-anxiety pills, which seem to help; she's sleeping now. I think it's the first sleep she's had in days. I don't know what to do; I've got a life; I can't stay here holding her hand all day; but I don't want her to wake up and find herself all alone. You gotta get your ass down here."

He'd never liked the bossy way his kid sister talked to him. "Give me thirty minutes."

After he'd hung up Carolyn said, "I haven't told the kids; I didn't want to worry them. When you come back just pretend you're coming from the airport."

"We'll have to tell them *some*time."

"Maybe he'll be back soon."

"It's been four days."

"I know, but we can hope."

A man didn't just go missing for no reason, and all of the reasons he could think of had bad consequences.

Chapter 3
The House With Two Cellars

The home ranch lay just south of San Jose, nestled in a cul-de-sac formed by an eastern spur of the Santa Cruz Mountains. The ranch was only 40 minutes from Foster City, and Jeff barely noted the miles as he sped south on 101, his mind a whirl of speculation as he struggled to come to terms with the situation, vacillating between anger and distress, first at the thought that his father may have abandoned his mother, second at the more likely possibility that his father was dead or dying. Perhaps he had wandered off on a mountain trail and broken a leg, fallen down an old well, or been killed by a mountain lion.

On one level Jeff was in crisis mode, calm and detached, focused and intent on taking charge of the situation and doing whatever needed to be done. It was the frame of mind he fell into when rushing to the hospital with one emergency or another, and there had been a number — Abby's appendicitis, Jake's cut fingers, Carolyn's concussion, his own cracked rib (they weren't an accident prone family, but stuff happens). On a more subliminal level he struggled to come to grips with the possibility that his father was no longer alive, and that the tension that had come to characterize their relationship would never be resolved. He loved his father, but he had a sense that his father was disappointed in him. It was obvious as much from what the elder Porter didn't say, as from what he did, the subtle looks of disapproval, the sighs, the way he always found some chore to attend to when Jeff came to visit.

Theirs had been a close, though reserved, relationship until Jeff developed his own interests in high school and college. Randall barely said a word about it when Jeff announced, with the brazen disdain of a teenager, that he had no intention of being a farmer, chained to a piece of dirt and living in a creaky old house that was too hot in the summer and too drafty in the winter. No, he had a bigger vision — he would be a National Geographic photographer and travel the world. He would sit in Paris cafés, stroll the cobbled streets of Rome, trek through Patagonia, and dive the Great Barrier Reef. It was a young man's fantasy, and if it was unrealistic, so be it; he was young and he would have his way. Randall just shook is head in dismay and said, "Get real."

But who was he to talk about "getting real?" Had Randall been realistic himself? Could he hold his own life up for inspection and say, "See what I've built; you would do well to follow my example"? On the contrary, Randall had held onto this property not on the promise of what it could be in the future, but on the antiquated and unrealistic vision of what it had been in the past. He might have left with his older brothers to grow almonds and corn in the Central Valley. But Randall had remained in upper Santa Clara Valley, which soon became colloquially known as Silicon Valley.

If observation had taught Jeff anything, it was that farming was a hard and unsteady life, a path to be avoided. It had certainly never been easy for his father. As the water table dropped with the growing population, Randall had been forced to drill deeper and deeper wells. There were good years and bad, but it was always one step forward, two steps back, so that little by little his financial situation became untenable. The nail in the coffin came in the 1990's when the local Planning Commission voted to change the zoning from agricultural to mixed agriculture and housing. Taxes tripled overnight. Encroaching housing developments, citing health concerns, sued to stop him from spraying his crops. It was all too much.

With mounting debts, he'd eventually been forced to sell off pieces of the ranch, and much to his amazement, with the change of zoning the land had become a good deal more valuable. The upper Chenin Blanc vineyard, now part of a municipal golf course, had netted them enough to pay off their loans and invest a good chunk in stocks. The peach orchard, now the proposed site of a county park, had made them financially comfortable. In his 60s, Randall found himself a "gentleman farmer" with half an acre of plums, half an acre of apricots, four acres of Zinfandel, and a little nest egg to supplement their Social Security.

All this was not lost on his son who, by the age of 40, had learned a few things from watching his father's financial ups and downs — that hard work was no guarantee of success, and it was better to be lucky than smart. Now, it seemed, his father's luck had run out.

Jeff transitioned from 101 to the Almaden Expressway, heading west, then exited onto surface streets, working his way south through a housing development that lay on top of what had once been a vineyard and an orchard.

The house stood in the shade of two enormous oaks and a laurel on an alluvial bench above a small seasonal creek, bordered on the east and south by a low set of rolling hills that were lush and verdant with grass in the winter and spring, and dry and yellow in the summer and autumn. A mile to the west the thickly wooded Santa Cruz Mountains rose steeply to 2,000 feet, covered on their lower flanks by oak and madrone, giving way to fir and redwood on the upper slopes.

The house was a compact, 2,700 square foot, two-story Gothic Revival with tall ceilings and narrow windows. Four bedrooms and a sewing room were upstairs. The office, parlor, dining room and kitchen occupied the ground floor. From the outside the house appeared to have changed little over the years, with the exception of gingerbread detailing added in the 1890's, and a twisted-brick chimney that replaced the one that fell in the 1906 earthquake.

Sometime before 1920 two and a half bathrooms had been added, the formal dining room shortened to make way for a laundry room, and the kitchen had been modernized.

As originally planned and laid out, it was to have had one large basement under the kitchen and dining room at the back of the house. However, when the workmen began digging they found a huge boulder smack dab in the middle of the proposed excavation. Rather than move the house, two smaller cellars were dug, one on either side of the rock, the root cellar on the south side accessed from the kitchen, and the wine cellar on the north side accessed from the dining room. They had retained their designations through multiple owners by virtue of the brass plaques affixed to each door, though neither cellar had ever been confined to its designated purpose. The boulder formed one wall of each cellar, the other walls being of adobe bricks that had been plastered over. The floors were of slate.

That the house contained two cellars was unusual but no secret. The real secret lay hidden for more than a century. In 1977 Jeff was 12-years-old and starting work on his geology merit badge. His father had given him a Boy Scout rock pick for his birthday, and for a week that summer Jeff and Buster, his Lab, scoured every part of their property, crisscrossing the alluvial bench, pulling rocks out of the streambed, roaming up the gently rounded, grass covered hills on the east, crossing the narrow valley and climbing the steep, forested slopes of the Santa Cruz Mountains to the west. All along the way he broke off chunks of rock to add to his collection — feldspar, quartz, mica, iron pyrite, flint and granite.

One evening over dinner he told of the progress he'd made and asked if he could take a sample of rock from the cellar.

"I don't think that would be a problem," his father answered thoughtfully. "You can't bring down the house with a rock pick. You know, we have some nice pieces of marble under the laurel there," his father added, gesturing to the tree outside the window. There had been a small graveyard under the laurel, but the roots had toppled over the headstones, and the wrought iron fence that had once surrounded the tree had all but rusted away. "Now don't be using your pick on the gravestones (that would be sacrilegious), but there are plenty of chips there for the taking."

The next day in the root cellar, by his father's neat workbench ("a place for everything and everything in its place," his father used to say), amidst stacked boxes of tax receipts, old magazines, historic papers, mementos, towels and bedding, and clothing Randall had outgrown (but had every intention of fitting into again, once he'd dropped a little weight), Jeff took samples from the slate floor.

Under the stairway he paused to strike the black boulder that separated the cellars and noticed a fissure. He gave it a good whack with the point of his rock pick. The point stuck. He leaned on the handle, but it wouldn't budge. He took his father's sledge-hammer and slammed the flat end of the pick. A large chunk of rock fell to the floor exposing a hole about the size of a silver dollar. He found a penlight in the workbench drawer and shined it into the hole. What he saw next took his breath away, and remained with him as one of the most vivid memories of his childhood. It was the moment that proved that anything and everything was possible in this life, and that he should always expect the unexpected. The light sparkled back from millions of purple amethyst crystals. It was tantamount to finding buried treasure.

In the ensuing weeks Jeff and Randall learned all they could about geodes. They found that the largest geode in North America (about the size of a UPS truck) was in Put-in-Bay, Ohio. Theirs was perhaps half as big.

Randall hired a man to help him cut a door-sized slab from under the stairs in the wine cellar, being careful to preserve as many crystal clusters as possible. They laid boards across the floor of the geode, and cut another door-sized slab out of the south side, making a tunnel that connected the two cellars.

Because of the unusual size and rare web of gold veins that ran through the crystals, the door-sized pieces fetched a premium price. Randall sold one to the Natural History Museum in San Francisco, and the other to a San Diego lapidary. In total, the pieces brought nearly ten thousand dollars, half of which he put into Jeff's college account. "I don't think we should take any more, because this rock supports the floor," he told Jeff and Rosie. "This is really special, but I want to keep this to ourselves. We don't want magazine and newspaper reporters bothering us for a story. There's no need to tell anyone about it. It can be our family's special secret." So Jeff and Rosie were made keepers of the secret.

Now as he turned his car onto the wooden bridge and started up the dirt drive to the old house, he felt a heaviness of heart. It was his boyhood home; it should evoke the comfort of family, of history, of continuity. Instead, it represented the past, when he wanted to embrace the future. And the thought of all that would be required of him if his father were really gone forever, was overwhelming. The anticipation of problems to come — the details, the obligations, the compromises, the strain on relationships, the demands on his time — threatened to drag him down. He had to stop thinking, stop speculating about possible scenarios. The only way to get through this was to focus on one thing at a time.

Chapter 4
Into Thin Air

He pulled to a stop under the old oak in the side yard and turned off the engine. The kitchen door opened at the back corner of the house and Rosie stood there glowering at him. She was dressed, uncharacteristically, in shorts, hiking boots and a wrinkled white shirt. She ran her fingers through her thick black hair, bounced the two steps to the side yard and strode purposefully toward him as though she were about to deliver a lecture to a miscreant child. She was four years younger, a well-preserved 39, yet she'd always treated him as if she were the elder sibling.

"It's about time," she barked. "I have kids to get back to. Where the fuck have you *been*?"

"Grenada and..."

"Do you have any idea all we've had to do these last four days?" she said, and by 'we' Jeffrey knew she meant 'I' — it was always about *her*. He had to be alert when his sister was speaking, because there was often a subtext that displayed itself through tone, or glance, or gesture. "We searched everywhere, and then there are all the papers to go through, looking for some clue (man, there are some things you don't want to know about your parents until after they're dead, or maybe never — I'm going home and burning a few letters and clearing out my drawers — I don't want anyone snooping through *my* stuff after *I'm* gone). And the cops...at first they were like *Could he have been having an affair?* Can you imagine? Pop, having an affair?"

"No, not really," Jeff replied truthfully, thinking that he *could* imagine his father being interested in another woman; he was a man, after all. But he couldn't imagine any woman being interested in his father. Anyway where would he have had the opportunity to meet another woman? — He spent his days on the ranch.

"The police didn't do diddly-squat until Tuesday afternoon, when I found his wallet and watch and keys on the workbench. Christ, Mom's been out of her mind. I just got her to sleep. Jesus, Jeff, you picked a great time to take a vacation."

"It wasn't a vacation. What can you tell me about Pop? What did you find?"

"There's nothing to tell; he's not here; there's no clue, end of story."

"Where have they looked?"

"Everywhere; everywhere on the ranch. There's no trace. We just don't know."

"The barn? The old well?"

"Whata you think? We're idiots?"

"What about the creek? The trails above the vineyard?"

"The cops brought dogs. They walked the entire perimeter and there's no indication he went off the property."

Jeff cast his mind about for hidden places on the ranch, a place where someone might not be easily discovered. He and Rosie had played hide-and-go-seek all over the ranch. Sometimes they hid in the brush by the creek, but the dogs would have found him there. Sometimes...

"The attic? Did anyone check the attic?"

Rosie frowned. "I don't know. I don't think I mentioned the attic. I forgot we even had an attic."

The trap door to the attic was in Rosie's old room upstairs. He pulled on the rope with a feeling of trepidation, hoping he wouldn't find what they were looking for. The door had a built-in ladder that extended to the floor. He looked at Rosie, took a deep breath, and climbed into the gloom until his head and shoulders disappeared into the hole.

"Anything?" Rosie asked in a hushed tone.

"I can't see very well. I need a flashlight and my iPhone is out of juice."

They both went quietly downstairs, through the dining room to the laundry room, where Jeff found a flashlight in the junk drawer. When he turned he pulled up short. Across the door to the wine cellar, a piece of plywood had been screwed into place over the doorframe. "What's with this?" he asked.

With glazed eyes and a vacant stare, their mother came shuffling around the corner as though sleepwalking in her flannel nightgown and alpaca slippers. She'd aged fifteen years in two weeks, Jeff thought. Her graying hair was disheveled; she had dark bags under her eyes, and the muscles of her face had become flaccid. "Your father closed it up last month; the stairs were getting rickety."

"You should be asleep, Mom," Rosie said.

"I couldn't sleep; I heard voices." She looked pleadingly into Jeff's eyes. "I'm so glad you're here." Then she wrapped her arms around him and began to sob into his chest.

Rosie cast her eyes to the ceiling and shook her head, as if to say, *Who's been here for you these last four days? Do I count for nothing?* "Honest to god," she mumbled disgustedly. "Let me take you back to bed."

Jeff felt his mother take a shaky intake of breath, as he stared at the wine cellar door. It occurred to him that with the door sealed shut, the only access to the wine cellar would be through the geode from the root cellar. "Did anyone check the wine cellar?"

His mother stopped crying and looked at Rosie. Rosie raised her eyebrows and shrugged. "Don't know."

There was no way to turn on the light in the wine cellar, as the switch was on the other side of the boarded up door. But he had the flashlight. In the kitchen he opened the door to the root cellar and flipped the light switch. A single bulb hung on a long cord from the ceiling. The passage through the geode was under the mid-point of the stairway, and as he turned the corner at the bottom of the stairs he noticed a glow emanating from within. That was new — his father had epoxied a small dome light onto the ceiling of the enormous geode. As Jeff stepped into the chamber his ears filled with a single note of such low frequency that it was almost inaudible.

Ahead he could see a black curtain draped over the opening to the wine cellar. Feeling queasy and steeling himself for the shock of finding his father's body sprawled dead on the floor, he pushed the curtain aside and found himself looking at a wall of wood that was angled out just enough to allow a man to squeeze through. Why his father would have blocked the way to the wine cellar was anyone's guess. He stepped sideways through the narrow opening. The low frequency thrum ceased abruptly as he stepped out and around an up-ended barrel. The wall of wood turned out to be the back of a rack of freestanding shelves that held an array of pots and pans, bulging burlap sacks, wooden bins and dry goods.

He panned the light across the floor and played the beam overhead up the stairway. Finding no evidence of a body, he ducked back behind the shelves, his head filling with that low thrum again, like the sound of a ship's engines, that made his bones vibrate and his stomach turn flip flops. He hurried back to the root cellar, shuddering with the easing of tension. His head was pounding. The after effects of an adrenaline rush always left him with a headache and depression, and he wondered if he could stave it off with a prophylactic dose of aspirin.

At the top of the stairs he switched off the light and emerged to find his mother and Rosie waiting anxiously. He shook his head. "Nothing."

His mother let out a moan of thanksgiving. "Thank god; then there's still hope."

"We should get you back to bed," Rosie said. "You need your sleep."

"I know; I know I do."

They escorted her back upstairs, Rosie solicitously holding her elbow, while Jeff mounted the stairs behind, in case she fell backward. She wasn't feeble, by any means, but lack of sleep and incessant worry had beaten the stuffing out of her.

She sat on the bed and nearly toppled over before Jeff eased her onto her back and pulled the covers up. She looked at both of her children, the fear plain in her brown eyes. "I don't know what to do," she said wearily, "but I need to sleep now. You two go home. Just let me sleep. I'll call you both tomorrow. I Just…." And then she was out, lost in the shifting scenes of drug-induced dreams.

They went back to Rosie's old room. She looked up at the gaping mouth of the attic and squeezed her brother's hand. "Thanks," she said. Jeff mounted the ladder, hoping not to find anything of consequence. He paused when he'd poked his head and shoulders through the opening. It was stifling. Dim light came from two dormer windows that hadn't been cleaned in decades. Cobwebs hung from the window frames and the rafters. The space smelled of dry wood and dust. He played the flashlight beam down the length of the attic and into the dark corners. There were old trunks and leather suitcases decorated with stickers; cardboard boxes with the contents labeled in permanent marker; a shoebox of postcards; a dressmaker's dummy; a hat rack; and a few items hidden under draped sheets to keep the dust off. There was nothing very big up here, because the trapdoor was small. It was a place frozen in time in his memory, for it had not changed since the last time he'd been up here a quarter of a century before. Nothing had changed, not one thing, and with a sense of relief he also noted there was no body.

Chapter 5
A Tableau of Domestic Bliss

He'd heard stories, now and then, about men who faked their own deaths and disappeared (an empty skiff found overturned, an abandoned car found in the parking lot at the Golden Gate Bridge), only to be discovered a year or two or ten later, living under an assumed name on a beach on a tropical island. They were usually high-powered executives with a background of financial impropriety or gambling debts. His father didn't fit the profile.

Back at the condo he found a note that told him Carolyn had taken the kids to the market. He unpacked, put some classic jazz on the stereo, poured himself a glass of Riesling, and downloaded photos to his laptop, while looping a series of thoughts over and over — was his father alone and injured, unable to summon help? Was he alive? Could he be dead? If he'd run away, what was he running from? Or was he running to...?

He tried to put it out of his mind by reading over his notes on Jamaica, and after staring blankly at the screen for several minutes, immersed in memory, he began to type:

> "What kind of birds are those?" I asked. The balmy night was alive with their song, like the peeping of a dozen ten-penny whistles, and an odd sound like wood tapping on a hollow gourd.
>
> "Dat's not birds, mon; dat's crickets," my host replied.
>
> Damn big crickets, I thought. They seemed to call and answer with a beat that insinuated itself into the

pulse of the island, blending so well with the calypso music coming from the beach restaurant that I wondered if the music wasn't subliminally inspired by the abundant rhythm of Jamaica's wildlife.

Is he running from a threat? Is he hiding?

The band was just ending its set as I sat down to dine on the terrace at the edge of the small curved beach at Round Hill, Jamaica's oldest resort.

Could he have been kidnapped? Could he have had a stroke? Can dementia come on so quick that no one notices until one day, confused, he just walks away? He could have fallen, hit his head and have amnesia.

Speculation led him no closer to the truth. There was nothing he could think to do that would help solve the mystery, so he resolved to put it out of his mind, as best he could, and get on with the things he did have control over. He resumed:

The restaurant serves an eclectic array of cuisine that mirrors Jamaica's cultural and ethnic diversity, as well as its island situation. Its 2.5 million people descend from Arawak, African, Spanish, English, East Indian and Chinese populations, all of whom brought their own style of cooking, including curries from India and chow mien from China. Some dishes developed locally, such as jerk chicken (slow cooked and spiced with Scotch Bonnet), which I enjoyed to the sound of the crickets and the lapping of water on the beach.

Once a hundred acre sugar plantation, later a...

He heard the garage door open and a moment later Jake came into the kitchen and set a canvas bag on the counter.

"Hey, Pop," Jake said, and opened the refrigerator.

Half a minute passed before Jeff addressed his ten-year-old. "You're letting all the cold air out."

"But I don't know what I want."

"I'm about to make dinner; don't fill up on junk."

"I won't."

"How was school?"

"Okay."

"What did you learn?"

"Nothin'."

"Nothing? You must have learned *something*." Jake took the milk out and turned around to get a glass. "Close the door; you're costing us money." Without looking, Jake reached back with his right leg and pushed the door shut.

Carolyn came in, put down a bag and her purse on the floor and ran upstairs calling, "Welcome back!" as though she hadn't already seen him earlier, and "I have to go to the bathroom!" adding, "Oh, by the way, I hate to bring it up at a time like this, but the kids' toilet keeps running, unless you jiggle the handle. Could you help unload?"

A moment later Abby came in hauling two heavy bags. At 14 she was at an awkward pubescent stage, gangly, with shoulder length strawberry-blond hair and a saddle of freckles across her small nose. When she saw him she called out, "Daddy!" He got up and helped her with her bags. Then she hugged him. It didn't matter how stressed he felt, his daughter always made him feel special. This was not something he took for granted. He knew that in a few short years she would turn her attentions toward her boyfriends, as she should, but for now he could enjoy her unwarranted adoration.

"Hey, Pumpkin," (he pronounced it Pungkin), "how's your week going?"

"Oh, it's horrible," she said, rolling her eyes to the ceiling and grinning with a mouthful of braces. "Mom is impossible when you're gone. It's always, 'do this' and 'do that,' and she's always crabby. And she can't cook — we always eat take-out when you're gone. I'm so glad you're back." They began to unload the groceries while Jake, foraging for food, ignored them. "Oh, and you won't believe what Linda did — she dyed her hair pink, and her mom was so pissed...I mean mad. But then her dad said she looked cool, so her mom let her keep it. And then she goes, 'I want to get my ears pierced,' and her dad goes, 'No way.' But her mom said it was okay, as long as she didn't get anything else pierced, so Linda goes and gets her ears pierced, and now her right earlobe is swollen up like a marble. So gross!" She began unloading the grocery bags. "How was your trip? Did you bring me a present?"

Jeff reached into his backpack and pulled out a rag doll he'd bought at the outdoor market in St. George's, Grenada. The chocolate colored figure was adorned with a head rag and a dress in the nation's colors — red, orange and green. He was mindful that it was, perhaps, a little young for his daughter, but nothing else had presented itself as appropriate.

"I love it!"

"Now turn it upside down."

She turned the doll over. As she did, a head appeared where the feet should have been. Jeff reached out and smoothed the dress down, and on this side the dress was rose colored. It was two dolls in one. The doll-maker, Anita Anderson (a large black woman with a Scandinavian name), told him she'd raised 10 kids on her doll business. "It was a vision from God," she'd declared.

"When are you going to take me on one of your trips?" Abby asked.

"I don't pay for these trips, Sweetie. They're only for journalists. Maybe someday I'll be able to afford to take you to some of the places I've been."

"Can Linda and Jessica spend the night?"

"I don't think so; this is a school night."

"Please, Daddy. Please!" She smiled her biggest metallic smile.

"Ask your mother."

"She'll say no. She always says no."

"Then don't ask me to say yes, or I'll get in trouble with your mother."

Abby pouted, pulled a cell phone from her pocket, and began texting as she slunk off to her bedroom. Jeff sat back down at the table.

Carolyn came back downstairs. "Oh, by the way, I got an email from the Honda dealer that says it's time to have my car serviced."

"I think we have more pressing business...."

"Of course, I mean later...after...."

They looked at each other knowingly. It wasn't yet time to tell the kids about their grandfather.

Jake plunked himself down at the table with a glass of milk and a peanut butter sandwich. He was growing taller and Jeff thought, with regret, that he was now too heavy to easily carry on his shoulders. To live with children was to continually lose them to time; three-year-old Jake was different than seven-year-old Jake. He missed those Jakes, but the ten-year-old Jake was a joy, too. "Aren't you going to ask about my trip?"

"Oh yeah, did you bring me anything?"

Jeff reached into his backpack and handed his son a small model of a bamboo raft.

"Cool. What are we having for dinner?"

"I don't know; I'll have it ready by 6:30 or 7:00."

Jake got up and went to his room, leaving a dirty glass and a half eaten sandwich on the table. Jeff finished it in two bites, and washed it down with Riesling.

Carolyn finished putting away the last of the groceries, then came up behind him, rested her hands on his shoulders and kissed the top of his head. "How did it go?" she asked quietly.

"It doesn't look good. No one has a clue." Carolyn kneaded his shoulders and it was only then that he realized how tense he was. "He left his wallet and watch and keys on the workbench. He didn't take any money or credit cards. The police walked the perimeter with dogs, and there's no indication he walked off the property. Rosie thinks someone must have picked him up."

"And your mother?"

"She looks done in, but then she hasn't slept for days. The doctor gave her pills and she was sleeping when we left. I don't know what more we can do."

"It'll be hard on the kids. I want to put off telling them for another day, until the weekend. He might turn up by then."

"Kids are resilient; you'll be surprised."

"I'm going out for a run. Run off the stress. I haven't been able to run in the mornings; it's too hard getting the kids off to school on my own — you have no idea. Oh, and I put your wine samples in the hall closet; we were tired of tripping over them."

While Carolyn jogged, Jeff cooked. At 6:35 he laid out four plates with salmon, peas and saffron rice, and lined them up on the kitchen counter. He called down the hall to the kids, "Dinner's ready!" Then he took his own dish to the table. In the course of a year they ate together only on holidays and birthdays. Exactly a dozen meals.

Later that Thursday evening Carolyn graded papers at the kitchen table. Jeff sat in his armchair in the living room, wondering what had become of his father. Jake played video games on his side of the bedroom; and Abby did her homework while texting two of her friends.

They were a loving family, and they might have presented at that moment a tableau of domestic bliss. But Jeff felt the foundation of their life was built on shaky ground. They'd been warned before buying the condo that given a certain type of earthquake, the landfill at the edge of the bay could liquefy and the whole town might sink into the sand. Now he felt that other forces lay unseen, waiting to swallow them whole.

Chapter 6
Lists

On the surface the ebb and flow of days often takes on a routine or pattern that is hardly disrupted by personal crises, and Friday was no different. From the moment he stepped through the doorway of *Gourmet Traveler* the pace quickened, with phone calls and a steady stream of people bustling into his office with questions or requests, piles of paper on his desk to be sorted through, reviewed, edited, checked for accuracy and funneled back into the system.

At 9:30 Rosemary Nealy, his editorial assistant, poked her head in. "You wanted me to remind you to call your mother."

Jeff was grateful for the nudge, and he was surprised that he'd been so involved that he'd managed to put his father out of mind for a few minutes. His mother sounded tired but lucid and he promised to come down to the ranch the next day.

At 10:00 Mike O'Malley, the Publisher, came rolling into the office. He was two hundred seventy pounds with curly white hair, dimpled cheeks and a twinkle in his baby blue eyes. He spoke in a high-pitched roar. "Jeffrey! Hey, buddy, how was the trip? You're looking good. Look at that tan. Drink a lot of rum?"

Jeff filled him in about the trip. "By the way," he added, "do you have a check for me?"

O'Malley looked perturbed. "Oh god, Jeff, don't ask...you'll get paid when I get paid; I'm expecting a check from Crystal Cruises this week. I'll cut you a check then."

"It's been three weeks."

"Advertising has been tight. You know Claudio's not worth shit; he couldn't sell ice to an Eskimo."

"So fire the little bastard," Jeff said coldly.

"You know I can't do that; my sister would have a hissy fit. Her poor little baby...you know."

"I'll gladly fire him for you," Jeff said.

"I can't," Mike lamented. "I can't. Don't even ask. Hey, have you heard the one about..." he began, and launched into another of his jokes meant to deflect serious discussion.

When Jeff got home that night, he and Carolyn told the kids about their grandfather. Abby took it the hardest. "You mean Grampa's dead?" she gasped.

"Your father didn't say that."

"He's missing," Jeff repeated.

"He ran away?" Jake asked, more intrigued than worried.

"I didn't say that, either. Missing is...well, missing. We don't know. It's possible he's been injured and can't get to a phone. Or he may have had a stroke and wandered off. We just don't know. All we can say for sure is he's missing. So we're going to the ranch tomorrow to give Gramma our support. And we want you to be prepared, because if Gramps doesn't turn up soon, there's bound to be some changes. I don't know what they'll be. Your grandmother may have to sell the ranch. We'll have to help out where we can."

Abby, who had been tearing up while he spoke, ran to her father and clung to him, a diminutive version of her mother. "I love you, Daddy," she said with a note of desperation that revealed a fear of abandonment that was almost palpable.

He wondered when he'd last said 'I love you' to his father. Longer than he cared to admit. "I love you, too, Pumpkin."

"Maybe I can help find Gramps tomorrow," Jake offered helpfully.

"You can sure try, bud."

In the morning, as everyone else slept, Jeff went quietly downstairs. He ate breakfast and perused the San Francisco

Chronicle. Then he laid out a legal pad and made a to-do list. He came up with nine personal and seventeen work related tasks. It was more than he could get done in three days.

Personal problems aside, he did have work to do. Within the parameters of his various duties he had enormous latitude — no one looked over his shoulder when he composed a photograph; no one told him what words to type — but there were deadlines. The printer had to have the files on a specific date in order to deliver the finished magazines to the newsstand distributor on time. There were penalties if they couldn't comply. He knew he'd have to work this weekend, if he had any hope of meeting that deadline.

But the uncertainty of his father's whereabouts was making it hard to concentrate. So often, he knew, the sentence, "he is missing..." was completed by the phrase "...and presumed dead." Yet he simply couldn't imagine a world without his father in it. He knew that was silly, because one day, if not today, his father would be gone. They all would, because the road of life was a one-way trip to oblivion. But he wasn't ready to write his father off just yet. Until he knew for sure, he couldn't accept that his father was dead.

Going back upstairs, he found Carolyn sitting on the edge of the bed, leaning on one arm in Gaugin-like repose, a baby blue towel wrapped around her head, another around her waist. Her breasts hung slightly to the side of her lean. *So soft*, thought Jeff, *so comforting to squeeze, and they move in such a fascinating way.* Pictures came to mind of jogging girls with jiggly breasts; calendar girls posed cat-like on all fours....

"What?" Carolyn asked.

He blinked. "I forgot why I came upstairs."

"You need a list."

"I *have* a list," he said, holding it up for her to see.

"Did you make an appointment to have my car serviced?"

"It's on the list."

She held out her hand and he obediently handed it over. She looked at it, the point between her eyes furrowing, her head bobbing in approval or understanding. Jeff waited for the pronouncement he was sure would come. Carolyn lowered the list and looked up at him. "You've over-scheduled yourself; you'll never get all this done," she said, handing the list back.

"That's not helpful," he said.

"I'm only stating the obvious. Why bother writing it down if you're not going to do it?"

"To remind myself of what needs to be done."

"What's the point?" She crossed to her dresser and took out a bra. "You need to delegate."

"I don't have a budget to delegate."

"Then you need to find more time."

"How am I supposed to do that? — There's only 24 hours in a day."

"Give something up," she said matter-of-factly. It seemed a simple enough thing to do.

"Like what?" he said with exasperation; it wasn't like he hadn't thought about it. He rarely read for pleasure anymore. He only watched two hours of television a week. He only got six hours of sleep a night. Like a passenger on a sinking ship, he had already jettisoned the excess cargo; there was nothing left to throw overboard.

"Give up the paper," Carolyn said, snapping her bra in place.

One part of his mind noted sadly that restraining her breasts in a harness took away their charm, while the other part of his mind answered, "You want me to be uninformed? I've read the paper everyday since I was 15."

"Get Newsweek instead."

"But I need the 'Food and Wine' section."

"Then buy a Wednesday paper. You can read the food section and Newsweek. That'll take maybe an hour and a half. That still saves you…" here she paused to calculate in her head "…more than three and a half hours a week. About 15 hours a month."

Jeff considered a moment, then added to his list:

• Cancel paper
• Subscribe to *Newsweek*

Carolyn asked, "Did you remember to deposit your check?"

"I didn't get a check."

"What?"

He threw off his robe and kicked off his slippers and as they talked he began to dress for the day. He sat on the edge of the bed, his back turned towards her. He really didn't want to get into it. "Michael says we have a cash flow problem," he said, pulling a blue polo shirt over his head.

"Uh, uh. *We* don't have a cash flow problem; *he* has a cash flow problem. So who else isn't getting paid?"

Jeff shook his head. "I don't know; Ralph said he got half, but that's not my end of the business." He stepped into his jeans.

Carolyn laid back down on the bed and propped herself on an elbow. *He's too nice*, she thought. She felt she had to take care of him or others would take advantage. *He has a habit of letting people walk all over him until he can't take it anymore and blows up.* He would have said he was accommodating and reasonable and then blew up, but it all came to the same thing. This would bring on a month of ranting about the injustice of it and the lack of ethics in the workplace. Then he would find a new job and the cycle would start all over again. *He's too trusting*, she thought. *He has somehow never learned that most people look out for number one.* "Let's not go through this again," she said. "Just tell him he comes up with the money, or you walk."

Jeff pulled on his socks. "It's not that simple."

"It's that simple from where I stand. Do you think Michael can't pay his personal bills? No, of course not. No, if you don't want to tell him, make me the bad guy. Tell him your wife says if he doesn't come up with everything he owes you by the end of next week, then you can't work for him."

"Goddamn it, Carol, I'm sorry I mentioned it. It's not that simple: Advertisers aren't paying on time, so we have a shortfall."

"Sweetheart, you just don't understand. *We* don't have a shortfall. Michael has a shortfall. He owns the company. *We* don't own it. It's his responsibility, and he has to understand we're not his cushion. I'm tired of this, Jeff. I'm really getting sick of this whole business. You have to stand up for yourself. Or stand up for me — is it fair that

Michael pays his bills and we can't? Is it fair that he can put out a magazine when he doesn't even pay his employees? It's not like you're an owner. Would you put up with it if you were a teacher? Or a factory worker? Or a postman?"

Jeff laced up his tennis shoes. "That's different. Publishing is..." Well, he really couldn't say why publishing was different. It was just that in his experience publishers often had financial problems. It was no wonder that Carolyn was tired of the same old litany of woe she'd heard from one magazine to the next. And she was also right about his role — he was an employee, not an owner, and he should expect to be paid on time.

"I'll tell him Monday."

"I think you should start looking for another job, something with a bit more stability. Maybe you could teach a course on editing at the community college."

"I don't know if the pay is any better."

"It can't be any worse than nothing," she said. "Anyway, it would do you good to step out of your comfort zone."

He suspected the last line had been lifted from one of the self-help books she was always reading.

"When do we leave?"

"I told your mom we'd be there by 10:30."

Chapter 7
Return to the Ranch

"Ranch work is your father's bailiwick," Carolyn said as they passed the blimp hangers at Moffett Field. "Your mother will need help."

"I'm no farmer. Besides, I have enough on my plate," Jeff said in a tone of irritation that he immediately regretted. He wasn't annoyed with Carolyn, or even the question. Carolyn always wanted to talk about a problem; it was her way of organizing her thoughts and working out solutions. Jeff avoided talking, because talk made him think about the very thing that was making him anxious. It wasn't that he could entirely dismiss a problem, or banish it from his thoughts (his subconscious was working on it full-time); he just hated to speculate on all of the possible outcomes, as each one came with its own set of problems and solutions, and in the end only one scenario would play out. He preferred to react to what was actually happening, rather than mentally preparing for a dozen different alternatives.

"Who takes care of paying the bills?" Carolyn asked.

"I don't know, actually. Mom, I think."

After his sister started first grade, their mother had worked as a legal secretary. At home there'd been a division of labor. She'd been in charge of the budget, the laundry and dinner. His father kept busy with the orchards and vineyards, and general maintenance.

"I'm afraid this is going to take a lot of our time (*your* time mostly)," Carolyn said.

She knew Randall's welfare had to be their first concern, but she couldn't help thinking about how much this would cost them. There would be little expenses that might not seem like much at the time, and yet they would add up by the end of the month (gasoline, fast food, odds and ends at the hardware store, wear and tear on the car, etc.).

"We'll just do what we have to," Jeff said. One way or another they would do the right thing. They always did. Not always to his benefit, Jeff's parents had instilled in him a willingness to assume responsibility, a reflexive honesty and the inability to lie. He looked in the rear-view mirror. "You kids been listening?"

"Yeah," they chorused from the back seat.

"You should be aware that we're going to have to be careful with expenses over the next few months. It's likely to be a lean Christmas."

Jake asked, "Can we get a dog for Christmas?"

"Lord, no," Carolyn blurted.

"We don't have room for a dog," Jeff explained. "And you have to walk a dog two or three times a day."

"I'll walk it!"

"What about when you go off to college?" Even as he said it, Jeff wondered if they'd have the money to send their kids to college.

"I'm only eleven!" Jake protested.

"You go off to college in seven years. A dog lives a bit longer than that, and I'd be stuck taking care of it."

"We could have a cat," Abby joined in. "Cats don't need much room, and you don't have to walk a cat."

"You kids don't seem to understand our predicament," Carolyn said. "Pet food, vet bills, animal license — it's expensive. We're not getting a pet!"

"It doesn't cost that much," Abby countered.

"Well, let's just add it up," Carolyn said reasonably, and proceeded to tally the expenses to a projected $450 a year. "A typical cat lives 16 years. So that cat ultimately costs" — she paused to calculate in her head — "more than 7,000 dollars."

Jeffrey always had mixed feelings about returning to the family home. The old house and the dwindling acreage that surrounded it always reminded him of obligations, failed expectations and broken dreams. It represented a parochial view of the world, a life lived within boundaries, a life looking backwards when he wanted to look forward. If his father was gone, that life would reel him back in like a fish on a hook. The thought was depressing.

For Carolyn, on the other hand, the ranch was the physical embodiment of the family. She thought about the old house with a sense of longing. Growing up the daughter of a career Air Force officer, she'd spent her childhood moving from one base to another, never staying in any one place long enough to call it her home. She envied Jeff his childhood. To have grown up here, with such stability and so much room, would have been her dream.

The dust had barely settled before Virginia came out the front door and down the steps to the car as they piled out. She still looked haggard despite carefully applied makeup.

Abby hugged her. "Hi, Gramma."

"How are you holding up?" Carolyn asked with concern.

"I keep thinking this can't be happening, and hoping I'll wake up and it'll all be over. I dream about it and then I wake up to the same nightmare; it never goes away. God, you think these things only happen to other people, and then you're the person everyone's reading about. Which reminds me, there's an article in this morning's paper; they sent a reporter out yesterday. I couldn't find a recent picture where he's looking straight at the camera; you know how he hated to pose."

Jeff noted the use of the past tense. "And the police?"

"Still nothing," she said. She gave her daughter-in-law and son perfunctory hugs, then turned to her grandchildren. "You all must be so worried," she said. "But we'll get through this. Your grampa will be back...soon." There was a long pause before she looked up at Jeffrey and finished, "I hope."

After Jake went off in search of his grandfather and Carolyn had taken Abby to the kitchen to make tea, Jeff asked, "Could Pop have squirreled away cash?"

"Impossible. I pay all the bills. I cash all the checks. I keep a strict accounting in QuickBooks. You know your father; he's never been on the cutting edge of technology, and he's never been particularly practical with figures."

"Have you looked to see if any money's been withdrawn?"

"That's one of the first things I checked."

"Unusual expenditures on his credit card?"

"Well," Virginia admitted, "that's another matter." She clamped her lips shut and stared a long while at the floor, gathering her thoughts. "Groceries," she said finally.

"Groceries?"

"I know, because I only shop for groceries on Tuesdays, and there were two extra charges on the credit card."

"When was this?"

"Last month, while I was visiting your aunt Connie. He must have been taking them someplace else; I'd know if he brought anything home."

"Why would he need groceries?"

"How the hell should I know!?" Virginia snapped back, then immediately apologized. "I'm just upset."

"I know; we all are." He gave her a one-armed hug and kissed the top of her head. "You didn't ask him?"

"About the groceries? No, I..." Why hadn't she just confronted him? Asked him point blank? "I mean, what would be the point? He'd just lie about it anyway, the way he lied about his 'walks.' I came back a day early from your aunt Connie's; I thought I'd surprise him. Only he wasn't here. He didn't come back until after dark. Of course he said he'd been out walking again." The thought that her husband could so willfully deceive her after so many years brought tears to her eyes. She felt betrayed.

"Any other unusual expenditures?"

"Nothing too startling. There've been some rather larger than usual charges at the hardware store the past few months, but I don't really keep track of every little thing he buys. It just goes under 'ranch supplies' (I don't have the actual receipts, just credit card charges)."

"Do you have enough money to pay the bills?"

"Of course — your father went missing, not our money."

"You might think about opening up an account in your own name. Just in case."

"In case what?"

"Well, if he isn't.... If he left on purpose, he could conceivably clean out the account."

"No, no, no. I know he was keeping something from me, but he wouldn't do that. I can't believe that of him."

"It wouldn't hurt to err on the side of caution. You said yourself, there were personality changes. It might be dementia or something; he might not be responsible."

"I'll think about it."

"Is there anything else I can do?"

"No, no you have your family to look after. I'll be alright."

"The grapes should be about ready to pick."

Virginia looked surprised. "I haven't even thought about the crops."

"Do you have a vineyard manager?"

"Has your father *ever* had a vineyard manager? He's too stubborn to delegate." She stared westward for a long moment, lost in thought. "I ought to let them rot, just to teach him a lesson," she said sternly, then recanted. "No, maybe it's not his fault. Maybe he's been hurt, or.... I can't decide if I should be angry or afraid. I just don't know. I'm not up to this."

"Can you afford to hire a vineyard and orchard manager?"

"We're fine. We're more than fine. We made a rather tidy profit on the sale of the peach orchard. So you don't need to worry about that. We can afford it."

Chapter 8
O'Malley Shows His True Colors

As was his custom on Monday mornings, Jeff sat in the conference room before an array of numbered wine glasses, evaluating the first of two flights of New Zealand and Chilean Sauvignon Blancs. He sniffed, tasted, spit into a bucket, and gave a point score based on aroma, flavor, balance, texture, complexity, length and finesse. But point scores alone didn't give a sense of style. For that he had to write a short description. The problem was that the English language was inadequate to the task of conveying the nuance of aroma and taste.

O'Malley had just passed the door when Jeff came out of the conference room. Jeff started to speak, but stopped when he heard O'Malley muttering, "Jesus, oh Jesus. Jesus fucking Christ."

Audrey Bickle, the myopic, mousey, part-time bookkeeper followed O'Malley down the hall clutching her laptop to her chest. "I wouldn't talk to him, if I were you," she said.

"What's wrong?"

"Stock market. Lehman Brothers folded today. He's lost a lot of money."

The mention of money reminded him that he'd promised Carolyn to give Mike an ultimatum today. He dreaded confrontations, and this was probably not the best time to demand money. He thought it might be better to wait, and went back to his office.

On Sunday he'd written up the "Where To Stay - Where to Eat – What to Do" sidebar on Grenada. Now he had to write the article. He spent an hour selecting and adjusting the best photos. Then he began to write:

> A large school of flying fish accompanied our
> catamaran back from Carriacou on a breezy September

afternoon. We watched them spring from the blue-green water, spread their wings, and trail shimmering droplets of water as they glided a hundred feet or more before splashing back into the sea. A brief tropical shower gave rise to a double rainbow that arched over Port St. George's, signaling our return to Grenada, the spice island of the Caribbean.

Chances are your pantry contains a small souvenir from Grenada (locals pronounce it Gre-NAY-da), for this tiny island of 110,000 people accounts for 20% of the world's nutmeg production.

His desk phone rang. Margie Young said in a secretive voice, "You have a policeman on line one."

It was a Lieutenant Hanes. "I was hoping you might be able to shed some light on your father's disappearance. Maybe there's some small detail that's been overlooked."

Jeff talked with him for a few minutes. It was obvious from the beginning that the police suspected discord at home. Jeff promised to keep him in the loop if anything more came to light.

He'd hung up and was standing in preparation to go to lunch, when O'Malley came through the doorway. He didn't look in his usual jovial mood. "What's this I hear about a cop calling? What's up?"

"My father's gone missing."

O'Malley's head snapped back and his expression yielded surprise. "Oh, is that all?" he blurted out. "I thought it was something to do with the business." He sounded relieved. "He and your mom probably got into a tiff. Hey, did you hear the one about the man and the woman who get into a head-on accident? It's a bad one. Both cars are totaled ..."

"No, Michael..."

"...but neither of them are hurt," O'Malley ploughed on, undeterred.

When the joke was finished Jeff said, "Yeah, funny. Listen, Michael, I had a talk with Carol last night, and the thing is, we can't pay our bills. I need a check."

"Oh, for Christ's sake," O'Malley said peevishly. "We went over this last week. You'll get paid, when I get paid."

"I can't do that anymore. I can't work without pay."

"So what are you saying? Are you refusing to work? Is that what this is? Because so help me, if we don't meet the deadline, I'll sue your ass for breach of contract!"

"We don't have a contract, Michael, but if we did, you'd be in breach of contract for not paying me."

O'Malley glared at him for a long moment, his face turning crimson with rage. Then cursing, he strode angrily from the room. "Son of a bitch!" he yelled at the end of the hall.

Jeff's stomach churned. An adrenaline reaction, he supposed. A couple minutes later O'Malley blew in, slapped a checkbook on the desk and leaned forward with his pen, muttering, "You're not irreplaceable, you know. Ralph filled in just fine when you were gone." He tore out the check and tossed it contemptuously on the desk. "I can't believe you have the gall to demand money after we just sent you on a five thousand dollar trip. I would've liked to go on that trip myself, but I was too busy *working!*"

Jeff could almost have written O'Malley's speech for him word for word, for he followed the same script as Jeff's previous employers.

"I was working too," Jeff reminded him. "I'm still working. And don't tell me it was a five thousand dollar trip; the tourist boards footed the bill. It didn't cost *you* a dime." It always amazed him how his employers would assign him to a press trip offered by a tourist board, then take credit for it and suggest the trip were somehow the equivalent of a paycheck. "The way *you* talk, you'd think I should pay you for the privilege of working here. That doesn't pay my bills." He looked at the check. "This isn't even half what you owe me."

O'Malley snorted. "Don't think I'll forget about this, buddy," he said, and as a parting shot reiterated, "You're replaceable."

Jeff watched him go without comment. He was too rattled to work. He called Guglielmo winery and the Santa Clara County Farm Bureau, and spent the rest of the afternoon following up leads on vineyard and orchard managers.

Chapter 9
First Harvest

On the last Saturday of the month Jeff and Jake got up early and drove to the ranch at sunrise. Jeff backed the tractor out of the barn and attached a small flatbed trailer to the trailer hitch. He drove while Jake stood behind, holding onto his shoulders. They trundled across the bridge and along the road to the entrance to the vineyard, where pickers already lounged around four beat-up pickup trucks. On the flatbed of a bigger truck were stacked 4-by-4-foot wooden boxes imprinted with the stencil: Property of Guglielmo Winery. A forklift transferred two of the boxes onto the flatbed at the back of the tractor.

Jeff scanned the men, looking for his Vineyard Manager.

"*Donde esta* Michael Gorman?" he asked.

A short, stocky man stepped forward. His countenance could have been found carved in stone on a Yucatan pyramid. "*Él será aquí más adelante.*"

"*Bueno. Dígale venir a la casa cuando él llega.*"

Jeff jumped down from the tractor. "Come on, Jake."

On the walk back up to the house Jake was in awe, having discovered a side to his father that he'd never suspected.

"How can you speak Spanish?"

Jeff looked sideways at Jake and smiled. From the time Jeff was ten, until he went off to college, his father had insisted he spend his weekends during harvest working side-by-side with the pickers. He'd dreaded harvest. It was hot, dirty, sticky, backbreaking work, and he rarely got through a day without either cutting himself or being stung by a yellow jacket. Try as he might to ingratiate himself with the pickers, it had always been an uneasy relationship. They'd made fun of him, talking among themselves in Spanish while sniggering and throwing glances his way.

When he'd complained to his father, Randall delivered a lecture that Jeff had never forgotten, because it was a history lesson. "Listen," his father had said, "our family came out here from the dust bowl of Nebraska in 1937, and the only work they could find was picking crops. Both of my grandparents, my father and uncles all picked crops for two years. They couldn't get other jobs because they were newcomers and there weren't many jobs to go around. They damn near starved. So when he bought this ranch, your grandfather always paid his pickers a fair price, because he knew what it was like to break your back for a buck. I asked you to help so you'd appreciate how hard their work is. Where would we be without them? Who would pick our crops? I'll tell you, it would be you and me, and we'd have to do it all. These crops don't just roll to market on their own. So give the crew a little respect."

"But they laugh."

"I'm sure they do, but put yourself in their shoes. They probably find it amusing that the owner's son is getting his hands dirty. If you want to earn their respect, work hard and learn a bit of their language."

By the time he was in high school he had learned enough Spanish to understand the jibes and gave as much as he took, in a good-natured way. And his father was right — he did eventually earn their respect. But the experience did nothing to assuage his growing aversion to farming.

To Jake he just said, "When I was your age your grampa made me pick grapes with the crew. That's how I learned Spanish."

"What did you say?"

"I asked them to send the Vineyard Manager by the house when he arrives."

Later, while waiting for the pickers to finish, Jeff sat in his father's office and perused photo albums he hadn't seen in many years. Jake came and looked over his shoulder. "Gramma says lunch'll be ready in five minutes. Who's that?"

"That's your great uncle, my Uncle Pete. There are some other people here you ought to meet," he said, flipping through the pages to introduce Jake to his forebears.

None of the photos were particularly artful, but they each captured a moment in time. A photo stopped time dead in its tracks. Memories were vague and fluid and unreliable. Photos were sharp and distinct and unimpeachable slices of time that you could examine in detail at your leisure. They also brought to mind long-buried memories. There were black-and-white photos of grandparents, aunts and uncles and cousins, and several pages of faded color photos from Jeff's childhood.

Turning the last page he found an old tintype had been tipped into the back cover, a macabre funeral photo he hadn't seen before. It had been taken at the front of the house, where a family gathered somberly around an open coffin that was propped upright against the porch steps, displaying the deceased body of a boy about ten.

The anonymous photographer had captured a whole world that had since passed away, Jeff thought — a horse-and-buggy world, a world before electric lights and telephones, before motorcars and airplanes, before refrigerators and washing machines, radio or television, before atomic bombs and satellites, computers and the internet. It was a quieter world, surely, a slower world, a world of traditional values and prejudices that had somehow evolved into the present, for better or for worse.

He took the album to the kitchen and asked his mother about the tintype.

Virginia frowned and shrugged. "He's been doing research on the house. I suppose it's the family that built it, the ones buried out back. The Kimballs, I think their name was."

"Buried here?" Jake asked. "Are there ghosts?"

"I've never seen a ghost."

"It's creepy. Why would they take a picture of a dead kid?"

"Post-mortem photography was common in the middle of the Nineteenth Century," Jeff explained. "It was a way to remember the dead. Sometimes it was the only photo the family had of a loved one.

They had to call in a professional photographer, because personal cameras didn't exist until the end of that century."

"Like the way they didn't have personal computers back in the old days when you were kid."

"Right," Jeff said, feeling positively historic.

Chapter 10
Giving Thanks

Early Thanksgiving morning Jeff tasted ten Barolos at the office. Then he sped quietly south along the nearly deserted 280 freeway under a ceiling of dark clouds that extended like a shelf along the entire length of the mountains. He set the cruise control to 65 miles per hour, sipped tea, and listened to Jeff Muldaur's *Private Astronomy, a Vision of the Music of Bix Beiderbecke.*

His cell phone chirped a few bars of "Ode to Joy."

Carolyn said, "Hey Sweets, what's your ETA?"

"I'm coming up on Saratoga; I guess that puts me about fifteen minutes out."

"We're on 101. I think you're about five minutes ahead of us. Is it raining there?"

"Sprinkling."

"Did you remember the champagne?"

"Got it."

It would be strange without his father. They were only just beginning to get used to his not being around. Still, they were denied the solace of pure grief, for how could you mourn a man who wasn't technically dead? Randall was in that Never-Never Land of "the missing." That he was probably dead didn't matter. With no body, no ashes to scatter, there was no resolution. There was simply a void where his father should have been.

He drove up the muddy driveway, tires crunching acorns as he pulled under the black oak at the back corner of the house. A light was burning in the kitchen. The rain had let up, but large drops fell from the tree limbs with each puff of wind.

He found his mother in the kitchen peeling potatoes. He hugged her and she responded with a pinched forehead and a listless hug back. "You feeling all right?" he asked.

"No, I have a headache, and I have too much to do. And it's cold. My back's been out of whack, and I don't feel up to lugging wood from the shed."

"Here, give me that peeler. Now you take some aspirin and lay down. I'll start a fire."

A few minutes later he heard the rumble of Carolyn's car passing over the wooden bridge, then the thump of car doors closing, the slap of feet running up the front porch stairs, and Jake calling from the entry hall, "We're here!"

Jeff set Abby and Jake to peeling potatoes. By the time Rosie and her family arrived, the potatoes were boiling and the kitchen was brimming with the tantalizing odor of roasting turkey. Tad, 10, and Timmy, 5, burst into the house calling for their cousins. The kids all gathered in the parlor. Rosie and J.C. came in, absorbed in conversation and bickering mildly.

Jeff enlisted J.C.'s aid in bringing in the wood. Jeff had mixed feelings about his brother-in-law. J.C. was a good conversationalist with wide-ranging interests and a depth and breadth of experience. He was one of those people who was comfortable in his own skin. But his view of the world was often black and white, whereas Jeff saw many shades of grey.

"And you? How have you been?" Jeff asked.

"Lousy," was the reply. "Besides all this business with your father, the banking crisis is killing us. I'm frankly afraid to look at it. We don't keep much in the bank; everything we have is invested in stocks and our house. The last time I looked our portfolio was down 40%, and our house is worth less than what we paid for it. It's been a bad couple of months."

"Are the potatoes organic?" Rosie asked. "I was watching the Food Network this week, and they asked farmers if they'd eat their own produce? Two potato farmers said they grew organic potatoes for their families, but they'd never eat the ones they sold to markets because they're so full of pesticides. It's no wonder cancer rates are so high."

Virginia came back downstairs and requested an aperitif. Jeff popped the cork on a Heidsieck Monopole Brut champagne and poured flutes for the adults.

When everything was ready they all took their usual places at the table. Virginia sat at the head of the table closest to the kitchen. On her right sat Abby, Carolyn, Timmy and J.C. On her left were Rosie, Tad, Jake and Jeff. The adults were all too aware of the empty place at the other end of the table.

J.C. picked up his glass and said, "I know you all aren't religious..."

"That's an understatement," interrupted Rosie.

"...so I won't say grace..."

"Hallelujah," Jeff added.

"...but since this is my tenth anniversary at this table, I'd like to offer thanks to this family for letting me be a part of it." They all raised their glasses and clinked those within reach.

"As long as we're toasting," Jeff said, waiting for everyone to look his way. He raised his glass and said, "To Pop, wherever he is."

"Here, here," J.C. said.

Virginia rushed from the room. Jeff pushed back from the table saying, "Sorry, that was stupid of me," and followed his mother to the kitchen.

She was shaking. He put an arm around her shoulders. "Sorry, I wasn't thinking."

"No, no, it's not your fault," she said, her words quaking with pent up emotion. "I just can't face it, not knowing. He's either dead, or he's sitting at another table. And I just can't stand the thought of either."

He hugged her and offered useless banalities.

"I need something to calm my nerves," she said, and broke away to go upstairs.

Jeff went back to the table.

Rosie looked to him and asked, "Should I go up?"

"No, she just needs a few minutes to calm her nerves."

"He better be dead, because if he showed up now I'd kill him."

The conversations started up again, and Virginia rejoined them after another five minutes.

"Hey, mom," Rosie said in a solicitous tone, "you know you might want to talk to your doctor about Prozac. It did wonders for me after Tad was born. I was depressed as hell, and that put me right again."

"I'll think about it," Virginia said. "The Xanax helps."

"Victory through biochemistry!" Carolyn quipped and sipped her champagne.

The conversation turned to Christmas lists and the economic upheaval. Virginia finished her third glass of champagne and asked for the Navarro Gewürztraminer.

Rosie looked askance at her mother and asked rhetorically, "Are you sure you should?"

"Mind your own business; I'm not your daughter," was Virginia's curt reply. "Maybe you should have a glass and relax."

"I can't; I mean, I shouldn't."

Virginia cocked her head and raised her eyebrows in silent inquiry.

Rosie took a deep breath and announced, "I'm pregnant."

There was a general outburst of congratulations from all the adults at the table. Then Carolyn said, "I thought you weren't going to take the chance on another boy."

"I know, but it's a girl."

"How lucky."

"Luck had nothing to do with it. We went to a clinic and made sure."

"But that's great," Carolyn enthused. "When are you due?"

"June."

"It'll be nice for the boys to have a little sister to dote over," Virginia said, beaming with glassy eyes and ruddy cheeks.

"I just hope she sleeps through the night better than the boys did."

"I can never get back to sleep, once I'm up," Carolyn said. "That's why Jeff always got up to feed them."

The conversation then split to either end of the table, the women talking about breast-feeding versus bottles, and the disruption of sleep that comes with a newborn in the house.

"You know, you set a bad example," J.C. said to Jeff.

"Why? What'd *I* do?"

"You set the bar too high. Here you were taking care of babies, and Rosie expects me to do the same."

"It wasn't that hard. I was freelancing at the time, so I was at home."

"I can't relate to babies. Until they can talk all they do is eat, poop and cry." He turned to Timmy. "Isn't that right, sport?"

Timmy had a mouthful of food and just bobbed his head. He kept on nodding and wiggling back and forth, as though he heard music that no one else could hear.

Then Rosie's voice rose above the chatter. "I got an email from Marie-Francoise Valette, you remember her? She said all of France is happy, but confused. Just when they thought they had us figured out, we elect Barack Obama."

J.C. spoke up. "It just goes to show that we're a collection of states with different viewpoints. There's not a lot of 'unum' in the 'plurabus.'"

"That's the truth," Rosie agreed; "it's like there's the east coast and the west coast and then there's this weird backward bunch of states in-between."

"Just because they don't agree with you, doesn't make them backward," Virginia said, annoyed, and poured herself another glass of Gewürztraminer.

"Yes it does," argued Rosie; "Republicans are reactionary."

"Might I remind you I'm a Republican?" J.C. said calmly, staring icily at his wife.

"You don't count; you're old-school. The new Republicans are run by the Religious Right and the Tea Party. They don't believe in science. They're stuck in some Nineteenth-Century time-warp. I'm glad I live in a progressive state."

"California is just as divided as the rest of the nation," Jeff said. "Liberal north, conservative south, and the Central Valley might as well be Oklahoma."

Rosie said, "You're right. I forget sometimes how different the Bay Area is from the rest of the state. I mean — can you believe gay marriage was voted down? People are so frigging mean."

"What's gay?" Timmy asked.

"It's like when a man loves a man," Rosie said matter-of-factly.

"I love Daddy."

"That's different."

"Why?"

"Just because."

"Because why?"

"When you're older," she said, reluctant to elaborate.

"I voted against it," Virginia admitted, staring at her daughter over the rim of her wine glass.

Rosie raised an eyebrow disapprovingly and said, "I can't believe my own mother is homophobic."

"God, I hate that term," Virginia said wearily. "Phobic means you have an irrational fear of something. I don't fear gays. I just disapprove of their lifestyle."

"Disapprove? You can't disapprove. It's like disapproving of someone being black."

"You know, when we were young, buggery was considered disgusting and perverted. We didn't hold parades to celebrate it."

Jeff wished his father were here now. No matter how politically charged the conversation, his father had always been a moderating influence.

"But you were for civil rights and women's rights. How is that any different from gay rights?"

"You can't choose your race or sex. I'm not convinced gays aren't just confused. I think it may be psychological."

"Mother, how can you be so frigging ignorant? It's been proven it's in the genes. Anyway, it's none of the government's business who we love."

"Isn't it? Every society has its standards, and government does set limits. The age of consent laws are the most conspicuous example. Laws against polygamy are another."

"Yeah? Well, when you were growing up, mixed-race marriages were illegal in lots of states. Now we have a president from a mixed-race marriage. Get with the times, Mom."

"Get with the times? Just remember that life is long and times change. So don't get to feeling so self-righteous just because you think you're progressive."

J.C. laughed, "Lord, I love this family! My mom never allowed us to talk about anything controversial. Sex, politics and religion were forbidden topics; there was never anything to talk about!"

Jeff raised his glass and looked down the table. "To friendly disagreement."

"I'll drink to that," Virginia said, and drained her glass.

After ice cream, Jeff took a picture of the table. Then the boys all scurried off together toward the parlor, with Abby following sedately in their wake like a mother duck.

There was an awkward lull in the conversation and a tension in the air until Jeff spoke up. It was his custom, on the day after Thanksgiving, to drive his family to a Christmas tree farm in the mountains to cut a tree for the condo. He offered to cut a second one for the ranch, but Virginia declined. "I don't think I'll have a tree this year; it would be pointless."

"We're still coming for Christmas eve. The kids'll expect it. Where will we put the presents?"

"Then you get one for the kids if you want, but don't do it on my account. I'd really rather skip Christmas this year."

"I'll put it up myself, Mom."

"Do as you like."

Rosie reached out and patted the back of her mother's hand in sympathy. With that gesture the meal concluded.

Chapter 11
Exit Stage Left

Jeff didn't have a religious bone in his body. To him, god was always god with a small "g." In all honesty, he thought the Judeo-Christian-Muslim idea of god entirely preposterous. Bible stories revealed a creator that was antithetical to the notion that god was either omnipotent or loving. Nonetheless, Jeff loved Christmas, or rather the secular version of Christmas — the Christmas of Santa Claus and Christmas trees, and of the great morality play of the past two centuries, Dickens' *A Christmas Carol*, extolling charity towards all, and the equanimity of spirit in the reconciliation of the past, the present and the future.

Every year Jeff had the best of intentions when the day came to cut the Christmas tree. And every year the day was spoiled by a lack of preparation, a lack of cooperation or an unwillingness to compromise. This year it was made worse by the necessity of buying, erecting, and decorating a tree for the ranch, a task that had previously fallen to his father.

In preparation, Jeff loaded the Subaru with rope, gloves, paper towels, plastic trash bags, a tape measure, hand wipes and an old blanket to protect the roof. He dressed in a flannel shirt, jeans, SF Giants baseball cap, and his oldest pair of tennis shoes. He directed everyone to bring extra shoes, because the ground was bound to be muddy and they didn't want to track mud into Gramma's house. Carolyn made sandwiches and placed plastic water bottles in all of the cup holders.

They hooked onto highway 92 heading west, passed over Highway 101 and continued up the flanks of the mountains, passing

The College of San Mateo as the four-lane highway crested the first ridge and snaked in serene arcs downhill two miles, crossed under interstate 280, narrowed to two lanes and passed into open space preserve. They crossed Crystal Springs reservoir, and wound up the mountain through scrub oak and cypress forest. Jeff was aware of the blessed silence from the backseat (the kids had finally outgrown their tendency to bicker). At the summit he turned the car south onto Skyline Boulevard.

When he glanced casually at the speedometer he noticed the light. "Oh Christ!" he blurted. "We're about out of gas."

"How could you let it get so low?" Carolyn asked.

Rhetorical questions irritated him. "Because I'm an ass," he answered.

"Don't be in a bad mood."

"Could you turn on the air-conditioning?" Abby asked. "I'm feeling a bit car sick."

"Slow down around the corners," Carolyn instructed.

They entered the redwood and fir forest and the road became windier. Jeff opened the front window a few inches to let in cool, fresh air.

"Pull over, I'm going to be sick."

There was no shoulder. He braked to a stop on the spongy redwood needles on the side of the road. Abby managed to get the door open before vomiting. She rinsed her mouth out. Then she and Carolyn spent five minutes walking back and forth in the dim light under the tall trees, while Jake played a video game on his Gameboy, and Jeff slid David Grisman's Christmas album into the CD player. Listening to the first carols of the season, he wondered how it was they could convince themselves each year that this was fun.

They gassed up at Alice's Restaurant and continued down the spine of the mountains, the road winding through the forest, breaking into sunlight along green rolling hills, and plunging back into the dimly lit redwoods.

At the entrance to the Christmas tree farm they picked up a saw and drove up a muddy service road, past parked cars and families in search of the perfect tree. Jeff parked under a small oak and they piled out.

He put on gloves and took the saw and tape measure. "I'm going to find Gramma's tree. By the time I cut it and get it on top of the car, you should have ours picked out."

The kids ranged energetically up the hill, leaving Carolyn behind as she tramped carefully over the uneven ground. Jeff smiled to himself. For once he wouldn't be in the middle of the bickering and indecision that seemed inevitable when his children were forced to make a choice.

He watched them go, then chose his favorite from the three trees nearest the road. After he'd cut it and hoisted it on top of the car, he sat on the tailgate and swung his legs and ate a turkey sandwich and sipped warm coffee from a commuter mug. He remembered other years when the rain was pelting, or the fog thick and damp, days so cold they'd had to come back to the car to warm up before continuing their search. Today was a beautiful, clear 70 degrees. He thought to call his mother to tell her they'd be coming with a tree, but there was no reception in the mountains.

An hour and fifteen minutes after they'd left, his family came down the hill. Jake led the way, glowering and stamping his mud-caked shoes as he crossed the road. It was easy to see who had won the battle.

"Stop!" Jeff shouted. "Off with the shoes. Don't get mud in the car."

Jake dangled his legs out of the car, took off his shoes and threw them vaguely in the direction of his sister, who was the next to come down the hill.

"Daddy," she whined, "tell Jake not to be such a baby."

"It's a lovely tree," Carolyn said, following behind. She had a glow in her cheeks, and joy in her expression.

Jeff gathered up Jake's shoes and put them in a plastic trash bag, and instructed Abby to follow suit. He opened the back door and thrust a sandwich into Jake's hands. "Eat," he commanded.

"I'm not hungry."

"You will be."

Then he grabbed his gloves and saw, and turned to his wife. "Lead on, Carol Lynn McTavish. Lead on."

When they were finished, they paid their money and returned the saw, then headed back to Alice's Restaurant, turned down Woodside Road and connected with 280 headed south.

"Do we have to go to Gramma's?" Jake asked grumpily.

"We do if you want a tree on Christmas morning," Jeff said.

"We could stay home for Christmas."

"And leave your Gramma all alone?"

"She could come to our house."

Jeff could see the logic in his argument.

Carolyn spoke up then. "We always stay over at the ranch Christmas eve. It's a tradition."

At the ranch Jeff pulled up by the front porch and went about taking the tree off the roof of the Subaru. Carolyn pushed the doorbell and knocked without drawing a response.

"Here," Jeff called, tossing her his keys. "It's the blue one."

She opened the door and called out, but the house was obviously vacant. When he'd got the tree on the ground, Carolyn took the top and he took the base and together they hauled it up onto the porch. "I should cut off another two inches from the bottom and get it into water as soon as possible. I'll get a saw from the barn. You get a bucket from the root cellar."

"I wonder where your mom is."

Jeff strode purposefully across the yard, aware that he was muddying his backup pair of shoes. He wondered if Carolyn had the presence of mind to take off her shoes before she went into the house. They'd all have to remember to clean their shoes before they got back into the car for the drive home. In the barn he paused a moment, waiting for his eyes to adjust to the dim light, then headed for the wall in front of the Chevy Malibu, where pitch forks, shovels, rakes, hoes, pruning shears, and saws were hung. He selected a triangular wood-saw.

A shape caught his eye and, sensing something incongruous, he stopped. It was a neat barn, with "a place for everything and everything in its place," just the way his father liked it. The tractor was parked at the far end of the stalls. His father's pickup truck was in the middle. And he stood in front of his mother's Malibu. So she had to be home. But she hadn't answered Carolyn's call.

He dropped the saw and sprinted back to the house, heedless of the mud on his shoes, heart pounding, on the edge of panic and trying to quell that panic, for he knew he had to be calm to respond to any emergency. He burst through the open door, nearly bowling over Carolyn who was lugging a pail of water toward the front porch, and flew up the stairs two at a time.

Carolyn put the pail down and stared after him. "Jeff?" No answer. "Jeff? What's wrong?" Jake started for the stairs. Carolyn reached out and pulled him back. Abby got up from her chair and stood beside them, looking up the stairs expectantly. After a minute Carolyn went upstairs herself. She heard whimpering before she reached the room. Jeff was on his knees beside the bed, his head bowed, his shoulders shaking. Virginia lay on her back, her pale face composed as though in sleep.

Chapter 12
The Mundane of the Macabre

He might have given in to grief then, had he not been forced to confront the procedural aspects of death. There were people to call, authorities to inform, wheels to be set in motion. So many details. He sent Carolyn and the kids home, saying he'd follow later in his mother's car. Then he sat calmly at his father's desk and started another list. He called Rosie first. After the fifth ring it went to voicemail.

"Rosie, I'm at the ranch. Mom...she's...Mom died this morning." On the word 'died' he suddenly broke down, as though speaking the word somehow made the abstract real. Time, that most precious commodity, had sailed serenely on, leaving his mother behind. In the end was the Word and the Word was Horror. "Sorry. Sorry," he said, his voice shaking. "Just call me."

He called the police and was told they would send the coroner and to wait there until he arrived.

The receptionist at the lawyer's office was obviously a gatekeeper, as she first said Mr. Blankenship was in a meeting, and then asked what the call was in reference to, and could she take Jeff's number and get back to him.

"No, I'll wait. This is an emergency."

She kept him waiting almost five minutes. "I'm sorry," she said, "Mr. Blankenship is tied up today. Can he get back to you on Monday?"

Jeff couldn't control his anger. "I'm sitting here with a dead body! I need to talk to him *now!*"

A moment later he heard a voice come on the line — a small, old, yet eager voice. "This is Paul Blankenship; can I help you?"

"This is Jeff Porter. Virginia Porter's son."

"Yes?"

"My mom has died, and I thought I should call you first."

"Oh, my god." Jeff heard him turn away from the phone and tell someone, "Virginia's dead." Then the voice came back louder. "I'm so sorry to hear, so sorry." There was genuine shock and grief in the voice. "Can I talk to your father?"

Jeff explained the situation as calmly as he could. Then he asked, "What do I do now?"

"Have you called the coroner?"

"He's coming." Jeff took a deep breath, trying to gather his thoughts. "I assume you have the will?"

"We do."

"When should we come in?" When there was no answer, Jeff further clarified, "For the reading?"

"Of the will? I'm afraid in this case it's not called for yet."

"What?"

"You said your father is missing. You may presume he's dead, but he is not *legally* dead."

This was not a complication Jeff had anticipated. "How long before we can declare him legally dead?"

"Seven years."

"Seven years!" The problems just kept multiplying. If his father were presumed to be alive, they would have no access to the bank accounts. "What do we do in the meantime? Who's going to pay the operation of the ranch? The house? The taxes? The upkeep?"

"We could petition the court to have an attorney appointed to oversee your parents' affairs until your father is found, or seven years has passed. I'd be happy to do that for you."

"I have to think," Jeff said, his mind reeling. If he had to have an attorney appointed, he'd ask his brother-in-law, J.C. Thatcher.

"Did my mother leave me and my sister anything?" Jeff asked, realizing how mercenary he must sound; but he had to know. "Did she have life insurance?"

"You know, it's really not appropriate at this time. Your parents each left everything to one another. So you and your sister will inherit only on the passing of the surviving spouse. But as I said, we can't declare your father deceased for seven years."

Jeff's phone began to beep, announcing an incoming call. "I have to take this call. I'm not sure what we'll decide. I'll get back to you."

It was Rosie. She'd obviously been crying, but had recovered enough to talk. "We'll be down as soon as I can line up babysitting for the boys."

"There's no point," Jeff said. "You can't do anything here. The coroner will be here soon, and they'll probably have taken her away by the time you get here. Is J.C. there?"

Rosie put him on and Jeff explained the problem of having his father declared dead.

"We don't want a court appointed attorney calling the shots," J.C. said. "Not even me. It just complicates matters, requires a lot of paperwork and filings and keeping the court apprised of expenditures. It's time-consuming and expensive, and we don't need the court looking over our shoulders."

"So how are we supposed to pay for the cremation, property taxes, upkeep? Carol and I have barely enough to pay our own bills." And it now occurred to him that without death certificates for both of his parents, he'd be unable to transfer legal ownership of the cars and the ranch. They'd be unable to sell anything. For seven years.

"Do you have your mom's ATM card? Credit cards? Pin number?"

"I don't know; I haven't checked. Let me look and I'll call you back."

He returned to the bedroom where his mother still lay as though asleep. On the chair beside her bed, Jeff found his mother's purse and credit cards. In her office (the sewing room) he found checkbooks, and a sheet of paper on which were printed her pin numbers and online usernames and passwords. Then he turned on her laptop which, thankfully, was not password protected, and opened her financial records. Everything was there — all the bills, the loans, the investments. He gave a great sigh of relief. All those years she'd spent working in a legal office had given her exceptional organizational skills. She'd made it easy for him. *Thank you, Mom. Thank you, thank you!* He called J.C. back.

"I have everything: Pin, usernames, passwords."

"How much is in the checking?"

"They've got a little over $12,000 in their checking, and another $20,000 or so in savings. They get monthly Social Security deposits, and a quarterly wire transfer from Morgan Stanley."

"How did she pay the bills?"

"Online banking, from their Wells Fargo account."

"Electronic transfer?"

"Looks like it."

"Perfect. Then we can just keep paying the bills as though they were alive — phone, utilities, automobile license fees, taxes, whatever, as long as there's sufficient money in the checking account. If we have to pay out of pocket, we can reimburse ourselves from the ATM. Don't cancel any credit cards — you can't use them in person, because you can't sign, but you can still buy things online (as long as the bills are paid, no one will know the difference). You'll have to notify Social Security of your mother's death. Also, cancel any health insurance they may have had; that's expensive."

When Jeff hung up he sighed with relief. There was no pressing need to sort through and dispose of his parents' possessions. It would have to be done, but they had seven long years to do it. In the meantime, they'd have enough to maintain the house and pay vineyard and orchard managers to keep the ranch running smoothly.

For the first time he hoped his father was dead, for then he would never have to come home to an empty house. And if there was an afterlife, Jeff thought, his parents presumably were together. It was small consolation.

He went back to his mother's room and sat by her bed. With the business end of death concluded and nothing to do but await the arrival of the coroner, a chasm of grief opened beneath him and he wept in earnest for the mother who would never awake and the time he could never reclaim.

That evening, as they sat (together for a change) at the kitchen table, Carolyn said, "We'll have to go back and clean out the refrigerator; all that food's going to go bad. You should make a list."

Jeff got a pad of paper and a mechanical pencil and wrote: 1. Clean out refrigerator.

"What else?" he asked.

"There will be bills. Find out how much the cremation costs. And speaking of expenses, you should put all the usual bills (utilities and such) on auto-pay." Then she turned to Jake, "Eat your vegetables."

"I don't like green beans."

"I don't like quinoa," Abby added. "It's weird."

"It's organic; it's good for you."

"Are we still gonna have Christmas?" Abby asked.

"Have the mail forwarded here," Carolyn said, ignoring her.

Monday morning Jeff called Ralph Denning and explained his predicament, leaving the Copy Editor with more responsibility than either of them was comfortable with. A little later O'Malley called, "Jeeze, sorry buddy; that's tough — your dad and now your mom.

Man, you've got some seriously bad karma going. Ralph tells me you've assigned some of your duties to him."

"Yeah, I have a lot on my plate at the moment. There's funeral arrangements," Jeff said (a gross exaggeration, but he didn't want to get into specifics).

Despite the overwhelming details in the aftermath of death, the magazine rolled inexorably on like the tide, pausing for no one and nothing. Since they were always working on three issues at various stages of completion, it was always a mental juggling act to keep all of the projects in motion. He was grateful to have a staff behind him. "We have all the articles in hand. We're still waiting on some artwork. And I've asked Ralph to coordinate with Claudio on the ads. You'll have to make sure they both move things along. Oh, and I forgot to ask Ralph to send me his edited copy — it always helps to have a second pair of eyes."

"Okey-dokey, I'll pass it on. Anything else?"

"No, I think that's it. I'll be in touch everyday, but I don't expect to come into the office until next week."

"Take all the time you need; Ralph's been doing a bang-up job in your absence."

O'Malley could be such a schmuck, thought Jeff.

The coroner called Wednesday. "I'm ruling this an accidental death," he said. "Your mother had a high blood alcohol level, combined with the sleeping and anti-anxiety pills we found by her bedside. I don't know why people don't read the warnings that come with prescription drugs, but they don't." Jeff nodded with his cell phone to his ear. "They're both in the benzodiazepine class, and there are clear warnings on both packages to avoid taking them together, and to avoid drinking alcohol in conjunction with these drugs. But there you have it. No one listens, no one reads." The coroner sounded annoyed, as though he were delivering a lecture. *A little too late*, Jeff thought. "I'm releasing the body to the Oak Hill Funeral Home."

A courier delivered the ashes the next week. They came in a clear plastic bag sealed with tape inside a small cardboard box. Jeff was working at home when the courier rang the bell. He accepted the box, put it on the kitchen counter, and went back to work. He knew his parents disliked the ceremony and expense of elaborate funerals, but this was the opposite extreme, entirely dismissing the solemnity of the occasion. Virginia, ever irreverent, had once flippantly remarked, "Don't make any fuss over me when I die; just toss me out with the garbage." With her ashes in a plain cardboard box, he could actually do just that. But funerals and memorial services were for the living, not for the dead.

He called Rosie. "I have Mom's ashes."

"What are you going to do? Did she say what she wanted?"

"No, she didn't say. I was thinking the Laurel tree."

There was a pause as Rosie considered. "Yeah, why not? That's as good as anyplace. She really didn't give a damn. Why should we?"

"You're too sentimental," he said sarcastically, but he knew what she meant. "You want to be there when I scatter the ashes?"

"No fucking way. I mean — she's gone to heaven or oblivion or wherever. Her ashes don't mean anything. I'd rather remember her in other ways."

"You want me to keep some ashes for you?"

"No thanks."

On Saturday they drove down to the ranch. Jeff dragged the dry Christmas tree off the porch and tossed it in the bushes by the stream. After they emptied the kitchen of perishables, Jeff addressed his family. "Okay, troops; it's time to say goodbye to Gramma. We're going to scatter her ashes."

"Isn't that illegal?" Carolyn inquired. "Don't we need a permit?"

"Probably, but who's to know?"

"It's not the way I'd do it, but she's *your* mother."

"It's what she wanted. My parents didn't believe in ostentatious funerals."

He picked up the box and a scissors and they all accompanied him out the side door to the dark laurel. A cold breeze scoured the yard, setting the leaves ashiver. Under the tree three, small, lichen-encrusted headstones lay toppled beside a large marble pedestal, upon which was carved "Erected by Mary Morse Kimball, 1916." The pedestal had been tipped up by thick roots that spread out from the base of the tree. "When I was a kid there was an obelisk with the names of the people buried here. These little stones were probably for kids, but the names and dates have worn off. Anyway, she loved this tree and I figured this was a fitting place to scatter her ashes." He opened the box and cut the top off the plastic bag. As he poured the contents around the roots of the tree, a gust of wind whipped some of the finer ash into the air where it wafted off toward the barn.

"You should wet that down before it all blows away," Carolyn said. Then she and the kids marched back inside.

Jeff dragged the hose over and sprinkled the ashes. Addressing the grey mud he said, "Love you, Mom. Say hi to Pop for me."

In the kitchen he tossed the cardboard box into the fireplace. He debated for a second about what to do with the plastic bag. The inside was still coated with a layer of his mother's grey ash. He hesitated only a moment, then wadded it up and threw it into the trash. Virginia had got her wish after all.

Chapter 13
Unemployed

Just three weeks later Jeff returned home with a heavy heart. Carolyn was wrapping presents in their bedroom. "Sit down, I have something to tell you," he said.

"They found your father?"

"O'Malley's shutting down the magazine. I've lost my job."

"Oh shit."

That evening they sat at the kitchen table and went over the finances. Carolyn made a list of outflows: mortgage, utilities, food, insurance, gas, cell phones.

"I don't want to be a doomsayer," she said, "but we really should plan on a worst-case scenario. Then we'll be prepared."

It wasn't a pretty picture: Without his meager income they'd be eating into their savings every month. Unemployment was on the rise; the stock market was in free-fall, and the housing market had collapsed. Prospects for a quick recovery were dim. Prospects for another job were even dimmer.

"Maybe you can freelance again," Carolyn suggested, "just for awhile, to make ends meet."

Jeff considered that possibility. Freelancing, writing articles and selling photos on spec to numerous magazines, had never been lucrative, though he had fond memories of working at the kitchen table with Abby in a playpen by his side. But with magazines and newspapers going out of business every month, the industry was littered with talented, experienced editors, writers and photographers competing for limited jobs. Supply and demand dictated that there would be few available jobs, and the pay would be ludicrously low.

Late evening a few days after Christmas Jeff sat on the bed, browsing for jobs on his laptop. Carolyn was pedaling a stationary bike, listening to music on her iPod and sweating profusely.

"Did your parents have a mortgage?" she asked.

"Who doesn't have a mortgage?"

"They lived there a long time. Could it be paid off?"

"It's easy enough to check." Jeff logged into his parents' bank accounts. "No mortgage payments, so I guess they paid it off."

"Wouldn't that be nice? Can you imagine if we didn't have a mortgage payment?"

"Dream on," Jeff said, going back to his job search.

She pedaled furiously for a couple more minutes, then stopped and turned off her iPod. "Virtually everything I make, after taxes, goes to paying the mortgage. Thirty-two-hundred a month. I was thinking, we could sell the condo, or if the numbers don't make sense, we could just walk away from the mortgage."

"What's the point? Apartments aren't cheap, either."

"We could move to the ranch. That house is just sitting there all paid off and empty."

"We've been over this before. It's a dump. You know what it would cost to renovate?"

"I know it needs a lot of work, but we could fix it up. We could afford to — think of all money we'd save each month if we didn't have a mortgage hanging over our heads. We might even be able to save enough for a vacation."

Jeff was silent. He'd worked all his adult life to distance himself from the ranch and all it stood for. Going back would be another admission that he'd failed the most basic standard of adulthood — self-sufficiency. He had become (as he'd once said of the ranch house) more of a liability than an asset, and the thought brought to mind a snippet of conversation he'd had with his uncle Ed. He'd been lamenting how hard it was to make ends meet on two incomes, when his uncle had replied in his characteristically acerbic manner, "A man who relies on his wife for support isn't really a man. It's time to grow up, get a real job, and stop whining." Jeff might have expected this from a man who once bragged he'd never changed a diaper, but the comment had nonetheless stung to the quick, and it still bothered him.

He started to object, but Carolyn interrupted him. "Sweetheart, before you say no, just think about it. This could be our last chance to have a house before the kids are grown."

"This *is* a house."

"Don't be argumentative; you know what I mean. Just think about it, please?"

She went into the bathroom to take a shower, and Jeff did think about it. And no matter how he looked at it, regardless of past resentments and his present feeling of failure, he knew she was right. It was the sensible thing to do.

"I'm not going," Abby said.

"Sweetie," Carolyn crooned, "just think — you'll have your own room."

"I'll stay with Jennifer."

"You'll make new friends."

"I don't want *new* friends. I want the friends I've had since I was in kindergarten!"

"You can finish out the year at Bowditch. We won't move before the end of the school year."

"I'm not going! You can't make me!" Abby shouted over her shoulder as she stormed down the hall and slammed the door.

Jake watched her go, then asked, "Can I have my own room, too?"

"Of course."

"Cool. Can I have a dog?"

"We'll think about it," Jeff said.

"Sweet."

Jake fairly skipped down the hall to his room.

"That was predictable," Jeff said.

"She'll like it once she has a room of her own and makes some new friends."

"I just wish she could think of it as an adventure."

"It's hard for her. She's like me; she craves stability."

"If you crave stability so much, why do you want to move?"

"You're not having second thoughts, are you?"

He took a moment before answering, "Well, I'm not crazy about the idea, but it makes economic sense." What he thought and did not express, was that it took the pressure off. Without a mortgage payment he could take his time finding a job that suited his particular talents, instead of taking the first thing he could find.

He went down the hall and opened the door. "Knock, knock," he said at the hanging sheet.

"Go away!"

He entered and found his daughter lying in a fetal position on the bed, tears in her eyes. He sat down next to her. "It won't be so bad," he said.

"You suck! It's totally unfair. You're ruining my life!"

"You know, your mother had to change schools every year or two the whole time she was growing up. She doesn't understand why you should be so upset, because she went through it time after time. She's looking forward to..."

"That's the point! She doesn't understand! *You* don't understand!"

She would have been too embarrassed to explain it to them. She'd been sitting next to the same boy, by virtue of their alphabetical order, for ten years. They had been through every grade but fifth grade together, and it was tacitly acknowledged that they would begin dating in high school. It had nothing to do with romance. It had everything to do with feeling comfortable. It would make it so much easier to mark those awkward firsts that every teenager had to face — the first time holding hands, the first kiss, the first dance, the first...whatever. And now she was being forced to go to a school where she knew no one. Where the other kids had a history together. She would be the odd girl out. It was a mean and terrible thing her parents were forcing her to endure.

"I know it'll be an adjustment," Jeff said. "But it has some positive points."

"Like what?"

"Your own room."

"Besides that."

That was the problem, Jeff thought. From her viewpoint, that was about all they had to offer. Jake had suggested one obvious answer.

"You could have a pet," he offered.

"I don't want a pet."

"Moving to the ranch will save us a lot of money. We'll be able to put something away for your college education. Maybe not a four-year college to start, but you could transfer after a couple years of community college."

"I'm not going to college. As soon as I'm 18 I'm out o' here."

"Yay!" came Jake's sarcastic cry from the other side of the bookcase.

"Jacob!" Jeff admonished. Then to Abby he said quietly, "When you're sixteen you can have your gramma's car; then you can visit your friends as often as you like. Besides, these days you can stay in touch with Twitter and Skype and texting and all that jazz."

"It won't be the same. They won't know who I'm talking about. They'll have different teachers. We won't have the same experiences. How would you like it if you had to work with all new people?"

Jeff let that question lie there for about fifteen seconds before he asked, "What do you think happens when you get a new job?"

"I guess I wasn't thinking," she said, sitting up.

"Look, I don't like having our lives disrupted any more than you do. But shit happens," he said. "Are you forgetting my own father has disappeared? My mother is dead? I've lost my job? I'd love to erase the last six months, but I can't. All I'm asking for is your understanding. We're trying to get through this the best way we can. I know it sucks. But it is what it is and no amount of wishing is going to turn back the clock. Can you please just cut us a break?"

Then she started to cry and threw her arms around him. He sighed and hugged back, wishing he could make it all better and knowing he was powerless to do so.

"For God's sake," Jake called, "take it to another room!"

Chapter 14
Preparing to Move

Late one evening Carolyn handed her plate to Jeff as he loaded the dishwasher. "I'm proud of you," she said.

"Why?"

"Because you've lost both of your parents and you didn't fall apart. You're still here for us. I know it's hard. I appreciate it."

He didn't feel he deserved any praise for holding it together. He wasn't as stoic as she seemed to think. He had cried for his mother and he silently mourned her each day with an edge of guilt. *If only I could turn back time and stop her from mixing alcohol and drugs*, he thought. But life didn't work that way. There *were* no second chances. Time did *not* stand still. Once gone, it was gone forever. Irrevocably.

It was disquieting to discover how little emotional control he actually had these days. Lately he'd found himself tearing up at the most inopportune moments. Phrases, songs and movies could cause tears to well up. Situations he'd once dismissed as mawkishly sentimental now struck him as profoundly touching and imbued with deeper meaning.

That he was emotionally skating on thin ice was obvious the day of Barack Obama's inauguration. A sea of people filled National Mall, while individual cameras captured select members of a weeping and enthralled audience. He did not usually fall victim to patriotic claptrap, but this day the clichés and the peaceful transfer of power brought tears to his eyes and a hitch in his breath. His usually healthy cynicism was entirely absent.

As for his father, in Jeff's heart he was stuck in emotional limbo, neither alive nor dead, neither here nor there, between now and then. How could he cry for a soul in stasis?

On a Saturday morning in late January they all drove down to the ranch. It was a cool yet sunny day with a slight breeze.

Jeff and Carolyn proceeded room by room, starting at the back of the house with the kitchen.

"I've always wondered why in the world there's a cast iron stove in the kitchen. It's an interesting antique, but it takes up so much room."

"I think they built the house around it. It weighs a ton. The only way to get it out of here would be to blow out the back wall and use a forklift."

"Okay, so it stays, for now," Carolyn conceded. "Why would anyone cover hardwood floors with linoleum?"

"Linoleum was the craze back in the day."

"Can you strip it off?" she asked. He made a note. They moved into the dining room. "Nothing to do here, except paint. And the drapes are shabby. Maybe just lace curtains to let in the light."

As they came down the hall they saw Abby, dressed in a baggy grey sweatshirt and jeans, arms crossed, leaning a shoulder against the parlor doorjamb and glowering in histrionic defiance of the whole proceedings.

"Hold that pose," Jeff said as he took his iPhone from his pocket and snapped a photo.

"That's not funny," she said.

Jeff held the iPhone out to Carolyn, who said, "Looks pretty funny from our side. Cheer up."

Jake came running in from the barn. "Hey, Pop, this is so cool! There's an owl in the garage!"

"I'm sure it has plenty of rats to eat," Abby said as if she'd been waiting to use the line, and tossed her strawberry blonde hair over her shoulder.

It was such a theatrical gesture that Jeff wondered where she'd learned it.

When they were done downstairs, Carolyn turned to Abby, who had sprawled on the parlor sofa. "Come on, young lady, we're going to take a look at your room."

"I don't have a room; I'm not moving."

"Humor me." Carolyn took her hand and Abby made a show of reluctantly being led upstairs.

Carolyn gave her daughter her choice of rooms. "The junk room is a bit small. Your dad's old room is the biggest, but if I were you I'd take Aunt Rosie's room; it has its own bath."

"I'd still have to share it with Jake."

Carolyn saw an opening and took it. "He can use the half-bath downstairs and shower in our room." This offer brought about an immediate change in her daughter's demeanor. The prospect of her own bath was just the enticement needed to win her over.

"And you'd have windows," Carolyn added in as cheery a voice as she could muster.

Jeff followed Jake out to the barn to look at the owl. It was probably a good thing to have an owl on the property, and Abby was right; it would eat rats and mice.

The barn was an old building; probably as old as the house, Jeff observed, but it had not been as well maintained. There were a few holes in the roof, the ladders to the loft were rickety, and some of the supporting timbers looked suspect.

Taking stock of the tools and machinery, he spied a tarp-covered lump on the workbench. Drawing back the edge he saw the obelisk.

"Hey, Jake, come here. This is that old gravestone I was telling you about, the one that used to be under the laurel."

It had cracked in half when it toppled off its pedestal, and it appeared as if his father had brought it here to repair.

Jake came to stand beside him, tracing engraved letters with his finger. Three were children. "They didn't live very long in the olden days, did they?"

"They didn't have vaccines or antibiotics. People died of all sorts of things: measles, mumps, small pox, pneumonia, appendicitis, farm accidents."

They were interrupted by a knock on the door, and Jeff turned to see Alan Murphy, the orchardist. They shook hands and Murphy slipped his hands into his back pockets. "I just wanted you to know up front, our inability to spray is going to impact the plums. We really should be using a fungicide. Also, I don't know if you're aware of it, but the trees are about 13 years old, and they'll only produce a commercially viable crop for another two to five years. I'd recommend replanting 15 to 20% of the trees each year, starting next year."

"I'm not sure we'll want to go that route. Shoot me an email with a cost estimate."

"Yes sir."

Jeff watched him go, feeling like the farmer he never wanted to be.

Jake must have picked up on the thought, for he asked, "Are you going to teach me how to grow stuff?"

Jeff shook his head. "There's no future in it."

That afternoon Jeff began boxing up his father's farm journals to make room for his archive of slide transparencies. The journals formed a kind of diary of a working farm. The elder Porter had handwritten notes on all procedures and expenditures since he'd started working the farm in the 1960s, chronicling pruning practices, replanting schedules, rootstock experiments, application of pesticides, dates of bud-break, irrigation regimen, harvest dates, sugar levels, a daily temperature log, equipment purchases, contract arrangements with various wineries for grapes, and with produce distributors for the plums, peaches, apricots and walnuts.

He also found similar journals that pre-dated his father's time, as well as a binder of historical documents. Among them was a bill of sale for redwood lumber and a payment made from August Kimball to one "John Glamis, carpenter," in 1855, suggesting that the house had been built in that year. Kimball appeared to be the original owner. Subsequent owners included the Marquette brothers and a William Bennett. There was an estimate from a contractor for repairs after the 1906 earthquake, notations from books and historical treatises about farming in the area, as well as a letter from Charles LeFranc concerning a dispute over payment for grapes for the 1882 vintage.

He was sitting in an armchair, staring out the window at the Santa Cruz Mountains stretching northward in a dark, diminishing line when Carolyn came in and kissed him on the top of his head. She massaged his shoulders with firm hands.

"I made some tea," she said. "What have you been up to?"

Jeff held up one of the earliest journals. "Just reading this, about the original owners, and thinking."

"About what?"

"About this room, this house, being a kid. You know that old saying, 'You can't go home again'? When you think about the way it was, it's not the *place* you're remembering, so much as the *time*. And you can't really recapture time, or how you felt then, because you're not the same person you were. Anyway, the only important thing is how you feel about it now. Now is all that matters. Does that make sense?"

"Perfectly."

"I'm just trying to see this place with fresh eyes," he said, as though trying to convince himself.

Chapter 15
Ghosts

Once the decision was made, preparing for the move seemed to take all of his waking hours. He called Rosie to enlist her contribution, arguing that any improvements would surely increase the value of the house, which would be to her benefit when the house was eventually sold. But Rosie was less than supportive. "We don't have a lot of extra money," she said; "it's all tied up in investments that've tanked. And it seems to me I'll be paying top dollar for new stuff that'll be used by the time we sell in seven years. So I wouldn't get *my* money out of it. There's nothing in this deal for me. Anyway, you can live in it without fixing it up. Mom and Pop did."

On a Tuesday he went to the county Planning and Building Department to find out how much permits might run. He faced an obese white woman of indeterminate age across the counter. He gave her the address and she called up the information on her computer.

She leaned forward, peering myopically at the screen. "It says here your father had the house placed on the National Register of Historic Houses. There are very special rules concerning Historic Houses. Just a moment." She waddled away and came back wheezing a few minutes later with a sheaf of papers concerning Houses on the Historic Register. "It's possible your father's house may qualify for a grant to help with renovation. You may want to look into it before applying for permits."

Jeff was uncertain what to do. It sounded as though applying for permits could be costly and time consuming. "What can we do without permits?"

The woman eyed him suspiciously. "Repairs under $500 are exempt. Anything over $500, or involving electrical or plumbing, requires a permit. And homes in the Historic Register are governed by strict rules; you can't make any additions. Your father must have known that when he had it placed in the Register."

Jeff thanked her and drove back to the ranch where he wandered the rooms with an eye toward what he might be able to fix himself. A coat of paint, new wallpaper and refinished hardwood floors would spruce up an otherwise drab room, and the cost would be negligible if he were to do it himself. Unemployed, he had the time.

Upstairs he entered his parents' bedroom. The pillow on his mother's side still bore the indentation of her head. Her slippers sat on the floor beside the bed, like patient puppies waiting for their owner to return. He found it strange to consider that all of these personal items were no longer of use to their owners, no longer even the property of their owners. They had become as orphans, items without owners.

In the drawer of his father's nightstand he found prescriptions for Simvastatin and Viagra, a tube of KY jelly, bottles of Aleve and Advil, Vicks VapoRub, a keychain without keys, three mystery keys, a box of bandaids, a travel alarm, a small flashlight, a compass, several pencils and erasers, a small folding picture frame with photos of Jeff's grandparents in their 30s, a sleep mask, a ruler, a solar-powered calculator, an antique pocket watch and two broken wristwatches.

The closet was filled with clothes that were too big for Jeff, and too out-of-style for Carolyn. And beneath the hanging shirts and skirts, coats and dresses there were shoes, perhaps thirty pairs, most of them dusty and showing signs of wear. He wondered if his parents had ever thrown out a pair of shoes.

It was a bit disturbing to find so much useless junk. It came from living in one place too long. He didn't want his own children going through his things and wondering why on earth he'd kept such rubbish. He made a mental note to jettison his own junk when they moved. He went out to the barn and came back with a large, plastic trashcan, and emptied the nightstands. There was precious little he cared to keep.

Then he turned his attention to his father's chest of drawers. He opened the top drawer with a sense of violation, as though his father might suddenly appear and scold him for peeking into his private drawers without permission. Inside the top drawer he found a jumble of rolled up neckties, tie tacks, a travel alarm, two more broken wristwatches, a flashlight, rubber bands and paper clips, three AAA batteries, six thumb tacks, two mechanical pencils, one antique fountain pen, a ballpoint pen, a blood pressure monitor, a Swiss Army Knife, miscellaneous buttons, miscellaneous receipts, two photo transparencies, a movie ticket and three baseball cards — all of the detritus of his parents' lives was now his to deal with. Every little thing. Every scrap of paper. Every bit of refuse shoved into a drawer to be forgotten. Every item saved in the unlikely event it would be of use one day. It would take weeks or even months to sift through it all. It would all have to be discarded or put away before they could move in.

Continuing to rummage through his father's drawers, he found two billfolds and a pair of gloves he'd given his father as gifts over the years, still in their boxes, unused. The next drawer contained pajamas and socks, all of the birthday and Fathers' Day cards Randall had received over the years, and a bundle of love letters from Virginia. The next drawer was full of sweaters, which Jeff piled on the bed for charity.

He opened the bottom drawer and stared in amazement. It was filled with clippings and magazines in which his photos and articles had appeared. His father had never praised his work, nor given any indication he was anything but disappointed in his son's choice of profession. Until this moment Jeff had been unsure if his father had ever read an article he'd written, or seen one of his published photos. There was a stack of *Gourmet Traveler*, the topmost issue bookmarked at an article on Wales he'd written the year before with some of his best photos. His father had obviously thought they were worth saving, so why had he never said anything? Why had he never offered a word of praise? *Or even criticism,* Jeff thought. He would have been content with criticism, any sign that his father took notice or was at all interested.

Over the next two months Jeff alternated between the ranch and the condo, working to clean up the clutter, hiring a broker to list the condo, making repairs that he felt competent doing himself, and hiring an electrician to tackle more technical problems.

In his parents' kitchen he fixed a broken drawer-front, stripped linoleum off the floor and refinished the hardwood. He replaced the sconces in the office, repainted three of the bedrooms, replaced shower heads in the bathrooms, replaced rotted boards on the porch, and painted over the dingy wallpaper in the office and the dining room with lighter colors.

There was something elemental about physical work, about seeing the tangible result to his labors that gave him an enormous sense of satisfaction. He might not be making money, but he was saving them money by doing most of the work himself, and that was a form of contribution.

There are moments in every life that serve as lines of demarcation to set apart what came before from what comes after. For Jeffrey Porter that line was as obvious as opening a door and stepping into an entirely different reality, and it happened over dinner.

One Saturday they had all gone to the ranch to help sort and clean, but Jake was distracted and Abby uncooperative, so it took longer than anticipated, and they found themselves not yet ready to leave when dinner time rolled around. Jeff found spaghetti and a jar of marinara in the cupboard. When it was ready they all gathered around the kitchen table. Jeff went down to the root cellar for a bottle of wine, while Carolyn served up the plates.

Returning with a Cabernet and a Zinfandel, he held them up for Carolyn's inspection. "Which will it be?"

She was considering the choice when they heard a voice shout out, as from another room, "Olly, olly oxen free!"

Everyone's head swung in unison toward the open cellar door. Jeff dropped the Zinfandel. It hit his instep and rolled harmlessly under the table. There followed a stunned silence as Jeff set the Cabernet on the sideboard and listened intently at the open door. Abby began to speak, but her father raised his hand in a gesture that cut her off in mid-sentence. He went halfway down the stairs and peered into the cellar. Then he came back upstairs, shut off the light and quietly closed the door. He retrieved the fallen bottle and set it on the table. His family was watching him now, waiting for some pronouncement.

"Well?" Jake asked.

Jeff uncorked the Zinfandel and poured two glasses of wine. He handed one to Carolyn and sat down at the table.

Looking considerably more shaken than he, she took her seat.

"Come on, Dad!" Abby said.

"You all heard that, right?" They just stared at him. He glanced toward the cellar door, then shrugged, smiled slyly and chanted, "'There's somethin' *strange*...in the neighbor*hood*. Who you gonna *call*?'"

"'Ghostbusters!'" Jake finished with glee. "I'll betcha it's Gramma."

"It wasn't her voice," Jeff said.

"There's no such thing as ghosts," Carolyn declared.

"They couldn't hurt us, could they, Daddy?" Abby asked.

"I don't think so, sweetheart."

"There are no such things as ghosts," Carolyn repeated slowly with conviction.

"I bet we could get on 'Unsolved Mysteries,'" Jake speculated with relish.

"No," Carolyn said firmly. "I'd appreciate it if all of you would please keep this to yourselves. It's not like we saw anything. We don't really know that there's anything down there. It could be a...I don't know...an echo of something, like a mirage. You see an oasis right in front of you and it seems real because somewhere that oasis exists, but not here. Our being able to see it is only an optical trick. And maybe this is like that, an auditory mirage."

"Who ever heard of an auditory mirage?" Abby scoffed.

"Well whatever it is, I'd rather you didn't go around talking about ghosts. People will think we're nuts."

"I think it's cool," Jake said. "I'm gonna get a ouija board."

Abby tossed her strawberry blonde hair over her shoulder. "I'm not moving into a haunted house," she said flatly.

PART TWO

Searching

Chapter 16
August Kimball

On a mid-April morning in 1870 August Kimball stood in his apricot orchard south of the barn.

Three rows away Owen, his eldest, called out. "What do you think, pa? Two weeks?"

He considered the question for a moment, his eyes roving over the hard fruit. "Yes, I expect so. Maybe three, if this blasted haze doesn't burn off."

He heard a shout of joy and turned to see Charles, seven, running barefooted down his row with the mutt yapping at his heels. In a moment August's heart sank, and then he felt badly of himself, for at the first shout his mind had played a trick on him. For a split second he had expected Ivan, dead from a rattlesnake bite eight months now, and when his mind made the instantaneous adjustment he was disappointed, and in his disappointment he rebuked himself for being unfair to Charles.

Ivan, who'd been just ten, had been his particular favorite, the one who hung around and kept him constant company, the one who cheered his days with infectious good humor and easy affection. He was not the first child they had lost, but August had not been the same after this one. He could not lose himself in his work, as he had when Molly died of the measles at four, because Ivan had always been at his side. In his mind, as he checked bud set and fruit, performed a graft or pruned a cane, he heard himself explaining to Ivan the right way to go about it. There were moments every day when he felt hollow, except for a lump of grief that seemed to stick in his throat. At times like this he chastised himself for being selfish, for over the last months he had not been much of a father to the others, particularly to Charles, who at seven looked much like his dead brother, but who was often distant with his parents.

He thought to make it up to Charles by inviting him to tag along. "I'm riding over to..." he began to say, when he noticed the youngster's bare feet and cut short the invitation.

Charles came rushing onward, mindless of his father's expression. The mutt bounded past. August caught his son by the arm, nearly jerking him off his feet.

"Gotta help Noah!" Charles yelled.

"How many times have I told you to wear your boots?" There was a fury in his voice that carried more weight than the rhetorical question. They all knew what their father meant when he asked that question: *Your brother might be here today if he'd been wearing boots. Boots might stop a rattler's fangs.*

Charles looked up into his father's eyes, saw the worry behind the words and was properly penitent. "Sorry, Papa."

August released his son's arm, knelt down, and hugged him gently. "I don't want to lose any more of you."

"I know, Papa. It's okay; I'll go put'm on."

Charles ran down the row a little slower now and cut toward the house. August stood up, took his hat off and ran his fingers through his short, salt-and-pepper hair.

"Owen, could you please saddle my horse? I'm going over to the pickers' camp to find out how the other growers are faring."

August paid a visit to the privy, informed his wife that he would be gone for an hour, and set out on horseback toward Guadalupe Creek.

Short, though solidly built, with light blue eyes and a brindled walrus mustache, he road with shirt sleeves rolled up his muscular forearms, a red bandanna tied around his neck, and a wide-brimmed black hat to shade his eyes. Fearing rattlers since Ivan's death, he wore long boots under his pants.

Sometimes the worry of raising a family seemed like a physical weight on his shoulders, though he had always assumed his responsibilities without complaint. Overall he was satisfied that he had made the right choices in his life, though each choice had profoundly altered everything that came after. He could not have foretold the outcome of his decisions as he made them, but each (leaving Pennsylvania for Oregon, the Gold Rush, buying into a business, marriage, children, planting the orchards and vineyards) had been necessary steps in the progression of his life. So that he now found himself looking over his ranch, secure in the knowledge that his wife and girls were tending to the house, his boys were learning to work the ranch, and life could hardly be better — if only he could stop grieving, let go of the past and embrace the future.

Rhubarb, the sorrel gelding, crossed the creek bed of Arroyo Calero south of the bridge, lunged up the far bank, and paused beside the vineyard of Mission grapes. Backed up against a natural amphitheater the climate here was warmer, the optimum spot to grow stone fruit and grapes.

He turned Rhubarb at a canter toward Guadalupe Creek and the Mexican encampment, a short ride of three miles. On the way he mulled over the previous week's sermon, an entertainment that occupied much of his time as he performed his duties around the ranch.

Reverend Winter's Easter sermon had been a rambling discourse on God's Great Plan. God has a plan for all of us, he had said. We are here to serve Him. But He works in mysterious ways etc. August had been turning the idea over in his mind, raising some interesting questions in the course of his contemplation. The idea of a Great Plan appealed to him, but he wondered if such a plan negated the possibility of free will. If God really had such a master plan, then society was working at cross-purposes to religion. If God planned it all, there was no use blaming criminals for their actions, any more than a man should take credit for his good fortune. He had been pondering those questions for four days now. The sermons were food for his soul, opening up avenues of thought previously unexplored.

He wanted to believe God controlled it all. That would take away all responsibility, leaving a man's fate in God the Father, whose love was all encompassing and unconditional. But he felt the reality of the situation must lie somewhere in-between. God, he thought, created us and gave us each a soul, which if cultivated and allowed to mature and develop, should lead us on the righteous path to heaven. Like salmon returning to the stream of their birth, each and every soul was born knowing the way home. So how was it that some men turned out bad? He thought that somehow, somewhere along the way, bad men lost God through selfishness, and in so doing they lost their own souls. They became pariahs in society.

So, August concluded, Man was naturally born with a propensity toward an end. God didn't oversee every little act. He just set us in motion with a soul that was predisposed to point toward heaven as a compass points north. A good man may make choices of his own but those choices were bound to point toward his ultimate salvation. Whereas a man whose soul had been perverted was without direction, like a compass that has lost its magnetism; he cannot find his way home to heaven, but blunders through life making choices that will lead to his perdition. So in the small everyday things he had "freewill," he could take a step to the side but still point in the right general direction, while in the larger sense his fate was cast.

The line of sycamores and oaks along Guadalupe Creek loomed ahead. August could see the tents of the Mexican encampment in the meadow to the northwest, in the curve of the creek.

But if the soul was predestined or designed to find its way home to God, August wondered, how did that affect the concept of original sin? Was Man then born innocent, or was he naturally barbaric and forced by the institutions of civilization — family, church, law — to be good? And if God is perfect, how is it that He made such an imperfect creation as Man? Ah, how the questions led one to another.

The Mexican camp was made up of thirty men and women and perhaps fifty children, a dozen large canvas tents, four wagons and eight mules. Charles Bowman, mounted on a dun mare, was speaking with the foreman of the group. August slowed Rhubarb to a walk and reined him in as he came abreast the mare.

Charles interrupted his conversation with Salvador Alamillo and nodded a greeting. "Gus."

"Charlie."

"Come to lure away my workers?"

"I've got nothing for them to pick yet. Our apricots are two weeks away, and the plums probably a month. How about you?"

"Same. Hey, did you hear about Delmas and Stevens? They used Chinese to prune their vineyards. Did a good job, too; went through those vines like locusts, and they don't charge as much as these Mexicans," he said with a twinkle in his eye and a sidelong glance at Alamillo, who frowned at the news. In the year since the completion of the Transcontinental Railway, laid off Chinese laborers had been roaming the countryside looking for work.

"Afraid of the competition, Sal?" Bowman teased with a hint of malice in his voice.

The Mexican grunted. "They work for nothing. They live like dogs." He spat at the ground in contempt. "They come here..." he began, and finished the thought with a fist to his palm, as though crushing a bug.

"I don't know, *Paco*, seems like them Chinamen offer a better deal. I might just go have a talk with them when it comes time to pick my trees."

"Is your crew staying here for awhile?" August asked Alamillo.

"Sure, Boss, we'll be here. We can do it. Just give us a couple days' notice. You don't need no Chinamen. You got beans and lettuce and onions, we pick those too."

August wasn't in the mood for small talk. He didn't like Bowman. He didn't trust a man whose wife always seemed frightened in her husband's presence. He left him to haggle with Alamillo and turned the sorrel back toward the ranch, eyes searching the sky for signs of a change in the weather.

Leaving Rhubarb tied to the oak nearest the house, he crossed the side yard. Lyddy and Betsy were out back hanging the wash on the lines. Carrie, their fourteen-year-old, was scrubbing clothes on a washboard on the porch outside the kitchen door. Before talking to

Owen and Noah about making more bushel baskets, he wanted a biscuit and a glass of water.

He had his foot on the bottom step of the porch when Emily, their three-year-old, came bursting out of the kitchen. The door bumped into the washtub.

"Papa! Papa! Papa!"

August scooped her into his arms. "Whoa, young lady. What's the matter, now?"

"A man bwoke you bottles."

"Would that man's name be Emily?"

She smiled sweetly. "I didn't bweak a bottle. The boogieman bwoke it."

"You know, I'm less upset about your breaking a bottle, than I am about your lying to me about it."

"I'n not lying!" she cried, pouting indignantly. "I *saw* him."

"Did you, now?"

Carrie drew an arm across her forehead. "Where's my soap flakes? I sent you for soap flakes."

"Sawwy," Emily shrugged. "I fo'getted."

August set her on the ground. Try as he might, he couldn't be angry with her. "We'll talk about this later. I'll clean up the glass. You help Carrie, now." He patted his youngest affectionately on the top of her head.

"Could you bring up a box of soap flakes?" Carrie asked as her father went into the kitchen.

Chapter 17
Palimpsest

Early Wednesday morning, the 14th of May, a late spring storm soaks the Bay Area. Jeff sees Carolyn and the kids off to their respective schools and dresses in his exercise outfit — long-sleeved polypropylene shirt, blue nylon warm-up jacket and pants, and Nike cross-trainers. He loads the back of the Subaru with the dozen cases of wine that have arrived at his door since January (as a reviewer he's on "the list" and samples come, regardless of the magazine he works for, or even if he's between jobs).

He drives south listening to his favorite version of Scheherazade, the 1958 recording of The Royal Philharmonic conducted by Sir Thomas Beecham, which always provides the proper mood for a storm. At the ranch he parks the Subaru by the back porch and carries the cases into the kitchen, and stacks them by the round table.

The old house is cold and damp, dark and quiet, and when he brings in the last case he takes off his raincoat and turns on all of the lights on the ground floor. He builds small fires in both the parlor and the kitchen fireplaces in an attempt to dispel the gloom.

Each bottle has to be inventoried, its pertinent information entered into a spiral notebook. The door to the wine cellar has been sealed shut, so he'll have to take the boxes down to the root cellar and pass through the geode to the wine cellar. When he finishes his inventory, he takes the cases one by one down to the root cellar and stacks them on the floor.

The dome light in the geode glows softly and at the far end of the tunnel he see the black drape and remembers the freestanding shelves that block the opening on that side. He doesn't think there is enough space to squeeze through carrying a case of wine. So he pulls aside the black drape, and nudges the shelves out from the wall with his shoulder. Then he steps into the pitch-black wine cellar. He pulls out his phone and flicks on the flashlight app. He sidesteps an upended wine barrel and two smaller barrels and pans the light around the cellar to get his bearings.

The light switch for this cellar is at the top of the stairs. *Didn't Mom say Pop sealed the door because the stairs were rickety? They look sturdy enough to me*, he thinks. He takes hold of the banister and shakes it. *Solid as a rock. Odd.* He goes up the stairs to flip the switch, but finds there is no switch. In fact, he finds that the only bulb that had hung from the ceiling has been removed. *What a nuisance.*

He goes back down the stairs and looks to the empty niche where he intends to store the cases. But the niche is full of bottles stacked on their sides. He picks one up to examine the label when the door at the top of the stairs opens (the door he knows to be sealed shut), framing a little girl of perhaps four, with curly golden hair, wearing a dress and pinafore. The very picture of Alice in Wonderland. She descends the stairs, her cherubic face lit by the candle she holds before her. When she sees him in the dim light she says in a small but very distinct voice, "Papa?" A chill goes up his spine. The bottle slips from his grasp and shatters on the slate floor. "God damn it!" he exclaims reflexively.

Then she is running back up the stairs. "Papa! Papa!" The door slams shut and he remembers to breathe. He's stunned. That was no ghost, no insubstantial echo from the past, no wraith. She was loud and clear, here and now. She hadn't walked through the door; she had opened it. But how?

He slowly ascends the steps and pushes open the door, and like Alice in reverse he pops out of the rabbit hole and into a world askew, at once familiar and unfamiliar. A short candle in a brass candleholder burns on the dining room table. At the far end of the dining room is an unfamiliar breakfront. He passes the table and crosses the hall to the kitchen. The windows, the fireplace, the cast iron wood stove are all in their accustomed places, but the rest of the scene is altered. Missing are the refrigerator, the electric stove and oven, the wall phone, the blender, toaster, coffee pot and microwave. A water pump sprouts above a copper sink. Outside the yard is bathed in sunlight, and the barn has changed color from a faded red to a bright white.

Beyond the back porch a short, plump woman in a long green gingham dress is hanging clothes on a line. Just outside the kitchen door he sees the back of a girl of thirteen or fourteen and a man holding the little girl with the golden curls. In the side yard a horse paws the ground under a small oak.

This is crazy, he thinks, as panic begins to seize him. He knows he can't be seeing what he thinks he's seeing. *I'm having one of those hyper-real dreams,* he thinks, and calms down. The details are marvelous (he can even feel heat emanating from the wood stove, upon which a pot of water boils). He turns the setting on his phone to camera. Why not document the dream? The door opens as the flash goes off, and he finds himself looking into the face of a mustachioed middle-aged man in baggy corduroy pants, a wrinkled, collarless shirt with sweat stains under the arms, and a wide-brimmed, flat-topped black hat. The man freezes in his tracks, blinks, turns, and rushes out the door. *I must have scared him. Now I'll wake up. I always wake up when I realize it's a dream.* The man runs to the horse, grabs a rifle from a scabbard and comes running back, kicking up dust in the side yard. "Everybody away from the house!" he yells. "Get Owen!"

He bangs through the door, pointing the rifle in Jeff's general direction.

I'm not waking up. A wave of heat rushes up Jeff's arms and legs to his face; there is a rushing sound and the world begins to go white. He kneels down on one knee, heart pounding, head swimming.

"I m-m-must be having a stroke," he says. "I think I'm having a stroke. Call 911."

"Explain yourself," the man says.

Jeff ignores him. The man's just an illusion. Jeff dials 911 and holds the phone to his ear. Silence. "No bars. No god damn bars!" he screams in frustration.

"Are you drunk, man?"

Jeff lets out his breath, lies down on his back and puts a forearm over he eyes. He realizes that he has never, until this moment, experienced true terror in his life. Fear maybe, but never terror, not the dread stark panic he feels as he realizes he could lose his essential self, that his sense of reality might be ripped from his mind. What does one have, if one's mind is gone?

He lies on his back for perhaps half a minute, his heart hammering so fast it is almost a thrum, then rises up on shaking elbows.

The mustachioed man says, "You don't look so well, mister."

Jeff draws in several deep breaths, the panic subsiding a bit, but the images remain. *If this isn't a hyper-real dream, then I'm awake and hallucinating. Or did I die in my sleep and this is the afterlife?* Whatever is happening, it is an oddly detailed and cohesive image.

"I think..." he starts to say, and loses the thought. "Help me up." The man pulls Jeff to his feet and Jeff can feel his grip, the physical reality of his presence. "I think I should go back and lie down. I should call my wife. I'm sick," he mumbles, and thinks *I must be going mad.*

He stands unsteadily and reaches out to lean against the nearest counter. The mind is indeed a mysterious place, for whether dream, or madness, or hallucination, or afterlife this is a seamless presentation, perfect in every detail. This is a vision of the house he grew up in, as it must have looked when new.

He's aware of the man with the gun, but he doesn't care. Visions, whether materializing in a dream or in the clouds of madness, have no reality, he tells himself. They exist solely in the mind of the beholder. He has, in his nightmares, fallen off cliffs and been hit by lightning, and like Wiley Coyote he has always awakened in one piece. If he is going mad, at least his madness is tempered by the comforting familiarity of the scene, and he's reminded of a line from *Paradise Lost*. "'The mind is its own place,'" he recites aloud, "and in itself can make a heaven of hell, a hell of heaven.'" He looks back over his shoulder and says, "Milton," in explanation of the quote.

"I know."

"So the question is, is this heaven or is this hell?"

"You're a might confused, ain'tcha?"

Jeff laughs out loud. "A bit," he replies. So strange of the mind to include balancing humor, as though to reassure itself that all is not lost.

He closes his eyes and thinks, *I'm ready to wake up now. Wake up, wake up.* But when he opens his eyes, it is just the same. "You know," he says, "I'd feel better if you wouldn't point that at me. Actually, I don't think you can kill me, but I'd rather not put it to the test, if you don't mind."

He crosses the central hall to the dining room, opens the wine cellar door, and reaches for the light switch, but it's still missing (of course). He turns on the flashlight app and descends the steps. He can hear the hallucination clumping down the stairs behind him.

"Where are you going? Come back here," the man commands.

Jeff hears the sound of the rifle cocking, but ignores it. *He's not real,* he reassures himself.

Under the stairs he steps around an upended barrel and pulls the drape aside.

"Holy mother of God!" the man exclaims. "Deliver us from evil!"

Jeff turns to examine him. He looks so real. This whole dream is so marvelously detailed. "Who *are* you?"

"August Kimball," the man answers with a straight face.

"Of course you are," Jeff replies sarcastically, "and I'm Santa Claus." He steps into the tunnel, his ears buzzing.

He jumps at a loud bang and the whine of a ricocheting bullet.

In the root cellar he runs up the stairs and flicks off the light. He feels weak and wants to lie down for a minute before calling Carolyn. She'll know what to do. *Maybe,* he thinks, *this is just a dream, a nightmare. If not, then I've gone mad, or else I've had a stroke and I'm lost in a coma.* He's terrified, and at the same time utterly exhausted. He walks down the hall to the office and lies down on the settee, and closes his eyes.

The rain is falling again. He listens to the water drumming on the roof and dripping from the eaves and is soon asleep, if he's ever been awake in the first place.

Chapter 18
The Gates of Hell

As the stranger stepped into the tunnel he took the light with him and the cellar was plunged into darkness. Fear shook August, he back-peddled and fell backwards over a small keg, cracking the back of head on the slate floor and involuntarily squeezing off a shot. The sound reverberated in his ears. He scrambled to his feet in the darkness, started toward where he knew the foot of the stairs must be, and once again stumbled over a small keg, falling forward and hitting his forehead on the banister. He sat stunned and waited for a full minute as his eyes adjusted to the faint light that stole around the edge of the door above.

When he came into the yard Lydia rushed to him. "Would you mind explaining what that was all about? Why were you carrying on so? Lord, you scared me. Owen thought he heard a shot. You didn't shoot that poor man?"

His children were all gathered around him now. "Lyddy, there's a tunnel under our house!"

"Gus, come now, you're talkin' nonsense. You've been hurt," she said reaching up to brush a lock of hair away from his forehead where a knot was rising. "Did he hit you?"

"No, he didn't hit me. I tripped. Twice." He swept her hand away.

"You didn't shoot him?"

"No, Lyddy, have you been listening to me? A tunnel under our house!"

"How would anyone dig a tunnel under our house without we knowed about it?"

"I don't know. It was strange. Did you see him?"

"We couldn't see much of anything through the windas; you told us to stay away."

"He was dressed so strange — he had a silk jacket, like a Chinaman, and shiny pants with stripes up the side like a clown, and funny shoes. You never seen anything like it. Then he holds up his hand and blinds me with a flash like lightning. Did you see that?"

"No, I can't say as I did; I was hangin' clothes."

"I did," Carrie affirmed. "It was like a flash of lightning, only there wasn't no thunder."

"That's right," August said, "and that's when I ran for my gun and told you all to stay away. But when I went back inside he was all wobbly and said he wasn't feeling well. Then he talked a bunch of nonsense, numbers and such. He said, I remember, he said 'There's no bars.' Then he got up and went to the wine cellar, and I swear a strange light went before him lighting his way. Then he parts a curtain and there's a tunnel with purple jewels aglowin'."

Lydia started for the kitchen door. August grabbed her arm and swung her around.

"Didn't you hear a word I said, woman?"

"I heard it; I just don't believe it. You got a nasty bump on your head and maybe you ain't thinkin' straight. I don't know what's going on here, but I aim to get to the bottom of it."

She pulled away and went into the house, followed by August and the rest of her brood.

"Hold up now," August said, pushing ahead. He picked up the candle that Emily had left burning on the dining room table, handed his rifle to Owen, and led them all down the stairs.

He stopped at the side of the freestanding shelves under the stairway and pointed to the black drape that hung between two of the stair supports behind it.

"I don't remember this curtain being here. Did you hang it, Lyddy?"

"Not me."

"Owen?"

"Not me."

August set the candleholder on the upturned wine barrel. "Owen, you take my gun and point it at the opening just in case. Everybody stand back." With a theatrical flourish he took the edge of the drape and flung it aside, revealing...a solid rock face. He stepped behind the shelves and slapped the rock with his hand. "It was right here!"

"Maybe you followed the fella down here and he hit you on the head and went upstairs and out the side door, while you was knocked out," Lydia suggested.

"He didn't hit me; I told you, I tripped. Besides, I know what I saw," August said.

"I know what you *think* you saw. But everyone knows a bump on the head can scramble your brains. Tunnels don't just suddenly appear and disappear. You're all mixed up, Gus; it's all in your head."

August was about to respond, then fell silent.

"What is it?" Lydia asked.

"What you said just now, about it being all in my head; it reminded me of something else he said. What was it? It was a line from Milton."

"You know I don't read naught but The Good Book."

"Pa's read everything," Charlie said with admiration.

"Not everything, but I have read Milton. It was a quote from *Paradise Lost*, about the mind making a heaven of hell or a hell of heaven. Then he says (the man, not Milton) — he says to me, 'The question is: Is this heaven, or is this hell?' Then he goes into that jeweled tunnel. Lyddy, I think we might've built our house over the gateway to hell."

"That's crazy," Lydia said.

"Maybe he's a magician," Owen offered, "from the circus."

August ran his hand over the rock face again. "I'm posting a guard at the top of the stairs. I'll take the first watch. Owen, you can take the next watch."

"Now you're just being silly," Lydia said. "What if he doesn't come back? Are you going to stand watch day and night for the rest of your life? There's work to be done."

"What choice do I have? I can't just go about my business when the door to the underworld could open any second! Maybe we should send for Reverend Winters."

"Lord, no! He'll think you're crazy as a loon."

"But if it's the work o' the Devil, he might know what to do."

"Suit yourself, but I don't set no store in that man's abilities. He's no Reverend Broadly. Now that was man you could trust. Anyhow, Winters is gone up to Sacramento, and he won't be back fer a week. What you need right now is to set yourself down and put a cool compress on yer head. You've addled your brains."

August looked confused. "Maybe you're right, but I still want to post a guard."

"You can leave Laddie down here," Charles said. "He'll bark if he sees anyone."

"That's usin' your noggin, young man," August said. "That's a good idea."

Lydia shook her head. "Well, I don't think it's necessary, but do what you must. In the meantime, let's get a wet washcloth on that bump and you lie down. We still have laundry to do and dinner to get on the table. Come on Carrie."

Carrie turned to Emily. "Bring up that box of soap flakes. You can help scrub."

Chapter 19
The Price of Opportunity

Jeff dreamt he was on a Mississippi steamboat moving upstream against the current. The riverbanks rose high on either side. He could only see as far as the next bend.

A gust of wind shook the front door and rattled him awake. He sat up and, remembering, felt a shiver of fear that his mind had slipped a cog.

Physically he felt all right. His heart wasn't racing. His head didn't pound. His ability to think didn't seem impaired. He debated calling Carolyn or driving to the hospital. But he didn't want to worry her unduly, and he didn't want to spend the night away from home being poked and prodded if it wasn't necessary. He felt a rising panic that he must be losing the ability to distinguish fantasy from reality, that he was caught in some kind of half-dream. Maybe it was a panic attack. He'd heard of panic attacks. Your electrolytes went off, your serotonin levels went wacky, or an imbalance of who-knows-what caused your brain to overload.

He went to the dining room and examined the wine cellar door again. The plywood was still screwed securely into the door jam. He went to the kitchen, comparing it to what he thought he'd seen, when the barn again caught his eye — the *faded red* barn.

He remembered the phone and took it from his pocket — four bars; no problem with reception. Then with trepidation he called up the last photo, and felt his stomach clench and a cold shiver run up his spine as he stared at a white barn and August Kimball coming in the door. He remembered Abby asking, "They couldn't hurt us, could they daddy?" Now he wasn't so sure. They were like no apparitions he'd ever heard of. August's hand was solid flesh and bone.

There was a slight chance, he thought, that he wasn't seeing what he thought he was seeing, that it was just a hallucination, or maybe he'd never really awakened at all. But he didn't seem to be dreaming; time was linear and there was no magical morphing. But that didn't mean he wasn't seeing things. And yet, they had all *heard* the "ghosts." And if they could be heard, why not seen? And if they could be seen, why not felt? Maybe it wasn't his mind, but Time that had slipped a cog.

He took a photo from the same position and swiped the screen backwards and forward. One red barn under a grey sky. One white barn under a blue sky, with a wide-eyed August Kimball caught in the open doorway.

He drove back to the condo, listening to Debussy's *Prélude à l'après-midi d'un faune* for its calming effect.

That afternoon, when the kids came home from school, he called Jake over and handed him the phone. "Tell me what you see."

"The barn at the ranch."

"Now swipe to the last photo."

"Cool! Did you do that in Photoshop?"

"Do what?"

"Turn the barn white. Who's the dude?"

"A neighbor, I guess you'd say."

"Can you teach me?"

"Later, maybe."

Jeff mulled over the facts as he knew them, while he made dinner — a mixture of wild rice and quinoa, grilled asparagus, and boneless, skinless chicken breasts sautéed in grape seed oil with crimini mushrooms and sprigs of rosemary. He wasn't just seeing things; Jake had confirmed that much. So it appeared their "ghosts" were no figment of the imagination, nor were they phantoms; they were solid and substantial. And if he accepted that, as he must, then what did that mean, and what were the possible consequences?

Had he been born in an earlier time — in August Kimball's time, for instance, he'd have had few, if any examples to draw from. But he'd been born into the latter half of the Twentieth Century when wormholes, parallel universes and alternate realities were part and parcel of the culture. The only real stretch here was in wrapping his mind around the reality of the concept, as opposed to mere fantasy. Millions did the same every day in blind acceptance of one religion over another. This was much easier; it took no leap of blind faith. If one could believe in the possibility of an afterlife, or in string theory, or in Einstein's concept that gravity warps time, it wasn't such a stretch to accept what his senses told him was real.

The proof was captured digitally on his phone. Jake had confirmed it. The questions now were: How should he respond? What were the possible consequences of making contact? Would they be safe? Were they safe *now*? Should he confess what he knew to Carolyn and the kids? And what did he really know?

There were obviously very real dangers — August had fired his rifle as he ducked into the chamber — but was the man inherently dangerous? Jeff didn't think so. He wasn't a psychopath; he was a family man and like any man he'd do what he had to, to protect his family. So Jeff wondered if he should try to reach out and make contact, or bar the entrance to the geode and pretend it didn't exist.

He called out that dinner was ready, knowing that each of them would wander in on their own schedules. For once he was glad they ate separately; he needed time to think this through. There were horrific dangers, and August Kimball was the least of it. If word leaked out and was believed, it could be their death warrant.

Stepping into the past also came with certain moral conundrums and obligations. Who, given the opportunity, wouldn't feel obliged to stop some of history's worst villains before they got started? It would be a simple thing to kill Adolph Hitler as a child and save millions of lives in the process. But what then? Wouldn't that also be erasing millions who were born as a result of World War II, of parents who would not have met if history hadn't unfolded in just the way it had? Might he even erase himself? Might there be another Hitler and another Stalin among the millions saved? There was no way of knowing, because any change in the past had unforeseen repercussions in the present.

The safest course of action would be to fill the geode with concrete.

But what of the possibilities? He felt a growing exhilaration as it occurred to him that knowing what was coming was like knowing the winning numbers in the lottery. Without exaggeration, knowing the future was a guaranteed ticket to fabulous wealth.

Yet it wasn't a decision one could make lightly or in a moment, and he resolved to sleep on it. Not that sleep would come easily.

After a fitful night's rest he arose early, wrapped himself in a robe, and half-hoping it had all been a dream, once again examined the photos side-by-side. Red barn. White barn. His stomach was in knots with equal portions of worry and excitement.

"You don't look well," Carolyn commented as he came out of the shower.

"Didn't sleep well."

"Take a nap once we're gone."

But he had no intention of sleeping.

In the kitchen he made a cup of coffee, ate a banana and two avocado and crab sushi, and nervously pondered his next move.

The most prudent course was to block the tunnel or fill it in. The next most cautious course was to do nothing. But what would prevent August from coming through to *this* side? Doing nothing was no safer than plunging into the deep end with your eyes closed. Momentous events had never taken the side of caution. Yet Life didn't dole out opportunities in equal portions or at prescribed moments and, once passed, opportunities were often lost forever. Still, their safety was at stake, and what opportunity was worth that risk? The logical course was to err on the side of caution, but the rewards were so tempting. Another person might have made a different choice. The timid avoid risk. The foolhardy take risks without regard to the dangers. On a continuum between the two, Jeff fell somewhere in-between, acknowledging the danger while moving cautiously forward. The anticipated reward, to say nothing of his abiding curiosity, thwarted prudence. Curiosity alone demanded further investigation. And after all, he reasoned (and not without merit), he took his life in his hands every time he got behind the wheel of a car. One took real-life risks everyday. Nothing was ever gained without taking *some* risk.

He just had to minimize the risk, and the best way to do that was to limit the number of people who knew. But how was he supposed to do that? Secrecy required subterfuge, and few people are good at keeping secrets. How many could win the lottery and never tell their family or friends? John Sutter would have been rich as Midas if he'd been able to keep the discovery of gold to himself and a few trusted associates. Instead, he lost everything as gold-hungry squatters stole his land from under him.

Could he keep it to himself? No one but August had seen him enter the tunnel. Which begged the questions: 'Why hadn't he followed? Had he already told his family? And if he'd told them, did they believe him?'

If they were to use this miracle as an opportunity, he had to pull August aside and explain the dangers they would face if anyone else found out.... And if worse came to worst he could always pump the geode full of concrete, couldn't he?

Once he'd seen everyone off to school, he looked through his wardrobe for an inconspicuous outfit and settled on jeans, a collarless cotton shirt, leather vest and an old pair of leather loafers. It would have to do.

He spent more than an hour composing a letter that attempted to explain why he had decided to take the risk, and instructing Carolyn to have the tunnel cemented shut. He signed it, folded the paper, sealed it in an envelope, and wrote on the outside CAROLYN: TO BE OPENED ONLY UPON MY DEATH. But that was stupid — what if he wasn't dead? What if he just couldn't get back for some reason? He crossed out DEATH and wrote DISAPPEARANCE, and stopped short as its meaning struck him full force. Why hadn't he seen it before? Pop! No wonder he had left his credit cards and money on the workbench in the cellar. They were worthless where he was going. Pop was on the other side, and he had to find him.

Chapter 20
Stumbling Back

Jeff could hear the dog whimpering in the wine cellar. He reached around the rack of shelves and tossed a piece of turkey into the darkness. In a moment he peeked, his flashlight illuminating the green glowing eyes of the mutt. He tossed another slice of turkey. The mutt padded cautiously forward and, tail wagging, wolfed it down. Jeff crouched down and held a slice out. The mutt sniffed his hand and licked it, then took the meat. Then he scratched the dog behind his ears. They came to an understanding. *Dogs are so easy to please*, Jeff thought. *If only humans were so amenable.*

Leaving the dog the rest of the meat, Jeff mounted the stairs and pushed the door open a crack. The dining room was empty. He let himself out the side door into the north yard.

For the next hour he lay at the northeast corner of the house. The white barn lay a couple hundred feet southeast. In the adjoining corral horses moved slowly with lips to the ground as someone forked hay from the loft above.

Sunlight filtered through a high, thin overcast, yet it was warm for all that and he was sweating. He waited, observing from a distance, hoping for a chance to meet August alone. At last August appeared leading a horse from the barn. He mounted and trotted off in the direction of the creek. Jeff stole along the side of the house to the corner of the front porch just in time to see horse and rider passing behind the trees that bordered the creek. Jeff followed down-slope angling away from the house, hopped over the narrow trace of Arroyo Calero and clambered up the far bank through a tangle of bushes and willow saplings.

111

Astride his horse August moved down a row between the vines. At the far end of the vineyard he got off and examined a vine or two, then remounted and rode along the far edge of the vineyard. He stopped, leaned over to look more closely at a vine, and headed back toward the road.

He saw Jeff at the end of the row, but was unconcerned until recognition set him on alert. Then he drew up short, shouted, "You!" with alarm, and started to withdraw the rifle from its scabbard.

Jeff held his palms up and said, "I'm unarmed."

The horse seemed unsure of its master's intent and took a couple steps forward, then back. Hand still on the rifle butt, August drew himself up straight in the saddle and demanded accusingly, "What are you?"

Jeff was taken aback. One might expect to be asked '*who* are you?' but not '*what* are you?'

"Just a man, like you," he answered, and then added, "though I have to admit, until yesterday I thought *you* were a ghost."

"You thought *I* was a ghost?" August let the rifle slide back into its scabbard. "*I* didn't make a tunnel appear under my house. I ask again: What are you? Where are you from? What do you want?"

"I don't have all the answers. This is one of those 'mysteries wrapped in an enigma,' yada, yada."

Jeff reached into his pocket and as he withdrew two photos he found himself looking down the barrel of a rifle again. "Whoa! Hold on now! Why don't you put that away before you hurt someone?" Once August had pointed the barrel skyward, Jeff advanced slowly and handed him one of the photos. "Here's the picture I took yesterday in your kitchen." August slid the rifle into its scabbard and studied the picture.

Jeff held out the second. "And here's a picture from the same angle that I took this morning."

August studied the photos side-by-side. "I don't understand."

"First, let me introduce myself." Jeff stepped forward and stuck out his hand. "My name is Jeffrey Porter."

August reached down to shake his hand with a firm grip. "I'm..."

"August Kimball; I know."

"Yes."

August swung down from the saddle. He was about Jeff's height. It was difficult to gauge his age because, like Jeff's father, he'd spent much of his life outdoors. Deep crow's feet spread from the corners of his light blue eyes, his skin was like tanned leather and his hair peppered with grey. Staring again at the photos, he shook his head uncomprehendingly. "What's this mean?"

"How to explain? Have you read *A Connecticut Yankee in King Arthur's Court*?" Jeff asked. August looked at him dumbly. "No? Okay, maybe it hasn't been written yet. How about Dickens' *A Christmas Carol*?"

"Yes, certainly."

"It's like that. I'm like the ghost of Christmas future."

"You're no ghost."

"Not exactly," Jeff assured him. "What's the date?"

"The date? Why, Tuesday April 19th."

"The year?"

"1870, of course."

Jeff turned and pointed above the tree line to the roof of the house. "I live in that house. I took that second photo this morning, on May 14th, 2009."

August let out a chuffing sound, smiled and arched an eyebrow. "Do I look like a simpleton?"

"I don't mind healthy skepticism, but how do you explain that?" Jeff asked, indicating the photos. "Have you ever even seen a color photo?"

"Could be a trick."

"It's not a trick. Look," Jeff said, snapping a photo of August and holding out his iPhone for him to see. August gaped in silence. "I grant you, it's a helluva lot better camera than you have in your time, but it's still just technology. It's the science of the future, not magic."

It took August a long moment to digest this. Then he said, "Tell me about the tunnel. Is the tunnel science?"

113

"No, that's a mystery. All I know is that this...(I don't know what to call it — this phenomenon, I guess is the best way to put it). This phenomenon could be an amazing opportunity, or it could be something like Pandora's Box."

"How do I know it doesn't lead straight to hell?"

"Do I look like the Devil?"

"The Devil comes in many disguises."

"You'll just have to trust me. We'll have to trust each other, because I expect we'll be seeing a lot of each other. And I need your help."

"With what?"

"Helping me find my father."

August nonchalantly tied the reins to a grape vine and looked up at the sky as though mulling something over. Then he flipped open a saddlebag and withdrew a revolver. As Jeff once again stared down the barrel of a gun, August said, "Show me."

Chapter 21
Falling Forward

In Jeff's day the dining room had been shortened in order to add a laundry room, which was entered by the side door. In August's time the side door still opened into the dining room. They stole furtively around the dining table. They could hear the girls talking and clumping about in the kitchen. August paused to take up a safety match to light a candle. Jeff stayed his hand, turned on the flashlight app, and led the way downstairs.

For a moment Jeff wondered if there might not be a time-matter paradox, whereby one cannot be in the two places at the same time. For undoubtedly August's body was already in the future, moldering in its grave. He had little time to contemplate the possible complications before he stepped into the chamber.

As August stepped through the opening he winced and shook his head. "What's that buzzing?"

"I'm not sure."

Sensing the source of the sound August reached up toward the dome light. "How does this lantern work? There's no flame."

"Don't touch; there might be a short!" Jeff said, then realizing that the term would mean nothing to August added, "It might not be safe. It's electric. Electric lights were invented around your time, I think. Everything runs on electricity now. You should get in on that; you'll make a fortune."

August paused to admire the purple crystals, while Jeff continued forward and, with a profound sense of relief, stepped into the root cellar and was assured that he had returned to his own time.

In the kitchen Jeff gave August some time to acclimate. The poor man was in a daze as Jeff explained the purpose of the refrigerator, dishwasher, coffee maker, rice maker, toaster, mixer and microwave. Then they proceeded across the hall to the dining room and the laundry room. August ran his hands over the washer and dryer and shook his head in wonder. "What do the women do all day, if machines do all the work?" Jeff let that one lie.

August straightened up suddenly, struck by a thought, and rushed out the side door to the laurel. He knelt down and picked up one of the three little marble headstones. He turned it over and brushed off the lichen. Then he picked up another. He opened his mouth to say something, couldn't find the words, hung his head and pooched his lips. A tear ran down his cheek. He knelt there a minute, then stood and cleared his throat. "Molly or Ivan," he said. "The stones are so worn I can't tell."

"Your kids?"

He nodded. "Molly was four when we lost her. Ivan...Ivan was ten." He stared fearfully at the third stone that lay among the leaves. "We've only lost two."

"Don't look."

"What's the year again?" he asked.

"2009."

Comparing dates they found they were separated by 139 years and 25 days (the length of about two lifetimes). The time of day likewise differed, being about an hour and forty minutes ahead on Jeff's side (one hour of which was accounted for by Daylight Savings Time).

"When you pulled that curtain aside and I saw the tunnel for the first time, I thought you were a demon," August said.

"A demon?" Jeff chuckled at the thought.

August hooked his thumbs under his suspenders and gave Jeff a sly smile. "You quoted *Paradise Lost*, and said something of heaven and hell, and I feared I must be in the presence of an inhabitant of one or the other. Based on your point of entry I was rather worried it might prove the latter. Though I'm pleased to say you do not appear to be a demon, but an ordinary man. Still, I'm not accustomed to seeing tunnels (let alone Time tunnels) suddenly appear under my house. How, if I may inquire sir, does it work?"

"I'm just a spectator to these proceedings, same as you. I have no idea."

On the front porch they sat down in rocking chairs and fell silent for some minutes, each of them lost in his own thoughts.

Finally August broke the silence. Taking Jeff's measure, he asked, "Do you believe in God's Divine Plan?"

Jeff resisted the pressure to speak reverently where he felt no reverence. Priests and witch doctors were all the same to him. So he replied honestly, "I don't mean to offend, but if there's a plan to all the mayhem in this world, there's a sick mind behind it."

"You're a Deist?"

"I'm an atheist."

"How can you not believe in God?"

"How can I, when all that's contemptible in Mankind is manifest in his gods? The god of the Bible is a reprehensible character by any standard."

"Reprehensible?"

"Yes, reprehensible — a vainglorious, insecure, murderous psychopath, and not someone I'd care to spend eternity with."

August eyed Jeff with obvious contempt and went on. "Well sir, I do believe in the Creator. I've often wondered if he has a plan, or if he put us here to make the best of it, the Deist point of view. But I have to believe something so queer as this must be the work of God or the Devil, and for the life of me I can't tell which."

"I don't know about a Divine Plan, but there are certainly opportunities here...and temptations...and unspeakable dangers. If word got out it'd be like the Gold Rush. Your military would want to use it to import modern weapons and find out the enemy's plans in advance. Your scientists and businessmen would want to steal modern technologies and hardware. In their eyes we would simply be in the way. We have to keep this secret."

August stroked his stubbled chin. "Lyddy wouldn't believe it anyway. She'd think I was mad. Are you married?"

"Yep. Two kids."

"They around here?" he asked, looking over his shoulder.

"They're all in school at the moment," Jeff said, and explained how they hadn't actually moved in yet. "The safest thing would be to plug up the passage, as soon as I find my father."

August nodded his head and ruminated on the tunnel for a moment before he spoke. "We can't fill it in. There's a reason for this. I don't know what it is, but there's a reason. God tested Abraham and Job and Noah and now, I believe, he may be testing me, or us. There exists, in this miracle, opportunities for good or for evil that we're probably unaware of."

Before Jeff could think of a witty rejoinder his phone began playing "Ain't Misbehavin'." It was J.C., who told him that he and Rosie would be unable to make it for Easter. "I broke my collar bone and it's painful to drive."

"How the hell'd you do that?"

"Took a header on my mountain bike."

"You're too old for bikes."

"Screw that. I do not intend to 'go gentle into that good night,'" he said, alluding to the Dylan Thomas poem. "They're going to have to drag me kicking and screaming to the grave."

"Good for you."

"Damn right."

When Jeff was done August asked, "What just happened? Who were you talking to?"

"It was my brother-in-law."

"You were talking into your camera?" He looked dumbfounded.

"Oh, it's a phone, too. Oh, I forgot you don't have phones yet, do you? A telephone is like a telegraph, only you speak into it. Alexander Graham Bell invented it around your time. The newest ones are wireless."

"Where does he live, your brother-in-law?"

"Marin County, north of the Golden Gate."

"And you can talk to him whenever you want?"

"I can talk to anyone on the planet. I can talk to someone in New York, or Paris. All you need is their phone number."

"Good god!" August exclaimed. "Imagine having a conversation with someone in New York while you sit in the comfort of your own home. It makes travel obsolete!"

He paced the porch in thought, and turning at the south end he looked up and saw around the edge of the trees the houses just beyond the vineyard. "My god, what town is that? How many people are there?"

"About a million in San Jose, seven million in the Bay Area."

"Lordy! How many in The United States?"

Jeff asked his cell phone, and answered, "Three hundred thirteen million."

"You got that from your camera? I mean phone? It tells you that?"

"It's kind of an all-purpose device," Jeff explained. "You can tell time, look up information, send messages, make lists, do math, play games, take photos, play music, read books, get directions, find your location by global positioning, connect to the internet..."

"The inter...what?" August interrupted.

"The internet. It's uh...it connects everyone to all the information. Some people are calling this The Information Age."

August nodded and rocked back and forth. "You say the tunnel isn't just another invention, but you must know how it works, else how did you close it the first time?"

"Close it? I didn't close it."

"After you left the first time I tried to follow, but the tunnel was gone, vanished, turned to stone."

Chapter 22
Practicing Patience

Any doubts Jeff had harbored that his father had chosen to remain in the past now exploded into the air like a flock of startled pigeons. What despair had his father felt at finding the door shut? Jeff shuddered at how close he must have come to sharing his fate. "Maybe there's a pattern to it. We'll have to figure out why and when, or we're screwed." It was a double-edged sword, for not only might he be trapped in the past, Jeff realized that if August were trapped in the present, he would become his responsibility. His mind flitted back and forth between the mind-numbing, frightful possibilities.

He had to keep focused on the goal. "I have to show you something." He went to the office and came back with a photo of his father.

August took one look and exclaimed, "Randall!"

"Yes! My father. I think he was trapped on your side of the tunnel."

"Oh, well now, that explains some things — he used to show up and leave at the oddest times, just for a few hours at first, doing odd jobs and pruning. Then he worked for us for about six months. He stayed in the old cabin at the bend in the creek. I never did know his last name."

"Could he still be there do you think?"

"No, he moved on three-four months past. Haven't seen him since."

"Any idea where he might have gone?"

August pursed his lips in thought, then shook his head. "No. I think he worked for Jenkins for a while — seems like I heard something. At any rate, you can show your pi'ture around when we go into town, though that might raise some eyebrows — no one's ever seen a color photograph 'round these parts before."

"I can make it look old. It only takes a minute."

August folded his arms and cocked his head. "Can I ask you a question? — Why'd it take you take so long to look for him?"

"We've been looking. I didn't know about the tunnel 'til yesterday...well, no, that's not really true — it's been there since I was a kid — I just didn't know what it could do."

"Your father must be a formidable inventor."

"Huh?"

"To make a passage through time."

"What? No, he was a farmer, *is* a farmer; he's no inventor."

"Well, someone made it. Or some*thing*. Or...." He broke off and furrowed his brow, staring at the mountain peaks. Then he muttered, "God or the Devil. God or the Devil."

At that moment Jeff didn't want to debate theology. "Whatever," he said. "I just want to find my father."

"We could ride around to the nearby ranches tomorrow and ask."

"You mean on a horse?"

"We're not going to walk it."

Jeff was chagrined. "I don't know how to ride. We don't have horses."

"How do you get around?"

"A car — an automobile. In the beginning they were called 'horseless carriages.'"

"Show me."

August walked around and around the Subaru shaking his head. "Does everyone have one of these?"

"Not everyone, but most people."

They got in and drove a figure eight between the house and the barn.

"What about horses? Doesn't anyone ride?"

"Rich people ride for fun."

August took off his hat and scratched his head. "This is gonna take some getting used to. What else should I know?"

Jeff was struck dumb by the enormity of what August didn't know, the world remade by technological and social changes, the dangers his progeny would face. August's generation had just endured the Civil War. Ahead, his children and grandchildren would live through a couple of major Depressions, two World Wars, and a succession of smaller yet deadly conflicts. "I think there's just too much to tell you all at once. Let's take this in baby steps, one thing at a time. Unless this...this Time Tunnel is temporary, we have a lifetime to fill each other in. What I'm most worried about now is how to gauge when it closes and when it opens, so we don't get caught on one side or the other."

On the way back to the cellar Jeff ducked into the office and gave August a pad of ruled paper and a pen. "Here, keep track of the time when you check the tunnel, and if it's open or shut. We might be able to discern a pattern. Leave the pad on that big barrel in the wine cellar. If you want to get in touch with me, leave a note on a shelf in the root cellar." August looked at the pen and pursed his lips.

"I'll need a nib and some ink."

Jeff showed him how a ballpoint pen works. August grinned like a kid whose been told he's going to Disneyland, revealing for the first time a set of yellowed teeth with a gap where his right eyetooth should have been. Jeff was taken aback, and saw him as Carolyn or the kids might see him for the first time. With his leathery skin, baggy pants, wrinkled, sweat-stained shirt, scruffy beard and questionable dentition, he would have fit in with the homeless population in San Francisco. In fact, he smelled as though he hadn't taken a bath lately. But Jeff kept his thoughts to himself, out of politeness.

"Can you teach me to ride?" he asked.

"I expect so, except Saturday afternoon, when we take our baths, and Sunday, when we go into town to pick up supplies and go to church."

They went over the time difference again. The hardest thing to remember was the day of the week. On August's side it was Wednesday. On Jeff's it was Friday, and he'd promised their realtor that they would vacate the condo between noon and 4:00 pm each Saturday and Sunday, so he could show the place. He'd also promised Carolyn that they'd move as much of the small stuff as possible to the ranch. Besides, there was no way he could get away on the weekends without raising Carolyn's suspicions. So an appointment was made to meet in three days' time (Jeff's Monday morning, August's Saturday morning) for riding lessons.

"What'll your wife say when I show up?" Jeff asked. "We'll have to come up with a back story to explain why I'm around and how we know each other."

"Why not stick to the truth? You're looking for your father."

Jeff saw him through to the wine cellar. He lit a candle and placed it on the upended barrel next to the pad and pen, looked at his wristwatch and wrote, "Friday, May 15, 2009, 1:53 pm — Open."

August looked at his pocket watch. Then to the left of Jeff's notation he wrote "Wed. Apr. 20, 1870, 12:09 pm."

August stuck out his hand and they shook. "I'm relieved you're not a demon," August said, though the strained smile and troubled look in his eye belied his doubts. "I can't say as I understand what this is all about, but I'll leave that in God's hands. He has some plan for us, I've no doubt."

Jeff was back at the condo putting lasagna in the oven when Jake came running in from the garage, dropped his book bag, called, "Hey,

Pop!" and sprinted for the bathroom. Abby followed, arguing with her mother.

"Everybody wears makeup, mom," Abby said, her tone dripping with condescension.

"I'm not giving you thirty dollars for makeup; you're too young for makeup."

"I'm going to *high* school in the fall."

"What difference does that make? You still don't need makeup."

"Everybody makes fun of me."

"Why do you say that?"

"Look at these freckles! I look like a freak."

"You look beautiful."

"I hate my face!"

"Oh lord," Carolyn said. "Okay, come upstairs with me. You can use *my* makeup; I'll show you how. The trick is to use as little as possible."

When Jeff called out, "Dinner's ready!" forty minutes later, they came back downstairs.

Abby continued to her room, a smile of triumph on her made-up face. Carolyn rolled her eyes. "Teenagers," she said.

Jeff scooped some lasagna onto a plate and poured a glass of Argentine Malbec. Carolyn followed suit, and asked, "How was your day?"

He'd never been good at dissembling, but he was okay with leaving out parts of the truth that might cause distress. He said truthfully, "I had a remarkable day."

"Oh?"

"I met a neighbor. He has horses. He's offered to teach me to ride."

"That'll be the day," she scoffed. "I can't see you as part of the horsey set."

"Horsey set?"

"Dressage. Polo. Isn't that a rich man's sport?"

"He's not like that; he's a farmer."

"I still can't see you on a horse. Have you *ever* ridden?"

"No, but I could learn."

That weekend at the ranch, unpacking boxes, painting and working on little repair projects, he felt the pull of the tunnel. It took all his will to resist crossing over as he took boxes down to the root cellar. It was like finding a treasure chest, and having the discipline to keep the lid locked. In the afternoon on Saturday he gave in to temptation and stepped through to the wine cellar. On the pad of paper was written:

"Wed. Apr. 20, 1870, 12:09 pm / Friday May 15, 2009: 1:53 pm: — Open.

"Wed. Apr. 20, 1870: 7 pm — closed.

"Th. Apr. 21, 1870: 6 am — closed. 8:04 am — open."

Calculating to his time, he wrote next to his notation, "11:01 am — still open."

On Sunday he checked the passage when he arrived (it was open), and spent the rest of the day upstairs, practicing patience. Late in the day their realtor called with the news that he had an offer for a short sale.

Chapter 23
Horsepower

"The sermon last week was on the sin of pride. I'm afraid I've been guilty of that one today. I felt self-important that God should have singled me out, among all the people in the world, to step into the future! And He had singled you out, to step into the past. But, as we don't know why, I think we should approach this miracle with a proper sense of humility. I don't know about you, but I'm a little frightened."

"That makes two of us."

A great shaft of sunlight spilled through the clouds and lit the green foothills to the east. Another opened overhead for a few seconds, sending a spreading warmth that only served to remind Jeff how cold he really was. August looked skyward, gauging the weather.

August had rushed him out of the house and across the yard with no introductions to two of his daughters and his eldest son, to whom he simply raised a hand while striding purposefully toward the barn. He saddled his sorrel Rhubarb, and put Jeff on Patsy, a mild-mannered black mare with a white diamond on her forehead. Then they'd started off side by side at a walk toward the hills. To Jeff it seemed bizarre to feel so far away from home, while actually being so close. He felt as though he were in another country. At each turn and vista he tried to imagine what the landscape looked like in his own time. There were a few landmarks from which to get his bearings — creeks, the eastern hills and western mountains. Yet even the hills were different, less eroded. It seemed the earth, that one thing he had always thought of as solid, was in reality quite malleable, shifting like a slow moving ocean over eons as people moved on its surface in the blink of an eye.

At the base of the hills, along a line of scrub oak, August gave him few pointers on riding. Jeff was no good at a trot, bouncing off the saddle and jarring his spine, but a canter was pretty easy to take, and he began to get a feel for it.

"You don't want to gallop her, except on the road," August warned. "There are lots of gophers around here and if she stepped in a hole at a gallop she'd break a leg, or throw you, or both."

Jeff didn't intend to gallop at all, road or not. He didn't feel that competent, nor was he at ease on horseback.

As he rode back and forth taking instruction, fragments of memory were jolted loose by the once again familiar sounds and smells of the country. He had explored this ground in detail as a boy, hiking up and down the creek beds in the dry season and ranging over the hills. His memories of that time were vivid, even after all the intervening years, because there is an intimacy and immediacy in being able to fully sense your surroundings, to feel the sun and the wind, to smell the sage and greasewood, to hear birds trilling, insects humming, leaves rustling. Riding over the same ground now, a century earlier, he experienced it all over again as for the first time.

After half an hour of practice he was getting the hang of it, and preposterous as it seemed, he was enjoying it. Of course riding had its drawbacks: it was dusty and physically tiring, and he wouldn't have wanted to commute to work on horseback, but he had to admit it was exhilarating, if for no other reason than that it was different, and being different it shocked his apathetic senses into an appreciation for minute details.

Satisfied with his progress, August turned Rhubarb toward a trail into the hills. One of the advantages of a horse, Jeff soon discovered, was that he could point it in any direction and let it go, then carry on a conversation without fear of going off the road, bumping a curb or shooting a red light. Also, as the original off-road vehicle, a horse was free of the limitations that were inherent in driving a car. There was a wonderful sense of freedom in being able to go in any direction, unrestricted by paved roads or rough terrain.

Jeff inquired about August's family and learned he was originally from Pennsylvania. He'd met Lydia in San Francisco, after he'd given up prospecting.

"In San Francisco in 1850 there were about, oh, I'd say nine or ten times the number of men than women. Women were scarce and precious. Good women, by that I mean *moral* women, were even scarcer, so I joined a church and some committees for the beautification of the city, and that's how I met Lydia. She was in the church choir, and we were on a committee to plant trees. The whole city was just a dirt pile back then, and in the winter it got awful mucky."

A dark cloud passed overhead and a smattering of rain hit the dusty earth and dampened the grass before passing on, giving the earth a rich, wet, herbal aroma.

"I've been thinking about what I'd like to do in the future, in your future, I mean," August said, "while we're waiting to see what God has in store for us. I'd like to take a ride in a car, and read your history books to see what will happen from here forward, in my time and my children's."

Having no idea what he was doing on Patsy, Jeff watched August and tried to imitate his decisiveness and composure. Rhubarb was like an extension of his body; he directed the sorrel across the landscape as one might direct a cursor over a video screen.

Patsy lurched so unsteadily up the steepening slope that Jeff found himself standing in the stirrups and precariously leaning on the pommel. August seemed to sit comfortably in the saddle and rock back and forth in rhythm with Rhubarb's movements.

August asked, "What would you like to do in this grand year of our Lord, 1870?"

Jeff was no historian. He had no sense of anything worth doing in 1870. He thought it might be fun to sail on a square-rigged clipper ship, or ride on a steam locomotive, but those aspirations seemed a bit ambitious at present. A trip, by whatever conveyance, would take planning and subterfuge to accomplish without arousing Carolyn's suspicions. He scaled down his ambitions. "I'd like to see San Francisco," he answered.

Near the top of the hills they stopped to survey the ranch and the half dozen farms that spread out across the valley floor to the base of the western mountains. It was a beautiful, pastoral scene, and yet Jeff knew it was also a hostile landscape where people would die young of some thoroughly innocuous and preventable diseases because they were entirely at nature's mercy. It felt reassuring to know that he could slip back through the passage to the relative ease and safety of the future.

August took off his hat and wiped his forehead with a bandana. Directing his gaze out over the valley he said, "I can't look at this without feeling God's grace." He leaned forward, saddle leather creaking, to stroke Rhubarb's neck. "But then you don't believe in God, do you?"

"Religion doesn't make sense to me." There was a long silence as August stared into the distance and sighed deeply. "Is that going to be a problem?"

"I shouldn't proselytize. A man's religion is his own business. But a man with no religion — I have to wonder where his moral compass comes from, or if he has one at all."

Jeff thought about how to respond to that, for if he were to keep the door open, it was imperative that they trust each other, and it would be a lot more pleasant if they had mutual respect and a liking for one another as well. August was his guide, as he was August's. On the other hand he felt disposed toward an honest, if not particularly diplomatic, approach. "I don't see that Christians have a monopoly on morality. Seems to me Christians are killing each other every day. And screwing me in business, I might add."

"What is it you do for a living?"

"I'm..." he paused, wondering how to answer that question. "I've done a lot of things, mostly in the realm of journalism, but I'm unemployed at the moment."

They started off again at a trot, when August abruptly reined in Rhubarb, muttering, "Damnation." There on the path, thirty feet before them, was a wickedly big rattler. August reached into his saddlebag and withdrew a revolver. He swung down from the saddle and handed Jeff the reins. "Hold him tight; he don't like gunfire," August explained, and walked ahead to take aim.

He needn't have worried about Rhubarb, who stood as though in a stupor as he squeezed off two shots. Patsy, on the other hand, reared, turned and bolted, jerking Jeff off the saddle and running back down the path. Jeff hit the ground hard, still holding Rhubarb's reins.

August came running up with a look of concern on his face and asked if he was all right. He sat up and examined himself. With the exception of a lump on the back of his head, bruised back and elbows, he was fine. Rhubarb snorted. Jeff got up, rubbing his back.

Then he noticed the tears flowing down August's face. Seeing the question in his eyes August said, "Rattler killed my boy last year," by way of explanation.

He put his gun back in the saddlebag, took the reins from Jeff's hand and prepared to mount. "I'll get Patsy," he said in a voice still quavering with emotion. Then staring at Jeff's loafers he added, "You know a rattler's fangs'll go right through them slippers. You ought to have a good pair of boots."

Then he swung into the saddle and loped off to retrieve the horse.

Five minutes later he came around a curve of hill with Patsy in tow. He stopped in front of Jeff and handed over the reins, his mouth clamped tight while his eyes exhibited a certain glee.

"What's so funny?" Jeff demanded.

At that August let go a blast of laughter that subsided into chuckle and played itself out with some half-hearted snorts. Now he let his mouth bend into a tight crescent, showing a row of slightly yellowed teeth. "A grown man who can't ride a horse!" He giggled. "Sorry, I can't help myself."

Jeff glared at him and choked back his indignation.

"We'd better get on down to the house. Luis-Diego is coming." He pointed.

Jeff scanned the land below and saw nothing, save a speck moving along the edge of one of the far vineyards.

"How can you tell?"

"I know his horse's gait. Besides, anyone else would be coming along the road."

"Who is he?"

"Vineyard Manager at Mirassou. They buy most of our grapes. Almaden gets the rest."

They started off path, and at once Jeff found himself lacking technique and frightened that Patsy might tumble end over end to the bottom of the hill, but Patsy was sure-footed and they got down without incident, though Jeff's inner thighs ached from tensing the whole way down.

Chapter 24
Searching

"My god!" Carolyn gasped as he undressed for bed. "What happened?"

"What?

"You're bruised!"

He didn't even feel the bruises; his thighs were so sore from riding. "I was thrown from a horse," he admitted sheepishly.

"A horse! What in hell were you doing on a horse?"

"I told you; August is teaching me to ride."

"He's not doing a very good job of it."

"It wasn't his fault. The horse spooked when he shot a rattler."

"Rattler! Jesus Christ, where were you?"

"The hills behind the ranch."

"You might've told me before we committed to move."

"There've always been rattlers. I killed three or four when I was a kid."

"It's news to me."

"It's nothing to worry about. You just have to be aware." He wasn't about to tell her August had lost a son to a rattlesnake bite. Besides, these days there was antivenom serum.

"Wait a minute — you said he shot it. He isn't a gun nut, is he?"

"No, he's just cautious."

"Anyway," she said in a needling voice, "I don't know why you're wasting your time riding horses when there's still plenty to do before we move in. Not to mention finding another job."

Jeff was momentarily irritated until he remembered the limitless possibilities afforded by the tunnel and all the money that he would undoubtedly make. That brought a smile to his face.

"You *are* going to look for a job, aren't you?"

"Don't worry; I have plans."

He slid under the covers. Carolyn got up for a glass of water, then joined him and shut off the light. He was just nodding off when she asked, "What made you want to learn to ride?"

"I thought I could cover more ground — to look for Pop," he said truthfully.

"What would you do if you found him? No offense, but judging by the way you disposed of your mother's remains, I don't see the point. You might as well let his bones lie wherever they are."

He didn't have a counter argument. He couldn't admit he knew Pop was alive. But her question — *What would you do if you found him?* — brought up more questions: Could they still move to the ranch? How would his father react to his losing another job? Would he be angry that his things had been given away? Would he be defensive about the repairs and changes that had been made? Worst of all, Jeff thought, would be breaking the news that his mom had died. Would Pop want to come back, knowing she was no longer there?

But he was getting ahead of himself; he hadn't found Pop yet. In the meantime they had to move forward as though nothing had changed. They were waiting on Wells Fargo for approval of the short sale. Assuming it went through quickly, they'd be moving to the ranch shortly after the kids began their summer vacation. He wanted the house move-in ready by that time, and more than anything he wanted Carolyn to be happy.

He had already arranged to meet two house painters to take bids on the exterior, which he intended to pay for out of cash taken from his parents' checking account. Pop could scream about it later.

Jeff met the first painter that morning at 11:30. The second wasn't scheduled until late afternoon, and as he knew the Kimballs would be back from church no sooner than three o'clock his time, he crossed over. So far, the data suggested that the passage closed every evening and opened every morning, though the exact time was inconsistent. Still, it seemed likely that it remained open during daylight hours.

He went directly to the barn and saddled Patsy. She was a docile creature, easy to handle and forgiving of his inexperience. He spent over an hour practicing to get her to make the transition from walk to trot to canter and back to trot, trying to move with her, giving her more or less rein as she needed. At the end of it he was still a rank amateur, but as in all things, incremental improvement could only be made through practice. Afterwards he watered her, put away the saddle, rubbed her down and gave her some oats. Then he hobbled back through the tunnel, his thighs aching.

He left a note for August. The next morning, as he'd requested, August was waiting for him in the kitchen. Lydia did a double take when he walked around the corner. "Where in...?"

"Yup, he's as quiet as a injun — like his father," August said. "He'll be coming and going, and I've given him permission to just let himself in, like family, so don't be alarmed when he shows up."

Lydia dried her hands on her apron and smiled at Jeff. She was a plump, worn little woman. "We hardly got to meet t'other day," she said. "Gus tells me you're Randall's son?" She looked to August, then gave Jeff an appraising gaze that was, he felt, a little reserved.

"Yes. We..." And here Jeff had to fabricate a story on the spot, which had never been his forte. "He came out West before us, and we lost track of him."

"You have other family?"

"My wife and I have a boy and a girl, eleven and fourteen."

"And your wife? Is she...?"

"She's staying in Denver with the kids until I get settled here — Carolyn's her name."

"Our Carolyn (we call her Carrie) she's seventeen."

Noah was in the kitchen. He spoke up with the tactlessness of youth. "Are you staying the night?"

"No. I'm just down the road. But I'll be visiting often."

"He's buying the old Steiger place," August put in quickly. This was a bit of spontaneous invention he had not rehearsed, and Jeff was quite impressed with how well he pulled it off.

"Steiger?" Lydia asked. "I don't know anyone by that name."

"You remember them — other side of Wild Cat Creek. They bought it from Pacheco, stayed until their eldest son died, and left...oh, must be six years ago."

"I thought I knew everyone in this valley. Did they go to our church?"

"No, they weren't church-goers."

"Oh, well...." She turned back to Jeff. "Are you a church-goer?"

"Not really," he replied truthfully. "I'm a skeptic."

"You should go," she said.

He didn't know if she meant he should go to church, or he should go, as in leave.

"I'm hoping he can help out around here while we look for Randall," August said to change the subject.

With the small talk over, she went back to work and the men went out to the barn, where August introduced Jeff to his eldest son, Owen, a tall young man of nineteen, with thick dark hair and hazel eyes. Whichever side of the family he got his height and dark eyes from, he didn't take after either of his parents. He was a good six inches taller than his father and broader in the shoulders.

"Help Jeff with his saddle," August said.

While Owen put the saddle on Patsy, Jeff reached in his coat pocket and brought out an apple to feed her.

Owen stopped what he was doing and stared open mouthed. "Where'd you get a apple this time o' year?"

"Supermar..." he started to say. He looked at the apple, trying to come up with a story. The little sticker said Product of Chile. He surreptitiously peeled it off and said, "I was up in San Francisco a few days ago, and this boat came in from Chile. Did you know that down below the equator their fall is our spring? They were selling apples on the dock."

"Lord almighty," Owen said appreciatively, "what I wouldn't give for a apple in April."

"It's all yours," Jeff said, pressing it into his hand. Patsy nickered a complaint. He stroked her nose and brought out a carrot from his other pocket.

They rode out to the cabin Randall had stayed in, a weather-beaten one-room shack with a flimsy table, two straight-backed chairs, and a small wood stove for heat and cooking. The place was now deserted and covered in a layer of dust. There was no sign he'd ever been there. They rode on to the Ginthers and the Siefferts, where Jeff showed a sepia-toned photo of his father. They were eager to be of assistance, but no one had seen him.

Thursday Jeff helped August with chores in the morning. Then they rode out to other farms. The Belfrages were happy for the company and offered refreshments, but were of no help. On the way August was full of questions — how many states were there in 2009? How much did this or that cost? What did people do with all the time their machines saved them? Which nations were friendly or unfriendly?

They rode on to the Bowmans', distinguished by a small grove of redwoods that towered above a weatherworn adobe with a hip roof and second-story veranda, a leftover from the Mexican era. Two red bougainvilleas grew up the posts at either end of the porch and reached across the upper gallery to meet in the middle. As they rode into the dooryard, Mrs. Bowman came out to greet them, wiping her hands on a towel, a smile on her face that turned to a grimace at the sound of her husband's voice yelling, "Get yourself inside!"

"But…"

"You heard me."

Eyes cast down, she hurried back inside, where she turned and peered around the door. A youngster peeked bashfully out from behind her skirts.

Charles Bowman came striding across the yard from the corral, pitchfork in hand, and stopped before them. He was a big man, tall and powerful, with a thick neck and a gruff demeanor. He raised an eyebrow and cocked his head, his body language signaling more confrontation than greeting. "Gus, what brings you out this way?"

"Charlie, this here is Jeffrey Porter. His father, Randall, used to work for me, and we're trying to locate him."

Jeff held out the picture. Bowman took it, glanced at it with a frown. "No. Never seen him."

"Maybe your wife…" Jeff began, but was cut off.

"She ain't seen him."

"Maybe if you showed her the photo…"

"She don't go nowhere without me."

"He might have come this way looking for work."

Bowman scowled and called back over his shoulder, "What about it, Mary? You seen any strange men?"

"No," she squeaked and closed the door.

"See," Bowman said, smiling.

"If you do see him," August said, "tell him to come by my place."

Bowman just stared, tight-lipped.

As they rode away Jeff couldn't help thinking that Bowman wasn't a man he wanted to turn his back to. He exuded a sense of pent up violence.

Chapter 25
A Clash of Cultures

All of the Kimball children, save Owen, were on their way to school when Jeff stepped silently into the kitchen. Lydia watched them go from the kitchen window, then turned and jumped. "My word! You gave me a fright," she said, patting her chest. "You should wear a bell. Would you like some coffee?"

"No thanks. Is August around?"

"Him and Owen are saddling up in the barn. You're sure you don't want coffee?"

"No, I'm fine, I'll just head out there then."

"Oh, Mr. Porter, I almost forgot." She dried her hands on the towel tucked into her apron and reached into a cabinet. "Your pa give me this envelope in case any o' his kin might come by lookin' for him."

Jeff thanked her and stepped out to the back porch. He read:

Dear Ginny, I can't explain how I got caught on this side. One day the opening in the rock just closed up. If you're here, you must have figured out a way to open it up again. I've hung around this ranch for several months now, sneaking into the cellar every few days to check, without any luck. I've about worn out my welcome here and need to get on and find work. I'll try not to wander too far, and I'll come back now and again to check. So keep the door open and be careful. Keep the tarp over the opening (it could be dangerous if the Kimballs find out). I'm so sorry for all the worry I must have put you through. Be strong. Missing you, Your Loving Husband, R.

It was a cool, breezy April day with high wispy cirrus streaking the sky. The air was filled with the pleasant scent of wood smoke, and the pungent aroma of rotting food and manure wafting from the compost pile by the barn. Jeff folded the letter and stuffed it in his pocket.

Patsy was already saddled. Owen was leaning against a post drinking a cup of coffee. He came upright when Jeff walked in.

"Your father around?"

August ducked under Rhubarb's jaw. He made the introductions. Then to Owen he said, "Tell Sal the apricots should be ready to pick next week, ten days tops, but he oughta send one of his boys out to check with me on Monday. I'm taking Mr. Porter here to look for his father. We'll go as far as Jenkins' place, be back by supper."

Owen threw out the dregs of his coffee and placed the cup on the top of the stall post. Then he mounted Patsy.

"Patsy is Owen's horse," August explained to Jeff, then turned to his son. "Which of 'em do you think is best for Mr. Porter, Owen — Ben?"

Owen looked appraisingly at Jeff. "You a good rider, Mr. Porter?"

"No, not really. I'd have to say I'm only used to gentle old nags."

"In that case I wouldn't recommend Ben. He's been a bit cantankerous lately, run me up against a fence last time I had him out." He turned to his father. "Why not give him Stormy. He never throwed nobody."

August stiffened and made a pretense of adjusting the saddle blanket on Rhubarb's back. "He hasn't been ridden in a long time."

"No, he ain't and that's a good reason to put a saddle on him now, afore he forgets how."

"He's not used to a grown man."

"He should get used to it. He's not old enough to put out to pasture."

"Right," August said, resigned to the ineffectuality of further argument.

Owen rode off across the yard and over the bridge.

August snatched a bridle and headed for the corral, calling over his shoulder, "Saddle Rhubarb for me." Jeff was cinching the girth strap when August returned leading a skewbald pony. "Stormy was Ivan's. He's hasn't been ridden in a while, but you just let him be and he'll follow along. He's a good..." He clamped his jaw together holding down the grief that rose in his throat, and went to the barn for a saddle.

If anything, Stormy was easier to ride than Patsy, obediently following Rhubarb and cantering to keep up with the bigger animal's trot.

The horses blew nickering jets of warm steam into the cool morning air. They rode north out the dirt track that skirted the arroyo.

Low over the eastern hills, the sun threw the shadows of the riders out across the ground and raised a low fog that settled ankle high in dry grass.

Jeff enjoyed the ride far more than he would, had this been a recreational affair; he felt more comfortable with purposeful action; he craved direction. This was simply transportation and as such he appreciated the efficiency of riding over walking.

About a mile out from the house Owen came across the field with Patsy at a gallop. He reined in hard in front of them, said breathlessly, "We got trouble, Papa," and headed back lickety-split in the direction he'd come with August and a frightened Jeff in hot pursuit.

They heard the commotion before they reached the end of the vineyards. The sound of shouting and wailing rose in waves above the heavy thudding of horse hooves, like the crowd noise at a baseball game. They crested a small rise and started down into the meadow with a clear view of the mayhem. The air was split with a babble of

Spanish and Chinese. The main body of the Chinese contingent, perhaps forty in all, all dressed in gray or black pajamas, was scurrying toward the creek, men, women and children running with bundles on their backs and hand carts rumbling behind. A few men trailed further back, uncertain whether to flee or to aid their fallen comrades, for there were two men lying insensate on the ground, and another writhing with the pain of a machete wound in the thigh and a knife slash across the stomach. Five of the Chinese men stood around the victims with clubs in hand, facing off the Mexicans who stood in a tight clump with machetes and curved harvest knives in hand. A screaming woman knelt over one of the prostrate figures.

Slowing to a canter August reached back into a saddlebag, brought out a pistol and fired it into the air. Rhubarb threw back his head in alarm. Patsy merely neighed and snorted without breaking stride, as though stirred from deep thought. Stormy, however, shied at the shot, coming to a sudden halt and nearly pitching Jeff out of the saddle. August stopped between the warring factions, glanced at the Chinese to ascertain the extent of the damage, then leaned on his pommel and turned to the Mexicans, his pistol draped limply, but authoritatively over his forearm. He puckered his lips and looked over the group reprovingly, before bringing his gaze squarely onto two men who stood in the center of the group.

"Salvador. Ruiz. What do you have to say for yourselves?"

Salvador Alamillo stepped forward, harvest knife in hand, and stripped off his shapeless hat as a sign of respect. "They come for our jobs. We tol' them go back. They keep on coming. So we stop them."

August looked out over the heads of the crowd. He ran his tongue inside his cheek, making it bulge. "You shame me, Salvador," he said evenly, and brought his riveting blue eyes back to the foreman. "You don't trust me."

Salvador looked abashed and puzzled. "*Si, tengo mucho respeto.*"

"Do we not have an agreement?"

"*Si, nos tenemous.* We have," Salvador said, turning his eyes to the ground.

"Do you think I'll hire these Chinese when I have an agreement with you?"

"No, señor, but there are others who hire them."

August turned toward the Chinese then and asked if anyone spoke English. A young man stepped forward and declared that he did, though in an accent that made the veracity of his statement doubtful.

"Do you need medical supplies?"

"Sup-supp-lices?"

"Bandages, herbs?"

"Herbs, yes."

"Good. Now tell your people there are no jobs for them here. Do you understand?"

The young man bowed gravely, turned and said something to the others. One of the men who had been knocked unconscious stood now, groaning and holding his hands to his bloody scalp. The men and woman picked up the other two victims and started back up the road toward the sycamores along the creek.

Ruiz shouted some orders in Spanish and the Mexicans began moving toward their wagons.

Jeff rode up alongside August. "Shouldn't we call a sheriff or something?"

August smirked and made sure Owen was far enough away to risk the sarcastic answer he was inclined to make. "Why sure, I'll just reach in my saddlebag for my telephone."

"Oh, yeah," Jeff said, chagrined at his stupidity. "How dumb. But you know what I mean. Somebody could ride for the sheriff."

"Why?"

"I think they killed a man."

"He was only a Chinaman."

Jeff was appalled and sat dumbstruck for several seconds before he found his outraged voice. "He was a human being!"

"Yes, but he was also Chinese, and the law don't apply to Chinese. Same can be said for Mexicans. No sheriff will waste his time, unless what they do effects a white man."

"That's disgusting; it's not right," Jeff blustered, and seeing no response in his friend's face, he added a barb. "It's not Christian."

"You may not approve, but that's the way it is. I take it that's not the way it is in the..." he glanced over his shoulder to find Owen close at hand and finished with, "...where you come from."

"No, it isn't."

"Good, I'm glad to see the human race is making progress."

August squeezed his knees to start Rhubarb walking toward the tents. There he cornered Salvador again and told him they would be needed toward the end of the next week.

Owen gave his farewells and set off for home.

August turned Rhubarb to the east to pick up the track they'd been following earlier. "You know," said August as they rode away, "it's tough for these Mexicans. They owned this land once. And I think when Vallejo and Pico were elected to the State Legislature; they hoped to have equal representation under the law. But it hasn't worked out that way. Some of the richer Mexicans still hold some sway. But the rest aren't much better off than the Indians. They're outsiders in their own country."

Jeff remained silent, thinking about how a reunion with his father might go. He could imagine his joy at being found, and yet he was the proverbial bearer of bad news. Congratulations, you've won the lottery! And by the way, your wife is dead, and your son has raided your bank account and moved into your house. At the same time, finding that his father was alive was like bringing back the dead. *He's still in the land of the dead*, he thought — for every living person in 1870 was a long time gone.

They inspected August's Hermitage vineyard on the way to Etienne Thée's, and after some pleasant but fruitless banter with the Frenchman, they set out for Thomas Jenkins' ranch, nearly at the base of the Diablo range, which was as far from home as August was prepared to take them.

On the way August had plenty of time to talk, and Jeff had plenty of time to listen. He'd grown up the fourth child of eight on a farm in Pennsylvania. "My mother was a schoolteacher before she married. Reading was her one indulgence. She wanted me to be a professor. But I was young and headstrong and wanted to see the world, so I headed west. I'm afraid I was a great disappointment to her."

He fell silent for a while, then asked, "Will my children live to see cars?"

"Oh, sure. There were lots of cars by World War One, and your twelve-year-old will..."

"World War One?"

"1914 to 1918," Jeff supplied.

"How many world wars have there been?"

"Just two. The second from 1939 to 1945."

"Did many die?"

"Something like a hundred million, I think."

"My word! Who won?"

"The U.S. We're the world's Superpower now."

"More powerful than England?"

"Oh god, yes. England is insignificant."

August seemed pleased at this news, though Jeff often wished the U.S. were as out-of-the-way and forgotten as New Zealand. Being a citizen of a Superpower came with its own set of problems and moral conundrums.

They found Jenkins at home alone, in a black suit, his wife and daughters gone visiting relatives in San Francisco. His farm was the most prosperous Jeff had seen, with a bunkhouse for the ranch hands he employed. Jenkins was a tall, lean, angular man near forty, with long brown hair and a wide smile. "Randall? Sure, he worked here January and February. Knew his way around a vineyard, I can tell you. He supervised the Coolies. They done a good job. When they finished pruning he moved on. They all did."

Jenkins insisted they stay awhile. They sat at a table under a wisteria arbor at the edge of his vineyard. A Chinese servant brought out dried apricots, cheese and fresh sourdough bread, and two of the estate's wines. The first was god-awful swill, the second a decent Zinfandel.

On their return to the ranch they rode side-by-side in silence. Deprived of conversation, Jeff lost himself in the moment — creaking saddle leather, the horses' rhythmic panting, the clop and thump of hooves, the smell of vegetation and horse sweat, the cooing of mourning doves, warbling of meadowlarks, and screech of hawks. And there was the buzz of hope and excitement from knowing at last that his father, though elusive, was still alive and still in the area.

Eventually August glanced his way and said, "You should come into town with us on Sunday. Show your photograph around. Maybe even post a picture at the General Store."

The ranch was a hive of activity when they returned. The kids had returned from school. Owen and Noah were mucking out horse stalls; Charles was feeding the pigs; on the back porch little Emily cut squares out of newspaper and talked with Betsy who was churning butter; and Carrie and Lydia were making pies in the kitchen.

August kissed Carrie on top of the head.

"Any luck?" Lydia asked, as she lined a pie tin with dough.

"Not much. Randall left Jenkins' place a couple months ago. No one knows where he's gone to."

"Well, just be patient; he'll turn up sooner or later."

August leaned over his wife's shoulder and kissed her on the cheek.

"Go on now!" Lydia said, blushing and pushing him away.

August smiled, grabbed a couple of biscuits from a bowl on the table and tossed one to Jeff. Then he gestured with a nod of his head and Jeff followed quietly to the dining room and down the wine cellar stairs.

Jeff's momentary anxiety eased as he ascertained the tunnel was still there. The randomness of its manifestations was cause for concern, but what was he to do? Life came with risks, and so far it seemed a safe bet that the tunnel would remain open during daylight hours.

Chapter 26
Graduation Present

Jeff was at the kitchen table, surfing the net when the kids burst in from the garage and hurried straight to their room(s). Carolyn came in shedding her paraphernalia; she slung her purse onto the kitchen counter, dropped her jacket onto a chair and tossed her keys onto the kitchen table. Then she turned on her heels, grabbed a tumbler from the cabinet and poured herself a glass of Riesling. She closed her eyes, pinched the bridge of her nose, and sighed, "How was your day?"

Jeff hardly knew what to say. Her question was a non sequitur. Her actions, so out of character, screamed for another reaction. So he answered her question with a vague, "I had an okay day," and reflected her question straight back at her — "How was *your* day?"

She sat down at the table and took a generous sip of the Riesling. "I'm just so pissed. I know, I know – I shouldn't get involved in my students' lives, but…" She shuddered and took another sip. "But sometimes they're so… It's so…so frustrating! So grotesque!"

"More drug problems?"

"God, no. Well…there's that, but that's not what's…" She sighed and growled and took another sip. Then she put the glass down and strode out of the room and down the hall to the kids' bathroom.

When she came back she seemed much calmer, picked up her glass and paced the room, talking while looking at her reflection in the sliding glass doors. "I have a student who is very smart, and very pretty, and very rich, and she has this incredible sense of entitlement."

"She pisses you off."

"Yes, she most certainly does. I gave her a B- on her group project, which drops her overall grade to a B+, and she comes into my office crying. She needs to get straight A's or she won't get the graduation present of her dreams. And do you know what her daddy promised to give her for graduation?"

"A car?"

"Nope."

"A trip around the world?"

"Nope."

"What then?"

"A boob job! I'm so incensed! This girl has the brains and the money to get into any college in the country, and her father is offering her a boob job! What kind of message does that send to this girl? — You're good, but you're not good enough. You can be smart, but if you really want to get ahead, you need sex appeal. And if you don't have it, you can buy it! Ohrrrrghh!"

"That's sad."

"You know what's *really* sad? — She doesn't need enhancement; she's already Miss Perfect. I have other girls who are just as smart, but they have no money and no looks. How far do you think *they*'ll go?"

"Whoever said life was fair?"

"It's not, is it?"

"It most definitely is not."

"Can you imagine a father even bringing up the subject?"

"I'd be embarrassed."

Carolyn went back to the fridge and poured the last of the Riesling and dropped the bottle into the recycling bin at the end of the counter. She sighed heavily. "It's a moral dilemma, because the B- on the final project reflects the combined work of three girls. The other two fell down on the job. Kimberly did "A" work for her part. But if I give her an A, she gets the boob job, and I really don't want to give her that. So if I stick to my guns and give a B+ for the semester I could prevent it. But then she won't have straight A's, which she's earned, and she'll need a 4.0 to get into Berkeley. I don't know what to do."

Jeff opened the fridge and pulled out an Oregon Pinot Gris. He poured a glass (his third) and said, "Give her the A, she's earned it."

"You don't have a problem with promoting elective surgery?"

"Look, here's how it plays out: If she doesn't get the boob job she'll feel she doesn't measure up to her father's standards; her self esteem will suffer; she won't get into Berkeley; she'll marry a bank clerk who will give her a good but boring life, and eventually she'll be a widow with a small pension and go to live with her daughter. If she gets the boob job she goes to Berkeley, marries the alpha male, lives in a mansion, has a career and a couple of kids, and travels the world for the next 20 years, until her husband dumps her for the trophy wife. Is one story better than another? Who knows? It's all in your point of view. I say, 'Let her be the architect of her own life.' If she's earned an A, give her an A, even if it means a boob job. The rest of the story is hers to make, one way or the other, and in the end she'll be the one to judge if it was good or not."

"Maybe you're right."

"I'm always right," he said, sniffing the wine, "except when I'm wrong."

"How often is that?"

"About half the time."

"You're a big help," she remarked sarcastically.

Jake came into the kitchen and peeled a banana. "Little League tryouts are this Sunday," he said.

"You know we're moving," Jeff said. "We won't be here when the season starts."

"I know. That's why I checked out San Jose's Little League online. The tryouts are at Lincoln High School, Sunday at 10:00 am. I even got directions off Google Maps."

"Good," Carolyn said, looking pointedly at Jeff.

The year before he'd been too busy with work. Too busy for the things that mattered most. "Sounds like fun," he said; "I look forward to it." And he meant it.

Chapter 27
A Trip to the Mall

It'd been a long time since Jeff had had a weekend unencumbered by to-do lists and work deadlines. The painters were taking the Memorial Day weekend off. The Porters had packed up all they could before their impending move at the end of the school year; and Jeff had reached a dead end in his search for his father. Saturday Jeff and Jake drove to Burlingame high school where they played catch and Jeff shagged grounders and fly balls.

Sunday, while Carolyn graded papers and Abby hung out at the local mall with friends, Jeff drove Jake down to San Jose for Little League tryouts. Jake was a pretty good second baseman, and confident he'd be drafted.

Afterwards they stopped by the ranch to see how far the painters had progressed. The back of the house had not yet been painted, but the front no longer wore a forlorn look. It gleamed pale yellow with white trim — a bright, hopeful house.

While Jake used a bathroom, Jeff ducked into the geode and wrote a quick note to August that he'd be there Wednesday (August's Monday) morning.

Wednesday he was waiting in the dining room when August came running up the stairs and burst breathlessly through the doorway. "Ah, good, you're here."

"Something wrong?"

"It's just that the passage was closed all day and all night Thursday (that would be your Saturday), and it's been open ever since I found your note Friday evening. So it's not as predictable as we thought."

Jeff tried to remember if it was closed the previous weekend. "That's a sobering thought. Sit down. Let's think this through. Or maybe you should go back — I have to take my chances; you don't."

August shook his head. "No, I'm not going back. I just thought you'd want to know."

He had asked to see the future, and Jeff figured the easiest thing would be to take him on a quick shopping trip to the mall to buy him contemporary clothing. But first he insisted August take a shower and change into a set of clean clothes. August looked suitably offended as Jeff herded him to the bathroom and showed him how the toilet and shower worked. Twenty minutes later he came out of the bathroom wrapped in a towel and smiling beatifically. "Warm water! That was heavenly! I don't know as how I've ever been so clean! And a privy inside — very comfortable." Then his brow pinched with worry. "What'll I tell Lyddy? I'm supposed to take a bath this afternoon. We take baths *every* Saturday. She'll think I've been to a bawdy house."

"You can roll in the dust when we get back. For now, put on these clothes."

August buttoned up one of Jeff's dress shirts, then stepped into a pair of khaki chinos and paused. "Where's the buttons?"

"That's a zipper. Pull up on the tab."

He did, and pulled it down again. Then up. Then down. "Will you look at that!" he exclaimed. "Now ain't that *some*thing?!"

Jeff gave him the full tour of the car, from the tires to the engine, but August seemed most intrigued by the red plastic taillights. Before he got into the car he happened to glance back at the house. "The chimney is different," he observed.

"Yeah, I don't know if it's true or not, but my father told me the original fell in the 1906 quake."

"Must have been a big one."

"It was, and the fire that followed it leveled most of San Francisco."

"We had fires in '50 and '51 took out the Financial District in the city, and big quakes in '65 and '68. Some said San Francisco was cursed. Maybe they was right."

Jeff got him settled and strapped him in.

"What are these restraints for?"

"In case of an accident," Jeff said, and added with mischievous nonchalance, "Car accidents kill about 30,000 a year in the U.S." and closed his door before August could respond.

They'd just entered the housing development when August screamed, "Stop!" He was squirming in his seat, eyes wide, frantically fumbling at the door latch. Jeff pulled to the curb.

"What's your problem?"

"We have to help that woman!"

"What, who?" Jeff asked, looking around.

"She's running from someone! She's not clothed!" He pointed as a young woman ran past.

"She's not running from someone; she's jogging. That's a jogging outfit."

"Jogging?"

Jeff explained the concept to him, then issued an edict. "Don't react unless I react."

At the mall they had not been inside for more than ten seconds before August grabbed Jeff's arm. "Wait!" He frowned, turned and stared. "Were those *girls*?" he whispered, a look of horror on his face.

Jeff glanced back at them. They were indeed teenage girls, of that clique who display a certain disdain for their elders by affecting piercings, tattoos and short, spikey hair.

"Those girls are wearing *pants*!"

"Very observant," Jeff replied sardonically.

It was all a marvel to August. He was like a three-year-old. Passing an electronics store, he stopped, as mesmerized by a wall of televisions as by a burning bush. It took Jeff five minutes to get him to move on.

In Kohl's he gazed upward in open-mouthed wonder.

"What?" Jeff asked.

August pointed at the illuminated ceiling panels. "It's like they brung the sun inside."

Jeff bought him a dark blue polo shirt, a couple of dress shirts, a pair of Khaki pants, socks, running shoes, and (in hopes he'd stop fingering his fly) a grey cardigan sweater with a zipper. When Jeff handed him a pair of jeans, August took one look at the label and exclaimed, "Looky here, that little Jew's company is still in business!"

"Quiet!" Jeff cringed, realizing that fitting in was going to require more than a new set of clothes. "In 2009 we do not refer to people by their ethnicity, race or religion. It's considered extremely impolite."

"I never heard *him* complain."

"Who?"

"Levi."

"You know him?"

"Everybody knows Levi. I bought my Sunday-go-to-meetin'-suit from him."

Before their return they stopped by the supermarket to pick up a few odds and ends. August followed Jeff around like an idiot, his mouth agape as much at the packaging as at the sheer abundance.

Jeff took some pleasure both immediately and in the following weeks in introducing August to modern technology. How delicious it was to show him the simplest, most ordinary item and watch his eyes grow wide with astonishment like a child in a toy store. Each day he saw the world anew through August's virgin eyes. He had thought nothing of turning on a lamp, or a TV, or a computer, or talking on the telephone. But as he told August of satellites orbiting the earth, and how computers connected to a repository of collected human knowledge, it sounded like science fiction even to him, and he'd watched it develop over the past twenty-five years. But he couldn't play the sophisticate with smug superiority for long, for every time he stumbled to explain how something worked, he was reminded how little he really knew. He lived in an age of miraculous machines, but he only knew how to turn them on, not how to make them. If forced to rebuild civilization from scratch, he was unprepared. For all intents and purposes he was a Stone Age man in a modern world. He couldn't even make a match, or extract metal from rock.

August began his letter rather formally, in a beautiful copperplate script: "*My dearest Lydia, if you are reading this I expect I've gone missing, and for that I must profoundly beg your forgiveness.*"

After a page or two of explanation and divine justification, he launched into a description of his first trip into the future, which concluded with the following passage:

"*Today I traveled several miles in a horseless carriage (also known as a car, or automobile), a contrivance controlled by pedals, levers and a wheel. You travel at tremendous speed in a cabin surrounded by glass windows. I was taking in the scenery when Jeffrey pushed a thin silver plate the diameter of a small pancake into a slot in the dash. You can, perhaps, understand my excitement when a moment later the most glorious music filled the air! The music of a entire orchestra the like of which I never heard before hovered like a hummingbird in the air, now coming from the left, now from the right and even behind, like as if I was sitting on the stage!*

"*Imagine rolling down a road as smooth as a billiard table, faster than a horse can gallop, in a chair as comfortable as any in our parlor, sheltered from the elements, the heat abated by a cool stream of air directed at your face, and any orchestra at your bidding. That is what the future holds in store for our grandchildren. I was entranced.*

"*After a short introduction the orchestra was accompanied by a man who sang in a most pleasing voice. On inquiry Jeffrey revealed that the singer had been dead for 15 years. Think of it. To be entertained by the dead! Never to lose the past. Today a king might travel in as much comfort in a private railway car, and might even carry a chamber orchestra with him, but not even a king can bring back the dead for a recital. These musical plates have done for music, for the ear, what the invention of writing did for knowledge and the invention of photography did for the eye. Yet Jeffrey takes it as his due. My Lord, the people of the future are a spoiled lot.*

"And that, dear one, is how I spent my first few hours in the future. So if I am lost to you, you will perhaps understand why I have been unable to resist going through that door. For there is something intoxicating about the future, something as exciting and stimulating as a gay party. Even now as I think of it I keep hearing the strains of music going through my head. Such luxury! Such a heady access to all that you can imagine! Such comfort! Such speed! And yet, for all its wonders, the future is not free of conflict. Human nature, alas, remains unchanged. However, knowing when the storms will strike will make it ever so much easier to find a safe harbor to wait out those storms. With God's guidance, we will prevail.

"Your devoted husband,

"August"

Chapter 28
Jeff Goes to Church

Two grey mules pulled the Kimballs' weathered grey buckboard over the dusty road to Pulgas. August, reins in hand, sat on the sprung seat beside Lydia. In the back the girls (Carrie, Betsy and Emily), and the boys (Owen, Noah and Charles) sat on facing benches in the wagon bed. Tied to the tailgate, Patsy and Rhubarb trotted behind. Jeff took up the rear on Honey. Once the wagon was loaded with supplies for the trip back, Owen and Noah would also ride horseback.

That morning Jeff had sat at the kitchen table drinking coffee, while the Kimball brood bustled about getting ready for church. "Where'd you get them clothes?" Lydia asked. "I never seen such a sharp crease in a pair of trousers. And a built-in collar, too. Are they foreign?"

"Yeah, I guess so," Jeff said, vaguely aware that the suit was from Sri Lanka (known as Ceylon in 1870), the shirt from Costa Rica, the shoes and blue silk tie from Italy.

Owen walked into the room as she was talking, cocked his head and added, "That's some necktie, ain't it?"

August came in, pulling on his coat. He shook his head. "Now, I know you're a stranger in these parts, so I'm going tell it to you straight. If you wear that neckpiece, you're going to be asking for a fight. Let me give you something a little less...flamboyant."

August helped Jeff put on a sort of floppy black bow tie. "That's better," he pronounced.

"Right smart," Lydia agreed.

Honey's canter was too fast for the mules and Jeff was still unable to keep from bouncing off the saddle at a trot. By the time they crossed Guadalupe Creek and came to the cluster of clapboard buildings that made up the village of Las Pulgas, he was covered in a coat of dust and felt like he'd been kicked in the kidneys.

There were half a dozen houses, a Presbyterian church, a General Store, a Livery, a Blacksmith, a post office, a barbershop that doubled as a dentist's office, an undertaker, a restaurant and inn, a saloon with rooms upstairs, a bakery, a law office and a sheriff's office.

Beyond Main Street on the north was a forlorn cemetery overgrown by dry grass and weeds, whose boundaries were defined by six poplars and a white picket fence. The town was long gone by Jeff's day, but the cemetery was still there, hidden behind a Target, Subway, Chevy's, Ace Hardware, dry cleaners, Jamba Juice and local bookstore.

They watered the horses and were leading them toward the hitching rails behind the church, when a dapper man with a handlebar mustache and bowler hat came hurrying toward them with an amused air. "Hey, Gus. Better not go back there! Richards and his whole family was sprayed by skunks, comin' into town this morning. Reverend says he's leavin' the back windows open, so's they can hear the sermon from outside. Hope the breeze don't change direction! Ha!"

"Is Reverend Winters back?" Lydia asked.

"Yup. Back from Sac he is."

"That's good; I didn't like that other fella too well."

They turned around and tied up in the shade of an oak at the side of Pulgas General Store. Noah, Charles and Emily went off to Sunday School.

The church was a small, white clapboard affair with a modest steeple and arched windows of amber glass that bathed the pews in golden light. They sat about half way down the right side of the aisle on a hardwood, straight-backed pew that seemed designed more for penance than for comfort. Looking around at the members filing in, Jeff understood the warm sense of community that the church engendered, and that that same sense of community spawned an "us versus them" mentality, an assumption of moral superiority that he found disturbing. He'd also spent enough hours in hotel rooms reading Gideon Bibles to know that no leap of faith could enable him to reconcile the inconsistencies found in that book. He thought the Devil himself could not have written a better condemnation of religion.

The Reverend delivered his sermon from a pulpit on a dais backed by a choir and a piano.

"Let us rise up and join our voices in praise of our Lord, Jesus Christ," the Reverend intoned, and thus began an excruciatingly boring hour. The message of the day, interrupted at various points by hymns and the invocation to "Let us now bow our heads and pray," was on the subject of obedience. "Some among us may wonder at how the stories of the Bible have relevance to our humble lives today," he began, and seemed to direct his gaze toward his wife in the first pew. "Let me assure you that the Bible tells us all how to live in accordance with the Lord's wishes. We all have our parts to play, and the Bible is quite clear on the proper division of labor. I quote from Ephesians, "'Wives, submit to your husbands as to the Lord. For the husband is the head of the wife as Christ is the head of the church, his body, of which he is the Savior. Now as the church submits to Christ, so also wives should submit to their husbands in everything.' And Corinthians confirms, 'But I want you to realize that the head of every man is Christ, and the head of the woman is man, and the head of Christ is God.'" Which set the tone for the whole sermon, the lesson being the "virtue" of submission to one's "superiors," and the inferior position of females. Jeff imagined Carolyn receiving this message with unbridled indignation. It was the sort of demeaning paternalism applied by Middle Eastern theocracies. The Reverend Winters bolstered his argument by citing instances where women, in defiance of God, had brought divine retribution down upon themselves and mankind. He ended with the warning example of Lot's wife turned to a pillar of salt. Several of the men glanced at their wives here and smiled indulgently, as if to say, "Women — they can't help themselves."

There was a pause toward the end of the service where a plate was passed around. Jeff knew he was expected to tithe some money, but he had no 1870 currency. He turned to August and through gestures let him know he had nothing to give. August passed him a few coins that he plunked into the plate.

At the conclusion of the service the pastor walked down the aisle and stationed himself outside the front door where he intended to thank the devoted for attending. Jeff tried to duck past him, but was caught by the sleeve.

"So glad to see a new face among the congregation," Reverend Winters said.

Jeff grimaced, nodded, and tried to pull away. The man held on.

"You're new to our community."

"He's with us," August said. "He's looking for his father, who used to work for me. Show him a picture, Jeff."

Jeff brought out an antiqued photo from his inside pocket.

"No, I don't think so," Winters said, shaking his head. "Did he attend any of our services?"

"No, I think it unlikely," August said.

"May I keep this? I'll ask around," the Reverend said, before turning to another of his flock.

Emerging from the stultifying confines of the church the sky opened above them and Jeff felt a wonderful sense of release. A caressing breeze and warm sunlight on his upturned face brought a flood of gratitude and joy at just being alive and free.

The people didn't so much disperse, as stream toward the General Store and the saloon. August and Lydia lingered to talk with friends. Noah, Charles and Emily were already by the family wagon, playing with a little terrier. Jeff headed for the Pulgas General Store where a group of men were gathering on the porch. Beside the front door, two pages of a newspaper were posted on the wall, just enough to whet the appetite. Anyone wanting more would have to buy the whole paper inside. Next to the paper was a corkboard where anyone could pin a note or free ad. Between ads for piano instruction and pigs for sale, Jeff pinned an antiqued photo of his father, under which he'd typed the following message: "Anyone knowing the whereabouts of Randall Porter, please contact August Kimball or Jeffrey Porter at the Kimball ranch."

Looking for an opening to show the photo around, Jeff sidled up to a knot of eight or ten men who stood in front of the posted newspaper. The topic under discussion was the Fifteenth Amendment, which had been ratified a month earlier.

"I believe every man has a right to live free, even negroes," said a skinny young man with pockmarked cheeks and a drooping mustache. "But they ain't like you and me. They can't even read. Givin'm the vote is like givin' the vote to children."

"It ain't just niggers, neither," a redhead in a derby and brown suit said. "Anybody can vote now, even Indians and heathen Chinese!"

"Dat's what I'm worried about," said a Scandinavian with a paunch that strained the seams of his worn overalls. "Dem Coolies dey work for not'ing, an' dey take yobs meant for white men."

"You're a old fool, Adelhard," came a booming baritone Jeff recognized. Charles Bowman mounted the wooden steps and made an imposing figure as he stood a head taller and a good deal wider than any man on the porch. "You don't know a good thing when you see it. Sure Chinamen work for next to nothin', but I say that's a good thing. The only ones they're stealin' jobs from is Mexicans. So I say, let the competition begin. I pay a quarter o' what I used to pay. I get them greasers to make a offer, then let the chinks counter-offer. Any way you cut it, the price goes down. We ain't never had it so good." There was a murmur of agreement among the men.

"Still," said the man with pockmarked cheeks, "you give the vote to Chinese, the next thing you know women will want to vote."

"Now that's just unnatural," Bowman declared. "Our preacher said so this morning, didn't he fellas?"

In the general affirmation that followed Jeff chimed in. "Excuse me, but has anyone seen this man?" He passed out a few flyers. There were shaken heads and several 'nopes.'

"Is he wanted for robbery or something?" one of them asked.

"No, he's my father. I'm just trying to find him."

"I think I seen him," a leathery little man said. "Wasn't he workin' for Jenkins?"

"He was, yes, but he's moved on."

"Is there a reward?"

"There might be," Jeff said. "I'm sure we can work something out, if you can point me in the right direction."

"Well, I'll keep my eyes open. Mind if I keep this here flyer?"

"Please do."

August stepped up on the porch then. "If you see him, tell him to stop by my place."

Jeff followed August inside the store, where Lydia and Carrie and Owen were busy putting together an order for supplies. August stopped, looked up at the clock on the wall behind the counter, then drew out his pocket watch, wound it, and set it.

"How do you know if that clock is correct?" Jeff asked.

August shrugged. "I don't, really, but it's what we all go by around here." He dropped the watch back into his vest pocket and surreptitiously slipped Jeff some money. "Buy yourself some clothes," he whispered.

Jeff did. He bought shoes and boots, two shirts, one collar, pants with suspenders, a frock coat, a derby, and a cravat.

While the Kimballs were busy loading the wagon with small barrels of flour, sugar and corn meal, sacks of beans, boxes of baking soda and baking powder, tins of coffee and rolled oats, a bolt of cloth, kerosene, soap, tobacco, a saw blade, ammunition and odds and ends, Jeff crossed over to the saloon where he showed his flyers around.

"He don't look zackly like this pi'ture, a bit older I'd say, but sure I 'member him," the bartender said looking at the flyer. "He ain't a regalar, but he's been in here before. Not for a month or more, though. I'll tell him you was lookin' for him next time he's in."

Next Jeff paid a visit to the Sheriff, who didn't remember seeing Randall. He nonetheless tacked a flyer on the wall and said he'd keep his eyes open.

Before the Kimballs returned home they had a light picnic at the back of the wagon. There were biscuits and cornbread with jam, hardboiled eggs, pickles, ham, beef jerky and tepid lemonade. Jeff was standing in the shade of the big oak, finishing off one of the eggs when August yelled, "What in tarnation?"

Everyone was looking up.

"Land sakes, boy!" Lydia screamed, "Get outa that tree afore you break your neck! And you'll scuff up your best clothes!"

Charles was grinning and dangling his feet from a high branch.

"Ah, Lord," August muttered. "Careful now. You shinny down to where I can catch you."

It took a minute for the boy to get down to the lowest branch, where he hung by his hands before dropping into his father's arms. "I oughta tan your hide, young man. You near scared your mother to death!" He said it, but he didn't mean it.

"You're huggin' too hard," Charles squealed.

August put him down. "Don't need to lose another one," he said somberly.

They got back to eating. Then August asked Jeff what he'd thought of the pastor and Jeff couldn't help needling his new friend. He was passably familiar with the Bible, and knew God was nothing if not capricious.

"I think your pastor was very wise to end the sermon where he did, with Lot's wife turned to salt for looking back. If he'd finished the story, he would've had to explain away how her daughters mourned her death by getting their father drunk, raping him and getting pregnant. But I guess in God's mind drunkenness and incest are no big deal, since they were never punished. It does make you wonder, though, what they were up to in Sodom and Gomorrah that was so much worse." Jeff had to wonder if August had actually read his Bible. What parts did he choose to believe, and what parts to ignore?

They rode home in silence, and once back August made a point of ignoring him. It was then that Jeff reassessed his adherence to honesty, for there was a fine line between honesty and lack of tact. He vowed he'd be more sensitive in the future (or rather the past).

Chapter 29
The Piano

Jeff's phone jangled off a bar of "Ain't Misbehavin'" as he crawled along the 101 freeway on his way home. It was Ralph Denning, who had gone to work for *Gourmet Getaways* in Mountain View. "The thing is," Denning said, "the Managing Editor quit and I gave them your name, so you might be getting a call." Jeff thanked Denning and hung up, thinking that he really had no interest in jumping back into that pressure cooker. The pace was frenetic, the demands relentless and the rewards inadequate. He was getting used to a slower pace of life without deadlines or a time clock, and he liked it.

Having done what he could to prepare for the move, and waiting now to see if his flyers would attract his father's attention, Jeff found himself with time on his hands and ten days to go before the end of the school year.

The next afternoon he attended a press and trade tasting of Italian wines in the Presidio overlooking the Golden Gate. He visited with old friends and made notes on the wines. Still, his heart wasn't in it. He felt caught between worlds.

He had no reason to return to the ranch, but the following day he couldn't stay away. He arrived around noon, checked the wine cellar to see if August had left a note (he hadn't), and spent the rest of the day puttering around the house arranging things, breaking down cardboard boxes for recycling, making signs to point to the garage sale they'd be holding at the condo on the weekend, and sorting through old slides, putting aside those he wanted to scan. Time slipped by unnoticed until he heard the faint strains of "Ain't Misbehavin'" issuing from his pocket at 4:46. He answered the phone.

"Where are you?" Carolyn asked, concerned.

"At the ranch. Sorry, I lost track of the time. I'll leave now."

"No, don't bother; you'll be caught in the middle of commute. You might as well leave later. I'll pick something up. Do you feel like pizza, tacos or Chinese?"

He could tell by her voice that she wasn't upset, and felt grateful he wasn't married to a complainer. "I don't care. Whatever."

"Call me before you leave."

"Okay. Love you."

The commute wouldn't thin out until 6:15, so he made himself a pot of tea and went back to sorting slides.

At 5:45 he paused in his work to check the notepad in the wine cellar, hoping for some word of his father, but there was nothing. Above he could hear the muffled pulse of music. He stole up the stairs to listen. It was coming from the parlor. He took off his shoes and edged down the dim hallway, careful not to show himself. The sun had passed behind the mountains and the valley was in deep shadow. From his angle the Kimballs appeared as ghosts reflected in the bay windows, all the family gathered around Lydia at the piano. Emily, Betsy and Charles sat cross-legged on the floor. August sat on a stool with a fiddle under his chin; Owen stood playing a guitar, and Noah thumped out a bass line on the gutbucket. With a hand on her mother's shoulder, Carrie sang solo, her young voice pure and lilting:

"There's a Land that is fairer than day,
And by faith we can see it afar,
For the Father waits over the way,
To prepare us a dwelling place there."

Then the whole family joined in the chorus:

"In the sweet by and by
We shall meet on that beautiful shore.
In the sweet by and by
We shall meet on that beautiful shore."

Carrie took the solo again in a voice of such plaintive sorrow that Jeff felt tears well up. It was the kind of thing that had been happening since his mother's death and he could not help it. He felt overwhelmed with love and pity for this long perished family. She sang:

"We shall sing on that beautiful shore,
The melodious songs of the blessed,
And our spirits shall sorrow no more,
Not a sigh for the blessing of rest."

The family joined their voices again, a little ragged as a group, with August and Owen the baritones and the little ones behind the beat:

"In the sweet by and by
We shall meet on that beautiful shore.
In the sweet by and by
We shall meet on that beautiful shore."

August and Owen then took up an instrumental bridge of the chorus, followed by Carrie and Lydia harmonizing:

"To our bountiful Father above,
We will offer our tribute of praise,
For the glorious gift of His love,
And the blessings that hallow our days."
And finally they all joined together again on the refrain.

On the ride home he couldn't get their ghostly reflections out of his head, nor the sweet sincerity of Carrie's youthful voice, a voice now long quiet in the grave. And he wondered when had families stopped gathering together? How was it that we could be so interconnected by electronic devices, and yet so isolated in spirit?

How was it that machines that purported to save us so much time, seemed to steal even more?

His thoughts must have shown on his face, for when he returned home Carolyn asked, "Anything wrong?"

"No, not really. I was just thinking about August."

"Oh?" Carolyn noted with interest, clearly wanting to elicit a more thorough explanation, but getting nothing from her husband. "You're getting on well?"

"With August? He's likeable enough, but we don't have much in common."

Jeff did not make friends easily she knew; he had always been too busy. In the seven years they'd lived in Foster City he had not made a single friend of any consequence. On rare occasions he might see a neighbor picking up the newspaper or retrieving mail from the mailbox, and they would wave and smile cordially. And nearly every workday, as he had sat at the kitchen table eating his breakfast, he had waved to an anonymous neighbor across the canal whose schedule placed him at his own table at the same time every morning. He did not even know their names. His socializing was confined to the office, wine tastings and wine luncheons.

Carolyn began opening cartons of Chinese takeout. "We weren't hungry earlier," she explained. She leaned around the corner and called, "Your dad's home! Dinner's ready!" Then she turned back to Jeff. "You may have to heat those up."

Jake came in looking cheerful, followed by his sister looking glum.

"Frick and Frack," Carolyn said.

"What?" Abby asked, her tone derisive.

"Nothing, just something my father used to say."

They bustled about scooping food onto plates and sat down at the table together for a change.

"Is he married?"

"August? Yeah."

"Kids?"

"Six, now. Three boys and three girls."

"What do you mean by *now*."

"I gather they lost a couple."

"Oh my god, how terrible! What happened?"

"I didn't want to pry."

Carolyn fell into a thoughtful silence, and finally said, "We should have them over for a barbecue sometime. I'd like to meet someone in the new neighborhood."

"Maybe later in the summer," Jeff dissembled. "I'm not ready for entertaining. I want to settle in first."

Jake burped.

"Jake!" Carolyn reproached with raised eyebrows.

"What?"

"We don't burp at the table."

"*I* do."

"Well you shouldn't."

"It's natural."

"It's impolite."

"That's stupid; everybody does it."

"You're so immature," Abby said.

"People don't want to hear it," Carolyn said.

"It's gross," Abby added.

"It's funny," Jake said.

"It's gross."

"It's not funny," Carolyn said.

Jake looked blankly at his mother, then farted.

"Oh for Christ sake!" Jeff exclaimed.

Jake laughed until tears streamed down his face. Carolyn rolled her eyes to the ceiling in exasperation. Abby hung her head and muttered, "I can't believe you're my brother."

Jeff thought of that family gathered around the piano and wondered at how far the human race had come.

Chapter 30
Apollo's Chariot

The week before school let out, the orthodontist removed Abby's braces, and they celebrated Jake's twelfth birthday with lunch at Round Table Pizza. On the way home Jeff's cell phone began chirping the notes to "Ain't Misbehavin'." It was J.C. Thatcher.

Jeff turned on the speakerphone. "Hey," he said.

"Hey, yourself," came J.C.'s bright, cheerful voice. "Just calling to inform you all that Sierra Lynn Thatcher arrived this morning at 2 a.m. Mother and daughter doing fine."

"You hear that, Jake? You share a birthday with your cousin!"

"Send pictures," Carolyn called out excitedly.

J.C. promised to send photos and to bring the baby for a visit the following month.

"Then you'll be coming down to the ranch," Carolyn told him, "because we sold the condo."

"Congratulations all around then. Big changes."

In a few minutes Jeff pulled into the parking lot at the Peninsula Humane Society.

"Speaking of additions to the family," Jeff began, "your mother and I thought you might like a dog for your birthday."

"Or a cat," Carolyn said.

Jake was struck dumb for a moment before erupting with a joyous shriek.

They held a garage sale on the weekend, and boxed up all but a suitcase each for the coming week. Monday morning Jeff saw his family off to school and, with nothing better to do, headed south with a load of boxes.

It had been his habit to multi-task on his drives back and forth to the ranch, but after a few days spent with August he had begun to feel the frenzied pace of 2009 distracting. Instead of listening to an audio book or ballgame, or making a phone call, he kept company with his own thoughts. He carried on an internal dialogue with his father, rehearsing different ways of breaking the news of his mother's death, of confessing that he was, yet again, unemployed, and that they'd moved to the ranch (and into the master bedroom). His father's imagined responses varied from inconsolable grief, to shock and outrage, to acceptance and forgiveness. Nothing was certain.

At noon the temperature had risen into the 90s, a wind was blowing down the valley, and Jeff sat on the porch in one of the rocking chairs drinking iced tea. In the past nine months his life had been turned upside down by the disappearance of his father, the death of his mother, the loss of his job, the decision to move to the ranch, and now the tunnel. He'd been taking a terrible risk in passing to the other side. It begged the question why his father would have taken the risk. Was it possible he hadn't recognized the danger? Or had he simply found the past irresistible?

August stepped out on the porch, pulling off his black, broad-brimmed hat, and wiping his face with a bandana.

Jeff poured him a tall glass from the pitcher. "Hot on the other side, too?"

"Hot enough. We're picking apricots today."

"Do you grow a lot?"

"Just an acre."

"How many bushels?"

"About a hundred and fifty."

"What do you do with them?"

"Well, of course we'll keep some for ourselves to dry and to put up in jars. The rest we'll take up to the rail yard at San Jose. It's easy now since we got the railroad. It used to take us a day and a half to drive four wagons up the peninsula. And that was in good weather. Today, we only have to drive it up to San Jose, and once we load the baskets on a flatcar, it'll be in San Francisco in two hours, rain or shine."

"How much will you make on it, if you don't mind my asking?"

"We'll clear about $600," August said. He sat down in the second rocking chair and sipped his iced tea. "Ice, now that's a real treat."

"Do you cook the apricots first?"

"Pardon?"

"Before you put them in jars."

"Yes, haven't you ever…?"

"No, never." Jeff closed his eyes and held the cold glass against his forehead. "How long does it take to pick a hundred and fifty bushels?"

"We'll have it done today — we have a Mexican crew picking, and our boys to load the wagons."

Jeff thought of his own children who never did chores willingly and would grumble if deprived of their video games or television. "You have a nice family," he said. "They work hard."

"They do. Speaking of which, when will I meet yours?"

"Soon. School's out on Friday. We're moving in next weekend. Which brings up another point, and I don't mean to offend, so don't take this the wrong way, but…well…modern Americans are very clean. We shower everyday."

"You're saying I'm dirty?"

"Well, by modern standards…"

"You want me to bathe more often."

"I want you to make a good impression."

"Okay, well I wouldn't mind using your shower again."

"And then there's your teeth."

"What about my teeth?"

"When was the last time you had them cleaned?" August cocked his head, raised an eyebrow and crossed his arms. "What do you brush your teeth with?" Jeff persisted.

August pooched his lips and looked annoyed. "I don't."

"Don't what?"

"Brush my teeth. Is that something you all do in the future? Like bathing everyday?"

"It is. Your teeth are stained."

"It's the tobacco."

"That's another thing — smoking is frowned upon; it's bad for your health."

"Anything else I should know?"

There was so much, where to start? "I'm sure you'll be surprised by some of the social changes. I don't think you're ready for that yet."

Late afternoon, two days after they moved in, Carolyn came out on the porch to look at the sunset. August was sitting in one of the rocking chairs.

"I'm sorry if I startled you, ma'am," he said, standing and respectfully removing his hat. "My name is August Kimball. Gus, if you like. I was just waiting for your husband."

"Oh, you're the horseman."

"Pardon?"

"You've been giving Jeff riding lessons."

"Yes, ma'am, that's right."

Carolyn went back inside to tell Jeff. "He's awfully polite. More old-fashioned than I expected."

"Old-fashioned – that's the perfect descriptor."

"Where does he live?"

"'A long time ago, in a galaxy far, far away,'" he quoted.

"No, really."

"Just a hop, skip and a jump," Jeff said, gesturing vaguely southward with a nod of the head.

He poured two glasses of Refosco and went out to the porch. "Care for a glass?"

"Don't mind if I do."

"I'm glad you're not a teetotaler."

"Didn't Jesus turn water into wine?"

"That's the story. When's your birthday?"

"October twenty-second."

"Well, no matter — I have a present for you." Jeff went inside and came back with *American History, Volume Two: The Civil War to the Present,"* and *The Fall of Empires: Europe in the Twentieth Century.* "This ought to bring you up to speed, but they come with a restriction."

"Yes, sir?"

"They may never be taken to your side. You can come over and read them anytime, but they stay on my side."

August nodded. "I promise." He weighed the books in his hands. "I suppose a man who knew what was coming might avoid some dangers."

"With a little planning your family might avoid wars and economic crashes for the next 140 years."

August sighed. "So many questions."

"You might say, 'So many answers,' because they're right there in those books. I wish *I* could know what was coming."

"Yes, it's a comfort." August opened *American History, Volume Two* and leafed through the first chapter, pausing to read the captions under the photos. "Since you say I can't take the books to my side, would you mind leaving them here on the porch? That way I could come over and read a bit after work each day. Maybe just a half hour, or so — I'll try not to be a bother."

"I'll leave the dome light on to make your passage easier."

"'ppreciate it."

They sat quietly enjoying the sunset and sipping their wine. Then Jeff asked, "Do you have gold coins?"

"'Course."

"What denomination?"

"Eagle and double eagle, ten and twenty dollars."

Jeff took out his phone and connected to the internet. "Holy cow! An uncirculated 1870 double eagle is worth fifteen hundred to twenty-five hundred dollars today!"

"That's a passel of money."

"Can you get me some?"

August looked sideways at Jeff and assessed his friend/neighbor/opponent/colleague. "Now, I don't want to take the wind out of your sails, but isn't Avarice one of the Seven Deadly Sins? It might not be wise to use this gift of ours for personal gain."

Jeff rolled his eyes. "You really know how to suck the joy out of the simplest pleasures."

"I'm thinking of your own welfare," August mumbled. "'For what shall it profit a man, if he shall gain the whole world, and lose his own soul?'"

"Oh Jesus!" Jeff cried in exasperation. "There's a saying in your time — 'Don't look a gift horse in the mouth.' Anyway, who gets hurt if we sell a few coins? Does it harm the bank? No. Does it harm collectors? No. Everyone's happy. And as to my soul — it will do my soul good to know I can help my family dig out from under a mountain of debt. I intend to make enough so my wife can quit her job (if she wants) and my kids can go to college. Is that too much to ask?"

August looked genuinely surprised. "Your wife works?"

"The bills don't pay them*selves*. She teaches high school."

"We don't allow married women to teach in our school district."

"Yeah, well, today a woman can work and vote and hold office!" Jeff snapped irritably. "So get used to it." He sipped his wine and rocked his chair and was so glad to be from here and now, instead of there and then.

"I didn't mean to offend," August said apologetically.

Jeff's energetic rocking slowly became more sedate as he relented. "No, of course you didn't. Sorry. I have to remind myself, we may live in the same place, but we come from different cultures. Sometimes your neighbor may not share your beliefs, and you ought to be able to live with that."

August was silent for half a minute. Then he asked, "What if I find him offensive?"

"You have to learn to live with it. People are always offended by *some*thing. They're offended by the color of your skin, or your religion, or your politics, or who knows what? You can't please everyone. But we can all get along if we're tolerant and do our best not to harm anyone."

"That's very Christian of you," August said.

In the next moment August's eyes went wide. He sprang to his feet, ran into the yard, and pointing above the mountaintops cried in a tone of wonder, "Apollo's chariot!"

High in the sun's last rays a golden contrail streamed out behind a tiny white cross.

"It's an airliner," Jeff explained, "airplane — a flying machine."

"It don't flap its wings. Is it like a balloon, then?"

"Not exactly." Jeff described the principles of aerodynamics, the use of ailerons, vertical and horizontal stabilizers, jet engines and contrails.

"How big is it?"

"From here to there," Jeff said, pointing to a distant tree. "Carries over three hundred passengers."

"Amazing."

"Follow me," Jeff said, and led him out back. A minute later a 747 came into view over the eastern hills, quietly descending through the twilight toward San Jose International.

"How heavy is it?"

Jeff took out his phone and did a quick search of the internet. "About 400 tons."

"My Lord!" August exclaimed. "And it still flies? Have you ever flown in one?"

"Many times."

"Where to?"

"All over the world."

"I suppose they're quicker than a train?"

"Five hours to New York."

"*Hours!*" August screamed incredulously. "It stretches the imagination. Five *hours?*" He grinned and his eyes were alight. "I've dreamt of flying, but I never thought it possible. What a wondrous time this future is."

It *was* wondrous, Jeff thought, but the modern age wasn't without its problems. August saw only the apple. He didn't see the worms.

But then, thought Jeff, *I guess every era has its worms.*

Chapter 31
Summer

Carolyn fell into her summer exercise routine, exploring nearby running and hiking and biking trails. She went out early in the morning before it got hot, and returned in an hour or so to spend the rest of the day tending to her vegetable-and-herb garden, and relaxing with a book on the front porch.

The heat surprised her, as the daytime temperatures were nearly ten degrees warmer than Foster City where the climate was moderated by proximity to the bay. The heat made sleep difficult and after a few fitful nights Jeff bought electric fans and window-mounted air conditioners for their bedrooms.

By July, with the price of two mortgage payments in the bank, they'd already saved over six thousand dollars and Carolyn felt like they were rolling in money. It was such a luxury and relief to see more money coming in than going out.

Jake was conspicuous in his absence. He spent his first days roaming the ranch with Buster, his Poodle-something mutt. Together they explored the barn, the creek, and the eastern hills.

Jeff took Jake to Little League practice on Thursday afternoons, and to games every Saturday. On other days Jake took his bike and ranged further afield, exploring the surrounding neighborhood to get the lay of the land. One day he came back to announce, "I rode to my new school. It's just twenty minutes. Pretty close to the mall."

"You'll have to show me," his mother said.

"Abby's school is right next to mine.

Abby asked him to show her, so the next day, feeling like a trailblazer, he led her on a bike hike to their respective schools, and thence to the mall.

Seeing knots of girls and boys her own age hanging out at the mall, Abby felt the loneliness of an outsider. They weren't her friends. She knew no one.

They split up, Jake to check out the game store, Abby to scope out the fall fashions. In one store she picked out a loud blouse with a piano key motif in black and yellow and blue. There were no free mirrors, so she stood behind another girl her own age, a girl with several earrings lining the edge of her ears, purple streaks in her hair and black lipstick. Abby looked over the girl's shoulder and held the blouse up under her chin.

"That's cool," the girl said. "Are you a musician?"

"Musician? No, why?"

"Hello? Piano keys?"

"Oh, yeah, no, I just liked it."

"It's cool though. You go to Leland?"

"Leland?"

"High School?"

"I guess; I'm new."

"What's your name?"

"Abby."

"I'm Angie."

And so began Abby's first friendship in her new home.

Trusting in providence, August began making a habit of showing up most everyday to read and watch the sunset from Jeff's porch. Coming and going unremarked wasn't difficult during the summer, for he could just slip through the rarely occupied kitchen and thence out the back door, then mosey around to the front porch like any friendly neighbor might do. Going the other way couldn't be simpler, as he and Jeff would take their conversation to the kitchen when the family was gathered in the parlor to watch TV, or else were in the their respective bedrooms. Jeff was less sanguine about passing through the geode, but he did occasionally join the Kimballs on their porch to watch a second sunset. He was even growing fond of the smell of pipe tobacco.

One evening as Jeff was making dinner, August appeared in the kitchen, looking glum.

"What's the matter?"

"Dickens is dead."

Jeff didn't know what to say (Dickens had always been dead). "So are you," he observed tactlessly.

"Ha!"

"I'm just saying."

"I guess that's so. I feel pretty healthy for a dead man."

"You look positively lifelike," Jeff chuckled, and abruptly stopped when he realized that he could probably look up the date of August's death, which cast a morbid pall over his small joke.

One balmy twilight August sat quietly in the parlor, mesmerized by a movie Jake was watching on television, while Jeff surfed the internet in his office. When the movie ended August sidled over to Jeff and whispered, "What's that thing called again? With the moving pictures?"

"You mean television?"

"Yeah, that's it."

"Just remember the Greek word *tele*, meaning 'from afar,' or 'distant.' So we have tele-graph, tele-phone, tele-vision, tele-photo, tele-commute, tele-evangelist...."

He might have continued if fate had not intervened, for at that very moment his laptop began ringing and he accepted a call from Rosie, who appeared onscreen holding baby Sierra.

"Hey big bro. I know we said we'd visit earlier, but with J.C.'s broken collarbone and one thing or another we haven't got our act together. So I thought I better introduce you to your niece before she's all grown up." She held her limp, drooling bundle-of-joy up to the camera.

"Could you get Carolyn?" Jeff asked August, and turned back to Rosie. "How's the collarbone healing?"

"Still sore," came a voice from off camera.

"You picked a hell of a way to get out of changing diapers."

"It wasn't intentional, I assure you."

August found Carolyn upstairs in what he knew as the sewing room. "Ma'am? Sorry to disturb you, but your husband would like you to come see the baby."

Carolyn put down her book, struck once again at this man's strangely formal mode of address. "Baby?"

"On the television."

"A baby on the television?"

"In the office."

"Okay," she said, still puzzled.

She followed him downstairs and was soon cooing over the baby. By the time the conversation ended, August was nowhere to be seen.

"He's an odd duck," Carolyn commented. "I can't imagine what you two have in common."

"He's not like anyone I've ever met before," Jeff said, "but he grows on you."

Jeff had always felt that you could tell a lot about a person by where he or she chose to spend time in Disneyland. Rosie had always headed for Fantasyland (no surprise there). His parents liked to mosey down Main Street, immersed in a rosy, nostalgic view of Midwestern America circa 1910. For his part, Jeff split his time between Tomorrowland and Adventureland. He loved the promise of the future, but was equally drawn toward adventure, a penchant satisfied by travel in real life. However, he couldn't fail but notice the irony that in all of his travels he had come across nothing more exotic, nor more familiar, than the trips under his own house. The 1870 he now knew was no sepia image lying dead on the page; it was alive and full of colors and smells and promise. 1870 was distinctly (if somewhat uncomfortably), a foreign destination.

Even so, he harbored no romantic notions about the past. It was his impression that 1870 was a time of few comforts, where daily chores were physically taxing, people were often dirty, medicine primitive, and ignorance and prejudice rife. There was little to recommend it but the solitude, and he'd had plenty of that as a kid. Nonetheless, the more time passed, the stronger the pull to explore.

As August put down his history book to watch the sunset, Jeff said, "I was thinking if my father was looking for farm work, he might have gone south. How far does the train go?"

"Gilroy."

"We ought to go down there and leave some flyers."

"He might've gone up to San Francisco," August said around the stem of his pipe.

"Could we get to San Francisco and back in a day?"

"Well, sure, this time of year with the long days. Since the Southern Pacific took over the line they've been running more trains. We're ten miles from the San Jose station. It takes a little more than an hour to ride there and stable the horses. Morning trains leave San Jose at 6:00 and 8:00 (that'd be 7:40 or 10:40 your time). First train back leaves San Francisco at 4:30 (6:10 your time). So I guess we could do it."

"I could take out personal ads in the newspapers, leave some flyers and maybe buy a few things. Collectors will pay a lot of money for old stuff."

"That's just plain foolish." August puffed on his pipe and blew a stream of smoke from the corner of his mouth. "I'll tell you what — I'll take you to San Francisco, if you'll take me for a ride in one of them airplanes."

"I don't know. Security has been really tight since 9/11. You need a driver's license or a passport to board a plane."

"What's 9/11?"

"September eleventh, 2001: Terrorists flew planes into the World Trade Center in New York. Killed thousands."

"I haven't got that far in the book yet."

"You won't. That book only covers through the Twentieth Century. We could probably rent a *little* plane. I'll figure it out."

"Do you have something you want to tell me?" Carolyn asked.

Jeff was in his armchair, surfing the net to learn more about antiques. He gave her a blank stare. "No. Why?"

"No reason. You just seem to be gone a lot lately. You don't tell me when you're going out, or where you're going."

"I'm just walking."

"Where is there to walk around here?"

"I walk up to August's and back."

"How far is that?"

"Not far. Just up the road."

"I wish you'd tell me when you're going out."

"Okay."

"Because it's a little like what your mother said your father was up to, before he disappeared."

"I'm not going to disappear. But as long as you've brought it up, I was thinking of driving August up to the city tomorrow. He doesn't have a car. We'll be back a little after nine."

"Just take your phone." She pursed her lips and stared at him appraisingly. "Anything else you want to tell me?"

He had a momentary fright that she had somehow found him out. "Nnnnno, not that I can think of."

"Nothing about money?"

"Oh, that."

"Yes, that. Did you think I wouldn't notice?"

"I was going to tell you."

"Where did it come from? Explain it to me: How does an extra five thousand dollars show up in our savings account? Did O'Malley pay up?"

"No, I told you I had plans."

"What kind of plans?"

"August had some old coins. I helped him sell them on eBay. He had no idea what they were worth."

"You aren't taking advantage of him, I hope."

"Don't worry; I'm taking care of him. I'm helping him out with a few things."

Carolyn shook her head, took a deep breath and sighed. "Keep me informed next time. I was worried you'd robbed a bank."

PART THREE

There and Back

Chapter 32
San Francisco

The Santa Cruz Mountains separate San Francisco Bay from the Pacific Ocean, with San Francisco at the northern end and San Jose near the southern end. During the Spanish era San Francisco was connected to San Jose by *El Camino Real*, The Royal Road, which linked all of the missions in California from Sonoma to San Diego, each a day's ride from the next. When the United States annexed Alta California in 1846, a stage line was established along this dirt track, and at each stage stop little towns sprang up. In 1850 the 49-mile journey took six hours at a cost of thirty dollars. The line ran three times a week during the dry months when it was possible to ford the numerous streams that ran down the mountains.

By 1864 passengers could make the trip in two hours by rail, at the cost of just $2. Today El Camino is a four-lane surface street, running parallel to highway 101, which carries traffic along the flats at the edge of the bay, while Interstate 280 runs parallel along the upper flanks of the mountains. And the once little towns have spread out like blobs of oil paint, one running into the next in a continuous sprawl the entire length of the peninsula.

Jeff had ridden steam trains before, but none so clean. The wood and brass gleamed, the plush red fabric was new, and frosted filigree accents adorned the corners of the windows. Jeff kept stealing glances at a comely young woman who sat alone at the end of the car. She sat very straight in her pink silk dress and wide plumed hat, and Jeff wondered how her life had turned out. He judged she was about twenty, and given some luck she might have lived to seventy or more — 1920 or beyond.

The tracks ran along the flats by the bay, paralleling El Camino Real. Miles of parkland separated each little town. At each stop Jeff jumped off to add his flyer to the ever-present bulletin boards. Between stops he sat silently staring out the window, trying to imagine how the future lay upon the geography of the past. Between Santa Clara and Sunnyvale and Mountain View there were farms with orchards and the occasional vineyard. Further north they stopped at a town called Mayfield that no longer existed by that name. In Burlingame and Millbrae, in place of strip malls, car dealers and housing developments, dairy cows grazed wide pastures, and he began to understand what his father had found so appealing. There was a point where the human footprint actually improved upon nature, where the land was neatly tended and the occasional house suggested order and safety. There was also a point past which was ugliness and disorder. Here was none of the unsightly clutter of the modern age: the unending pavement, clogged freeways, strip malls, stoplights, signage, telephone poles and wires.

But all was not bucolic, for as they approached San Francisco a dozen smoke stacks belched dark clouds of coal smoke and a thin blue haze of wood smoke veiled the entire scene.

Low buildings spread out over the hills like the stubble of new mown grass, whereas he knew a later season when the hills were dwarfed by a luxuriant growth of skyscrapers.

"Holy shit!" Jeff exclaimed as they rounded Potrero Hill.

August looked around nervously and said *sotto voce*, "You mustn't use profanity in public. What is it?"

"Mission Bay."

"What about it?"

Jeff chuckled to himself. "Well, it's still called Mission Bay, but there's no bay there anymore. It's all filled in from the Embarcadero to Hunter's Point. It's all warehouses, apartments, a hospital, and a ballpark."

"Ballpark?"

"Baseball."

"Ah, they still play then?"

185

"It's big business. People are passionate about sports."

"I like a good game of billiards, myself."

In a minute the train pulled into the station at Third and Brannan. Jeff watched the young lady in pink disembark into the arms of an elderly man with a top hat and white mustache (her grandfather?) who escorted her to a waiting carriage.

Outside the station was a large bulletin board with hundreds of notes tacked up — help wanted, seeking employment, lost and found, rooms to rent, real estate for sale, horses and wagons for rent and sale, ads for everything from hotels and restaurants, to barber shops and dress shops, and notices from people trying to connect with one another ("Billy Drady, be here Monday morning July 25, Cecille"). Jeff moved some of the other notices to make room for his flyer and tacked it up.

It was a quiet day. A flag before the Verona Hotel was beginning to flutter in the morning breeze. A squad of feral dogs trotted single file across Third, looking purposeful on their westward commute.

Jeff and August mounted a horse-drawn trolley for the short ride up Third Street. Two to three-story brick and wood-framed buildings lined the dirt street, and projecting up above them all were the steeples of churches. Jeff had come with a hundred flyers, intent on posting them all over the city. In his own day he would have tacked them to telephone poles, but there were no telephone poles in 1870. There were, however, a few telegraph poles, and when the trolley stopped near one, he dutifully jumped out and tacked up a flyer with a photo of his father on each one.

The trolley stopped at every block to let passengers on and off. At Third and Howard, a newsboy for the *Daily Alta California* called out, "Prussia Battles France!" August bought a paper and scanned the first few paragraphs.

"Do you know about this? Who wins?"

"If I remember my history correctly, France invaded Germany and Louis Napoleon and his 100,000 man army were taken captive. You can read all about it when we get home. And save that paper; it's a collectable."

When they disembarked at Market Street Jeff stopped and looked up and down the wide thoroughfare. Three blocks to the east, the bay was a forest of masts before the looming presence of Yerba Buena Island. "Where to from here?"

"I thought I'd take you to my favorite bookstore. Then we'll stop by the *Morning Call* and the *Alta California*, so you can place your ads. After that we'll stop by my father-in-law's hardware store."

They turned west down Market Street, a wide cobblestoned thoroughfare with two sets of tracks for horse trolleys, and wide sidewalks fronting one to four-story buildings. Now it was time for Jeff to gawk. There were relatively few pedestrians. Beggars and street musicians were absent, and in place of the whine of electric buses, squeak of air brakes, surge of internal combustion engines, and wail of sirens echoing between tall buildings, he heard the sound of people in conversation and the slow clop-clop of horses' hooves on cobblestones. Along the sidewalks people strolled and chatted and window-shopped. The length of the street, horse trolleys, carriages, Hansom cabs, jitneys, delivery wagons and drays plied their trade. The scene also came with its own peculiar stench of horse manure, rotting garbage, cooking food, wood smoke and human waste.

"Do you recognize anything?" August asked.

"Not really. Not much survived the '06 quake."

In his derby hat and frock coat, Jeff felt like an actor in a period play, and he wished he'd taken the time to break in his high-topped shoes. They started west past a policeman who cordially saluted by tapping the brim of his hard hat with the tip of his billy club.

Midway down the block they came upon GILBERT'S Musical Instruments and Sheet Music. The double doors were flung wide and the tinkling notes of a piano spilled out into the street. Jeff pulled August inside. A bald, round-faced man with a walrus mustache sat at an upright piano playing a lively dance tune. He looked up, nodded and asked if he could help, while his fingers never missed a beat. Jeff said they were just looking. The man nodded as his fingers crawled over the keys.

Cellos and harps stood on the floor beside pianos and an organ. Smaller stringed instruments hung on the walls. Brass instruments, woodwinds, tambourines, harmonicas and Jews' harps filled two glass cases, and a rack of sheet music stood along the back wall.

"Some of this music ought to be collectable," Jeff said, though he had no idea what might be considered valuable in the future. He took a few minutes to browse, picking up "Camptown Races" and "Old Folks at Home" by Stephen Foster for no other reason than that he recognized them, and a couple others that piqued his curiosity by virtue of their titles and cover ornamentation: "Close the Door Gently for Mother's Asleep" by C.S. Fredericks, and "Marching Through Georgia" by Henry C. Work.

At Market and Fourth, across the street from St. Ignatius College, August said, "This is the place," and they entered Bay Book & Tobacco. The store was deep, with shelves reaching nearly to the fifteen-foot high ceiling. Tall street-side windows and gas lamps lit the interior. A thin man with a pencil mustache and dapper beige suit came around the counter to greet them. "Ah, Mr. Kimball, I'm so glad to see you. The latest Collins novel arrived yesterday. I was getting ready to send you a note."

"Mr. Swain," August said, giving a nod and a smile. "I'd like to introduce you to Mr. Porter. He's looking for...well, you tell him, Jeffrey."

"I'm looking for first editions, if possible, with a preference for leather bound."

"Literature, history or biography?"

"Literature."

"Authors?"

"Dumas, Hugo, Austen, Dickens..."

"Ah, Dickens," Swain said with a sigh. "There's been quite the run on his books since his untimely death, as you can well imagine. I'm sure we have something, but I'm not sure about first editions. By the way," he said, turning to August, "the new issue of *Overland Monthly* is out this week with a notable tribute to Dickens by Bret Harte."

The name Harte struck a cord with Jeff. "You wouldn't by any chance have anything by Mark Twain?"

"Sam Clemens? Well, sure, we have both books — *The Celebrated Jumping Frog of Calaveras County*, and his newest, *The Innocents Abroad*, which is really not much more than a compilation of the articles serialized in the *Alta California*, but it's sold like hot cakes. You have a copy, don't you Mr. Kimball?"

"I do. It's a bit irreverent, but it has its humorous moments. Nothing so amusing as his lectures on the Sandwich Islands, though."

Swain chuckled, "By god, he's good on stage, ain't he? Not as funny as Artemis Ward, I think, but then no one ever was."

Swain turned back to Jeff. "Mr. Clemens used to frequent our store before he moved East. He was kind enough to leave us a few signed copies. They may be first editions."

After some direction from Mr. Swain, Jeff browsed the stacks of new and used books looking for familiar titles. They lingered too long, and eventually left with their treasures stuffed into a carpetbag August had furnished for the occasion. Jeff had a signed first edition of Twain's *The Innocents Abroad,* and first editions of The *Celebrated Jumping Frog*, and Louisa May Alcott's *Good Wives*; as well as a used (though well cared for) 1816 edition of Austen's *Emma* in three volumes, all worth a small fortune at auction. August had purchased a pouch of pipe tobacco, the current issue of *Overland Monthly*, and the novels *Lothair* by former Prime Minister Benjamin Disraeli, and *Man and Wife* by Wilkie Collins. The entire load had set them back a staggering $23.10.

Chapter 33
Shopping for Antiques

They crossed Market and started up Powell Street, which in 1870 was paved in brick and bordered by two to five-story buildings and wide concrete sidewalks. There were few pedestrians, fewer buggies, and cable cars had yet to be invented. Imposing churches stood where hotels would one day rise above Union Square. The square itself was full of small trees planted in the triangles created by the intersection of four walking paths that met at a flagpole in the center, which in due course would be replaced by a 97-foot-tall monument commemorating Admiral Dewey's 1898 victory at the Battle of Manila. Jeff handed the heavy carpetbag to August, discreetly withdrew his iPhone from a coat pocket, and snapped a few photos. His misgivings of inadvertently introducing modern technology to the past had faded with the realization that even were he to lose the phone, it might startle the first person to pick it up, but its use would be a mystery, the battery would soon die and it would simply appear a curious bauble with no discernible purpose. It was certainly nothing that could be reverse engineered, for history had to play out step-by-step for the dream to blossom into a vision, the vision to become a possibility and the possibility to become reality. Technological advance required time and infrastructure to bring to fruition.

Before the Trinity Episcopal Church at Powell and Post (where a Saks Fifth Avenue stood in 2009) they caught a Hansom cab and headed east. Pedestrian traffic remained sparse as the cab turned down Montgomery Street catty corner from the Gothic Masonic Lodge. Where Jeff had expected to find a city of open spaces and flimsy wooden buildings, he found grand architecture of mostly

Italianate design rendered in brick and stone. There were, no doubt, areas to the west where building had yet to expand, but the Financial District of 1870 was a place of established commerce. Here were offices and retail stores — ticket agents, dentists, apothecaries, importers, wine merchants, furniture stores, dry goods stores, shoe stores, stationers, clothiers, jewelers, hotels, bars and art galleries.

The clock atop the J.W. Tucker building read 12:35, Jeff noted as the cab rolled sedately along Montgomery Street, leaving them just four hours. Save for bricks between the trolley tracks, the street itself was dirt. Before the block-long Lick House hotel, open buggies and closed cabs and delivery wagons parked at the curb. In the next block, the street in front of the Occidental Hotel was torn up for repairs (some things in the city never changed) and they were forced into a single file behind other buggies.

In front of Kane O'Leary & Co., they were stopped as a dray unloaded some wine barrels. "Quick, give me five bucks," Jeff said, and jumped from the cab. Three minutes later he came back with a bottle of La Tâche Burgundy. He held it up for August's inspection and grinning said, "Three fifty!" and tucked it into the carpetbag. They passed The Russ House hotel and Thomas Houseworth & Co. Optical Instruments, and came to a five-story building of balconies and arched windows that would have looked at home in Florence, Italy. There they turned west up the undulating cobblestones of California Street and pulled to the curb between the German Savings & Loan Society and the offices of the *Daily Alta California*. August paid the cabbie and they went inside.

The counter was unattended. Jeff rang the bell. They heard a rustle and squeak as a man tilted back in his chair so that his head showed through an open doorway. "Desk clerk is out to lunch," he said around a mouthful of sandwich. "What can I do for you?"

Jeff filled out an ad form. Under the category "INFORMATION WANTED" he wrote:

"SEEKING RANDALL PORTER, last seen working on farms near San Jose. His son, Jeffrey Porter, requests that any news of his present whereabouts be sent to the Kimball Ranch in Almaden Valley."

"Hungry?" August asked.

"Famished."

"Follow me."

Outside a thick cap of fog sat atop Twin Peaks and a cool breeze had begun to blow from the west. They marched back down to Montgomery and walked a block to Sacramento Street where they stopped in front of the What Cheer House hotel and restaurant. A sign in the window read: "FIRST-CLASS LODGING 50¢ PER NIGHT. Extensive Library, Museum and Reading Room free to all Guests! No women allowed on premises."

"We could eat here," August said. "The food is always good and cheap, but they don't serve alcohol. Or we could go around the corner to Miners', which is a bit more expensive, but they have wine and beer."

Jeff opted for Miners' on Commercial Street, which turned out to be close to both the U.S. Mint and the offices of the *San Francisco Morning Call*. Before lunch, Jeff stopped at the *Call* and placed a duplicate classified ad. At the mint, August exchanged bills for five newly minted double eagle gold pieces and handed them to Jeff.

At Miner's they ordered oysters, salmon, filet of sole, sourdough bread, and a bottle of California white wine — totaling 50¢ including tip.

"I can't believe they can sell a bottle of wine for 10¢. It's not bad, either."

"How much do you pay for a bottle?"

"For a Sauvignon Blanc of this quality, I'd guess eighteen to twenty dollars."

"And the food?"

"A meal like this would set us back at least thirty-five' dollars," Jeff said.

"But you say you can turn those four coins into ten thousand dollars?"

"Something like that. I wish we could get hold of a double eagle from the Carson City mint. Now that's a true rarity, worth fifty times as much."

"And how much do you figure you can get for them books, if you don't mind my asking?"

"If we're lucky, I'm thinking they'll bring in as much as twenty or thirty thousand dollars."

"So you could make thirty thousand dollars from one hundred twenty?"

Jeff nodded with an impish grin. "Sounds preposterous when you put it that way, but that's the gist of it. Of course you have to consider the government will take a third."

"A third? Really?" August gasped and shook his head in disbelief.

"Maybe more — depends on your tax bracket."

"Well, let's say you had thirty thousand *after* taxes. What could you buy with that?"

"Thirty thousand could buy a nice car. Or pay for our groceries for the next three years. Or a couple of really nice family trips to Europe."

August picked at his salmon for a minute, lost in thought. "I don't mean to rain on your parade, but it seems like you're more interested in making a profit than in finding your father."

"Well, finding Pop is the most important thing, but that doesn't mean I should pass up an opportunity along the way. An opportunity like this doesn't come along everyday."

They fell into silence as they both mulled over the possibilities and finished their meals. Finally August spoke up. "I don't want to seem ungenerous, but your money is worthless here. How are you going to pay me back?"

"I'm sure I could provide you with some things that would make your life easier, even if they don't make you richer. Do you have toilet paper?"

The nine blocks between the restaurant and Vallejo Street were quieter and not as grand as the Financial District. Apartment houses, neighborhood stores, saloons, brothels, wholesalers, warehouses and dance halls stood side-by-side along the narrow sidewalks.

"Isn't the Barbary Coast somewhere around here?"

"We're on the edge of it."

"It doesn't look so dangerous."

"Even a lion has to sleep. If you wander these streets at night, you risk waking up tomorrow with empty pockets or on a boat to China."

Hillman's Hardware was in a two-story brick building with barred windows and two great, black steel doors that sealed the entrance at night. The white haired gentleman behind the counter lit up when August walked in. "Gus, what a surprise! Did you stop by to see Lulu?"

"No, I'm sorry, Bert; we don't have time today; we have to get back to the ranch. But give her my love. I'll make a point of staying over next time. I just brought Mr. Porter up here to buy a few things. He's looking for some firearms."

"Colt revolvers, to be precise," Jeff said.

"We have a few in stock," he replied to Jeff, and turned back to August. "But first, you've got to fill me in. How is Lydia? How are my grandchildren?"

While August updated Albert on family gossip, Jeff browsed the isles looking for other items he might turn to a profit. There were hand tools and brackets and fittings of all kinds, paint and varnish, thinner and brushes, buckets, brooms, wire and winches, pulleys, nails, brass cleats, screws, copper sheeting, copper pipes, brass pipes, hinges, rope, pots, pans, saws and saw horses, maps and charts, chains and small anchors — almost anything a man might need. But nothing was either light enough, or valuable enough, to entice him to buy.

Looking back on it, that's when everything started to go wrong. A sudden influx of customers occupied Albert and his assistant for twenty minutes. Then Albert brought out four Colt .44 caliber Army revolvers with walnut grips, each in its own velour lined case with flask, bullet mold and cap tin. They each cost $20, plus $5 for the case and accessories.

"We'll take them all," Jeff said.

August could see Jeff was fidgety. "We have to hurry if we're going to make the 4:30 train," he told Albert, who took his time finding two burlap bags large enough to fit the boxes, and twine to tie them shut. Jeff gave him a flyer to post in his window.

It was 3:25 by the time they set off for the Embarcadero in search of a cab. Cabs were plentiful at the foot of each pier along the bayfront. At the foot of Broadway they found a landau, settled into their seats and lowered their loads.

"These won't be the easiest things to carry when we get back to the horses," August said. "Why'd you want four?"

"I would have taken more, if he'd had any."

"You know I can't afford to do this very often; we spent over one hundred and thirty dollars today. Some people might not think that's much money, but I believe 'a penny saved is a penny earned.'"

"You'll get it back, don't worry."

They were stopped by traffic at the Pacific Street Wharf, where freight was being unloaded from a newly arrived ship. Jeff watched the flow of people and wagons, wondering how to get the best price for his treasures. Should he sell them online directly to collectors, or would he be better off approaching an auction house?

Seeing a message board at the end of the pier, he jumped out and tacked up a flyer.

Soon they were able to move forward, but only for a hundred feet before they were stopped again. Minutes passed before they were able to slip through a gap between a water wagon and lumber dray. The path closed again at the end of Washington Street. They were caught in an old-fashioned traffic jam. August checked his pocket watch: 3:47. He asked the driver to turn back to Jackson Street, and take Battery to Brannan.

In retrospect they would have done better to leave the cab, walk past the traffic jam, and catch another cab. As it was, they arrived at the train station just a minute too late.

"Oh Fuck!" Jeff exclaimed, watching the caboose disappear down the tracks.

August paid the driver, then quietly leaned close and admonished Jeff in an avuncular tone. "Not in public. You could be arrested."

Frantic, Jeff turned to the cabbie. "Can you catch up at the next station?"

"Well, sir, it's sixteen blocks to the Valencia Street station, and even if we took it at a gallop, we couldn't catch her before she left. Besides, these horses ain't up to it; they've been hauling a cab all day."

Jeff's heart was hammering as he turned back to August. "Oh god, what are we going to do? Carolyn's going to kill me! When's the next train?"

August consulted the board. "7:00. That's the last train."

"When does that get us home?"

"Well now, let's see. It's two hours to San Jose. So 9:00. Then we'll have to rouse the livery stable, get the horses saddled. So 9:20 — 9:30. But it'll be pitch black; it's almost a new moon, so we'd have to take it slow on the road. Probably get in-between 10:45 and 11:00."

"Past midnight my time. This is a disaster! The tunnel will be closed!"

"We can stay over at my in-laws. They'd be happy to have us."

"We can't stay overnight; Carolyn will be frantic!"

"She'll just think we were delayed. It happens."

"Not in my time, it doesn't. She'll expect me to call. She'll try to call *me*. Even if my cell phone ran out of juice, she'd expect me to borrow one and call. Oh, Jesus, how am I supposed to explain this? She'll think I've been killed." Then an idea struck him, and he said excitedly, "We can take a boat! I'll pay whatever it takes."

August looked at him with amusement. "Not possible. Alviso slough silted in years ago. Even if you could get a boat through those shallow waters, at night, it would take eight hours by boat. There's nothing to do but wait for the next train. Come on, we'll go have dinner and a beer."

Chapter 34
In the Dog House

Knowing he would catch hell from Carolyn, he nevertheless felt immense relief at finding the passage still open at 12:33 in the morning, *praise be to God in heaven,* and Jeff mounted the stairs wondering how to minimize the fallout. He decided he should sleep on the settee in the office. When she discovered him asleep in the morning, he could say he hadn't wanted to disturb her, and that way she wouldn't know how late he'd actually come in.

He set the burlap bags and carpetbag on the dining room table and sat down to take off his leather-soled shoes, so as not to wake Carolyn with his clumping around on the hardwood floors. Only then did he realize he'd neglected to change out of his period costume in the cellar. *Screw it,* he thought. He was too tired to go back down the stairs. He stole down the hall to the office in his stocking feet, aware that the lights were blazing in every room. Carolyn, who was herself resting on the settee, sprang to her feet. "Oh, thank god," she cried in a shaking voice, "what happened? Where were you?" Her immediate concern was evident in her tone, which began to change as she took him in and found him in one piece. "Why didn't you call? I thought you'd been in an accident. I called all the hospitals! Are you all right? Why are you dressed in those clothes?"

"Oh, uh, I...I...I went to an antiques convention with August. I'm sorry, my phone ran out of juice."

"Your phone ran out of juice? Is that all you can say? You had me worried half to death! I was sure you'd been in an accident. You couldn't have borrowed a phone? You couldn't have sent an email? Something? What the fuck were you thinking!?"

"I...I had a little too much to drink and fell asleep," Jeff improvised.

Carolyn stood feet apart and arms akimbo, glaring. "You think getting drunk is an excuse? Did you ever once think of *me*? Or the example you were setting for our children? Did you think how worried we'd be? How terrified? I thought you were injured or dead! I wish you *were* in the hospital — *that* I could understand. *That* I could forgive. But here you come stumbling in drunk in the night..."

"I'm not drunk."

"You said..."

"I fell asleep."

"Weren't you with August?"

"Yes."

"And he fell asleep, too? He couldn't call? Did he forget *his* phone, too?"

"He doesn't have a phone."

"Where did you sleep?"

"In the car."

"Whose car?"

"Whose..." Jeff started to say, and it suddenly dawned on him that he'd left the Subaru in the barn all day and Carolyn likely knew it. His excuse about driving August into the city wouldn't fly. "August's car."

"Yesterday you said he didn't have a car."

"He got it fixed."

Carolyn scowled at him, her eyes at once hurt and angry. "Are you having an affair?"

"No, god no!"

"Then where were you all day?"

"I told you; I was with August. We were in the City."

"Maybe you should just be quiet until you have your story straight. Have a nice night on the couch, you fucking bastard!!" She stormed passed him and bounded up the stairs in tears. In a moment the door to their bedroom slammed. Abby and Jake stood in their pajamas at the top of the stairs, looking scared.

"Are you okay?" Abby asked.

"Yeah, I'm just…I'm very tired. Your mother is upset, and…well, she has a right to be, but it's okay. Go to sleep. Everything will be all right in the morning."

They both stood there looking down on him, more in shock than disapproval. Parents weren't supposed to fight, or get in trouble, or have emotions, or be at a loss for words. It was upsetting.

"Go on now, go to sleep."

But no one slept particularly well that night.

In the morning his excitement outweighed his sense of guilt. Carolyn found him at the dining room table with his treasures spread out before him and his laptop open to auction websites.

"What are you doing with guns in this house?" she asked in a perturbed tone that let him know she was still annoyed and spoiling for a fight.

"They're antiques."

"I don't want guns around the children."

"They won't be here long. We're going to sell them to collectors. They're worth a lot of money."

"How much did you pay for them?" she asked more in exasperation than from curiosity.

"They were cheap; twenty-five bucks apiece."

"Why are you wasting your time on twenty-five dollar antiques, when you should be looking for a job?"

"They're not worth twenty-five dollars; they're worth a lot more."

"How much more?"

He hadn't wanted to tell her this way. He'd wanted to keep it a secret until he'd actually made his fortune. He'd fantasized about surprising her with a check, or a car, or plane tickets to an exotic vacation. But the dismissive tone in her voice was like a slap in the face, and he reflexively slapped back with the truth. "About six grand apiece. Maybe more."

"Sithawhaa?" she blurted, her words becoming stuck in the intersection of conflicting thoughts and emotions. "I thought you said twenty-five dollars?"

"That's what we paid."

"You mean these are worth twenty-four thousand dollars?"

"About that."

"Where did you find them?"

"August's father-in-law has a lot of antiques."

"So-o-o...let me get this straight — August's father-in-law sold you these guns for one hundred dollars, and you can resell them for twenty-four *thousand* dollars?"

"Yep."

"You can't do that."

"Why not?"

"What do you mean, 'why not?' It's unethical! You have to give them back."

"I can't; he's dead."

"I'm confused. *Who's* dead?"

"August's father-in-law."

"I thought you said he sold you the guns."

"*Oh what tangled webs we weave, when first we practice to deceive,*" thought Jeff, trying to extricate himself from the hole he'd dug. "I misspoke. I meant, August's father-in-law got them for twenty-five dollars apiece."

"And he's dead?"

"Yes."

"And August inherited them?"

"Something like that."

"What does that mean? Either he did or he didn't."

"He did."

"And he's given them to you to sell?"

"Yeah, he doesn't have a computer. He hasn't a clue how much they're worth, or where to find buyers."

"What are you getting out of it?"

Jeff sat silently looking Carolyn in the eye and resenting the third degree. He wasn't good at dissembling. He took a sip of cold coffee and leaned back in his chair. "Fifty percent."

"Does he know what he's giving up?"

"He'll do fine. If it wasn't for me, he would have given this stuff away."

It was only then that she seemed to see the rest of the stash arrayed on the table "How much are the coins worth?"

He weighed whether it was better to lie or tell the truth. But he'd already let the cat out of the bag, so what did it matter? "About ten thousand."

"Ten thousand! And the books?" she asked, casually picking up *The Celebrated Jumping Frog of Calaveras County* and leafing through to the title page. "Oh my god, it's signed!" She shook her head and put the book gently back on the table, then turned on her heels and started for the kitchen. A moment later she turned back. "I thought you said you went to a convention last night?"

"Right, an antiques convention."

She cocked her head and eyed him with suspicion, but said nothing and went back to the kitchen, where he could hear her knocking about opening cabinets and drawers and the refrigerator. A minute later she called out, "You should still be looking for a job. Selling a few antiques isn't a career."

"There's more where this came from," he called back. Little did she know there was an unending supply.

Chapter 35
Back to School

That night, after the lights were out, he reached out and touched Carolyn's back.

"Don't," she said.

So much can be conveyed by tone. Said one way, 'Don't' might be a plea, as in 'Please, don't.' Said another it might be an imperative, such as, 'Don't touch that; it's hot!' Carolyn's tone implied a threat — 'Don't you dare.'

"It's been two weeks," he said.

"It might be two years — I don't have sex with men I can't trust."

"I hope you don't trust any *other* men," he quipped miserably.

"It's not funny. I can't trust you to tell me the truth."

"I haven't told you one lie," he said, inwardly cringing at that lie, for he had told a few, small, white lies.

"You haven't told me the whole truth. Where were you, really? "

"In the City, like I said. We went to a music store and a bookstore, and we went to August's father-in-law's hardware store. That's the absolute truth."

"You said you went to a convention."

"Well, there were hundreds of people selling antiques, and if that isn't a convention, I don't know what is."

"What else were you doing?"

"Nothing, just…. Nothing."

"Just what? Tell me."

He cursed himself for not keeping his mouth shut. Lying to her was like lying to himself. Every time he heard distrust in her voice, he wondered if they might not be better off if he just filled the tunnel with concrete. What did it matter if in keeping her safe he destroyed their relationship? For now, though, he had to give some explanation or risk alienating her even further. Once again he resorted to the truth. "Putting up fliers."

"Fliers? For what?"

"To find Pop."

Carolyn rolled onto her back. "Why in the world?" Then she softened. "Oh honey, your father's dead. You must know that."

"He's...." Jeff struggled with how much to tell her, and remembered his own council. Keeping the tunnel a secret was the surest way to ensure their safety. "I don't want to talk about it."

"You need to face the facts. Wishing isn't going to change things."

Jeff sighed and rolled away from her. Losing his parents and losing his job was hard enough. Losing Carolyn's trust was harder still, for she had always been his supporter and confidant. They had always been a team. They had built a better life than most, he knew, and though they'd had their share of troubles, she had made them so much easier to bear. But he'd made up his mind; he couldn't share this with her, not if he wanted to keep her safe.

As evening came on he sat on the porch swing feeling like a man out of time. The sun had dipped below the Santa Cruz Mountains and now pinked the lines of cirrocumulus overhead. In the distance he could see a line of white lights snaking down Highway 17.

He waited for Carolyn to go upstairs to get ready for bed before stealing through the tunnel. His ears popped painfully as he stepped out from behind the black sheet (there was often a pressure differential passing from one time to the other). He had hoped to catch the end of another sunset, but upon stepping into the darkening dining room he could see the first stars appearing in the twilight sky above the laurel, and heard the family already gathered around the piano in the parlor. They were playing a lively instrumental, and Jeff sat down at the dining room table to listen. The music ceased abruptly amid cries of laughter. Then Owen, Carrie, Betsy and even little Charles joined in a rousing rendition of "Camptown Races," accompanied by a gutbucket and Noah's harmonica.

Soon after the music ended, he could hear August reading aloud to the family from Disraeli's *Lothair*.

Jeff quietly passed back through the tunnel. Carolyn and Abby had gone up to their bedrooms. Jake was still watching television in the parlor, stroking a prostrate Buster. Jeff walked around the room perusing his library. He pulled out a volume of Roald Dahl's short stories. During a commercial break he said, "What would you think if I read to the family after dinner every night?"

"Whose dinner? We all eat at different times."

"Well, how about I read from 8:00 to 8:30?"

"Depends on my homework. What do you want to read?"

"Short stories."

"I guess that would be okay. But it can't be on Mondays or Wednesdays or Thursdays — I have shows I watch. And Abby watches that stupid reality show on Tuesday."

Jeff slipped the Dahl book back into the bookcase.

By the end of summer Abby had slipped back into her former sullen self. Her old friends were busy getting ready to start high school. They didn't call as often, or have time to visit. She'd strained her friendship with Angie by being too needy. They still met at the mall, but always in the company of other girls, and Abby felt like a tin can tied to a bumper. She trailed behind, trying to get a feel for the hierarchy and history of this strange bunch of teenagers. When they laughed and reminisced about former classmates and teachers, Abby had no idea who they were talking about. She had nothing to contribute. She was miserable.

She spent the week leading up to the start of school nervously trying to decide what look to present to her new classmates. It seemed of supreme importance that she be perceived as "cool" — that all-inclusive yet nebulous term that implied acceptance. On the big day she came downstairs in pajama bottoms, a gossamer white blouse, and a strange looking piece of pastel knitted headwear with earflaps dangling to her shoulders.

Carolyn said, "Go upstairs and get dressed and I'll drive you to school."

"I *am* dressed."

"You're not going to school in that," Carolyn said in dismay.

"Yes, I am."

"No, you're not. You can see right through that blouse, and no daughter of mine is going to school in pajama bottoms."

"Everybody's doing it."

"I don't care who's doing it; it's not acceptable."

"You want me to go in a slutty mini skirt instead?"

"No," Carolyn said firmly. "You'll wear normal clothes like a normal 15-year-old."

"You have no idea what you're talking about."

"Oh, really? What do you think I've been doing for the past nineteen years? Babysitting high-schoolers like yourself. Now get back upstairs and put on a decent outfit, or you'll find yourself grounded for…."

"Yada, yada, yada," Abby interrupted impudently, striding past her father as he came into the kitchen.

"What was that about?"

"She thought she was going to get away with wearing pajamas to school."

"At least she isn't pierced or tattooed."

"Thank god for small favors."

Abby came back in tight black jeans with a studded belt, a short black t-shirt that bared her belly button, and rather inexpertly applied black eyeliner. "Does this pass the teacher's test?"

Carolyn eyed her with disapproval. "I don't like it, but it'll have to do. Let's go."

Jake sped off to school on his bike, eager to start seventh grade with its lure of different teachers, different subjects and a new group of classmates to meet. His enthusiasm, infectious good humor and complete lack of concern over his peers' opinion of him, made him naturally popular. For him, it was all an exciting adventure.

Chapter 36
Questions and Rumors

Since their summer excursion to San Francisco, Jeff was less inclined to risk being trapped like his father, though even he was now becoming convinced there was a pattern. The portal was always open by 8:30 in the morning and remained open until late at night. But if it was so predictable, why had his father been unable to return? Looking over the logs, he could see that the time August had noted the doorway was closed had been getting progressively later. Did that mean it changed with the seasons? Even if it did, how would that account for it staying open past midnight? Was he just lucky, or was there a mechanism at work here? Now that he thought about it, he had never personally found the portal closed. He only had August's word that it did. Might the tunnel only appear to disappear on August's side? Maybe his eyes were fooling him. Jeff had the feeling that if he closed his eyes and took a leap of faith, he'd be able to walk through that rock as easily as Marley's ghost passed through Scrooge's door. He wanted to put the question to August.

That afternoon, hours earlier than usual, August let himself into the kitchen and said without preamble, "Saw Rich Ginther in church this morning. A friend of his stopped by and saw your flyer, and he thought he recognized your father. Said he'd seen him supervising a bunch of Coolies picking fruit in Livermore Valley sometime in June. Does your father speak Chinese?"

"No. He speaks a little Spanish, but no Chinese."

"Still, it tallies with what Jenkins told us."

"How long does it take to ride to Livermore?"

"Hold your horses. Now first of all, I can't be trotting off on a wild goose chase every time we hear a rumor. Besides, you can't get to Livermore, search for your father and get back in a day. And then there's the bartender in Pulgas who said one of his patrons thought he saw someone who answered the description, with a Mexican crew down around Morgan Hill a month ago. Now he can't be in two places at once, and he wouldn't be working with both Chinese and Mexicans. So you can't know if it was really him. Even if it was, he could have moved on by now."

"If you'll lend me a horse, I could search on my own."

August smiled and patted Jeff on the shoulder. "I wouldn't recommend it."

August's patronizing tone and lack of faith in his abilities rankled Jeff, for despite August's more weathered appearance, Jeff had determined he was the elder by four months. Yet there was something about August's attitude that gave the man a more authoritative demeanor, at least on his own ground. Their roles were somewhat reversed when August was on Jeff's turf.

"Riding isn't all that difficult," Jeff said.

"No, but what would you do if your horse threw a shoe? Or stepped in a gopher hole? Or just refused to go? Do you know when to rest a horse? Or how much and when to water them? See, it's not all about the riding. And besides, a horse can sense confidence or the lack of it."

"I haven't had any trouble yet."

"Patsy and Stormy — they're pretty mild mannered, and they tend to follow Rhubarb when we're out on the trail. But when they're alone even they can be cantankerous. I wouldn't feel right letting you go on your own. Besides, if your father is around, eventually he'll see one of your flyers, or classified ads. No need to look for *him; he'll* come to *us*. We're not going anywhere."

Jeff conceded the point.

"Now, I'm gonna get out of these 'Sunday-go-to-meetin'-clothes' and then I thought I'd come back and read up on some history."

August came out to Jeff's porch a few minutes later dressed in the blue dress shirt, chinos and running shoes that he kept in a box in the root cellar. Jeff couldn't help thinking that he looked like a duck out of water. There was something in the way he moved in these clothes that seemed unnatural, a buoyancy in his step, a formality of gesture, as though he were an actor on a stage.

"It's not easy keeping the Sabbath on a ranch," August said, settling into a rocking chair. "There's always plenty to do, and animals to care for."

Jeff didn't believe in 'keeping the Sabbath,' but he understood how hard it was to keep from working when there was work to be done. When he was working it seemed there was always something to attend to. Since he lost his job he'd been forced to slow down, take a step back and make better use of his time. He'd always let work distract him from what he was working for — time to engage in personal pursuits, time to connect with his family.

"I hope you don't think me rude, but I'm just going to dive into the next chapter of this book," August said, holding up *American History, Volume Two: The Civil War to the Present.*

"Keep in mind when you get to the end that the book is about ten years out-of-date. It stops at the end of the Twentieth Century."

"It's all new to me."

"Before you settle down to read, I have a question," Jeff said, and asked him about the possibility that the tunnel might only *appear* to be closed.

"I'm sorry to disappoint you, my friend, but I've run my hand over that rock. It's solid all right. You were lucky the other night, because it closed almost as soon as you went through."

Jeff shook his head, pondering the news. "I'll be in the office if you have any questions."

He went back to his office to work on the commentary for a photo book tentatively titled, *Vineyard Seasons.*

Looking up from his work, he could see August through the open door, slowly rocking and turning the pages of a story yet to be written.

Chapter 37
Antique in the Eye of the Beholder

Predictably, Jake settled into his school routine immediately. At the end of the first week Jeff opened the front door as he returned from the hardware store, and saw Jake bounding down the stairs two and three at a time to land with a thud in the entry. He wore a backwards baseball cap, a T-shirt emblazoned with "No Fear," baggy shorts, and high topped basketball shoes. "Hey Pop, I'm going over to Teddy's."

"Who's Teddy?"

"Guy lives down in the housing tract. He's got a dog, too. Come on, Buster. See ya later, Pop!"

Jake and Buster skipped out the door and down the front steps. Jeff watched him go, hoping he would never lose his easy-going confidence.

The one-year anniversary of Randall's disappearance passed without fanfare. Jeff was not one to memorialize unpleasant events. Carolyn settled into a new and shorter commute to her school. The Zinfandel was picked and trucked off to Guglielmo winery. And Jeff spent his time thinking about how to maximize the anticipated returns from the antiques business. He hadn't realized how much pressure he'd felt about their financial situation until relieved of the burden. The recession ground on, unemployment increased by the month, but their bank account was growing thanks to the absence of a mortgage and the $940 Social Security check that arrived in his parents' checking account each month, money that he siphoned off through cash withdrawals at the ATM. Everything that Carolyn made could now be banked.

During the summer Abby's oldest friends had visited three times, and she had spent a few days and one sleep-over at Jenny McClarty's, but as time went on her old friends had called less often and when they did she had nothing new or exciting to report to keep their attention. She began to feel like what she was — an outsider. She felt no less an outsider at her new school, and unlike Jake, who was naturally gregarious, she had no facility for making new friends. She became withdrawn, sullen and petulant and spent most of her time in her room feeling sorry for herself. What little interaction she had with her parents was unpleasant, fraught with complaints, her answers to their well-meaning questions curt and insolent.

"You could at least be civil," Carolyn said.

"You don't know what it's like."

"Don't whine at *me*; I was a military brat," Carolyn reminded her; "we had to move eight times when I was growing up."

"It wasn't hard for *you*. *You* didn't have any friends!"

There were a lot of slammed doors and hateful stares. And then, suddenly, it was over. A month after she started school the fog lifted, her mood lightened, her answers became courteous, and she seemed to have reconciled with her circumstances. One day she was glaring from behind bangs, wearing goth black, and disdainful of all she surveyed. Then seemingly overnight her color palate softened along with her demeanor, and her long strawberry blonde hair was braided into a crown upon her head.

"What happened to *her*?" Jeff asked rhetorically one evening.

"I'd like to think she's found a new friend, but no one's been by to visit, so I expect it's a boy."

Whether it was a boy, a girl, or a teacher who inspired her, or something she'd read and taken to heart, her parents were just grateful to have their old daughter back again. She still spent most of her time in her room, but she no longer complained about homework or a lack of friends.

Six weeks after their brief excursion to old San Francisco, Jeff contemplated the bottle of La Tâche that stood on the table beside the other collectibles, knowing he could never pass it off for what it was. For wine aged. So, for that matter, did most paper. He'd thought the sheet music and newspaper might be collectable, but on further reflection he realized they would be seen as reproductions because the paper wasn't yellowed or brittle with age. The books might even be suspect, unless they were printed on acid free paper, which did not yellow. As for wine, only fortified Madeira or Port, properly sealed with wax, might survive 140 years. Any table wine would long ago have turned to vinegar. Of course not all collectables betrayed their age. But some did, and without the proper markers they might be construed as replicas or forgeries. The problem was how to artificially age them.

He considered this as he surfed the internet for the best places to sell antiques. Earlier in the summer he'd sold two of August's twenty-dollar gold coins for a smidgen under five thousand dollars on eBay. As the seller he'd been charged a 10% transaction fee. Traditional auction houses charged the buyer 13%, which might discourage buyers, although he'd seen the way an auctioneer could whip an audience into a frenzy of competition and greed to ensure inflated prices. But searching for the results of traditional auctions on the internet was proving fruitless. The websites for Sotheby's, Christie's and Butterfield all went out of their way to be opaque.

He gazed at his treasures and fell into a reverie of hopeful speculation. He knew he'd have to be careful not to flood the market, but the potential was limitless. It was like standing on the threshold of King Tut's tomb. He'd seen the traveling exhibition of artifacts from that tomb, and had seen firsthand how, given the right circumstances, even wood and fabric could last a millennium. He was puzzling over the problem of aging antiques, as he imagined Howard Carter's amazement when first he beheld the tomb, and was suddenly struck by a brilliant idea: They would fill a vault with valuable antiques and seal it shut, then pass back to the future and open it. Voila! — Authentically aged antiques! The logical place for a vault would be the wine cellar, where it would lie undisturbed for the next 139 years. To be sure, there might be obstacles to overcome. Humidity, or the lack of it, might pose a problem — too much and there could be mold or rust; too little and wood and leather could crack. Earthquakes might cause the vault to cave-in. Some items might simply deteriorate over time.

Remembering newsreel footage of Carter on the threshold of the tomb, another scheme took the stage of his imagination. He could "discover" a letter that disclosed the location of a secret vault filled with riches, and sell the television rights to film its opening. It might even be a national sensation, and would be far more lucrative than the antiques themselves, which could then be sold en masse to a museum to be exhibited as "The Treasure of Almaden Valley." But almost as soon as he imagined television crews wandering around the cellar, he gave up the idea as far too dangerous.

A vault to age antiques, however, was still a good idea. There was only one problem: To fill the vault he needed 1870 dollars.

He put the scheme to August, who eyed him coolly. "I don't think this miracle was put here to make you rich."

While Jeff didn't believe in the theory that there was a rhyme or reason behind this phenomenon, by now he understood that August was of a different frame of mind. This was an impediment to his plans. He'd spent years working for very little money, often trading his time for nothing more than perquisites – press trips with little or no remuneration that had given him a wealth of experience, but had not benefited his family a farthing. Now he saw a way of making up for his shortcomings, of giving his family the advantages of wealth, and the thought excited his imagination. Carolyn could retire (or not, as she pleased). Abby and Jake could go to college and have a fighting chance at living interesting and fulfilling lives.

August didn't understand his situation, for despite his prejudices and relative ignorance, August was a self-made man. He'd come to California with nothing, and had built a thriving business that supported his family. What more could a man ask? But Jeff could see that August didn't see it the same way. August saw Jeff's toys as a measure of success. Jeff saw August as an obstacle to giving Carolyn the freedom that wealth could bestow.

"Your objections are duly noted," Jeff said, "but until you're certain of the reason, humor me. Maybe God wants us to be rich. Have you ever thought of that?"

August sighed audibly. "Well, He certainly don't want to make me rich. I don't see where I'm benefitting from this arrangement. And I can't afford to keep funding you; I have a duty to my family."

Maybe that was more to the point, Jeff thought. "There must be some way I can return the favor. If I could find something for you to sell, something that might be of benefit here…. Of course we can't bring modern technology into your time if it might disrupt the natural course of progress. Anyway, most of our technology is electronic and you don't even have electricity yet." He racked his brains trying to come up with something from the present that could benefit August's past. It would have to be something that could be produced cheaper, or something that couldn't be reverse engineered. "Stainless steel. Now that's something you could probably sell here — pots and pans. Your neighbors would all be willing to pay for something like that."

"I have a ranch to run. I don't have time to sell pots."

"Then there's knowing the outcome of certain events. What about sports? What's your favorite team?" August looked at him blankly and only then did Jeff remember there were no professional sports teams in 1870. "How about horse races? How about the Kentucky Derby?"

"The what?"

"Well there must be some sporting events you can bet on," Jeff said.

"Bet? No, I don't believe in gambling."

"It's not gambling if you know who's going to win."

August stared out across the valley and seemed to be looking inside himself. After a minute's consideration (and much to Jeff's surprise) he said, "Yes, I guess that's so."

"Also, it's probably worth your while to know that there's a big economic collapse coming soon and it'll last almost a decade. And then there's the phylloxera epidemic."

"What epidemic?"

"The phylloxera epidemic. It's a louse that kills grape vines. Even now it's decimating the vineyards of Europe, and will soon destroy all the vineyards in California planted on vinifera roots. But native American vines are immune. So in the next decade or two every wine grape vineyard in America and Europe will be grafted onto native American rootstock. You can get a head start on that and not lose a vintage. I can get you virus-free rootstock already grafted over to Zinfandel or Cabernet."

"Oh!" August said, perking up. This was something he could understand. "I wonder if...." August trailed off into his own thoughts.

"If what?"

"Nothing. Just, 'God works in mysterious ways his wonders to perform.' Now then, tell me more about this epidemic."

Chapter 38
A Vault

"For pure return on investment, there's nothing like stamps," Jeff said, as August pumped water into a bucket. "They're not half so glamorous as art, or coins, or jewelry, or furniture, but stamp collectors will pay a fortune for old stamps. One and two cent stamps (mint, unhinged) are worth two to four thousand dollars apiece. The lowest price I've seen is about eight hundred dollars! Of course we might drive the price down if we flooded the market."

"I'm still not comfortable being a party to this."

Now it was Jeff's turn to sigh. "Listen August, with your fifty percent you'll have a nice nest egg in the future. You can buy whatever you like for use on my side (you could even buy a car, if you want). And you can bring anything back to your side, as long as you clear it with me first. Tools would be okay, and clothes, food, sundries — most anything you might find in a supermarket or hardware store. You'll see; this is going to be good for both our families. Incidentally, I bought a set of pots and pans and some glassware for Lydia."

Jeff felt positively Machiavellian as Lydia unpacked the boxes with exclamations of gratitude and joy. Owen, however, was far more interested in the packing material — styrofoam, plastic bags, corrugated cardboard boxes and transparent tape. He pestered Jeff with questions about their manufacture, which Jeff deflected easily by pointing to the small lettering on the box: Made in China. "You'd have to go to China to find out how they do it." Owen just shook his head and puzzled over the mysterious materials.

"Honestly," Jeff said, continuing his conversation with August on the front porch, "we could just fill up a strongbox with stamps and bury it under the porch here, and dig it up on my side. It could be that easy. But I think the guns and books would do better in a vault. I don't suppose you'd care to donate a few of your own books to the cause? You have a nice library."

They watched a dust devil whirl some dry leaves by the bridge. "Reading is the one passion I inherited from my mother. She believed in the instructional value of a good story. She still sends me books from time to time. But there are a few volumes I wouldn't mind parting with. I don't know if they'd be worth anything, but you're welcome to them. Thank you for Lydia's gifts, by the way."

"My pleasure," Jeff said. "You know, the Chinese dug a lot of the early wine caves in Napa Valley. We could hire them to dig the vault. It doesn't have to be particularly large, maybe four feet deep, four feet wide, six feet tall. Just a small closet, really."

"You don't need to dig. There's a recess in the wall of the wine cellar. We'd just need to take the bottles out."

The sound of hooves on the bridge alerted them to a visitor. Charles Bowman reined in his dun mare before the porch. He raised an eyebrow and looked suspiciously from August to Jeff and back. "Charlie, what can I do for you?"

"Gus," Bowman said, with a slight nod of the head and a wary look at Jeff. "Have you started picking yet?"

"No, not yet. We'll probably start next week or the week after."

"Do you have a crew?"

"We've used Salvador Alamillo's boys for the past four years, same as you."

"Uh huh." Bowman scratched his stubbled cheek, weighing his words. He let out a loud sigh. "Does he give you a special rate?"

"No, why would he?"

"I just thought maybe you had connections."

"No more than you."

"I just thought maybe you did, 'cause didn't you say you was lookin' for a man named Randall?"

"That's right."

"My father," Jeff added hopefully.

"Uh huh. You wouldn't happen to know where I could find him, now would you?"

"No," August said, "we're still looking."

"Still looking," Bowman said slowly, giving them a sidelong glance. "You're sure now?"

"Yeah, of course. What are you getting at, Charlie?"

"Well I'll tell you, a funny thing happened a couple days ago when I went looking for a crew to pick my Mission vineyard. The Mexicans wanted twice what I paid to have my trees picked in June. I told'm they'd take my price or I'd go to the Chinese. Now, what do you suppose they said?"

"I don't know, Charlie; you tell me."

"They said they had some agreement with Mr. Randall, that the Chinese won't work south of Guadalupe Creek. Now the Mexicans won't take less than two dollars a head per day. I wonder, who the hell is this Mr. Randall, and why is he puttin' a lid on free competition? Then I remember you was lookin' for a man by that name. Now I got grapes about ready to pick, and the goddamned greasers got me over a barrel, and I ain't happy about it, not one bit. So you tell Randall I'm lookin' for him."

"Calm down, Charlie. First of all, we don't know it's the same man. We're looking for Randall Porter. Did they say Mr. Randall, or Mr. Porter?"

"What difference does it make? You know the way they talk. I only know the son-of-a-bitch is costing me money, and he's gonna pay."

"Hold on now. Let's just assume we're talking about the same man. What makes you think he can control the price of labor?"

"He's running those Chinks ain't he? And he don't allow free competition, does he? That costs me money, plain and simple. It costs all of us."

"Well, I suppose that makes sense," August nodded. "The smaller the labor pool, the more we're likely to pay. Then again, Sal's always done a good job for a fair price."

"It *ain't* fair! Two dollars a head is extortion! They can't raise the price like that without warning; the crops'll rot."

"You can't force a man to work for less than he's willing to work for, Charlie. Besides, it's not much more than we paid last year. Sal knows if he charges too much, we'll just go to Miguel Rivas."

"Rivas is working on Ortega's rancho down by Morgan Hill."

"Well, let's not get ahead of ourselves. It might not come to that. We can probably work out a compromise. It's not an insurmountable problem."

"There wouldn't be no problem if the Chinks bid on the work. That's why a bunch of us is looking for this Randall fellow. He needs to be taught a lesson. Are you with us, or ag'in' us?"

"There's no sense in doing anything rash, Charlie."

"If a man picks my pocket, he's gonna pay. If you call that rash, so be it." Bowman started to turn his mare around.

Jeff spoke up then. "If you find him, and it's Randall Porter, tell him I'm looking for him."

Bowman glanced over his shoulder and chuckled maliciously. "This ain't gonna be a social call, junior." Then he spurred his horse and the animal jumped forward and trotted across the bridge.

Jeff felt a new sense of urgency in his plans, and acknowledged to himself for the first time that he had embarked on his quest for riches as much to still his father's disapproval as to provide for his family. The dread he felt in anticipation of their next meeting was twofold — he had to break the news of his mother's death (a death in which he felt at least partly complicit), and he had to admit once again to the loss of yet another job and the confirmation of his failure in his father's eyes. He could do nothing to soften the blow of the former, but a burgeoning bank account would ease the criticism he expected to come his way.

They watched Bowman disappear behind the bushes and trees that bordered Arroyo Calero.

"I've never liked a man who wears spurs," August said.

"Do you think it's him? My father, I mean?"

"Probably."

"You think we should look for him, too?"

"Where would we look? All we know is he's likely north of Guadalupe Creek. He could be in Napa Valley for all we know. No, just sit tight. Someone will see the ad in the newspaper, or see one of your flyers."

"What if Bowman finds him first?"

"Your father is a grown man. Anyway, I expect Bowman and his cohorts are more bark than bite. His kind is all bluster...usually."

Chapter 39
Keeping Secrets

When Carolyn returned home from school she found the Jake rocking listlessly on the front porch sipping an iced drink. "What are you doing out here?" she asked.

"It's too hot in my room," Jake complained.

"Turn on the air-conditioner."

"It takes forever."

"Where's your sister?"

Jake shrugged. "She was going to lay down; she had a headache."

The house was stifling. Carolyn propped open the front door and went upstairs to open windows and start a cross breeze flowing. She paused in front of Abby's door and rapped softly. "I have aspirin, if you need it, Sweetie." She could hear the hum of the air-conditioner, and went back to the porch.

"Where's your father?"

"I dunno," Jake said, "probably Mr. Kimball's."

"Where is that, exactly?"

Jake shrugged. "Up the road, I guess."

"If you're so hot, why don't you go down to the cellar? It's cool in the cellar."

Carolyn dialed Jeff's cell phone and heard it ringing in the kitchen. She found it on the butcher block. There was a text alert. She touched the screen and read: "Left 2 messages. Has your # changed? New editor quit. Job is yours if u want it. Call A.S.A.P., Ralph."

That brightened her mood. She didn't want Jeff to think she'd been snooping, nor did she want to take away from his excitement when he told her the news. So she set the phone back on the counter and went upstairs to lie down on the bed under the air conditioner, where she promptly fell asleep.

When Jeff slipped back behind the shelves he found Jake sitting Indian-style on the plank floor under the dome light.

"Whoa!" Jake exclaimed. "Where'd you come from?"

"What are you doing here?"

"Playing video games. It's too hot upstairs."

Jeff searched his son's face for signs that he knew more than he should, but Jake returned his look with a guileless expression. "You shouldn't be down here. There are rats."

They went upstairs together.

An hour later Carolyn found Jeff in the kitchen preparing dinner. "Where were you?" she asked.

"When?"

"When I got home."

"When was that?"

"An hour ago."

"An hour ago? Probably in the wine cellar. There's evidence of rats; I was setting traps. I didn't know you were home."

"I've been upstairs napping."

"Sleep well?"

"I tried to call earlier; you didn't pick up."

"I didn't think I needed to carry my phone around when I'm home."

"It might be a good idea," she said, careful not to sound needling. "What if I had car trouble? Or the kids might need a ride or something. Or somebody might leave a message."

He glanced over at the counter, saw his phone and picked it up. He stared at the screen a moment, poked it and stuck it in his pocket.

"Any messages?" she asked, hoping to draw him out.

"Nothing important," he said, and went back to grating cheese.

Carolyn decided to eat at the kitchen table with Jeff that evening. It was a good dinner of tilapia coated in panko, twice baked potatoes and zucchini and mushrooms in a white sauce, served with a Sauvignon Blanc.

"How are your new students?" Jeff asked, sipping his wine. "Any standouts this year?"

"One girl who writes the most elegant prose. Most of them write the way they talk. I can't tell you how many end sentences with '...and stuff like that.'" She squeezed some lemon on her tilapia and asked casually, "How about your day? How is the job search going?" She waited expectantly, suppressing her enthusiasm.

"Same old, same old — it's a tough market."

Carolyn ate silently, wondering why he would lie and how she could tell him she knew he was lying without disclosing that she'd been snooping. She wondered which carried the greater offense, and decided that lying was worse than snooping, particularly as she had not set out to snoop. She pushed her plate away and said, half apologetically, "When I called your phone I heard it ringing. I picked it up." Jeff didn't say anything. She continued, "I saw the message."

"It's not a job I want. You wouldn't want me to take it."

"What more are you looking for?"

"I have other plans."

"This isn't about antiques again, is it? You can't make a living selling antiques; you don't know the first thing about the business."

Jeff felt annoyed that she would read his private messages, shamed at being found out and taken to task for it, and contrite in his guilt, and still he felt compelled to keep his secret, for their safety was paramount. Yet the need for secrecy was eating away at what bound them together. Instead of feeling that they were working together as a team (them against the world), they were being pulled apart. "I have a few irons in the fire, trust me."

"You ask me to trust you and then you lie. You stay out late, worry me half to death and offer lame excuses. You disappear at odd times and I can never get hold of you because you refuse to take your phone. You're turning into your father! So what do I have to look forward to? Are you going to just disappear one day, too?"

"I'm not planning on it."

"What exactly are you planning? You keep talking about plans. What plans? Since we moved down here you've just been sitting around, riding horses and doing god-knows-what with Gus."

"Why is this an issue now, after all of the crummy jobs I've had? Now that I finally have a chance to bring in some serious money, to make a contribution, you want me to give it up to work for another magazine that will undoubtedly fail in another six months. Anyway, they're offering a lot less than I was making before."

"It's not about the money."

"It is about the money. Now I can make a difference."

"I've never begrudged you the money."

"For which I'm eternally grateful. So why start now?"

"I didn't marry you because I thought you'd make me rich; I married you because you're not boring. I could have married Dennis Stone. He'd have made good money. But he was boring. I'm boring. I've got boring covered. But you have an adventurous spirit; you make my life more interesting. I may not be able to go on all those trips with you, but I can live vicariously through your adventures."

"My adventures haven't exactly added to the kids' college account."

"Don't worry about the kids; they can get scholarships, or take out student loans. You're not an antique dealer; you're a photographer and a writer."

"It doesn't pay the bills."

"Don't worry about the bills. The bills get paid."

"Maybe I'm tired of working for publishers who stiff me, tired of knocking my head against the wall. That job is no different than the last one, or the one before that. It's just another chance to go down with a sinking ship. Print publications are dead."

"So find somewhere else to use your talents. You've got to do something. I don't mind your not making much money, but speculating in antiques is a dead end. That well is going to run dry, and it's not something you're suited to."

Abby said, "Can you just stop it? Daddy is doing the best he can. Cut him some slack."

Jeff and Carolyn looked up to see Abby standing at the edge of the hall, arms crossed, looking stern and surprisingly adult. Jeff was grateful for the unexpected support.

"Besides," Abby added, "I thought we were saving tons of money moving down here."

"We are," Carolyn acknowledged. "We're finally putting some money in the bank. That's why I want your father to take a job he's good at, not just something for money."

"He's an adult; let him do what he wants."

Chastised, the elder Porters sat in silence until Abby had filled her plate and walked out of the kitchen. Carolyn finished and stood up. "Just promise me one thing."

"What's that?"

"Tell me when you're going out."

"Right."

"And carry your phone."

"I'll try to remember."

"And don't keep secrets."

He was about to answer affirmatively but stopped himself before he could make a promise that he'd regret breaking. He cleared his throat. "What if..." he began, trying to come up with a plausible reason for keeping a secret, "...I were planning a surprise party?"

"That's different. I mean something important."

"What if it's in your best interest?"

"What could be in my best interest that I shouldn't know about?"

"I don't know, what if...your doctor told me you had three months to live?"

She looked suddenly sober. "I'd want to know. She didn't call or anything, did she?"

"No, you're perfectly healthy, as far as I know."

Carolyn let our her breath.

"What if...it's a matter of National Security?"

"Don't be ridiculous."

"What if I was working on something with August, and I didn't want to share it until it was finished."

"That's it, isn't it?"

"I am working on something. It's something important, but I really don't want to talk about it until it's finished."

"Are you going to give me a hint?"

"No."

She rinsed her plate and put it in the dishwasher. "I don't like secrets."

He almost said, *"It's for your own good,"* but had the sense to restrain himself. That would only lead to questions that would cause her more worry.

"It isn't illegal, is it?"

"No, that I can promise you."

She left without another word and he felt enormous relief. By his personal interpretation of morality, admitting to keeping a secret, even without revealing what that secret was, relieved him of the obligation to tell the whole truth. He no longer had to wrestle with his conscience when he dissembled or indulged in a bit of misdirection. He had not known the weight of guilt until it lifted from his shoulders. Once Pop was back, there would be no reason to keep secrets, no reason to keep the tunnel open. They could fill it with concrete, or do whatever needed to be done to keep them all safe. Until that time he was free to pursue his ends without interference or subterfuge. He sighed with satisfaction and poured himself another glass of wine.

Chapter 40
Other Perspectives

Jeff was toweling off after a shower on the first Saturday of October when he heard Carolyn calling for him in an accusatory tone that suggested a quarrel was in the offing. He really couldn't feel self-righteous; he had only himself to blame. She was not naturally shrewish. But he had given her reason to doubt him, and that put a strain on their relationship. He decided to get dressed before confronting the problem.

He found Carolyn in the kitchen.

"Where were you? I've been calling for you," she said crossly.

"I was in the shower. What's up?"

She marched past him, crossed the hall to the dining room, and pointing at the three gun cases said, "Your son was playing with a *gun*! In *our house*!"

The kids both sat at the table with the old newspaper spread open before them.

"I was just looking at it," Jake said in his own defense.

"It's nothing to worry about," Jeff said. "It's not like a modern gun. It doesn't have cartridges; it has a ball and cap. It takes gunpowder and several steps to load it. None of those guns has ever been loaded."

Having her thrust so easily parried, she seemed momentarily flustered. "He didn't know that," she said weakly.

"It's not like I pointed it at anyone," Jake said to his father. "I'm not that dumb."

Jeff addressed Carolyn. "I understand you don't like guns, but these are harmless museum pieces."

"You know I don't like guns."

"I know, and you know they're valuable and I'll get rid of them just as soon as I figure out how to get the most we can for them."

Carolyn looked from father to son and back again. Then she sighed with resignation, placated for the moment. "I was going to make myself some Cream of Wheat. Does anyone want some?"

They all did, and she turned back to the kitchen.

"Listen to this," Abby said, reading from the July twenty-first 1870 edition of the Daily Alta California:

> "'There are only 1,175 whisky shops and lager beer saloons in San Francisco at present. Fifteen or twenty have failed and closed within the past few weeks. Three restaurants and two second-class hotels have failed within the last few days, owing to the impecuniosity of the customers.'

"*Only* a thousand whisky shops and saloons? *Only?* How many people lived in San Francisco in 1870?"

"About 150,000, if memory serves," Jeff said.

"They must've all been drunk!"

"What's impecu...impecuni...?" Jake asked.

"Impecunious means impoverished, without money," Jeff said. "So businesses were apparently failing because they were losing customers. It was at the beginning of a depression."

"Is that like a recession?" Abby asked.

"Same thing."

She scanned the paper and in a moment said, "Yeah, see, here it is again." She read:

> ### "'Business Depression in California.
> 'The great cause of this unfortunate dullness of trade is, as is well known, the Pacific Railroad, which was dreamed of and hoped for as the great blessing of the State.

Hitherto our businessmen have enjoyed a protective tariff laid by nature in separations by mountains and deserts of three thousand miles. The simple fact is that California is now brought near the Eastern States, and must compete with the economical Yankee and the saving German, whose habits of expense are different from his extravagant Western counterparts. For the first time since the foundation of the State, there is talk of economy, and the need is felt of retrenching every branch of expenditure. It is an unpleasant position just now for the business community of California, with their 'free and easy' ways, but it is a healthy one. We can look with no pleasure on such extravagance as has prevailed in the Pacific State. The reckless habit of the people has not been favorable to the cultivation of the best types of character. Nothing is so wholesome for a community as the exercise of self-denial and habits of economy. Had it not been for the introduction into California of the most economical race of laborers and producers in the world — the Chinese — the State would long ago have been ruined by its extravagance.'"

"That's an interesting editorial," Jeff said, "but it's off the mark. I've been doing some research of my own and that depression wasn't just in California; it was global and lasted a decade."

The cycle of economic boom and bust had not changed much in a hundred and forty years, Jeff thought. Only now illegal immigrants from Mexico, and factory workers in China provided the cheap physical labor, while imported workers and outsourced office jobs to India provided cheap intellectual labor.

Jake sniggered.

"What?" Abby asked.

"Read that," he said, pointing to a headline that read "John and Sambo."

Abby read aloud:

"'A New Orleans correspondent of the New York Herald, writing of the effort of Chinese labor in the South, says: On the same plantation there are employed some fifty or sixty negroes, whose quarters are but a stone's throw from the Chinese encampment... At first they were reluctant to speak on the subject, but a way being found to loosen their tongues, spokesman No. 1 (a stout, powerful negro) gave his opinion: 'I dun care; dey can do me nuffin. Dar's too much work, anyhow. S'pose dey turn me away here, den I goes somewhere else; that's all.

'A narrow chested, worn-out darkey, employed as a sort of makeshift watchman around a plantation house, was emphatic in his opinion — and found many to agree with him— that 'them men would never do the work.'

'Why not?'

'Well, dey ain't got the strength.'

'The youngest and weakest of the Chinese, meanwhile, would have found little difficulty in doubling this old darkey up and dropping him into the Mississippi. The more sensible of the colored hands seem to appreciate the gravity of the experiment. It is not likely they will attempt any organized opposition to the introduction of Chinese labor into Louisiana. There was an attempt to get up an anti-Chinese labor Convention at Baton Rouge, some time ago, but it fizzled out.'"

Abby looked up from the paper and said, "Wow! They could never print this stuff today."

"They sure made blacks sound stupid," Jake said.

"I hate to say it," Jeff said, "but that dialect is probably pretty accurate. Remember, it was only five years after the Civil War. That man had probably been a slave his whole life and never educated. It would be surprising if he *didn't* speak in dialect. And face it — kids in inner city poor neighborhoods today speak a kind of dialect that would sound pretty stupid if you wrote it down."

Abby said, "It makes you wonder how we'll sound to people in the future. I mean, like, IMHO, abbreviations sound kind of stupid even to me, LOL."

"Exactly."

"Imagine if all you knew of the world was what you read in this newspaper," Abby said.

"Is it so different now?" Jeff asked.

"We have TV and the internet," Jake interjected.

"But the opinions don't vary much across the media. It's the same message. They're still the opinions of the day. What sounds ignorant to you might sound perfectly reasonable to someone in 1870, and what you think is reasonable today might sound ridiculous when you're my age. In my own lifetime the role of women in society has changed. The way we think about divorce has changed. The way we think about gays has changed. The way we think of race has changed (when I was born, this country would never have elected a black President). An awful lot of what passes for humor on TV would have been considered obscene. Times change, as your gramma liked to point out."

"But they had a lot less information," Jake said.

"That's true."

"Having more information doesn't necessarily make you smarter," Abby said.

Jeff looked at his daughter with new respect. Where was that little girl who spent her time fatuously gossiping with friends on the phone? She'd been replaced by a thoughtful young adult. The disruption of the move and transition to high school had somehow transformed her. Instead of rebelling, she had matured.

"I have a friend," she went on, "who's very nice, but I don't think she's ever had an opinion of her own. She believes everything her parents tell her. And her parents are religious. I don't think she's stupid, but I can't understand how she can believe some of that stuff."

"You and me both," Jeff said, thinking of August and Lydia. "People are taught to be rational in everything but religion."

"And love," Abby added.

She really was becoming a little adult, he thought.

They all ate Cream of Wheat at the little round kitchen table.

"Who stole all the toilet paper?" Carolyn asked. "I went down to the cellar this morning to get some, and it's vanished. I just bought a big pack on Thursday." She looked from Abby to Jake, who both shrugged.

"I'm afraid I gave it to August," Jeff said.

"All of it?"

"He has a large family."

"Does he? Why haven't we seen them?"

"They don't get out much."

"Can we talk about something other than toilet paper at the table?" Abby whined.

"You'll have to run out to the store today," Carolyn told Jeff, "I just put the last roll on. I don't know why you would give away the whole pack."

"Mo-o-om!"

"Sorry."

Chapter 41
A Riddle Solved

Sunday the first breath of autumn came on a cool breeze that wafted down the valley. Jake was off to the movies with Ted, his new best friend from school. Jeff and Carolyn were off to the nursery to buy potted ferns for the parlor and a ficus for the dining room. Abby elected to stay home to work on a school project.

Meanwhile, on a still, hot Friday morning in early September, Noah, Betsy and Charles all piled into the little trap pulled by Clarence the mule (so named because he was as stubborn as August's cousin Clarence). Lydia and Emily stood by to see them off.

"Carrie is not sick; she's faking," Betsy grumbled as she settled into her seat beside Charles. "She just wants to get out of the math test!"

"Now, that's no way to talk about your sister," Lydia scolded. "She's not feeling well."

"She was just fine last night," Betsy pointed out indignantly, folding her arms and glowering at her mother.

Noah pulled the accordioned top up to give them shade. Then he took up the reigns and they were off across the bridge. They parted two horsemen on the far bank. Lydia and Emily watched the trap trundle down the dusty road until it disappeared behind the willows.

The two horsemen stopped in front of her.

"Is *señor* Kimball at home?" Salvador Alamillo asked.

Lydia squinted at him, pointed toward the barn and said, "Hayloft."

Owen, in the corral, had already seen them. "Pa! We got company!"

August put down his pitchfork and climbed down the ladder. He found the men standing by their horses, hats held deferentially in hand.

"Sal, Miguel," he said, acknowledging the men. "What can I do for you?"

Salvador looked to Miguel, who looked away as if embarrassed. Then he looked back to August without actually making eye contact. "I...*we*...," he began, "we want to know if you need your grapes picked."

"We're probably two or three weeks away, but sure. Is there some problem?"

"Well, we jus' want to know if you want us to pick, like before." Salvador gripped the brim of his hat in both hands and stared at August's chest. "Because we have to charge a little more than last year."

"I heard that," August said. "Two dollars a head per day; is that right?"

Salvador and Miguel both nodded nervously.

August nodded back at them. "That's fine."

"Because we have families to feed, you know."

"You've always done a good job for a fair price. I don't have any complaints."

Salvador relaxed and finally looked into August's eyes. "You know, a lot of people they're not too happy, because, you know, the Chinese they work for nothing. They takin' our jobs. But then Mr. Randall he say he keep them *norte de arroyo Guadalupe*. And now we want to work, but a lot o' people, they don' wan' to pay. They think two dollars is too much."

"I understand. I'd like to show you something. Wait here."

August went into the house and came out with one of Jeff's flyers. He handed it to Salvador. "Is this Mr. Randall?"

"*Sí!* That's him! He's a good man. He listened to us. We sat down and he made the Chinese listen. Now everybody's happy. Except some of the owners."

"Do you know where I can find him?"

Salvador frowned and shook his head. He turned to Miguel and asked, "¿*Usted sabe dónde él puede encontrar señor Randall?*"

Miguel spoke animatedly for a minute — too fast for August to catch all the words. Salvador translated. "He says last he know was three weeks ago. Mr. Randall and the Chinese they were picking prunes somewhere by Saratoga in the mountains."

"Thanks so much," August said, shaking his hand. "That's very helpful."

"You know Mr. Randall?"

"He did some jobs for me. His son is looking for him. If you see Randall, give him this flyer."

"Sure, boss." Salvador folded the flyer and slipped it in his shirt pocket.

August and Owen were finishing their chores late in the afternoon, just as the youngsters returned from school. Noah pulled up to the barn to unhitch Clarence. He was in a good mood. "Teacher says we can have the next three weeks off for harvest!"

"Good. Then I can put you to work."

"Aw pa! That ain't fair."

August smiled at the thought of more hands to work on the weekdays.

It had been a hot, windless day and he was drenched in sweat. He took a towel and a wooden bucket out to the pump and kicked off his shoes and stripped off his shirt. He filled the bucket three times and three times he dumped the contents over his head. Then he toweled off and went upstairs to change into clean clothes.

At the top of the stairs Betsy was pounding on the girls' bedroom door. "Carrie! Open up! You can't lock me out; it's my room, too!"

August paused to rap on the door. "Carrie, are you all right?"

Her voice seemed to come from a long way away. Then there was creaking and a thunk and the door opened. Carrie's face was red and her forehead glistened with sweat.

"Gosh, you really are sick!" Betsy said.

"I'll be all right. Could you bring water for the basin and a wash cloth?" She closed the door again. Betsy scurried off to get water. August retired to his room to get dressed. He wanted to break the news to Jeff that Randall had actually been spotted not too far away.

Jeff was enjoying the tang of cooler temperatures and the clarity of air that came with the fall. It had been a good day, the first that he and Carolyn had spent alone in months. They came home from the nursery with a good deal more than they'd intended, and transplanted their new plants into several decorative pots that they placed around the parlor, the office, the dining room and their bedroom. Besides adding color and natural grace, the plants served as their personal stamp on the house and made them feel less like interlopers.

They all ate an early dinner at the kitchen table — a simple dinner of shrimp in garlic-lemon-butter sauce, angel hair pasta and peas. Afterwards, as mountain shadows stole across the valley, Jeff switched on the lights and loaded the dishwasher. Remembering that August was likely to show up at sunset, he went to the root cellar and turned on the light to make his passage easier.

He had just strolled into the parlor, where Carolyn sat grading papers, when August appeared on the porch looking concerned. He came in, acknowledged Carol with a "Ma'am," and a nod of his head, and signaled to Jeffrey that he wanted to talk in private.

"Come on," Jeff said, "I'll pour you a glass of Pinot."

Carolyn watched them go, wondering how they'd met and why they spent so many hours in each other's company. They seemed an unlikely pair. What had prompted Jeff to befriend his opposite?

In the kitchen August spoke in a low, but urgent tone. "I tried to come through a few minutes ago, and the tunnel was gone. So I was going over the log to see if we'd ever found it shut at this time, when it just opened, like magic."

"When was this?"

"Just now."

"Oh my," Jeff said as a thought blossomed. "Follow me; I want to try an experiment." Jeff led August to the root cellar door, gave him a flashlight and showed him how to use it. "Now go back through. When you're on the other side call to me and stand back. I'm going to turn off the dome light and see if anything changes. I'll turn it back on in a minute or two."

When August called, Jeff turned off the light, turned on his flashlight app and descended the stairs. At the mouth of the tunnel he called softly to August. No response. He went through himself. The geode still opened to the wine cellar, though it was obvious it wasn't August's cellar, but the cellar as Jeff had last seen it more than a year ago, before his father had sealed the door shut. What had his mother said? "Your father closed it up...the stairs were getting rickety." The stairway now appeared sturdy enough. He puzzled over this anomaly as he made his way back to the root cellar and up the stairs. He flicked the light switch. A minute later August came into the kitchen. "Yes, siree, that did it: When you turned off the light the tunnel disappeared. It was solid rock for a good minute. Then the light come on and the tunnel reappeared."

"Well I'll be damned," Jeff said. "It's the electricity." He went down the stairs following the wire that branched off from the single bulb that hung from the ceiling. The wire ran along the ceiling and down the wall and into the chamber, where it connected to the dome light. "I don't know how it works, but it's the electricity that does it. That must be how my father was trapped. My mother must have seen the light on and no one in the cellar and turned off the switch." He sighed. "Wow. It was so simple."

Later, Carolyn was on her way to load the washing machine when she noticed the corner of a paper sticking out of the carpetbag. When Jeff wandered into the parlor, a little after 9:00 p.m., she held it up and asked, "What does this mean?"

"It's just a flyer."

"I know it's a flyer; I'm not stupid." She read, "'SEEKING RANDALL PORTER, last seen working on farms near San Jose. His son, Jeffrey Porter, requests that any news of his present whereabouts be sent to the Kimball Ranch in Almaden Valley.'" Jeff just blinked and said nothing. "Well?"

"Well what?"

"When was he seen? Where? By whom? What has August got to do with anything? Why send word to *him*?"

Once again he was caught, and once again he found it easiest to tell the truth, even if it wasn't the whole truth. "He was working for August."

"When?"

"Until January."

"When were you going to tell me?"

"I didn't see the point. You'd only worry."

"Yes, I'd worry! Of course I'd worry! What are we supposed to do if he comes home? Why did he abandon your mother in the first place?"

"I don't have all the answers."

"Oh, lord! Have you told Lieutenant Hanes?"

"No. The police aren't going to look for a missing person if that person is an adult and left of his own free will."

"I can't believe this. I know you were only trying to protect me, but keeping secrets is worse; trust me." She went to him and laid her head on his shoulder. "Why would you want news to be sent to August?"

Jeff hugged her tight as he came up with a plausible answer. "If Pop saw the flyer and he knew I was looking for him, he'd naturally go to Foster City, and we wouldn't be there. If I gave this address, he might stay away (he probably doesn't know Mom's passed away). But he might go to August's if he knew I was looking for him."

"Oh, Sweetie, I'm so sorry. It would be so much easier if he were dead." She immediately regretted her words, but that didn't change the sentiment.

Chapter 42
Trouble

August was working in the two-acre Carignane vineyard behind the house, stripped down to his undershirt and perspiring profusely. He mopped his face and neck with a bandana and looked longingly westward, where creamy fog spilled over the crest of the mountains like a frozen wave. Later that afternoon he knew a cooling breeze would come whistling down the bay, but for now the sun baked the little valley. He was walking the rows, tasting the grapes to assess their ripeness and mentally calculating the tonnage per acre, when George Koeppler arrived on his pinto. He tied his horse to the hitching rail at the water trough and met August at the edge of the vineyard.

"Gus," he said, extending his hand.

August shook it. "What brings you out this way? I don't suppose it's good news."

"Why do you say that?"

"Well, it's harvest time, George, and there's hardly a year goes by that one of us don't need some help, what with broken equipment and such. What can I do for you?"

"Actually, I've come to tell you — after you left church yesterday, a bunch of us was sittin' around chewin' the fat, and Bowman got to talking about holding our ground on prices. He says what with the Chinese stayin' up north, the Mexicans think they can charge a premium to pick. But if we all stick together we can hold the price the same as we was payin' the Chinks."

August frowned. "You know what the Mexicans are asking for don't amount to much more'n we paid last year. I don't see what all the fuss is about."

"Well I tell ya, a Chinaman is worth two Mexicans. They work faster and for less, and they do a better job. But if the Mexicans think they can raise their price 'cause they scared the Chinese off, they got another thing comin'."

August watched a red-tailed hawk land on a fence post and bend down to tear at the mouse in its talons. "Well, George, I've never hired the Chinese. Don't have anything against'm, but I've always been happy with the Mexicans. Alamillo, Ruis, Ortega, they've all done a good job for me. I don't begrudge them a fair wage."

"Well now, Gus, that's the problem. If you was to pay'm more'n we're willing to pay, then you get your crops picked, while ours rot on the vine, and pretty soon everyone is paying the same high price. That don't make sense. That's what I come to warn you about, 'cause Bowman was sayin' there's just a few of us who might scotch the deal, an' he singled out you and Watson and Pinault as the most likely culprits."

"What's he going to do if I don't join his little rebellion?"

Koeppler looked abashed and scratched the back of his head. "Well, I don' rightly know, but we thought maybe you'd think different if you knew all your neighbors was holdin' the line on a price increase."

"Well now, I'll tell you what, George," August said, taking the man's arm and turning him gently toward his horse, "I'll think about it. I appreciate your coming all the way out here and letting me know what my neighbors think. But in the end a man's business is his own business, long as he's honest, and I'll do business my way, and you can do business your way. Isn't that the way it's done?"

"Course, Gus. A man's got to make up his own mind." At his horse Koeppler turned worried eyes on August. "But you'll think about it?"

"I'll think about it," August said.

"Okay, that's good, Gus. That's good."

Koeppler mounted and road away. August pumped water into a bucket, dipped his bandana in it and wiped his face.

Owen joined him at the pump and poured a ladle full of water over his own head and drank another. They watched Koeppler's horse trot up the slope on the far side of the bridge.

"What'd he want, Pa?"

"Trouble," August said.

Chapter 43
Flight

Ever since his first foray into the modern world, August had longed for more. Though not a timid man, it had not escaped his notice that, with the exception of their rides to neighboring ranches and their one excursion to San Francisco, Jeff had also confined his horizons to the ranch. There had been reason for caution. They had never been sure whether the tunnel would be open or closed. They had supposed that they were less likely to be caught out during the daylight hours. It was a foolish conceit, he now realized, for until they had discovered the mechanism, they had been at continual risk. Now it was a simple matter of flipping a switch. Switches and buttons ran the machinery of the future, a future he ached to see.

It was Saturday for the Kimball family. They were up at first light. The boys went out to feed the animals, while the girls stoked the stove, gathered eggs, milked the cow and set the kettle on to boil water. They made a breakfast of eggs, bacon, buttermilk pancakes, baked apples and cornbread with butter and apricot jam, milk and coffee. At the table August charged the boys with cutting and splitting wood (a task that would take them all day). As the girls cleaned and geared up for bread and pie production, August told Lydia that he'd be out inspecting the vines.

He lingered over a cup of coffee in his stocking feet, and when the girls were chattering at the sink, he stole silently into the dining room and down the wine cellar stairs.

It was Monday at the Porters, and all but Jeff had left for school. August showered and dressed in his new outfit. Then they set off for the Hiller Aviation Museum at the San Carlos Airport.

On their trip to the mall they had never left city streets. On highway 101 August was alarmed by the speed, dismayed by the number of cars on the road, and relieved to see that Jeff was relaxed and in control as he kept up a constant patter.

"I'm sorry I can't get you up in an airliner. It's a different experience than the little plane we'll be going up in. An airliner is much quieter; you have a tray table, an entertainment system, restrooms (well, you'll see, because they have a fuselage of an airliner at the museum). Little planes are a lot louder, and they don't fly as high. Do you get motion sick? It could be a bumpy ride."

"Bumpier than a trot?"

"No, probably not."

The further they drove, the more disturbed August became by the unrelenting development. There was no telling where one town left off and another began. Where were the familiar landmarks? Where were the farms, the streams, the pastures? — All had been paved over by a sea of buildings that lapped up the sides of the mountains like a tide of concrete.

The museum and airport were half an hour north, built on fill at the edge of the bay. They spent more than an hour in the museum, which housed replicas of John J. Montgomery's gliders and the Wright Brother's Flyer, antique biplanes, a Grumman Albatross, various helicopters, and the cockpit and first class section of a 747.

When they were done, they walked next door to Diamond Aviation, where Jeff had arranged for an hour's tour of the Bay Area in a Cessna 172. August sat in the backseat, so he could scoot from side to side for the best view. As they were taxiing to the end of the runway, the pilot offered them gum. August took the proffered piece and tapped Jeff on the shoulder. Jeff lifted August's earphones from his head and yelled over the roar of the engine, "You chew it. It helps equalize the pressure in your ears. Don't swallow it. When you're done with it, spit it in a Kleenex."

August shrugged, looked perplexed, and yelled back, "What's a Kleenex?"

Jeff dug in his pocket and handed him a tissue. The pilot glanced over at Jeff with a questioning look and mouthed, "A bit slow?"

"Amish," Jeff offered. It wasn't exactly the truth, but it would explain a multitude of August's quirks.

As the little plane rose into the air, August gaped in wonder at the receding ground. He was thrilled by the perspective and at the same time overwhelmed by the magnitude of the changes spread before him. Below, tiny cars streamed down the highways like lines of busy ants. The sheer number of people, the evidence of human habitation, and the frenetic hive-like activity amazed him. People were everywhere.

They flew up the peninsula, skirting west of San Francisco International Airport, then back toward the bay, over the Bay Bridge, past towering skyscrapers and along the waterfront. They passed low over the Golden Gate Bridge, swathed in fog, and turned south along the coast at a thousand feet. The fog thinned along the beaches of Pacifica and Half Moon Bay. The little plane dropped down to five hundred feet and sped down the rural coast, over artichoke and pumpkin fields and Christmas tree farms. At Santa Cruz they climbed to three thousand feet and turned east, passing over fluffy white clouds that clung to the spine of the mountains. Then they descended into Almaden Valley, where they circled the ranch for a minute as Jeff took pictures, before turning north again, running parallel to the ridge line as they flew back to San Carlos Airport.

August was silent and preoccupied as they clambered out, overwhelmed by the new perspective he'd gained in the past hour. He had seen the future. He had seen the world as from heaven. Jeff thanked the pilot and August shook his hand vigorously. Then they started back to the car.

"You're awfully quiet, August," Jeff said. "What'd you think?"

August stopped and grasped Jeff by the shoulders. "By god, that was something to remember!" he said, his voice quavering with emotion, then added as an afterthought, "You can call me Gus."

They arrived home just after 2:00 pm. Carol and the kids wouldn't be home until 3:30. Jeff made a couple sandwiches and offered August (Gus, he reminded himself) a chilled glass of Gruet Blanc de Noirs sparkling wine, "To celebrate your first flight."

August grinned proudly as they clinked glasses. "Just think, in this grand year of our Lord, 1870, not one man on earth has flown in a plane, save one. That's a humbling thought. I only wish I knew why."

"Does there have to be a reason for everything?"

"I'd like to think there is."

They lingered on the porch for over an hour, as August talked excitedly about what he'd seen from the plane, the way you could see the drainage patterns on the land, the vast number of cars flowing into and out of the city, the changed landscape, the way that height made human endeavor seem insignificant, "...except for them buildings in the city. My Lord, they're taller than the hills." Then more to himself than to Jeff he murmured, "Ivan would have loved to fly."

Jeff, who could only imagine the horror of losing a child, said, "I expect he has his wings already," not really believing it, but hoping it offered some solace.

When he was ready to leave, August said, "Thanks for a remarkable day. It was very generous of you."

"Not really. You need to remember you have a large credit here in the future. Those coins I sold early in the summer fetched a good profit. You have at least five thousand dollars sitting in my checking account, and there'll be a lot more once we sell our latest stash. This antiques business is going to be like hitting the mother lode. We'll have to figure out how to convert that to cash on your side, but you'll be rich here. You're already rich. Just think, you don't have to grow your food anymore; you can go to the supermarket and buy it."

August looked amused. "I can grow my own."

"But now you can buy anything you want, anytime you want it."

"That reminds me — the girls really like that...um...paper."

"Paper?"

"For the outhouse."

"Ah."

"And I wouldn't mind some more of that gum. Now that was like a little dessert that went on and on." August stared at the wall for a moment, thinking. "How much do you reckon we'll make?"

"As much as we want."

"Could I afford a plane?"

"Sure, but you can rent one a lot cheaper."

"Let's go over to my side," August said. "I have a few things to add to that stash."

In the wine cellar Jeff changed shirts and pulled on boots, and August changed back into his working clothes.

"I've got some books might be valuable," August said, finally showing some enthusiasm for their joint venture, "and an old flintlock."

"And don't forget about stamps," Jeff reminded him.

The kids arrived back home at 3:25. Carolyn followed a few minutes later, carrying groceries. She took a pack of paper towels and a box of dishwashing detergent down to the root cellar and put them on shelves. She was careful to turn the light off as she left the cellar.

Chapter 44
Trapped

Heart hammering, Jeff rubbed his hand over the stone where the opening should have been. He took a deep breath and tried to calm himself. Then he went upstairs to inform August.

August led him a little ways from the house, so they could talk in private. "What're you going to do?"

"Well, I can tell you what I'm *not* going to do. I'm *not* going to do what my father did, which is walk away. I'm going to camp out in the cellar. I need a pole, or a ladder — something to lean against the rock. When someone turns on the light, the pole will fall, and I'll know immediately, even if I'm asleep."

"I have some fence posts that'll do the job."

"I'd like a blanket and pillow, if you have any to spare, and something to eat, if you can manage it. I guess you'll have to keep the family out of the cellar for the time being, or they'll wonder what I'm doing down there."

"That won't be easy; the girls go down there for flour and sugar."

"Take what they might need upstairs. Tell them there are some big rats down there and you've set traps, and not to go downstairs without your permission."

The cellar was dark, lit only by a single candle that threw a small circle of light. Jeff pulled the rack of shelves further out, drew the curtain aside, and leaned two fence posts against the rock where the opening should be. He sat on the hard slate floor and leaned his back against a barrel, cushioned by a feather pillow.

August had given him a book to pass the time, but he hadn't the patience to read. His mind was occupied with the consequences of this catastrophe. Unless the passage opened before midnight, he would be in deep trouble. He'd deflected Carolyn's questions before, but what excuses could he offer now? He had to question whether he could keep it from her for much longer without doing irreparable harm to their marriage. After all, marriage was built on trust. At the same time, he could envisage it all blowing over as nothing of consequence, once he made his fortune. If, a month from now, he apologized for being secretive and presented her with a check for a quarter of a million dollars, it would go a long way toward ameliorating the situation. But that didn't do anything to diffuse the confrontation that would inevitably come if he were to simply disappear without explanation for a day (or two, or ten). He racked his brains for the best way to spin it. The hours ticked slowly past. The candle dwindled. The longer he sat there, the more uncomfortable and depressed he became. It was cold in the cellar. He dozed.

He awoke to the sound of music. Someone was playing the piano, accompanied by a harmonica, guitar, fiddle and gut-bucket playing a lively instrumental. Soon thereafter the instruments reached a crescendo and abruptly stopped to cries of laughter, clapping and the murmur of approval. Then Owen, Carrie and Betsy, accompanied by piano and violin, blended their voices in a sweet rendition of "Beautiful Dreamer." Jeff couldn't imagine his own children being unselfconscious enough to deliver such sentimental lyrics without twisting them into a comical or cynical statement. The modern world was distrustful of sentiment, as if it were merely manipulative histrionics. In the Nineteenth Century, where living to adulthood or old age was largely a matter of luck, sentiment gained authenticity. It was something he had come to appreciate in the past year. The loss of his father and death of his mother had brought home the fleeting nature of life and love, and now often left him near tears at the most unexpected and inopportune times. Jeff was contemplating this when he realized the music had ceased, and now August was reading aloud to the family, a steady drone with the cadence of sentences that he couldn't quite make out.

The candle guttered out. Eventually the door above opened and August peered in, holding a lantern at arm's length. He closed the door and came back in a minute with a glass of water, a knife, half a loaf of bread, a jar of jam, and some cheese. He said not a word, but went back upstairs and in a few minutes returned dragging a straw-filled tick mattress, an extra blanket, a couple of candles and matches, and a chamber pot. Then he sat down on a small, upturned barrel, put his hands on his knees and said, "How are you holding up?"

"Bored to tears and worried about how I'm supposed to explain this to Carolyn."

"Would it help if I took the blame?"

"Unless I was held under duress, I have no excuse."

"I could say Betsy fell down the well and...no, that wouldn't work. How about you went for a ride up into the mountains and your horse threw you and you were lost?"

Jeff brightened at that suggestion. "That might work if you back me up," he said, "but only if I get back soon. If it's more than a day, I don't see how I could explain it away."

"We could say we were exploring a mineshaft and got lost. It could take days to find your way out of a mine."

Jeff agreed with the suggestion, though he doubted Carolyn would fall for it.

"I'll leave you the lantern."

When dinner time rolled around and Jeff was nowhere to be found, Carolyn started to worry, but only a little. His unexplained disappearances were too frequent to elicit real alarm. She tried his phone and got his voicemail. She texted him.

The only evidence of what he'd been up to that day was a nearly empty bottle and two champagne flutes on the kitchen table. Who had he been drinking with? If not for the numerous times of late when he'd suddenly disappeared, only to show up an hour later with August, she would have suspected another woman. Under the circumstances, she thought it more likely that he and August had cooked up one of their schemes and lost track of the time. She would have to insist on getting August's phone number and address. She made a box of macaroni and cheese and heated up some chicken-apple sausage, and took it to the parlor to eat in front of the TV.

When he did not show up by the time she was ready for bed, she was still not too worried, but she was a little angry and disappointed that he could be so inconsiderate. He'd surely come in late with some lame excuse. She meant to deny him the luxury of their bed and locked the door before going to sleep.

In the morning she expected to find him on the settee in the office, but there was no sign of him. The bottle and flutes were still on the kitchen table. Now she had a choice: She could go to work as usual, or call in sick and wait for her wayward husband. The more she thought about it, the more annoyed she became. She had no intention of giving up her sick days just to sit at home and worry. It would be unfair to her students. And what would she do with herself while waiting? No, it was better to keep busy, to keep her mind off his selfishness. She went to work. The kids didn't even notice his absence.

In the morning Jeff awoke to the sound of feet tromping on the boards overhead, and muffled voices as the Kimballs got ready for breakfast. Betsy's voice rose strident and clear as she ranted about her elder sister. "Carrie's still in bed. She says she's not going to church and won't help with breakfast. It's her turn to milk the cow."

"Maybe she doesn't feel well," Jeff heard Lydia say. "Get Charles to help you."

"He won't help; he's helping Noah."

"Emily, why don't you go help your big sister?"

"She's no help," Betsy objected; "she can't milk a cow. Can't you get Carrie to come down?"

"We shouldn't bother her. Besides, I'm trying to get this bread in the oven and the hamper filled for lunch. Why don't you take Emily here and she can gather eggs."

"She breaks eggs."

"Do not," Emily protested.

There was scuffling, then footsteps and a door slammed. A while later the whole family was gathered in boisterous conversation in the dining room overhead. Jeff's stomach was rumbling. He hoped they'd leave something behind. Soon orders were given and everyone filed out.

The door above opened and August came down the steps. "Any luck?"

"Not yet."

"We're about to head out to church. I've left some cornbread and hardboiled eggs in the pantry. There's some coffee warming on the stove, and a pitcher of milk in a water bath in the sink. We'll be back around 1:30."

"Hopefully I'll be gone by then."

"I'll keep my fingers crossed. Oh, and Carrie is staying home (she's not feeling well), so be quick and quiet when you go upstairs."

Jeff waited ten minutes before stealing upstairs, gathering his breakfast and returning to the cellar. He ate slowly and tried to read by lantern light, but the book, *Miss Marjoribanks*, didn't hold his attention, being the work of an expert in circumlocution. His mind wandered and he found himself thinking about his father. He wondered how he was fairing in his new role as foreman to a crew of migrant farm workers. He thought back to his youth when he'd followed him around the ranch. His father had always been a taciturn man, more inclined to show than to tell. And though he had never been overtly affectionate, Jeff had always felt loved as a child. Their later falling out, he now realized, had more to do with sensing his father's disapproval than with anything he had actually said. Now, if he needed proof that his father took an interest in his chosen life, there was that drawer full of old articles. And he thought that if the Fates held a lottery to select one's parents, he could have done a lot worse than his own mother and father. They had their quirks, but they were quirks he was comfortable with, and he only hoped he could do as well by his own children.

He supposed that one of the reasons he and his father had grown apart, was that their experiences diverged as Jeff began to travel. Randall had never wandered very far from home, and seemed to have little curiosity about other cultures. Now, however, they had taken the same trip back in time, and had a lot of notes to compare. Jeff was turning that thought over in his mind when the fence posts fell into the tunnel.

Chapter 45
Siren Song

"Wait! Leave the light on!" he yelled and sprang through the opening, heart racing.

"Dad?" his daughter called.

He raced through the geode and let out a squeal of relief. "Ah, lord, thank you!"

"What're you...? Sorry, I didn't mean to..."

"Is your mother home?"

"Not yet."

"Was she very angry?"

"Why would she be angry?"

Jeff stopped, flummoxed by her cluelessness. Could he have slipped in time? How could he be gone and not be missed? "You...didn't know?"

"Know what?" she asked cautiously.

"How long have I been gone?"

"What? I don't know. Gone where?"

"Wait, I'm confused. What day is it?"

"Tuesday."

He shook his head. "Date."

"October sixth. Why?"

"She didn't say anything last night, or this morning?" Abby frowned and shook her head. "And you didn't notice I was gone?"

"Not really."

"Well I was," he said. "I was in the wine cellar and someone turned off the lights." He began to mount the stairs. "I tripped and banged my head," he added, working on a plausible excuse for Carolyn by trying it out on his daughter first. "And when I awoke it was dark and I couldn't find my way out."

It wasn't a very believable excuse, but it was all he could come up with on the spur of the moment. Famished, he went immediately to the kitchen to make a quesadilla in the microwave. The clock on the microwave indicated it was ten minutes past noon.

"Wait. Why aren't you in school? Is it a holiday?"

"I had a headache," Abby said.

Jeff texted Carolyn that he was okay and would explain everything when she got home. She did not text him back.

When Jake returned from school, Jeff went out to the porch to await Carolyn's arrival. Ten minutes later her Civic crossed the wooden bridge and came up the slope. She didn't even glance his way, but drove on to the barn. She came in through the kitchen door and he awaited her arrival on the porch, bracing for the expected fury and ready with his feeble excuse. When, after ten minutes, she didn't make an appearance, he went inside and, taking a deep breath, turned the corner into the kitchen. Instead of Carolyn, he found Abby putting fruit into a blender.

"What?" she said.

"Have you seen your mother?"

"She said she was going to take a shower. Do you want a smoothie?"

He took his blueberry-peach-strawberry-banana smoothie back to the porch, wondering if putting off the confrontation was merely adding to the pressure, like a boiler building up steam, which would make the eventual blow up that much more powerful.

He rocked, thinking about Carolyn and August, his mother and father, antiques and riches. Already emotionally exhausted, the rocking and the soporific effect of a full stomach lulled him to sleep.

He awoke at 5:17 with a crick in his neck. The sun perched atop the western mountains. He went to the kitchen to start dinner, put a beef tenderloin into the microwave to defrost, and set potatoes to boil. He sautéed broccoli in olive oil, poured in a quarter cup of broth, brought it to a boil, covered and removed the pan from the stove. He transferred the potatoes to the mixer, added half and half, a pinch of garlic salt and half a stick of butter, and ran the mixer until the potatoes were thoroughly mashed. Next, he emptied a jar of gravy into a little pot and set it to warm on the stove. Finally, he broiled the steaks and placed everything on serving plates on the table. Then he called out that dinner was ready.

Jake was the first to arrive. "All right, steak! My favorite! Thanks, Pop." He sat down at the kitchen table to eat. Jeff didn't know what it was about the ranch that made his kids gravitate to the table instead of wandering off to their rooms or the parlor, but it was becoming a habit.

Abby came in, followed shortly by Carolyn, who smiled at him as though nothing untoward had happened. "Thanks for dinner," she said pleasantly. They all sat around the table and Carolyn asked the kids about their day, studiously avoiding addressing Jeff, whose stomach was too much in knots to do more than pick at his food.

Jake left first. Abby lingered over her dinner, sensing the coming argument and wanting to be part of it.

"Don't you have homework to do?" Carolyn asked.

"It's not his fault," Abby said. "He was confused. He didn't even know what day it was. He's doing the best he can."

Carolyn bit her lip and raised her eyebrows, then with a nod she gestured for Abby to leave.

When they were alone, he said, "Okay, go ahead and ask."

"Ask what?"

"Where I was last night."

"Who am I to question you?" she asked with a frosty stare, while carefully keeping her voice free of emotion. "I'm only your wife."

"I was in the wine cellar."

"All night? Sleeping in the wine cellar?" she asked.

"Honest to god, I was in the wine cellar, and someone turned off the light," he said as truthfully as he knew how, before sliding into the real lie. "And I tripped and hit my head, and then it was dark and I couldn't find my way out."

Carolyn chuckled politely. "Your next wife had better be really dumb, because no one with any intelligence could possibly take you seriously." She got up from the table, took her plate to the sink, and coolly added, "Your pillow is on the futon in your mother's office."

It could have gone worse, he thought, hoping that her reference to his "next wife" was merely a rhetorical construct, and wondering if anything was worth losing his wife's respect.

When he'd finished loading the dishwasher he found everyone had gone up to their bedrooms.

He was too emotionally keyed up to concentrate on reading or sorting photographs. Instead he watched a couple of sitcoms, but in his current mood the one-liners fell flat and the laugh tracks depressed him. At 9:00 he turned off the TV, and not relishing a night on the futon, stole through the tunnel. It would be 7:20 on August's side, just about sunset, and he thought he might share a glass of Scotch with him. As a precaution he taped the light switch in the on position and taped a note over it: "LEAVE LIGHT ON."

He found the dining room dark and empty and warm. The last glimmer of twilight gave just enough light to maneuver. Through the open windows he heard a fiddle, gutbucket and guitar playing a rollicking jig that ended in a burst of laughter. From the direction of the sound he could tell they were playing on the porch. They played another instrumental. Jeff sat down at the head of the table where he could hear better. Then he heard the first bars of "Oh! Susanna" struck on the piano, and there was a good bit of shuffling as those on the porch moved inside. The piano was joined by banjo, gutbucket and harmonica. Noah took the solo part and the rest joined in on the chorus. It was a different song than the sanitized version Jeff had been taught in Boy Scouts. When Noah cheerily sang the line, "I jump'd aboard the telegraph and trabbled down de ribber, de lectrie fluid magnified, and kill'd five hundred nigger," Jeff could only cringe.

Noah was still singing as Owen came down the hall with a candle and entered the kitchen. He put down his candlestick and pumped water into a glass. Turning around, he could see Jeff across the hall.

"Mr. Porter! What are you doing sitting in the dark?"

"I didn't want to disturb you all. I was just listening."

"You're welcome to join us."

When the song ended August called, "Who are you talking to?"

"Just Mr. Porter," Owen shouted back.

"Bring him in here."

Jeff followed dutifully, uncomfortable about intruding on their intimacy and unable to think of a graceful way to extricate himself. "Sorry," he said, wincing as he looked at August. "I really ought to be going. I just heard your singing and stopped to listen."

"Come sing with us, Mr. Porter," Lydia begged. "I'm sure you have a fine voice."

"Oh, no, I don't…"

"You must know some songs we don't."

"Oh, yes," Betsy cried, "we're so tired of the same old songs."

Then they all piped up in encouragement, and he felt a blush rise to his cheeks. Though he could carry a tune, he'd always been self-conscious about singing.

"I'm afraid I can never remember all the words," he said. He was sure that the few snippets of songs he remembered from the 1970s and '80s would be incomprehensible to them.

"It doesn't matter," Lydia said. "Just sing us what you can recollect. Anything new would be appreciated."

But what would be appropriate? He knew part of only one Nineteenth Century song, gleaned from a Disney cartoon, and though it probably wouldn't be a hit for another twenty years, he thought they might like it. He sang:

Daisy, Daisy, give me your answer, do!
I'm half crazy, all for the love of you!
It won't be a stylish marriage; I can't afford a carriage.

256

But you'll look sweet upon the seat of a bicycle built for two!

When he finished they all looked at him with blank, quizzical faces.

"Sorry, that's all I can remember."

After a moment of awkward silence Lydia said, "It has a nice tune. Uh...what's a bicycle?"

It hadn't occurred to Jeff that bicycles had yet to be invented.

"Oh, oh!" August cried like a school kid who has the right answer. "I know, I know — it's a two-wheeled vehicle."

Thinking of the two-wheeled horse cart he drove to school, Noah asked, "Like a trap?"

"Well, not exactly," Jeff replied, "but close enough."

Lydia turned to Carrie. "Give us 'Hard Times',"she said.

Carrie stood by her mother, brow furrowed and glistening with sweat. She took a deep breath and as Lydia and Owen began to play she sang in her pure, sweet voice:

Let us pause in life's pleasures and count its many tears,
While we all sup sorrow with the poor.
There's a song that will linger forever in our ears;
Oh hard times come again no more.

Lydia joined her for the chorus:

'Tis the song, the sigh of the weary,
Hard times, hard times, come again no more.
Many days you have lingered around my cabin door;
Oh hard times come again no more.

Carrie's hand went to her side and her voice quavered as she picked up the next plaintive phrase:

While we seek mirth and beauty and music light and gay,

There are frail forms fainting at the door;
Though their voices are silent, their pleading looks will say
Oh hard times come again no more.

Lydia played piano, Owen guitar and Noah harmonica for an instrumental interlude. Then Lydia and Carrie began the chorus together, but Lydia had to finish alone. Carrie stopped midway through, a hitch in her breath and a tear coursing down her cheek. "I'm not feeling well," she said, and turned to make her way upstairs.

"Poor thing," Lydia said.

Noah, watching her go, asked softly, "Do you think it's because that was Ivan's favorite song?"

Lydia shook her head. "It's nothing to do with that. She's a young woman now. It's just female complaints. She'll be all right with a little rest."

Later that night Jeffrey lay awake for a long while listening to the sounds of a sleeping house. Eventually, convinced he would get no sleep on the futon, he got up and crept along the landing in the moonlight to their bedroom door. The door was unlocked. He let himself in and stood silently by the door until, reassured by her rhythmic breathing, he quietly undressed and eased himself into bed. He turned on his side and restrained the impulse to reach out and touch her, wondering if the tables were reversed, would he be as patient with her? If she had stayed out all night, he would have been in a panic, and when she returned he was certain his sense of betrayal and concern would have shown itself in anger. But expressing anger wasn't in her nature. Anger didn't solve anything; it was just a symptom of frustration. He was pretty sure she would forgive him his secrets, especially since he was only trying to protect them. But would she understand that? Had he ever said as much? Had he even apologized? *Oh hell*, he thought, *I've been an ass.*

Chapter 46
Appendicitis

Jeff made a Mexican salsa of diced raw onions, tomatoes, tomatillos, small sweet peppers, salt, lime and one Serrano chili. He sautéed ground beef with onions, chili powder and coriander. He julienned lettuce, grated Monterey Jack, opened a container of sour cream, and set up a taco station on the counter. Finally, he made a bowl of guacamole and opened a bag of taco chips. Then he opened a bottle of well-chilled Mexican beer and called, "Dinner's ready!"

Jake came bopping in a moment later with Buster at his heels. "Oh yeah! Taco-o-o-os!" he crooned.

"No dogs in the kitchen," Jeff reminded him.

Jake rolled his eyes but didn't argue. He put Buster on the back porch with some kibble.

Carolyn joined them a minute later, cool though not hostile. She assembled her tacos and sat at the table with Jake. Jeff made his own and then went to the hallway to call for Abby.

"Don't yell; she's got a headache," Jake warned.

"She's had a lot of headaches lately," Jeff said. "Maybe she needs glasses."

"I don't think she really has a headache," Carolyn commented. "She just wants her privacy."

They devoured their dinner in short order, mouths too full to carry on a conversation. Then Jake filled one paper bowl with salsa and another with chips, and led Buster upstairs.

When they were alone Carolyn said, "I wish you wouldn't spend so much time with Gus. I think he's a bad influence."

"Bad influence?" He could sometimes be annoying — sanctimonious, bigoted, and far too religious to Jeff's way of thinking, but a bad influence? "He has his faults, a bit of a Bible thumper, but he's the most responsible man I've ever known."

"All I know is you're not at your best when you're around him. You're secretive. I know you've lied to me."

There was no point in denying it any longer. "I am sorry, my love. Truly." He reached out to take her hand, but she withdrew it. "I admit I've told a few small, white lies. Or not lies really, but..." He struggled to come up with a suitable explanation for his dissembling, but there was nothing he could say that would excuse the facts.

"I can't even get hold of you when you're with him."

"There's no reception over there."

"What's his phone number?"

"He doesn't have a phone."

"Then tell me his address."

There was a pained look on Jeff's face. "I'm sorry I've had to... to keep certain things from you, but if you'll just accept that it's for your own good..."

"For my own good?" she asked incredulously. "That's what scares me. What do I need to be protected from? And don't you think I'm old enough to determine if it's for my own good?"

"Just give me another month or so. Then everything will be back to normal." That wasn't exactly the truth either, he thought. But he did think that once they'd made a killing with the antiques and Pop was back home, he'd have no reason to go back. He would go maybe once or twice a year for another load of antiques. Though he had to admit he would miss the quiet evenings on August's porch and the easy camaraderie he shared with the Kimball family.

Carolyn took a cup of tea to the parlor and sat down to compare the old edition of *Seeds of Revolution* with the new, revised version that she was obliged to teach this year. None of the changes were substantive, but merely served to generate another edition (and hence more revenue) for the publisher.

"Daddy!" Abby called, rushing down the hall, fear in her voice. She skidded to a halt, glanced into the office and back at the parlor, caught her mother's eye for an instant, then ran back down the hall calling, "Daddy!"

The urgency in Abby's voice put Carolyn instantly on the alert, though the fact that she had rushed off looking for her father was an indication that it was not something she wanted to share with her mother. She had probably seen a mouse or a rat. Only then did it dimly register in Carolyn's mind that Abby had not come from upstairs, where she'd ostensibly been lying down with a headache. Carolyn set down her book. There was hurried talk in the dining room, none of which she could make out, then she saw Abby and Jeff hurry cross the hall to the kitchen. She got up and walked down the hall. The kitchen was empty. She opened the back door and stared into the moonlit night toward the barn, listening intently. The wind soughed through the big oak, and there was a faint hum of distant traffic.

Carolyn was puzzling over their sudden disappearance when she heard a commotion at her back, at first muffled, then louder.

"Move the goddamn shelves; I can't get through!" There was a scraping sound and a jumble of raised voices.

She moved closer to the kitchen table and could make out August's voice raised above the others, a note of panic in his commands. "Damn you, woman, go back! Do as I say!"

A woman's voice, sharp with alarm: "She's my daughter, too!"

"Now!" — his voice fairly growling with anger.

"Mama," a young man's voice pleaded. "Come on."

August again: "Owen, make sure she.... Take her back. Upstairs! I don't have time to argue. Keep everyone out of the cellar!"

Then Jeff's voice, in that calm, ordered tone he adopted in a crisis: "Abby, call up to me when they're through, and I'll turn off the light." There followed deep grunting as of enormous physical effort, and heavy steps on the stairway. Then August burst through the root cellar door, red-faced, wide-eyed and panting, with a girl in his arms.

Carolyn quickly pulled a chair out from the table and August sat, cradling the girl against his chest. "My daughter," August said. "She's not well." That was plain to see. The girl, young woman really, was pale and glistening with sweat, panting in quick shallow breaths.

"Now!" Abby called. Jeff switched off the light and held the door open for her. A moment later Abby bounded into the room, her sleeveless blouse and tight jeans drawing a sharp contrast to Carrie's green gingham dress.

Jeff said, "I'll get the car and bring it to the back door." He rushed off, the screen door slamming behind him.

Carolyn stood looking at August, his daughter and Abby, waiting for an explanation. "Could someone please tell me what the hell is going on?"

"I think Carrie has appendicitis," Abby said.

"Is your family living in our root cellar?"

"Sorry ma'am," August replied, "I dasn't say."

Jeff returned and helped August carry his daughter to the car. He put them in the back seat of the Subaru. Abby took the front passenger seat. Jeff turned to Carolyn. "I don't know when we'll be back."

"Oh no you don't!" Carolyn yelled, and before he could strap himself in she had opened the back door and jumped in beside August. She sat quietly, observing. Now there was plenty of time for explanations, and she finally had a captive audience.

"How long have you been living in our cellar?"

August didn't answer, deferring to Jeff, who looked to his daughter, who said, "Don't look at me."

"How long have you known?" Jeff asked Abby.

"Me? Three weeks. I followed you one day."

"Has anyone else seen you?"

"I don't think so. Just Carrie. We've been meeting when we can, but it's not easy; it's a big family."

"Tell me about it. Has she been on our side?"

"Once. She was supposed to come last Sunday (their Sunday, I mean), and when she didn't come I went downstairs to look for her, and that's when I turned on the light and you showed up."

They were on 101 now, speeding north. Carrie leaned against her father, eyes closed. At one point she raised her head, looked bleary eyed at the passing lights and groaned, "I'm scared."

"Nothing to be scared of," August assured her. "Jeff knows what he's doing."

They pulled into the emergency room entrance. Abby and August each took an arm and helped Carrie stagger through the door

.

Jeff hopped back in the car and pulled forward into one of the spaces marked for emergency room visitors.

"Are you going to tell me what's been going on?" Carolyn asked.

"This isn't the time or place. I have to talk with Gus first."

"So you can get your stories straight?"

"There are decisions that have to be made that concern the safety of his family, as well as our own. I promise you will know all you need to know by this time tomorrow."

The waiting room where patients were admitted was sealed off from the emergency room by a locked door. The receptionist sat behind a thick plexiglass window with a louvered hole that allowed communication. The Kimballs had already been ushered into the emergency room. Abby had taken a seat in the waiting room. "We came in with the Kimballs," Jeff said.

"Only one family member at a time can accompany the patient," the receptionist said with curt finality.

"You'll need me. My friend won't be able to fill out the forms."

"Please sit down, sir."

"He won't understand the half of it. He doesn't have a social security number, phone number or address."

"Is he developmentally disabled?"

"He's Amish. He's staying with me and he doesn't have any money. I'll have to guarantee payment."

Money was the magic word. "Step to the door on your left," the receptionist said.

"Amish?" Carolyn asked. "You didn't tell me he was Amish."

The receptionist buzzed him in.

Alone with Abby in the waiting room, Carolyn asked, "What do you know about all of this?"

Abby leaned forward so that her strawberry blond hair hid her face. "This is between you and Dad. It's not something I can discuss," she said, sounding far more mature than her fifteen years. "But you should know he was only trying to protect us."

"Um humm," Carolyn said appraisingly. "Well, that's nice to know."

At Carrie's bedside, Dr. Quackenbush said, "Assuming there're no complications, an appendectomy is a simple operation, nothing to worry about."

"Oh god," August pleaded, "can you give her some whiskey for the pain?"

The physician raised an eyebrow, clearly wondering what kind of crackpot he was dealing with.

"He's Amish," Jeff offered.

The doctor relaxed and smiled comfortingly. "Oh, well, we have something better than whiskey. We'll put her to sleep; she won't feel a thing. I'll go see if the operating room is ready."

When he was out of earshot August whispered, "Why do you keep saying I'm Amish? I may be from Pennsylvania, but I'm no Mennonite."

"The Amish don't believe in modern ways, so when you seem like a duck out of water, it's an easy way to explain your ignorance."

"You're calling me ignorant?"

"Don't get your hackles up."

"No more ignorant than you — I doubt you could harness a team of horses, let alone butcher a pig."

Carrie groaned and grabbed the handrail of the gurney with white knuckles.

"Not much longer," August said, taking her hands in his. "The doctors will take good care of you."

An hour later in the surgical waiting room, Carolyn stopped her pacing and said, "We forgot all about Jake." She turned to Abby. "Can I borrow your phone?"

"Didn't bring it."

Jeff held out his. "You should always remember to carry your phone," he said with a snigger.

Jake picked up after five rings. "Yup?"

"We're at the hospital with Mr. Kimball. His daughter is sick. I just didn't want you to be worried."

"Okay."

"You weren't worried, were you?"

She could almost feel the shake of his head over the phone. "I didn't even know you were gone; I was playing video games and had my headphones on. Good thing I had my phone on vibrate."

"I don't know when we'll get back. Are you all right all alone there?"

"I've got Buster for company."

"Okay, then. You call us if you need anything."

"Okay, Mom. No problemo," he said, and before she could wish him sweet dreams, he hung up.

It was past midnight by the time Carrie was out of post-op. The operation had gone well, with no complications, though as an extra precaution she was being kept in the I.C.U. for observation overnight.

They drove back in silence, pulling to a stop by the back porch at 1:47 a.m., thoroughly exhausted and Carolyn still in the dark.

PART FOUR

Something Found

Chapter 47
Letting the Cat Out of the Bag

Tues, Sept 13, 1870 — Th, Oct 8, 2009

The sun was already up when Jeff awoke to a light knock. Carolyn stopped snoring and rolled onto her side. He slid into his robe and answered the door.

It was Jake. Jeff put a finger to his lips, stepped into the hall and closed the door behind him.

"Sorry to wake you up," Jake said. "I just figured you'd want to know I was heading off to school. Is Mr. Kimball's daughter okay?"

"She had an appendectomy, but she's fine. We're all staying home; none of us got much sleep. You need anything before you leave?"

"Lunch money."

Jeff returned to the bedroom and came back with some bills. Then he saw Jake out the front door and watched him ride his bike down the slope and across the bridge. It was a bright day under a mackerel sky.

He went to the kitchen and started the coffee pot and went upstairs to dress, too awake now to go back to sleep. He carried his clothes into the office, so as not to wake Carolyn, dressed and was about to go out for a walk, but paused long enough to scribble a short note that he'd be out for an hour. Then he pocketed his phone and went out the kitchen door.

He walked south past the barn and the apricot orchard, and down a slight slope to Arroyo Gonsalves where it trickled into Arroyo Calero. Arroyo Calero, periodically fed by the Calero Reservoir, flowed throughout the year, and in another month both streams would be flowing full freshet from the first of the autumn storms. He hopped Arroyo Calero at a narrow, and scrambled up to the dirt road. He walked for five minutes, then turned around and stopped, taking in the valley and the distant edge of the housing development, and remembered the valley as it had been in his youth, not so unlike August's time, and felt a sense of (if not destiny) inevitability. Connection. He began to understand what August meant when speaking about his god's plan. What Jeff felt was something like a religious revelation, an understanding of where he stood in time, and a surrendering to the inevitable flow of events that would take him where it would, as a stream bore flotsam toward the sea. He might swim against the current for a time, but eventually he would be borne downstream. He wondered whether souls — for despite not believing in any conventional conception of the creative force, he did believe in that individual expression of creation known as the soul — he wondered whether souls flowed toward the source of creation as streams flowed into the ocean, which fed the clouds, whose rains filled the streams, *ad infinitum*. Was that a Hindu or Buddhist concept?

When he strode into the Kimballs' kitchen Lydia screamed and dropped a plate, which shattered on the hardwood floor.

"Oh! Oh! Lord, you gave me a fright!"

"I'm sorry. Is Gus up yet?"

Lydia clenched the edge of her apron. "Where have you taken my daughter?"

"We took her to a doctor — a better doctor than you have around here."

"I seen that...that..." Her eyes darted toward the dining room. "I seen that jeweled tunnel," she said in a shaky voice.

"Not to worry. All will be explained in time, my dear. Is Gus up yet?" he asked a second time.

"He's in the privy out back."

Betsy and Emily came in with a basket of eggs, saw Jeff and froze. Betsy took a belligerent tone, demanding, "Where's my sister?"

"Betsy!" Lydia responded reflexively, "Is that any way to speak to your elders?"

Jeff smiled, tousled Emily's hair, brushed past Betsy, and held the door open for Noah, who was coming in with a pail of milk. Outside he took a deep breath of morning dew edged with earthy whiffs of manure and the sweet-sour scent of rotting fruit.

The door to the privy slammed shut as August came out, cinching his belt. He looked like he hadn't slept a wink. As soon as he saw Jeff he threw up his hands and said, "What are we going to do?"

"Let's take a walk," Jeff said, and they did.

When they returned half an hour later, the family was gathered at the dining room table around a breakfast of bacon, biscuits with honey and butter, milk and eggs. Conversation ceased abruptly. The Kimballs looked to Jeff in anticipation and wariness. Little Emily glared and shouted, "We want Carrie!"

Jeff smiled benignly back and turned to August. "How much time do you need?"

"Ten minutes."

"I'll be back soon."

August sat at the head of the table, laced his fingers together and stared solemnly at each of his children and at Lydia. "Carrie is in good hands," he began. "She is in God's hands." There was a collective gasp, Lydia cried "Oh, no!" and he quickly corrected himself. "No, no, I don't mean to say she's died. But she is in God's hands. You may be wondering, some of you, what you saw yesterday in the root cellar. You'll recall last spring, when we had an intruder and I hit my head. I said then we'd built our house over the gateway to hell."

"Lord God," Owen said, dropping his coffee cup onto the table.

"Lordy, Lord, Lord," Lydia cried.

Betsy squirmed and bit her knuckle.

Emily looked to Betsy and began to whimper.

Noah stared dumbfounded, and Charles grinned with expectation, as though he had just been promised a bag of candy.

"Well, I was wrong. It's not the gateway to hell; it's more complicated than that. The Lord has chosen us, among all the people on earth. He has sent his messenger to show us the way, and that messenger is Mr. Porter. You may have noticed he's a little different. In fact, he is not of this world." There was another collective gasp. "In this year of our Lord, 18 hundred and 70, he has not even been born. He has been sent here to point us toward the future. And the message he brings," August began, raising his voice to full stentorian roar, "SHALL BE OBEYED!" He slammed a hand flat on the table in punctuation, making the plates and flatware jump. "The Lord has spoken, and He says no one...I say, NO ONE..." and here he paused to glare at the youngsters menacingly, "...no one — *under the age of sixteen* — may enter that cellar. You remember..." he hissed, swiveling his head from child to child, eyes wide, doing his best to inspire fear, "...what happened to Lot's wife? Turned to a pillar of salt she was! This is the Lord's command, and NO ONE SHALL BREAK IT without bringing the wrath of God down upon this house!" He stood up abruptly, knocking over his chair and growling, "DO YOU UNDERSTAND ME? Say you understand, for all our sakes. Our very lives depend upon it!" Emily and Charles were crying. Noah and Betsy trembled as much with the fear of their bug-eyed father as with the promised wrath of God. Owen sat stunned to silence. "And the Lord has told me that no one is to breathe a word of this outside of this house. For if anyone beyond our house finds out, we shall all surely perish. YOU – MAY- TELL- NO - ONE! Not your best friend. Not Reverend Winters. NO ONE! Do you understand?"

They all muttered, "Yes, Papa."

After a moment's silence Charles raised his hand.

"Yes, Charles?"

"Is it a bad place where he comes from, like Sodom and Gomorrah?"

"It's a strange place of fearsome violence, the whole world at war. It's a place of many dangers. But it's also a place of many wonders, things you can't even imagine. It's a place of great abundance and temptation, and a place where everything you think you know is turned on its head — I've seen women wearing pants, and girls with purple hair. It's a place where people fly through the sky, and where you can have a conversation with someone a thousand miles away as easy as they was sittin' across the table. I can't tell if it's the End of Days, or the Beginning of something new and wonderful. It can be a frightening place, if you're not strong in spirit. It's not a place for children, and that is why you must wait until your sixteenth birthday to be allowed entrance. And when that happens, I will be there to guide you." Here he paused to right his chair. "Owen, there's a lock and hasp in the workbench in the barn. We'll place it high on the outside of the wine cellar door. And we'll put a hook and eyebolt on the inside of the door." He glared at the youngsters and finished, "To discourage the curious."

Carolyn and Abby were both awake and sitting quietly at the kitchen table when Jeff emerged from the root cellar. Carolyn wore a bright orange, v-neck blouse and blue jeans. Abby wore a light blue sweater with the sleeves pushed up to her elbows, and black peg-leg jeans. Carolyn put down her coffee. "Taking care of our guests?" she asked sarcastically, resting her tired cheek in the palm of her hand and cocking her head at him. "When were you going to get around to telling me?"

"Well, I was hoping I'd never have to tell you. The more people who know, the more dangerous it is."

"Dangerous for whom?" Carolyn asked.

"Abby, you haven't told anyone, have you?"

"What, and have everyone think I'd gone insane? No way. Besides, I got to thinking about what the military might do."

"That's what I was worried about. I still don't want Jake to know. Not 'till he's older."

"What the hell are you talking about?" Carolyn asked, looking from one to the other. "What has the military got to do with it?"

Jeff looked to Abby. "You want to help me out here?"

"It's not what you think, Mom."

"And what is it you think I think?"

"You think the Kimballs are living in our basement."

"And you're saying they're not?"

"Right."

"And how do you explain last night? I heard what I heard. It's obvious why the wine cellar is sealed shut."

Abby threw back her head and stared at the ceiling, gathering her thoughts. "Daddy?"

"No, I think it's better she hear this from you."

Abby took a deep breath and let it out with a whoosh. "It's like the dead have come back to life. I mean, they're all dead, long dead, but they aren't really. They're here, now."

"Oh, come now, you're being ridiculous. Are we talking about zombies?" Carolyn laughed, incredulous.

"It's more like another dimension."

"Oh, now it's like Twilight Zone, or Star Trek. Sure." Carolyn waited impatiently for the punch line, but none was forthcoming. "Okay now, what's really going on?"

Abby looked to her father. "I think it's easier if we just show her."

Jeff nodded. "Okay."

"Mom, I think you should go to the bathroom first."

"I don't need to go."

"Then don't blame me if you wet your pants. I did."

Abby led the way, holding her mother's hand.

As they mounted the wine cellar stairs Carolyn reminded her daughter, "The door is sealed."

"No, it's not. And it doesn't lead to where you think it leads."

Now Carolyn stopped and pulled back. "You're scaring me."

"It's nothing to be frightened of," Jeff said. "As a matter of fact, it's a History teacher's dream. Remember, open eyes, open mind." With Abby pulling and Jeff gently nudging from behind, they mounted the stairs.

Chapter 48
Introductions

Tues, Sept 13, 1870 — Th, Oct 8, 2009

After instilling the fear of God into his children, August said, "Noah, I'm putting you in charge of your brother and sisters. You can finish eating outside. Then I want you all to harvest the potatoes behind the barn. Out with you now; I want to talk to Owen and your Ma alone." When the back door had closed he cleared this throat and laid his hands flat on the dining room table. "I may have embellished the situation a little bit," he said, "but I didn't exaggerate the danger." He quickly explained, in the simplest terms possible, the appearance of the tunnel, where it led, and the threat it posed. "The danger is real enough," he concluded, "but so are the benefits. It may be a good thing, if we don't abuse it. The future is full of miracles. I know for a fact that Carrie would've died last night if we hadn't taken her to the other side. We should count our blessings."

At that moment Carolyn stepped into the dining room staring into the faces of the three eldest Kimballs. August, a familiar face, stepped forward. "Mrs. Porter, I'd like to introduce you to my wife, Lydia, and our eldest son, Owen."

It wasn't until she'd shaken their hands that she saw the room out of the corner of her eye. Her eyes darted back and forth; she gave a shriek, and clapped a hand to her mouth.

"No, no," Carolyn said, eyes and head swiveling this way and that, she rushed across to the kitchen and stopped dead in her tracks. "Holy crap!" Carolyn blurted.

Jeff caught her as her knees began to buckle.

"Oh, dear," Lydia said.

Eyes wide and fully alert Carolyn lurched toward to the counter, looked out the window, and shrieked again. Then hyperventilating, her heart beating like a hummingbird, she saw white dots dance before her eyes as though she were swimming in a pool of Alka Seltzer. She held onto the counter and bent her head low. "Shit, shit, oh god, oh god," she whimpered, shaking all over. Jeff rubbed her back.

"It's okay, Mom," Abby said.

Owen pumped a glass of water and handed it to her. She took a long drink and muttered a "Thank you."

August stepped forward. "Well, I don't know quite what to say. I guess I should just say welcome to 1870."

"They really are wearing pants," Lydia said, more as an observation than a judgment. "Do all women wear pants in...wherever you're from?" She turned to August. "What's the name of the place they're from?"

"It's not a place," Abby said; "it's a time. We live here in 2009."

"And the answer to your first question is mostly," Carolyn said. "You can wear whatever you want. Some women wear dresses."

"Awful short dresses," August put in. "I seen'm."

Carolyn took a deep breath and gulped more water.

Owen caught Abby's eye and extended his hand. "I'm Owen," he said, blushing.

"I know. I've watched you all from the attic windows. Carrie and I."

"Can we go to her?" Lydia asked, looking first to August, then to Jeff and Carolyn.

"In a little while," Jeff said. "Maybe Carolyn can drive you."

"He don't mean in a carriage, neither," August added. "You're gonna ride in a car — that's a horseless carriage."

Carolyn took a deep breath and stood up, clinging to Jeff. "Are you really Amish?" she asked Lydia.

"Amish?" She turned to August. "What's Amish?"

"It's a Mennonite sect, dear," he said and addressing Carolyn said, "No, ma'am, we ain't. That's just something your husband says to explain why we don't know what everybody thinks we ought. Same as I might call him a city slicker to explain why he can't harness a team o' horses."

"Did you know our Carrie is really a Carolyn?" Lydia said. "We just never call her by her given name."

"Lyddy, why don't you show Mrs. Porter around?"

"Why, don't she know the house she lives in?"

"It's a little different on their side."

They all followed as Lydia led Carolyn around the ground floor.

Carolyn pointed out where the half-bath and laundry room had been added. "It's really not that different. I wish we had some of this furniture; you can't get carved wood like this anymore."

Jeff whispered to August, "This is going better than I expected. Lydia seems to be taking it all in stride."

"Well now, that's the advantage of reading the Bible. Every day she has her head in that book, and it's chock full of miracles. It's not such a stretch."

Carolyn said, "Gus, didn't you say you had other children?"

"Yes ma'am, we have two boys and two girls out picking potatoes behind the barn," August said. "You'll meet them later, but don't tell them anything about...about where you're from. They don't need to know details. Not 'till they're older."

"Speaking of which," Jeff said, "what did you tell them?"

"They only know there's a gateway to a strange and dangerous place that they're forbidden to enter before their sixteenth birthdays. I've made it plain they're not to tell a soul."

"You struck the fear of God in'm," Lydia said with a wink.

"Fear will keep them quiet for now," August said, "and by the time they turn sixteen they ought to be mature enough to appreciate the danger."

"I'm only fifteen," Abby said, "and *I* understand perfectly. I mean, can you imagine what would happen if the CIA found out?"

"What's the CIA?" August asked.

Jeff momentarily thought of telling him *The Culinary Institute of America*, but kept his wit to himself and said, "Central Intelligence

Agency. It's a secret branch of government. They have a reputation for eliminating anyone and anything that poses a threat to the country. And anything capable of manipulating time would be at the top of their list."

"What are we going to do about Jake?" Abby asked. "I mean, I love my brother, but he *is* only *twelve*."

"Put the fear of God into him," Lydia said.

"It wouldn't work," Abby said, "we're not religious."

Lydia looked gobsmacked. "Not...you're...you don't...?"

"No, we don't," Carolyn confirmed.

Jeff was proud of her for not sugar coating the message, professing agnosticism, when in truth there was little in the Bible, Koran or Bahagavad Gita that made any sense to either of them, save the admonition common to all ethical philosophies to 'Do unto others as you would have them do unto you."

Lydia looked to August. "I thought you said they was messengers from God."

"Well, I might have exaggerated that part."

"You might...well...I...humph!"

"I wonder if Jake will even notice," Carolyn said. "Gus has been coming and going for months and *I* didn't notice. None of us did, except you, Abby."

"I wouldn't've known," Abby said, "if I hadn't gone downstairs and heard Dad talking to Mr. Kimball in the tunnel, and I followed. Freaked me out."

"If it's just the six of us..." Carolyn began.

"Seven," Jeff corrected. "You forgot about Carrie."

"Seven then. If it's just the seven of us, and we're discreet, who's to know? We'll just have to be careful around Jake."

"Can you take me to Carrie now?" Lydia asked timidly.

"Let's all go," Jeff said.

Lydia was only too happy to get out of the car when they returned three hours later. "I don't as how I'm ready for these new fangled machines," she said, eyeing the Honda Civic with disapproval. "A body could get killed agoin' that fast."

Chapter 49
Loading the Vault

Wed Sept 14, 1870 — Fri Oct 9, 2009

The first gold rays of morning were painting the leaves of the laurel, when the squawk of a Steller's jay stirred Jeffrey toward consciousness. He was in that half-dream state, where reality swims in and out of view, and he was aware of the weight of his limbs and the rhythm of his breathing. He wasn't yet ready to think. Carolyn scooted her back toward him until they touched. He rolled on his side and spooned her and was soon dreaming again. He was walking through a tube as long as a basketball court toward a sunlit space at the far end, where he saw the silhouette of a man who seemed to be waiting for him.

Carolyn sneezed, resettled herself on her back, and draped an arm over him.

"Are you awake?" he asked.

"I am now. I hope you're not looking for a kiss; I have morning mouth."

"A kiss isn't necessary. Are you going to work?"

"No, I called in sick last night. I need time to think." She lay there for a half minute staring at the ceiling. "I hope this doesn't sound crazy, but is there a time portal under our house, or was all that just a dream?"

"It wasn't a dream."

"I'm worried."

"About what?"

"About keeping people from finding out about you-know-what."

"If worse comes to worst we'll just snip the wires."

"What wires?"

"The wires from the light switch to the tunnel. If you left the light off and went through with a flashlight, you'd end up in *our* wine cellar, not the Kimballs', because the path through the geode only exists in our time. There's something about the wires to the dome light that makes it manifest in the Kimballs' time. When the light's off, there's no opening on their side. That's how Pop got caught on the other side, and why I was trapped overnight on Monday — someone turned off the light."

"*I* turned off the light. I didn't know."

"I didn't know, myself, until last Sunday. All these months we couldn't figure out why sometimes August found it open and sometimes he found solid rock."

"You should have told me."

"I thought the fewer people who knew, the better. But Carrie's appendicitis sort of blew the doors off the secret. We couldn't just let her die, could we?"

"No, of course not. But you should have trusted me."

Jeff opened his mouth to defend himself, but thought better of it. "You're right, I should have."

"I take it you haven't found your father?"

"We think we know where he is. I might be able to find him, but it would take more than a day, and I couldn't be away that long without freaking you out, so that hasn't been an option."

"Well, now that the cat's out of the bag, go find him!"

"I'll go as soon as we take care of some unfinished business. I don't know how Pop will react to us being here, to Mom being gone. We might have to move. I'd like to put some money in the bank, just in case."

"On the bright side," she said, "I'm beginning to see the potential in antiques."

They were still in their robes when they saw Jake and Abby off to school.

"He doesn't suspect, does he?" Carolyn asked.

"He hasn't a clue."

"I want to go back. I know it might be better if we limited contact, but I just have to see it again, to prove to myself it's real."

"Of course, and I don't think there's any point in limiting contact. The Kimballs all know."

"Will they keep quiet?"

"They are (as Gus has pointed out) a 'God-fearing' family. So my best guess is yes, they'll keep quiet or face eternal damnation."

"That won't work with Jake. But if we all start tramping back and forth, he'll figure it out."

"You think so? I think he's like most kids. You go down to the cellar, you come back up. The neighbor comes; the neighbor goes. Kids don't really pay attention to what's going on in the adult world." Jeff looked down at Buster lying on the rug. "Isn't that right, Buster?" The dog looked up with sad eyes and thumped the floor listlessly with his tail. "If he's not playing video games, or with Buster here, he's off to Ted's house."

"I suppose."

"Let's take a shower. Then I'll call the hospital to check on Carrie, and we'll pay a visit to the Kimballs."

The door at the top of the Kimballs' stairs was locked. A pinned note read, "Pull string for bell." He did, and heard a tinkling on the other side of the door, then the sound of a chair being dragged, a lock being sprung, and Lydia opened the door. Her lips turned up in a small, strained smile as she stepped aside to let them in. They passed through the dining room and crossed the hall to the kitchen, where Betsy and Emily stood furtively by the stove, eyeing them both with

279

trepidation that Jeff attributed to their new status as Messengers from God.

"Girls," he said brightly, "you haven't met my wife. Carolyn, this is Betsy and Emily."

Carolyn crossed the room and held out her hand. "Pleased to meet you," she said. Betsy took the proffered hand, but Emily stuck one thumb in her mouth and grabbed hold of Betsy's blue gingham dress.

Jeff turned to Lydia. "The doctor said Carrie can come home the day after tomorrow."

"Oh, that's such a relief! Can I see her today?"

"I took the day off," Carolyn said. "I'll drive you."

Carolyn was too discreet to ask Lydia's age, but she could extrapolate from Owen's age, which put Lydia at about her own age of forty, give or take a year. But there the similarities ended. Carolyn was trim, fit, energetic and well educated. Lydia's education had ended at fourteen, and eight pregnancies, the death of two children (three if you counted a miscarriage) and a lifetime of physical labor had left their mark on her careworn face.

Running a household with a boatload of children was no task for the fainthearted. Nonetheless, Lydia felt overwhelmed by the pace of the future. With Carrie's crisis, there had been no time to ease her into it. The lights, the speed, the gadgetry, and the gender bending mores confounded her. She found herself uncharacteristically timid in Carolyn's presence. On their drive to the hospital, she took furtive glances at the pants, shoulder length hair, sunglasses, bared arms and ankles, and the assertive way Carolyn maneuvered the car through traffic, and felt they had little in common.

Then Carolyn broke the ice by saying, "Tell me about your children."

By the time they were on the way back they'd found a mutual bond.

"I think your Carrie must be a good influence on Abby. She was getting to be such a pill, and then the last few weeks…"

"Pill?"

"I mean she'd become difficult, rebellious."

"Well now, I can't say as Carrie has ever give me a speck of trouble. She's my sweet one. Now, Betsy, on the other hand, has her moods. And Jake? Is he difficult?"

"No, he's easy. Our only real problem with Jake is getting him motivated to do his schoolwork. He's an enthusiastic kid, but not very focused."

"It's just the two, then?"

"Just two."

"Well, you still have time."

"But we don't plan to have any more."

Lydia's mouth lifted in a wry smile and she blushed as she said, "It's not something you plan for; a man has his needs, after all."

"Well, actually, we *can* plan in our time. There's a pill to prevent pregnancy."

Lydia looked askance, blinked and shook her head in disbelief. She was quiet for a full minute before saying, "I can't imagine. It's hard, sometimes, but I count each one of them as such a blessing."

Carolyn checked her rearview mirror and side mirror and changed lanes. As her eyes slid off the side mirror she saw tears streaming down Lydia's cheeks. She remembered Jeff saying they had lost two children. 'Just two,' she'd said. Eyes discreetly trained on the road ahead, Carolyn counted her own blessings.

While Carolyn drove Lydia to the hospital, Jeff and Gus set about loading the vault. It was just a broom-closet sized recess in the wall opposite the geode, three feet wide, six feet high and two feet deep, with two shelves that were stocked with bottles of wine made by Almaden and Mirassou, from the Kimball's own vineyards. August and Owen and Jeff moved the bottles to other bins in the corner.

Owen had purchased as many postage stamps as the postmaster in Pulgas would allow. There were four sheets of one-cent stamps with a violet profile of Benjamin Franklin, two sheets of green Washington three-cent stamps, and two sheets of six-cent stamps with a carmine red profile of Lincoln. Altogether they represented 800 stamps worth over $700,000 at current market value. Jeff reasoned they would have to be careful how the stamps entered the marketplace, for flooding the market would surely make them less attractive to collectors. He slid the sheets into the front cover of *Innocents Abroad*. He laid the book flat on the lower shelf, topped by *The Celebrated Jumping Frog*, and next to *Good Wives* and the three volumes of *Emma*. He placed the sheet music and the July twenty-first, 1870 newspaper on top of the books, and covered them all with a supple cloak of tanned buckskin. They placed the four Colt revolvers in their display cases on the upper shelf, and covered the boxes with a sheet of canvas.

"I hope that's enough protection," Jeff said. "Too much or too little humidity could cause a lot of damage over that much time."

August stepped back and assessed the meager selection in the dim light of the lantern. "It don't look like much," he said.

"Any suggestions, short of robbing a bank?"

"You say folks'll pay for most anything that's old?"

"To a point."

August considered thoughtfully. "Owen, whyn't you go up to the attic. Bring down that old mantle clock, the one that runs fast. And those two paintings, the ones that used to hang in the dining room." He turned to Jeff. "What about old newspapers? I saved a couple from the end of the war, and another when President Lincoln was shot."

Jeff straightened up and appraised his companion. "You've been holding out on me."

"I didn't want to excite your greed."

An hour later August deemed it a proper treasure. On the floor under the shelves he'd added the historic newspapers, two silver candlesticks, a flintlock musket, *Uncle Tom's Cabin*, *The Marble Faun*, *The Gorilla Hunters*, *Five Weeks in a Balloon*, and *Little Dorrit*, two paintings of San Francisco by George Henry Burgess, some costume jewelry and $150 in circulated coins, including three gold pieces.

"Will that be enough to buy a car?" he asked Jeff hopefully.

"A whole fleet of cars."

"What about one of them airplanes like we flew in?"

"What was it you said about greed?"

"Well, I've been thinking about that. If God doesn't want us to profit from this, he'll just cause this vault to cave in, and that'll be the end of it."

"That's a logical assumption," Jeff muttered, "if you believe in divine intervention."

"And if we're meant to learn a lesson in the folly of giving in to Temptation, I guess we'll learn that too."

"It might be easier if God just came out and told you straight away."

August shot him a withering glare. "He don't work that way."

"How *does* he work?"

"In mysterious ways."

"Now that's the first right thing you've said."

The remainder of the afternoon was spent concealing the vault behind a wall of adobe bricks. When they had finished, Jeff turned off the light switch in the root cellar and turned on his flashlight. Then he passed through to his own wine cellar, where plastered walls gave no indication that the vault had ever been breached.

The next morning Jeff called Christie's and Sotheby's, explained that he'd found a cache of antiques, and arranged for an appraisal the following week.

Chapter 50
Smoke

Th Sept 15, 1870 — Sat Oct 10, 2009

Saturday morning, Carolyn arose with a charged sense of anticipation. She showered and ate breakfast while the house slept. At 8:30 Jake took a bowl of cereal into the parlor to watch cartoons. At precisely 9:00 a.m. she rang the bell at the top of the wine cellar stairs. "Coming!" Lydia called. Carolyn waited as she heard a chair being dragged across the floor, a key rattling the lock, the lock springing open.

"This is such a nuisance," Lydia complained. "Gus wanted the lock out of the children's reach, but nobody asked me if *I* could reach it."

She was, Carolyn noted, barely more than five feet tall. "Are you busy?" she asked, observing the open windows and the heat emanating from the wood-burning oven.

"Well, I um...," Lydia said, glancing toward the kitchen. "I was just cleaning up after breakfast. The girls are churning butter. The boys are workin'. I was just fixin' to start work on the midday meal. You can help if you want. I'm planning on shepherd's pie, corn on the cob, tomatoes, spinach, bread and cornbread, brains and apple cobbler. Then this afternoon we'll gather up the wash (Tuesday is our usual laundry day, but what with Carrie and all the excitement Monday night, we just didn't get it done this week)."

"Did you say 'brains'?"

"Pickled calf brains. Would you care for some?"

Carolyn grimaced. "Not my favorite. When do you have to have lunch ready?"

Lydia glanced at the clock on the mantle and said, "It's 7:30. We try to eat around noon, so we have about four and half hours."

"Let's hurry and clean up then," Carolyn said, and added with an air of mischief, "We're going to have some fun today."

By the time noon rolled around, Lydia had had her first hot shower; the laundry was washed, dried and folded; and a quick trip to the supermarket saw the center of the dining room table turned into a cornucopia of deep-fried chicken tenders, buffalo wings, chicken-apple sausage, French fries, macaroni and cheese, Caesar salad, fresh pineapple, seedless grapes, and pitchers of iced tea and chilled orange juice.

Carolyn slipped away and went back home. She found Abby sitting on the parlor floor bent over three coffee table books: *American Album, The West,* and *American Century.* Abby looked up when her mother walked in and said, "I always wondered why you taught History; it seemed so boring. All these people in black-and-white photographs were so…historical."

"They *are* historical."

"I know, but I mean they didn't seem real, somehow."

"What I try to get through to my students is that the way we live and think now didn't just spring from nothing. Our society is an evolution from what came before."

"Men had it a lot easier than women back then. Women couldn't even vote."

"No, that's true, but women didn't have to fight wars. Speaking of men, do you know where your brother is?"

"He and Buster went off to Ted's."

"Would you like to lunch on the other side?"

She did. Jeff, who had been quietly listening from the office where he'd been writing more copy for *Vineyard Seasons,* asked if he was invited.

The three Porters, along with Betsy and Emily, had all gathered in the dining room when Lydia went out to the back porch and rang the triangle that hung from the eves. August, Owen, Noah and Charles all stopped by the water trough to wash up before coming inside. Lydia was beaming. "Mrs. Porter has brought us a feast!"

The atmosphere was convivial and the food was consumed with gusto. Nothing went to waste.

Owen was the first to get up. "I better get back to work. You coming, Noah?"

"I'm comin', too," Charles cried, as though work was his favorite pastime. He grabbed another chicken tender and followed his brothers outside.

A moment later Owen came back in. "Pa, I think you better come out here."

At that the whole table arose and went into the yard. Owen was pointing to the west where a plume of white smoke rose off the valley floor. Orange flames licked out of the smoke at the base of the column.

"Looks like the Watson place," August said. "We better go see if we can lend a hand."

After some discussion as to who would go and who would stay home, August, Owen, Noah and Jeff all mounted and rode off to the northwest, leaving the women and a protesting Charles behind.

By the time they arrived half an hour later, the Watsons' barn was a pile of crackling embers. The heat was intense and the air alive with sparks. Herbert Watson and two of his sons were on the roof of their house, pouring buckets of water onto the wooden shingles. Two more were using pots to douse sparks on outbuildings. Mrs. Watson was leaning out the dormer window to take in empty buckets. Francis Pinault was pumping water, while his two sons, the Watsons' daughter-in-law and the two Watson girls still living at home, formed a loose bucket brigade from yard to roof. Other neighbors were conspicuously absent. There were eleven ranches in the vicinity, and only two were represented at the calamity. The three Kimballs and Jeff all tied up their horses and helped lug water.

It was nearly an hour later when the sparks abated and Herbert climbed in the window.

"I think we got it under control," Herbert said to August, "but I could sure use your help. I managed to let the animals out of the barn, but they all ran off south. If you could just bring back a couple of horses, then my boys can ride out and find the rest." No sooner had he uttered these words than a troubled look of realization wrinkled his brow. "Damn it! The tack room went up with the rest of the barn; I don't have any bridles. For that matter, most of the feed went up with the barn. What'll I feed the animals?"

"Let's go talk to Francis."

Thoroughly exhausted after pumping water for an hour and a half, Francis Pinault sat on the edge of the water trough by the pump, flanked by his two sons. His suspenders hung down to the ground and his sweat soaked undershirt clung to his body. Jeff, Owen and the Watson boys joined them. August explained Herbert's dilemma. Between the Kimballs and Pinaults, they had seven horses and five lariats. The Watson's missing stock consisted of four cows, five horses, two sheep and a sow with a litter of six. After a few minutes discussion it was decided that Owen Kimball, Robert and John Watson, and Dudley and Elmer Pinault would ride after the missing horses and cattle. "We can rope them and put them all together with the mules in the corral back by the trees there," Herbert said. Jeff and August would ride back to the ranch, and return with a wagon of alfalfa and grain for the animals, and spare saddles and tack.

"You never think how much stuff you store in a barn until you lose it," Herbert said. "Tack, pitchforks, tools, feed. It's a lucky thing the carriage was back o' the house."

"Any idea how it started?" Francis asked.

"I have my suspicions," Herbert said, squinting through smoke-reddened eyes. "Last week I got a visit from Pete Campbell. He implied there would be trouble if I paid the Mexicans what they were asking. I told him I'd do what I damn well pleased and he could put that in his pipe and smoke it."

"I got a similar visit from Koeppler," August said.

"And I got one from Sieffert," said Pinault.

"Yesterday Sal Alamillo's boys picked my Carignane vineyard, and o' course I paid'm what they asked. I didn't think two-dollars a head was unreasonable. Then on the way to Almaden, Bowman, Sieffert, Ginther and Belfrage stopped the wagon."

"I'm surprised Belfrage would go along with that," Pinault commented.

"Anyway, they said they was the Almaden Growers Association and my grapes was harvested illegally."

"I never heard of any Almaden Growers Association," August said.

"Well, it just so happens that Almaden Winery sent a man out to check the vineyard before we picked, and he was riding back in the wagon. So he says those grapes belong to the winery, and if they didn't get out o' the way he'd make sure the winery didn't take *their* grapes. So they let the wagon pass. But...," he gestured with a nod of his head toward the smoldering embers, "now this. I can't prove it, but it doesn't take a great intellect to put two and two together."

They rode away with red-rimmed eyes, reeking of smoke, soaked with sweat, smudged with soot, horses snorting and stamping. August sneezed, pulled a handkerchief from his pocket, blew his nose, folded the cloth and stuffed it back in his pocket. He glanced sideways at a silent Jeff. "Thanks for helping; I appreciate it. You didn't have to come; it ain't your fight."

"No worries," Jeff said. He hadn't even thought twice about it, he now realized, because somewhere along the way August's problems had become his problems.

Chapter 51
Carrie Comes Home

Fri Sept 16, 1870 — Sun, Oct 11, 2009

Jeff drove with Carolyn at his side. Carrie sat in the back between her parents, looking tired but happy and craning her neck for a better look at all she'd missed on the night drive to the hospital.

The wind was whistling down the valley in great gusts as they parked under the big oak by the front porch. Abby was the first to greet them. "You saved my life," Carrie said, embracing her friend. "If you hadn't gone for your father, I would have died." Abby grinned with pleasure at the commendation. August helped Carrie toward the house, her legs so weak they shook as she mounted the porch stairs.

Before returning to their home, Lydia put a hand gently on Carolyn's arm and invited them all to dinner that night.

"Can I help?" Abby asked.

"If you'd like. We'll start cooking around three. Dinner is around six."

When the Kimballs were gone Carolyn asked, more to herself than to Jeff, "Now what'll we do about Jake?"

"Leave that to me," Jeff answered.

After he'd escorted the Kimballs through the tunnel, Jeff turned off the light and headed for the office. On the way paused to put away the coffee table books that Abby had left on the parlor floor. One was open to a photo of a family lined up before their sod house. It brought to mind the tintype he'd seen tipped into the back of one of his father's photograph albums. He remembered there had been an open coffin and stopped, wondering if the child in the box had been Carrie. He pulled out the album in question. The photo was, indeed, of the Kimball family, but the child was a boy — Ivan, no doubt, dressed in his Sunday best for his trip to eternity.

Carrie's words to Abby ("You saved my life") echoed in his head, and set him to musing on the consequences of their actions. He did not believe in divine plans or preordained ends. He did, however, believe in Destiny, in the sense that one's personality, strengths, weaknesses and character offered predictable outcomes. But saving Carrie had dubious consequences. If she had died without intervention, what then of all the lives she would now touch as she moved forward, ad infinitum? If their simple act of compassion had irrevocably altered the future, then the present he now found himself in was materially different from the present he had awoken to on Monday. If he were to search her genealogy online, he was certain he could map certain changes. Presumably she would marry (had married) and had children. It was a strange twist to speculate where her life might lead in her future, while at the same time knowing that on this side of the tunnel her life had already been lived, her course had run, her influence had already passed to her progeny, ripples on the pond of time.

Jeff went outside to stroll through the blustery yard, stuffing his hands in his jeans pockets and puzzling over the moral implications of the changes, witting and unwitting, in which they were complicit. The guns he'd bought, for instance, might have been destined to assist a suicide, commit a murder, foil a bank robbery, or fulfill the dark fantasies of a jealous lover. They had instead become harmless museum pieces. The ends to which they might have been put had been forever altered. Likewise, in agreeing to save Carrie he had exercised god-like power. And though he could not discern the changes he'd wrought, they were immutably present.

In the barn the wind shook the old timbers and rattled the doors. He drew back the canvas tarp and ran his hands over the marble obelisk. Then he took a pad and pencil from the workbench drawer and copied the names. Kimball was carved near the bottom in bold relief. Higher up the names were smaller and cut into the stone:

In Memory of
Lydia, nee Hillman b. 1829 – d. 1872, Beloved Wife and Mother
August b. 1828 – d. 1894, Beloved Husband and Father
Rest in Peace
Owen 1851 – 1912
Molly 1853 - 1854
Noah 1856 – 1896
Ivan 1859 – 1869
Charles 1863 – 1886
Emily 1866 – 1872
1st Lieut. Charles Morse Kimball 1871 – 1898

Lydia and Emily would both be dead in two years, implying death by illness (most likely something that could be cured by antibiotics, or prevented by vaccine).

Carved into the separate base was the legend: "Erected by Mary Morse Kimball, Thomas Kimball, Carolyn Kimball Bennett, Elizabeth Kimball Volkenant 1916." Presumably Carolyn Bennett referred to Carrie, and Elizabeth Volkenant referred to Betsy. Was Mary Morse Kimball August's second wife, or a wife of one of the boys? Who was Thomas Kimball? These were questions that might have remained a mystery a decade earlier. Now it was a fairly simple matter of spending a few hours researching the records on a genealogical website.

Back in his office he went online and soon found a public family tree posted by Charlene Volkenant, with links to census records, and photocopies of marriage and death certificates.

Carolyn stretched half-recumbent on the settee, legs propped on an ottoman, a book in her lap.

"What are you reading?" he asked.

"*Outlander*. Very sexy." She smiled coyly.

He ignored the look, laced his fingers behind his head and leaned back in his pneumatically adjustable, ergonomically correct desk chair, and stared up at the ceiling.

In a minute Carolyn asked, "What are you thinking about?"

"I was wondering if we did the right thing saving Carrie."

"What a question! Of course you did; you have a conscience," she said straightening up and putting down her book. "You couldn't just let her die."

Couldn't he? He wondered. What of those who never would be? What of their unborn children? The consequences grew with each generation like compound interest. Of Carrie's six children, four had lived to adulthood and married, and three had borne children. At each generation the ripple effect grew larger, for children and grandchildren took spouses who, had Carrie not been spared, would have taken other spouses. And what of Carrie's husband, Bertram Bennett? Whom would he have married, and how many children, grandchildren and great-grandchildren might they have had?

He did not even mention Lydia and Emily's imminent deaths, for he had not yet decided whether to intervene. Mary Morse Kimball, as it turned out, was August's second wife. August had adopted her son, Charles, who had died of yellow fever during the American occupation of Cuba after the Spanish American War, but not before fathering a daughter by Gertrude Jenkins. Raised by August and in the company of half-brothers and sisters, Charles's life may have taken a different course had his mother married someone else. If Lydia were to survive, Mary and August's son Thomas and all of his progeny (which currently numbered over 400), would all cease to exist.

Jeff sighed. "But think about it — she has grandchildren and great-grandchildren alive now who shouldn't be here."

"Why not?"

"Because if she'd died they wouldn't be here. And other people who were here, aren't now, because of what we did, what *I* did. Doesn't that raise ethical issues in your mind?"

"It's not logical. In Carrie's world you and Abby exist, so there's no scenario where she would have died. You have to take yourself out of the equation."

"Oh, lord!"

"*Que sera, sera,*" Carolyn said as she sat on his lap. "I'm proud of you. You did the right thing. And I think you're pretty clever to come up with the antiques scheme, even if it's not your forte." She put her arms around his neck and kissed him on the forehead. "You know what you should do? Go back to San Francisco and take a zillion photos. Of course they'd have to be in black-and-white, but you'd have the greatest archive of old photos. You could print photo books and sell them in San Francisco at all the hotels, bookstores and tourist spots."

"That sounds like a plan."

"And this time I want you to take *me*. We'll make a vacation of it."

He kissed her neck. "I'd love that. We'll stay at The Lick House or The Occidental."

"I think I'll lie down before dinner. Want to join me?"

"No, I think I'll work on my book."

She arched an eyebrow and whispered, "I wasn't talking about sleep."

Jeff caught her meaning. "Oh. Must be some book. I'll go shave."

Jeff awoke near evening, after a long nap. He drove to Round Table and brought back a pepperoni pizza with extra mushrooms. Jake returned from his diurnal wanderings just before sunset, followed by an exhausted Buster.

"Your sister, mom and I are going to the Kimballs' for dinner. I got you a pizza."

"Cool."

Jake took the pizza and a glass of milk to the parlor, where he lay on the floor in front of the TV.

A little while later Abby came back to inform them that dinner was ready.

"What are we having?" Jeff asked.

"Chicken. It was so gross! They cut the head off. "

"What did you expect? Chickens don't grow in cellophane."

"Give her a break," Carolyn said, "she's a tender soul; she won't even kill a spider. And I have to admit, if it came to slaughtering animals, I don't think I could kill anything with a face. I'd probably confine my animal protein to fish (they don't scream, and they don't have facial expressions)."

"Did you know a chicken can run around without its head?" Abby asked.

"I'd heard that," Carolyn said.

"Betsy thought it was hilarious."

Jeff taped over the light switch and left a sign reading, LEAVE LIGHT ON!

On the way through the north cellar he grabbed a couple bottles of wine to add to the feast.

The table was laid with a banquet of chicken stew and dumplings, boiled ham, mashed potatoes, celery, corn on the cob, fried parsnips, cornbread, biscuits, honey, strawberry jam, milk, coffee, tea and apple pie.

When they were seated, August said, "Owen, if you'll do the honors?"

The Kimball family bowed their heads in unison and Owen said grace. "Bless us, O Lord, and these thy gifts, which we are about to receive from thy bounty, through Christ our Lord. Amen."

As they were eating Jeff said, "I feel like we ought to reciprocate. We should set a date."

Lydia turned to Carolyn, "That would be nice. I'll help you cook."

"Oh, I don't cook," Carolyn admitted. "Jeff does all the cooking."

Lydia glanced curiously at Jeff.

"I like cooking," Jeff said; "it's therapeutic."

Carolyn felt a gentle tug on her sleeve and turned to see Emily looking earnestly up at her. "Are you a witch or a angel?" Emily whispered.

Not knowing what August had said to 'put the fear of God in'm,' Carolyn was unsure how to answer. "Why do you ask?"

"Papa says people fly where you're from."

"I'm not sure how much I should tell a little girl," Carolyn said, looking to August and Lydia for guidance and finding none. "I'm neither, though I have flown on occasion. Maybe one day, when you're much older, I'll take you high above the clouds."

"I knew it; you're a angel!"

Carolyn chuckled. "Let's just say I aspire to be."

Chapter 52
Turning the Other Cheek

Sun Sept 18, 1870

Reverend Winters addressed a tense congregation on Sunday morning. Conversation before the service usually revolved around the weather and harvest, impending births and betrothals, accidents and politics. This day, however, the talk was only of the Watsons' fire. As the only witnesses, the Kimballs and Pinaults answered questions while everyone waited for the Watsons to arrive. People had already begun filing through the front doors before their buggy pulled up beside the willow at the back.

The Kimballs occupied the next to last pew on the right. August eyed his neighbors with suspicion. Sieffert, Belfrage and Ginther had already declared their allegiance to Bowman. Were there others? August suspected the majority of this congregation (made up of ranchers, dairy farmers, shopkeepers and their families) was ignorant of the tension. Most had heard about the fire, were curious about the details and sympathetic toward the family, but few knew of the veiled threats and the possibility of arson.

The Watsons came in last, taking their usual pew, five rows from the front on the right. Herbert looked straight ahead, an expression at once grim, serene and resolute. All eyes watched them file in, and the knowing few glanced to Bowman on the left side of the aisle, to watch his reaction. He made a point of looking away.

The Reverend Josiah Winters held his hands out palms downward as a silent instruction to sit. Whether by design or divine inspiration, the sermon spoke to the tensions of the day. As the murmur died down and the last straggler was seated, he began. "Today I am reminded of the grace of forgiveness. Forgiveness is what sets Christians apart. We may pray to the same God as the Jews (our Lord himself was a Jew), but whereas the Old Testament metes out justice an eye for an eye and a tooth for a tooth, in the New Testament Jesus teaches us compassion and forgiveness. Our Heavenly Father was a harsh taskmaster, but He sent His son to walk upon the earth that He might better understand man, His highest creation. Jesus walked among his fellow men and saw what was lacking in mankind. He saw the perversion of selfishness and greed and envy, sins that twist men's souls and set one man against another in an endless cycle of misery. Christ knew that the only way to break this cycle is through the grace of forgiveness. He knew that a man bent on revenge poisons his own soul, for he tells us the Kingdom of Heaven is within us. If we can forgive our enemies, we shall not lose the Kingdom within us. We shall be blessed. Christ, in his Sermon on the Mount, Gospel of Matthew, says, 'whosoever shall smite thee on thy right cheek, turn to him the other also. And if any man will sue thee at the law, and take away thy coat, let him have thy cloak also. And whosoever shall compel thee to go a mile, go with him twain.' It's a hard thing to love thine enemies. It's easy to mouth the words, 'turn the other cheek,' yet who among us has not carried revenge in his heart? It's a natural response. It's part of our baser nature. But Christ asks us to be better than our base selves. He shows us how to find the divine within us, by following his precepts. Let us pray."

They all bowed their heads and the preacher invoked the deity in a monotone. "Dear Lord, help us this day to hear thy words and know thy will. Teach us to be humble. Teach us to be kind. Teach us to extend a helping hand to our fellow men. And teach us to forgive those who would do us ill. Amen. Please stand."

The Reverend then turned to the choir of four men and six women, who stood on the dais behind the pulpit. On his signal they led the congregation in "Blest Be the Tie That Binds."

"Let us be seated," Reverend Winters intoned. He took a sip of water as everyone sat and the hymnals were put away. He continued, "Christ practiced what he preached. Imagine: As he hung dying on the cross, he so loved his fellow man that he forgave even those who put him to death. Remember and reflect on his words: 'Forgive them, Father, for they know not what they do.' The Gospel of Luke, Sermon on the Plain, tells us in Christ's own words, 'But I say unto you which hear, Love your enemies, do good to them which hate you, bless them that curse you, and pray for them which despitefully use you....' In both Matthew and Luke you find the Golden Rule, which regardless of the translation implores us to 'Do unto others, as you would have them do unto you.'"

The sermon continued on in like fashion, with occasional pauses for prayers and hymns. At the passing of the collection plate, Winters said, "I know you're all aware of the misfortune that struck one of our own this past week. I'm calling for a barn-raising party for the first Saturday of November. Please dig deeper in your pockets for this worthy cause, and know that we stand together to help one another in time of need." When the plates had been passed and collected, Winters said, "Let us close with The Lord's Prayer," and the men and women spoke as one as they recited by rote:

"Our Father who art in heaven, Hallowed be thy name.

Thy kingdom come, Thy will be done on earth, as it is in heaven.

Give us this day our daily bread.

And forgive us our trespasses, as we forgive them that trespass against us.

Lead us not into temptation, but deliver us from evil.

For thine is the kingdom, and the power, and the glory, forever. Amen."

August finished reciting the prayer with much on his mind. As a member of the church, he felt part of the greater community. But that community was held together by a tacit agreement to adhere to the Golden Rule. He had been happy to lend a hand or loan a tool when needed, and he had been confident when in trouble that his neighbors would step in to help. In this he had not been disappointed. But those had been instances of circumstance, a broken tool, a shortage of material, a sickness in the family. The current situation, if Watson's suspicions were correct, was more a matter of economic alliance than circumstance, and one's neighbors could not be counted on if money were in play.

"And now," said Reverend Winters with more liveliness than he'd shown during his sermon, "I'd like to announce the date of the harvest dance, which will take place six weeks hence on Friday, October twenty-eighth. Those wishing to be part of the planning committee, please see me after the service."

With that the organist began to play and Reverend Winters gathered up his *Bible* and walked solemnly down the aisle. Ushers opened the front doors and Winters stood on the front porch to thank his congregation for coming. The pews were emptied in an orderly fashion, starting from the back. As the last member filed out the door, the music rose to a crescendo and abruptly ceased.

August felt invigorated and cleansed. He'd been given a lesson to contemplate, a compass to heed, a direction to follow. If not for these weekly reminders, he thought life would seem pointless and self-serving. He wondered, how could the Porters could be so blind? How lonely they must feel in their godless universe.

When Charles and Emily were retrieved from Sunday School, they accompanied Lydia, Carrie and Betsy to the Pulgas Bakery, while August, Owen and Noah sauntered over to the General Store, as much to replenish supplies as to witness the collision of wills that seemed inevitable. Adding to his anxiety, he knew a fisticuffs was not out of the question, and he might be obliged to step in to help Herbert, who was not noted for his physical prowess. In the middle of the street Herbert Watson came upon them from behind. "Did you hear about Miguel?"

August stopped and turned. "Martinez? Sal's right-hand-man?"

"He was beaten by men in hoods."

"How bad?"

"He'll live."

"Thank God."

"The Mexicans have moved their camp closer to Almaden winery."

Francis Pinault joined them before they mounted the porch where a band of men was already embroiled in a political discussion. Herbert paused at the door and caught Bowman's eye.

Bowman said, "Tough luck about your barn. What'd you think of the sermon today?"

"Seems like if you want to be forgiven, you have to forgive others. Isn't that it? As the *Bible* says, 'Whatsoever a man soweth, that shall he also reap.'"

"Uh huh."

"Then I'm sure we'll see you at the barn-raising."

Bowman sniggered and turned away.

Five minutes later August, Francis and Herbert were inside placing their orders when a shout came from outside. "Smoke! Somethin's afire! Charlie, ain't that acomin' from your place?"

"God damn it to hell!" Bowman bellowed.

Herbert Watson had to clamp his mouth shut to keep from smiling.

Chapter 53
If a Branch Falls

Mon Sept 19, 1870 — Wed Oct 14, 2009

In the early morning hours of Wednesday, the 14th of October, 2009, the first storm of autumn swept in from the Pacific. In the grey before dawn the wind whipped the branches of the apricot trees, and the big oaks creaked in complaint. Then dark clouds spilled over the mountains and let loose a torrent. All along the mountains the little streams and dry creases soon filled with water running downhill through the wild forest and into the cities, where storm drains channeled the deluge underground to the bay.

At the ranch the dry earth soaked up the water like a sponge and, when the earth was full, the water ran down in muddy rivulets to fill Arroyo Calero on its way into the storm drains at the edge of Almaden Estates. The wind-driven rain lashed at the windowpanes and woke Jeff from a fitful sleep.

He pulled on his robe, stepped into his slippers and went downstairs to start the coffee. He put rice in the rice cooker and was frying two eggs when he heard a loud crack, followed by a horrendous crash of metal and glass. He ran down the hall, threw open the front door and peered out.

Caroline called from the top of the stairs, "Did you hear that?"

"Fuck. You'll have to take my car to work today."

"Why?"

"A branch just flattened yours."

The kids came out of their rooms, bleary eyed but alert. They came downstairs and looked out from the bay window in the parlor.

"Holy shit!" Jake exclaimed, immediately realizing the profanity that he usually kept from his parents' delicate ears, and amended, "I mean 'cow.'"

"You kids might as well get ready for school," Carolyn said. "We'll take your father's car."

"Why didn't you park it in the barn?" Jeff asked.

"Between the tractor, your mom's car, your dad's truck and the Subaru, it's a bit of a squeeze. Seemed easer to park outside."

"*C'est la vie*. I'll call the insurance company when you leave for work."

"What's that smell?"

"Oh damn," Jeff cried, annoyed with himself. He'd forgotten to turn the heat off the eggs.

In the kitchen, he opened the window to disperse the smell, and cleaned the pan. Abby came in and spoke quietly. "You know, I'll bet if you go to the Kimballs and saw off that branch before it grows big...."

The logic dawned on him. "Rrrr-right. That makes sense. It might be hard to explain to Jake, though."

"Just tell him it's a replacement car."

He made four omelets, set three on plates on the kitchen table, then took his own to the parlor and stared out at the branch and the crushed car. The sky seemed to be lightening and the rain slackening, though the wind had not abated. Could altering the past change something that had already happened in the present? He was puzzled. Since he'd already made the decision to saw off the offending branch, presumably that branch had not grown over the ensuing century. So how was it that it had fallen on the car? If intensions to change the past were realized, wouldn't the results already be manifest in the present? But the branch still lay on the car. Likewise, if he intended to age more antiques by placing them in a strongbox buried under the front porch, wouldn't they already be there? What was it Carolyn had said about saving Carrie? "In Carrie's world you and Abby exist, so there's no scenario where she would have died." But he had not been born until 95 years after Carrie's appendicitis, so during all that time he did not exist in Carrie's world. She had grown old and died before he was born. To complicate matters, he was now 44 and she was only 17. She hadn't existed in *his* world until he was 27, and there had been no interaction between their worlds until his father had installed the dome light a year earlier. Like contemplating eternity or infinity, it was all too much for Jeff's meager brain.

When the rain abated mid-morning he pulled on his mud boots and crossed to the barn for a pole saw. On the back porch he kicked off the muddy boots, slipped on some old loafers and passed through the tunnel. On the other side it was sunny with a high haze. He found August in the office and explained his mission. August followed him outside. The oak, which would grow to an impressive height and girth over the next 139 years, was here a scrawny adolescent. The branch, which would one day grow as wide as his shoulders, was barely wider than his wrist. Jeff raised the pole and began sawing.

"You've lost some weight," August observed.

Jeff looked down and saw that his middle-aged paunch had indeed shrunk over the months since they'd moved to the ranch. He hadn't noticed before, but the increase in physical activity had had an effect.

He sawed, squinting against the sawdust that drifted down, and breaking a sweat before the branch fell to the ground. Returning to his side, he looked out the parlor window. The Civic was gone. He took the pole saw back to the barn, where he found his Subaru parked in its usual space.

He called Carolyn and left a message on her voicemail. "Just thought you'd like to know, you'll find your restored Civic in place of the Subaru."

She called back during a break between classes. "What was that cryptic message about?" she asked.

"I just didn't want you to be surprised. My Subaru is back in the garage, so your Civic must be in your parking space."

There was a long silence. "Yes. Why wouldn't it be?"

"You didn't take the Subaru this morning?"

"No. Are you feeling all right?"

Now it was Jeff's turn to be silent, as he contemplated her answer. "I'm fine. I need to go."

"You're worrying me."

"Never mind, I'll tell you about it this evening."

He walked around the house searching for anomalies, but found nothing amiss. How was it that Carolyn had no idea what he was talking about? If this Carolyn had left for work in her Civic this morning, where was the Carolyn he'd seen drive off in his Subaru? How was it that he could remember that morning's calamity, and she couldn't? There was no doubt in his mind that it had happened the way he remembered it. He puzzled over this problem all afternoon, finally coming to the conclusion that the family he'd awakened with that morning was on another timeline. His own timeline wasn't linear; it included a doubling back in time and coming forward again, complete with any repercussions that his actions in the past might incur. By sawing off the branch, he'd established a new timeline for his family. As he was the only one of his family present in the past when the change occurred, he was the only one with a memory of a tree branch that no longer existed in 2009. Logically then, he had to conclude that multiple timelines must run concurrently. There was a world where a branch destroyed Carolyn's car, and a world where that never happened, a world where Carrie died of appendicitis, and a world in which she lived to old age. Multiple worlds obviated any prohibition against changing the past, since no world was more valuable than another. Thus armed with a justification, he determined to save Lydia and Emily when the time came, and to have the Kimballs immunized against measles, mumps, rubella, pertussis, diphtheria, tetanus, polio and hepatitis. Why take chances?

Chapter 54
Opening the Vault

Tues Sept 20, 1870 — Th Oct 15, 2009

When he'd seen his family off to their respective schools, Jeff entered his own wine cellar with the rock pick he'd been given as a boy. At the top of the stairs he flicked on the light switch, which illuminated the single bulb that hung from the ceiling. Then he set to work. The plaster came off the surface of the wall in chunks, kicking up a fine dust. The first bricks he removed were in line with the lower shelf and confirmed that nothing inside was missing. He worked carefully, but quickly, and inside of an hour he'd pulled down enough bricks to reveal the two shelves and floor below.

The antiques had aged as gracefully as was possible over such an extended period. The once supple buckskin crumbled as he pulled it away, but the items it protected were in remarkable condition. The leather bindings of the books were almost like new. The newspapers, while delicate, had barely yellowed in the complete darkness of the vault. The guns and paintings looked almost new.

The Christie's agent arrived first in a silver Mercedes. He was about fifty, with salt-and-pepper hair and bushy eyebrows, wearing a light grey suit with a blue dress shirt and a loosened tie. He got out looking bored and checked his watch. Jeff went down the porch stairs to greet him. The man introduced himself as David DeGroot, and handed Jeff a card.

"So, what are we lookin' at? What am I here for?" DeGroot asked impatiently, as a black Mercedes came tearing across the wooden bridge, coasted up the long slope, and eased to a stop beside them. A man in his mid-thirties hopped out. He wore a blazer, an open necked shirt, and khaki pants. He quickly proffered his business card and energetically declared, "Richard Muldaur, Sotheby's. You can call me Rick."

DeGroot looked displeased. "I wasn't aware the competition would be here."

"As I understand it," Jeff said, "your auction houses take a 13% commission from the buyer."

"That's right," DeGroot said.

"That's standard," Muldaur seconded, nodding in agreement.

"So it's in your best interest to get the most you can."

"Right," they chorused.

"When you give an appraisal, do you guarantee a minimum bid?"

"We don't work like that," DeGroot said.

"It's not standard policy," Muldaur agreed. "It's impossible to know for sure what someone will pay for an item."

"I want a piece of that 13%."

"First, let's see what you've got," DeGroot said.

Jeff had laid the treasures upon the dining room table.

"Quite amazing," Muldaur said reverently as he surveyed the lot. "It's like a time capsule, all dating to the 1870s, I'd say. Beautiful condition. Let's be careful here. Take these." He handed white cotton gloves to Jeff and DeGroot.

"How did these come into your possession?" DeGroot asked.

"I found them in a trunk in the attic."

Muldaur took out his phone and began snapping pictures. "This is a remarkable find," he said. "Remarkable."

DeGroot picked up the newspaper with the headline announcing the assassination of Lincoln. "We also arrange for private sales to select clients and museums."

Carolyn came home to find the men still examining the stash. She stood in the hall looking in and was soon joined by Jake, who took one glance and asked what was going on.

Carolyn put a finger to her lips and escorted him into the kitchen. "Your father found some more antiques, and he's having them appraised. Don't disturb them."

"No problem," Jake whispered, only vaguely interested. He took a glass of milk and a cookie and went upstairs to play video games.

In the dining room, Muldaur and DeGroot were cataloging the treasure, taking photos with their smart phones, checking prices online, and making audio entries for each item. "This is truly an amazing find," Muldaur said, picking up *The Celebrated Jumping Frog....* "A first edition of Twain's first book. Of everything on the table, this is probably the most valuable piece. I've seen a pristine copy like this go for 75,000 dollars. Of course I can't guarantee you could get that. Some of the gold coins are in mint condition. The guns are museum pieces. The books are flawless. Just off the top of my head (no guarantees here, of course) I'd estimate the total to be worth somewhere around $200,000. We might get more, if we're lucky."

Jeff made a show of looking disappointed. He casually opened *The Innocents Abroad.* "Wouldn't Twain's signature make it more valuable?"

"Of course," Muldaur began, and stopped with his mouth agape as a sheet of stamps slid out.

"These ought to be worth something, "Jeff said innocently.

"Oh yes!" DeGroot laughed. "Yes, indeed!"

Chapter 55
Supply and Demand

Wed Sept 21, 1870 — Fr Oct 16, 2009

"Damnation," August muttered, pointing toward the northwest corner of the Mission vineyard where a group of four deer were munching grapes. "Every year it's something." He reached into a saddlebag and drew out a pistol. "I should have brought a rifle; could have put some meat on the table." To Jeff he warned, "Hold on to your pommel." Then he raised his gun and fired.

Rhubarb flinched. Jeff held tight to Honey's pommel as she jumped and skittered backwards, neighing. Patsy tried to bolt, but Owen kept her in check.

"Hit anything?" Jeff asked.

"Nah — you can't hit a barn door with a pistol. Anyway, I only wanted t' run'm off. Every year we have some problem with birds and deer. Two years ago we lost most all the Carignane to boar. They love fruit."

"Why don't you fence it?"

He put his gun back in the saddlebag and sniffed. "Deer'll jump an eight or ten foot fence. Boar get under it. I used to station Owen up on the far hill there with a shotgun towards the end of the season, to scare off the critters, but then they come out at night, anyway. So what's a man to do?"

"You ever try scarecrows?"

"Nah, a scarecrow only works in a field crop. They don't work in orchards or vineyards — don't know why."

A great shaft of sunlight spilled through the clouds, lit the golden foothills above Arroyo Calero, and sent a spreading warmth that only served to remind them how cold it really was. August looked skyward, gauging the weather. They left the road, following Arroyo Calero toward the Hermitage vineyard. Jeff flicked the reigns to move Honey abreast of August and said, "I ordered you some Zinfandel grafted onto American rootstock, so you can start replanting in the spring."

"How much do I owe you?"

"Nothing. Once we're paid for the antiques, you'll have about half a million dollars to play with."

"How much is the rootstock?"

"A grafted Zinfandel vine will cost you three dollars and seventy five cents. So 1,000 vines, with tax and all, would be around 4,000 dollars. I can order more, or different varieties, if you want."

"I'll make some computations when we get back."

Cloud shadows moved across the valley, and far to the northeast the clouds parted and bathed Mount Diablo in a chiaroscuro of warm light against a cloud darkened sky.

"We hardly ever get rain before October," August said eyeing the sky suspiciously. "Funny, in Pennsylvania it rains all summer."

"You still have family back there?"

"My family came to the New World in 1609. Seems like one way or t'other I'm related to just about everybody in Pennsylvania. All my family, what's left of them, is there. My older brother, my sisters, my ma. Nephews, nieces, lots of cousins. I haven't seen any of them since I came out in '48, though I get a letter now and then. We lost Ada to consumption before she was twenty, and my older brother, Ethan, was killed during the battle. All my brothers were too old for the army, so you might think they'd be safe enough up there in Pennsylvania, with all the fighting in the South. They never figured on the war coming to them. When the fighting started Ethan went out in the yard to watch and caught a bullet. Damned foolish way to die."

"Are you ever tempted to go back and visit?"

"I've been thinking about that ever since they finished the railroad last year, but it's a long way, and I'm not sure I want to see them old and wore out. In my mind they're all still young."

When they reached the Hermitage vineyard, August leaned down, picked a grape, tasted and spat. "Good. We'll go talk to Sal about getting these picked tomorrow. Let's hope the rain holds off."

They regained the road that paralleled Guadalupe Creek and cantered toward the Almaden winery. Half a mile ahead they could see the white tents and wagons of the Mexican camp, set beside trees at a juncture where a side road crossed a small bridge. Quite a few men were on horseback.

"Looks like they're getting ready to move," August said.

As they closed the distance August recognized a few of the horses, including Koeppler's Pinto, Bowman's dun mare, and Ginther's Palomino. The horsemen faced Pete Campbell and his young son Douglas. Behind the Campbells ten Mexicans sat dangling their legs from a narrow dray piled with empty lug boxes and pulled by a large white draft horse. When he saw them Campbell called out, "Hey, August. We have a situation here; these men won't let us through."

August looked up and down the line. Six rifles were out of their scabbards. Nick Belfrage and his two eldest sons; Rich Ginther and his eldest; George Sieffert; Bowman; Koeppler and his sons, and Francis, Dudley and Elmer Pinault.

"What the devil?" August exclaimed. "Francis?"

Francis rubbed his stubbled cheek. "Well, you know the more I thought on it, the more I could see we shouldn't be fighting our neighbors. We got to stick together."

August addressed Bowman, whose central position, size and demeanor suggested power of authority. "What's this all about, Charles?"

Bowman twisted in his saddle. "We're not lettin' these greasers pick anyone else's fruit until they pick ours. We got first dibs. You and Campbell are at the back of the line."

August edged Rhubarb around Pinault and trotted past the wagon into the center of the camp. Jeff had no choice, as Honey obediently followed. The women and children had withdrawn past the last tent, surrounded by perhaps thirty men armed with nothing but knives and sticks. A handful of armed men gathered with Sal Alamillo behind the chuck wagon.

"What's going on, Sal?" August asked.

""They want us to pick their grapes, but they don't pay. They shot into our camp."

"Anyone hurt?"

Sal shook his head.

The sound of horses on the bridge made everyone look up. Sheriff Fisher and the eldest Campbell came at a gallop. Sal, August, Owen and Jeff gathered around Pete Campbell.

"All right now," Fisher said, "the first thing is everyone is going to holster their weapons." He waited until the men on horseback had all complied. "You, too, Sal."

"I don't got no holster."

"Put it down on the ground, then."

The sheriff's deputy crossed the bridge then, taking up station behind the line of horses.

"Who's going to speak for the ranchers?" Fisher asked. "Tell me what's going on here."

All eyes went to Bowman, who cleared his throat and said, "The thing is pretty clear, sheriff. These goddamn greasers refuse to pick my grapes. My grapes is shriveling on the vine, whilst they go off to pick other vineyards. I've had enough. Now they're gonna pick my grapes for free, or they won't pick anybody's. And when they're done, I want them arrested for burning my barn."

"We didn't burn no barn," Sal protested.

"We seen him," Belfrage said.

"That's right," Ginther agreed.

August had to speak up then. "Now, Nick, Rich, you know that ain't true."

"You callin' us liars?" Belfrage demanded.

"I'm saying you were with the rest of us at church. You can't know for certain who burned Charlie's barn. None of you can. For that matter, some people think you all burned Herb Watson's barn."

"That's a lie!" Bowman shouted.

"I'm not saying you did," August said. "But there are those who suspect as much." August fixed Francis Pinault with a knowing look.

"And they hurt Miguel," Sal put in.

"That's bull pucky," Belfrage said.

"We saw you," Sal said, standing his ground.

"You couldn't've seen us," Ginther said; "we...." He was cut short by Bowman's backhanded slap to his midsection.

"You wear hoods, but I know your horses."

Fisher looked from the horsemen to Sal. "How is it that all this is going on right under my nose, and I don't know anything about it? Doesn't anyone here have respect for the law? I've a mind to arrest the lot of you 'till this is sorted out. I would, too, if our jail wasn't so small. Now, Sal, why don't you just smooth this over and pick Mr. Bowman's vineyard. Then we can all get back to business as usual."

"He don't pay."

"They're askin' too much," Bowman complained.

There ensued a long discussion about the prevailing cost of picking.

"It all started when that bastard's father took the Chinese away," Bowman said, pointing at Jeff. "If I ever get ahold o' that son-of-a-bitch..."

"You'll make no threats around me," Fisher said, "or you'll spend the night in jail while I think up some charges. You're all going to abide by the law. Is that clear?"

He was just a man, and not the biggest or strongest among them, but he had the weight of his office on his side. In the end a compromise was worked out. Four crews were divvied up and sent on their way. Pete Campbell and August contracted for the following days.

Leaving the camp August said, "That was a near thing. It's lucky the sheriff arrived before it got out of hand."

Jeff was quiet on the way home. Bucolic as it was, it was a hostile landscape, and men were only a part of it. There were dangerous animals out there — mountain lions, wild boar, and bears. There was no fire department, minimal police, and only the most rudimentary health care. Here on the farms that spread across the valley, were those who would die young of some thoroughly innocuous and preventable disease or infection, because they were entirely at nature's mercy. It felt reassuring to know that he could slip back through the geode to the relative ease and safety of the future.

Chapter 56
On the Road

Th Sept 22, 1870 — Sat Oct 17, 2009

"You know, you could just quit," Jeff reminded Carolyn, as they dressed Saturday morning. "You don't have to work now."

"I like my job, although it's nice to have a choice. What about you? Don't you miss work?"

"I miss feeling relevant, but I don't miss having to beg for my paycheck, and I don't miss the pace. Especially the pace. Everything was always so urgent. Everybody needed something *yesterday* — it was never fast enough. Until these past few months, I never understood the appeal farming had for my father. It seems like the faster you go, the less you see. I was so busy running around seeing the broader world, I couldn't see what was right in front of my face."

"Now you can slow down, and you can afford to take me with you."

"That would be nice. We can travel together for a change."

"See? Who said money can't buy happiness?"

"You still have to have a good attitude. Anyone can be miserable."

"That goes without saying. So why are *you* miserable?"

"Do I look miserable?"

"You don't look happy."

He took a minute to consider. "The tunnel still bothers me. We don't know how it works. What happens if it just stops working? What happens if there's a power failure?"

"I thought *I* was supposed to be the worry wart."

Jeff let out a big sigh as he packed his saddlebags. "Come here."

He enfolded her in his arms and drank in the comforting scent of her. "I should have told you earlier. It's been a big relief to have someone to share the burden."

"Don't think of it as a burden. Think of it as a privilege."

He kissed her forehead. "I love you."

She smiled and kissed his lips. "Do you have everything you need?"

"Everything but the kitchen sink. I'm taking Honey, and Gus is lending me Stormy as a packhorse (so Pop will have a ride, if I find him). I have two changes of clothes, extra socks and underwear, gloves, flashlight, compass, canteen, mummy bag, tent, toilet paper, wet wipes, insect repellent, SPF 40 sunscreen, Sterno, waterproof matches, collapsible umbrella, topographical map, fifty feet of nylon rope, some freeze-dried food, peanut butter, bread, jerky, granola bars, a bottle of bourbon. What am I forgetting? Oh, and...(I hope you won't be too upset) I bought a Smith & Wesson handgun."

Carolyn pushed away and fixed her eyes on his. "Only in the direst emergency."

"Of course."

"God, I hate guns."

"I don't expect I'll have to use it"

"Please don't. Please be safe."

"I'll do my best."

"I'm going to be stressing out until you come back."

"I know. I'll make it quick."

"Just be safe."

"That's the first order of business," Jeff replied.

It was not likely to be a dangerous trip, but there were so many incalculable risks and variables. He'd given up speculating how his father would receive the bad news. There was nothing left but to find him and bring him home, and let the chips fall where they may.

"How will you explain my absence to Jake?"

"Press trip."

"But I'm unemployed."

"You had press trips when you freelanced."

A knock came at their bedroom door. "Daddy?" He opened the door and Abby flew into his arms. "I don't want you to go."

"It'll only be for a few days. If I haven't found him in a week, I'll be back."

"Don't get hurt."

"I'm not planning on it."

"Let's see you off," Carolyn said.

"Jake is downstairs watching cartoons," Abby cautioned.

The three of them went quietly down the stairs. Engrossed in the TV, Jake lay on the parlor rug, chin cupped in his hands, oblivious to their passage.

"I've said it before and I'll say it again: You don't want to gallop her, except on the road," August warned. "If she stepped in a gopher hole at a gallop she'd break a leg. If she landed on you, you could be crushed. Don't run'm too hard; you don't want to get'm lathered up. And give'm a rest every hour. Don't forget, they need water, but don't let them drink all they want. Horses ain't the brightest animals; they'll drink themselves to death if you give them half a chance. Stormy will follow behind readily enough, but be careful not to snag the tether. You can store most of your gear in her side-bags. Remember to re-cinch the saddle, and loosen it when you stop to rest and give'm water." August sighed and swept a concerned gaze over Jeff's face. "I'd send Owen with you, but I need him here. We're picking today and tomorrow. When you come to a town, post us a letter so we can mark your progress."

"What's the address?"

"Address? Why, Kimball ranch, Almaden Valley. There's only one."

"Right, of course."

"If you're gone more than ten days, I'll send Owen after you."

The threat of rain the day before had passed away in the night. The air was crisp, and as the morning sun warmed the ground, the dew turned to vapor that hung in wisps over the fields.

Lydia came out with a cloth napkin into which she'd bundled some biscuits. She stuffed them into the already bulging canvas bag slung over Stormy's saddle. "For the road," she said. She was soon joined by Emily and Carrie. Jeff tied his frock coat, the tent and a small collapsible shovel to Stormy's saddle. Then he hugged Carolyn and Abby, and mounted Honey.

August shook his hand. A shout of "Good luck!" rang out from the barn. Jeff turned to see Owen and Noah leaning on pitchforks, hands raised in farewell. Then he stood in the stirrups, clicked his tongue, gave a flick of the reins, and was off, trotting down the slope and across the bridge. He stopped to look back only once.

It had been two weeks since the last rumor of Randall's whereabouts, which placed him somewhere in the Santa Cruz Mountains above Saratoga. It was a mere twenty to twenty-five miles, a short drive even on surface streets with stop signs. A horse might average a sustained ten miles an hour on a flat road, but Jeff had no way to predict the condition of the roads, nor the stamina of his horses. He could tell from the topographical maps that his way would be impeded by numerous streams. In half an hour he reached Guadalupe Creek, where he let the horses drink. He took a couple of photos, then he led them across the bridge into Pulgas, where he dutifully headed for the post office. He was posting the note when Rich Ginther came in with a handful of letters to mail. He was a short man with tight lips, close-cropped hair and deep laugh lines around his eyes, but he didn't look like laughing when he saw Jeff.

"Morning," Ginther said gruffly.

"Morning," Jeff mimicked, keeping it civil. He didn't really know the man, nor any of the neighboring ranchers really. With the exception of Bowman, they'd all been perfectly cordial back in May, when he'd first been searching for his father. Jeff wondered how long it would take August to mend those friendships after this latest disagreement. He was an independent man, but independence had its price. This was a community that relied on one another when the need arose.

Up to Pulgas it had all been familiar ground and did nothing to arouse Jeff's anxiety. But once he passed the town he was in unfamiliar territory — familiar enough in his own time, criss-crossed by streets and highways, paved over from the foothills to the bay, but utterly foreign to him now. The main road branched north toward San Jose. They followed the road angling northwest from Pulgas, along the base of Blossom Hill.

August had not given him particularly detailed instructions, but all of it had been cautionary. So Jeff was careful, urging Honey into a canter for ten minutes (which was about all his own back could take), then walking her for fifteen minutes. Twice they had to stop as Stormy halted to pee.

He rode on in silence, whistling from time to time, lost in thought, for this was the first time in many months that he'd spent in solitary communion with himself. The air was redolent of dry grass and sage and nameless vegetation both familiar and unidentifiable. He sneezed, and reaching into his pocket for a Kleenex, he came out with the paper on which he'd written the names and dates on the obelisk. It set him to wondering if he could influence the dates on that stone, and reflecting on the sweep of history a lifetime could encompass. His own great-grandparents, born in the 1890's, had seen the end of the horse-and-buggy era, the advent of motorcars and airplanes, the fall of European monarchies, the rise of American dominance, two World Wars, a Great Depression, radio and television, the atom bomb, rockets and men on the moon. Their society, too, had changed, as conventional morality and decorum had been turned on their collective heads. Behavior once condemned was now accepted, if not encouraged. Like most people, Jeff was a man of his time. He found the prescribed guidelines of August's era unnaturally restrictive and irrational. Yet August seemed content enough. You'd never see him on a therapist's couch struggling to find himself, or wondering how he fit into the scheme of things. On the whole, Jeff thought the human species had not improved much in the past 140 years. For all our imagination, inventiveness, intelligence, curiosity and compassion, the darker side of human nature guaranteed that envy and greed, selfishness and fear, intolerance, mean-spiritedness and evil were still in force in the world.

Coming to a stream he stopped to water the horses, then tied them in the shade of a scrub oak and paused to eat a sandwich and granola bar. A sudden fatigue overtook him then and he lay down in the dry, prickly leaves for a short rest. He awoke to the nervous whinnying of the horses. About fifty yards upstream, a mountain lion slunk along the edge of the trees, eyes intent on three deer that had come to the water's edge to drink. Jeff got up and took his handgun from the saddlebags as a precaution. The deer drank, then suddenly perked up, ears swiveling like antennae. The cat crouched, muscles tensing. At the same moment the deer turned and bounded up the far bank. The cat sprang out of the grass, down the bank and across the stream in a vain effort to chase. Then she stopped, her tail twitching, and her head swiveled as she turned an evil eye in Jeff's direction. The horses were pulling against their restraints. Jeff stepped out from behind Honey, raised his gun and fired. It kicked hard in his hand. At the report of the shot, the cat flinched and Stormy reared, pulling the tether until it snapped the branch it was tied to. She tore off at a gallop in the direction they'd come. The cat paused long enough to give Jeff a disdainful glare and slunk back into the trees. Jeff swore to himself and set off on Honey in pursuit of his packhorse.

Chapter 57
The Old Man on the Mountain

Th Sept 22 & Fri Sept 23, 1870 — Sat Oct 17 & Sun Oct 18, 2009

They ambled into the small village of Los Gatos about one in the afternoon. The day had turned warm and Jeff took off his hat to wipe a forearm across his brow. He tied the horses at the water trough in front of the saloon and went inside. There were just three patrons, two playing checkers, one eating a plate of liver and onions.

He explained his mission to the bartender who shrugged and wiped the bar with a damp cloth.

"Never came in here, far as I know."

The smaller of the two checkers players spoke up in a high voice. "The Chinee cleared out two-three weeks ago. Moved north. I tink dey had a white foreman. I'm purty sure. You 'member dat, Hank?"

Hank, a big lump of a man with a slouch hat, stared into space a moment before answering. "Yup, I recollect he was a old man. I think Albert hired them to pick his apples."

"North, you say?"

"Yup," the short man answered. "Prob'ly north o' Saratoga. They's plenty o' apples up there."

Jeff drank a warm beer and asked for directions.

"Directions? Why, you cain't miss it. That there is the Los Gatos-Saratoga Road. Lord, it's but six miles!"

"It's easy goin' afore the mud season," Hank added.

The road, such as it was, might have been only six miles, but it was six miles over difficult terrain, crossed by innumerable streams and narrow canyons. What would have taken fifteen minutes in a car on a paved street, took Jeff almost two hours. It was, nonetheless, a beautiful and quiet landscape with the tall, dark mountains looming on his left as he rode in the shade of oaks and elms, madrone, fir, laurel and redwoods.

When he came into the sleepy village of Saratoga, half a dozen men were lounging on the porch of the general store/post office. Jeff passed by with a wan smile and nod of his head as he continued to the pump and water trough in front of the livery. He watered the horses and refilled his canteen, then tied the horses to a hitching rail and walked back to the store. They all eyed him warily.

"Howdy," a young man greeted him. "Where you from?"

"Almaden Valley."

They all nodded.

"Where you goin'?"

"Looking for a man," Jeff said and handed out three flyers. "My father."

A man in a rocking chair leaned forward and spat tobacco juice into the dusty street. "Yeah, I seen a man looked kinda like'im. He was with that Chinese bunch that went off east to Plotkin's farm."

"Nah," another spoke up. "They come back through here last week." He pushed his hat up and scratched his forehead. "Seems like I heard they was up t' Congress Springs pickin' apples."

"Lemme see that," another said, snatching the flier from his companion's hands.

"No-o-o-o sir," drawled yet another. "They was pickin' walnuts over to the Pierce place."

"Nope. Apples."

"Walnuts."

"Apples."

"You're all wrong," a lean, middle-aged man leaning against a porch post said. "They were going to Luigi Martini's on Montebello

Mountain. I saw Luigi at Barger's last week. He said he'd contracted with Chinese to pick his apples and grapes. Of course I don't know if your father is with them; there's no way of telling for sure without going up the mountain." The man spoke with such authority and with his grammar all in order that the rest of the group fell silent. "I'm headed that way tomorrow; I could point you in the right direction."

Jeff had been reconciled to sleeping on the ground. Now finding himself in a town and faced with a layover, he boarded the horses at the livery stable and went in search of a room.

He might have been better off on the ground, though the discomfort and smell of the bed over the saloon was only partially to blame for his lack of sleep. He'd agreed to meet Bert Beynon, for that was the man's name, shortly after sunup. Having no alarm clock, he found himself waking every hour to check his pocket watch by candlelight, until the candle guttered out shortly after 3 a.m.

Fortified with coffee and scrambled eggs, they set off at 7:30 on the Saratoga to Mountain View road, which ran northeast down a mild alluvial slope until it broke out of the woods and into open parkland. It was a chilly morning. Beynon's horse trotted, so of course Honey followed suit, and while Jeff prided himself on his recently acquired riding skills, he still found trotting a bone-jarring gait. Beynon rode in silence for the first half hour, then proceeded to pepper Jeff with questions — had he been West long? How long since he'd seen his father? How did his father happen to fall into the company of Chinese? Did he speak Chinese? Etc. When they were above Cupertino Beynon stopped and pointed to the north.

"You'd do best to cut across open ground here. You'll pick up the road that follows Stevens Creek into the mountains. After about three miles you'll come to a small lake. That's the beginning of Martini's property. Can't miss it."

They split up then, Beynon following the road and Jeff striking out over open ground to the creek. There he watered the horses and took this moment of privacy to squat in the bushes and relieve himself which, though mildly disgusting, was not as horrifying as he'd imagined.

The road followed the creek under a dense canopy of trees that changed subtly from willow, oak and sycamore on the lower slopes to fir and redwood as they plodded uphill. The air was cool and smelled of moss and ozone. In spots the trees arched over the road and stream to form a tunnel, and Jeff was forced to lean low over Honey's neck to keep from being swept off the saddle by low-lying branches. As they gained higher ground the road occasionally broke out of the trees and crossed a meadow of dry grass and mustard. At a particularly steep fall the road left the tumult of rushing water and zig-zagged up the mountainside, emerging at a small lake, hardly more than a pond. Jeff could see a few rows of a vineyard spilling over the edge of the ridge above the lake, and a thin column of smoke rose above the treetops just visible beyond that. The way up to that ridge was achieved by way of five long switchbacks that led to the summit.

He could see by quick perusal that four fifths of the vineyard was already picked. A crew of men, women and children could be seen laboring down one far row. Further along the undulating ridge top a few men perched on ladders, harvesting apples. Jeff trotted down to the vineyard workers and asked to see the foreman. He was met with an uncomprehending stare and a gesture to continue on towards the orchard. At the edge of the orchard he was pointed to another picker, who said, "Mistah, he ovah…" followed by a gesture up a gentle slope to the far end of the orchard near the edge of the forest, where he could make out a tent and a small camp fire, and men on ladders in the apple trees. He urged Honey forward. At the top of a wooden ladder at the end of a row an old white man was dropping apples to a Chinese woman below who put them into a bushel basket.

Jeff's heart sank as beheld the thin, swarthy old man with a thick white beard and long white hair flowing out from under a straw hat. This emaciated Spaniard (for so he took the stranger to be) was clearly not his father. He reined in Honey and let his disappointment take hold, and weighed his options. It had not occurred to him there might be more than one Anglo supervising a band of Chinese. For that matter, it seemed unlikely there was even one. He watched the old man lean out to reach outlying fruit, and envisaged a prolonged search, wandering about the countryside with no ability to contact his family. Where might he go? Livermore Valley, perhaps, Napa, Sonoma? There was no telling where his father might have gone. He wished he had August's knowledge of this place and time, and for a minute considered simply going back and waiting until after harvest, when he might enlist his friend's assistance. But by then the trail would be cold, for harvest would have concluded and no work would be done until winter pruning. And who was to say if the various bands of itinerant laborers would still be together in January?

Chapter 58
Reunion

Fri Sept 23, 1870 — Sun Oct 18, 2009

He was about to turn away when he caught the whistled fragment of a familiar tune. He stopped and listened intently, making sure he wasn't deceiving himself, for faintly borne on the breeze he could hear the unmistakable strains of *Sentimental Journey,* a 1940's tune glaringly out of place in 1870. This man, whoever he was, must know his father, and with great excitement Jeff nudged Honey forward. The Spaniard glanced at them as they advanced uphill and stopped whistling, but he continued with his picking. He was not quick, but worked methodically, plucking apples in a kind of rhythm and dropping them to the woman below. When he was ten feet away Jeff reined in Honey, took off his bowler and said, "Excuse me, sir, but I couldn't help overhearing..."

At these words the man yelped, dropped an apple, opened his mouth to speak and could do no more than whimper. He clambered down the ladder and advanced, eyes wide, limbs shaking. "Jeffrey? Oh, Jeffrey!"

Jeff was off the horse in a second, staring into his father's eyes. But for the eyes and voice he would not have recognized him. He seemed to have aged ten years in the past fourteen months since Jeff had last seen him. He'd lost at least forty pounds; his hair had grown long and turned entirely white; he wore a long white beard, and deep wrinkles creased his leathery skin. They hugged one another tightly, Randall unable to speak.

"It's all right, Pop. I've come to take you home."

Randall laughed with overwhelming relief and moments later the laughter turned to sobs. "I'm sorry; I'm sorry!"

"It's okay, Pop. It's okay."

The Chinese went discreetly about their work as though nothing was amiss.

When he'd regained his composure Randall said, "I couldn't get back. The passage...."

"I know."

"You're not...?"

"No, we can go back."

Randall put his arm around Jeff's shoulders and turned him toward the tent. "I have to get my things together. Oh god, what must your mother think. Is she...?"

"She's gone, Pop."

"Gone?" Randall pulled away. "She'll understand when I explain. She'll...."

"Pop, Pop," Jeff said, locking eyes with his father. "She's gone, Pop. She...died."

For a long moment he stood there silently, then moaned, "Oh no, oh god, oh no, oh Ginny," a lost, frightened look in his eyes. "This can't be. Oh god, oh no, no, no," was all he was capable of uttering. He seemed about to faint, then sank to the ground. "Oh god, how?"

"She'd been taking pills to relieve her anxiety, and we had wine at Thanksgiving dinner. It was an accidental overdose."

"Ginny, Ginny," Randall muttered, rocking back and forth. He looked dazed and very, very old. "Oh Ginny, god damn it, this can't be happening. This can't be happening!"

"I'm so sorry, Pop," Jeff said. There was so much more to say, but now didn't seem the time. Randall leaned over and vomited in the dirt. Jeff went to the horses and came back with a pint of bourbon. Randall rinsed his mouth and spit, then took a generous sip and swallowed and coughed. He handed the bottle back to Jeff. "I wasn't the best of husbands, I know. I...I've never been much of a talker."

At this frank admission Jeff couldn't help but utter a glum chuckle. "No," he agreed. Randall had never shirked from answering a pointed question, no matter how inconsequential or controversial. He had always had a ready answer but had rarely offered an opinion of his own volition.

"Your mother loved to talk. It drove me crazy. She…" He buried his eyes in the crook of his arm and began to weep in earnest.

Jeff stood uneasily by, then patted his father on the shoulder and walked away to give him privacy. There was something unsettling in observing his father's vulnerability. He had always viewed Pop as strong and unflappable, reserved and (he thought) tacitly judgmental. Even as Jeff had grown into adulthood, competent in his own sphere, he had never grown out of the subordinate position of a child seeking the favor of a parent. They'd never even had an adult conversation where his opinions carried equal weight, though to be fair their conversations had mostly consisted of Jeff's complaints, followed by Randall's terse, unappreciated advice. In Jeff's mind, Randall had achieved an almost god-like status by virtue of his imperious silence. Now diminished by age and unmanned by grief, he assumed more human dimensions. This fundamentally changed their relationship.

When Randall had cried himself out he went to Jeff and gave him a fierce hug. "I'm so glad to see you, son," Randall said, wiping his eyes.

"Pop, there's something else and you may not like it."

Randall let out a long, shaky breath. "It can't be any worse."

"No, but…well, for the longest time we thought you were dead, and I lost my job…"

"I'm sorry to hear that."

"…And we moved to the ranch."

"You've come home? But that's *good* news."

"We took the master bedroom."

Randall shook his head. "Doesn't matter; I won't need it, not without your mother."

"We threw out a lot of your stuff."

"It's just stuff, son; it's not important. I wasn't looking forward to going back to an empty house. It'll be good to have company."

"Rosie had a baby girl; her name is Sierra."

"Wonderful, wonderful. Have I been away that long?"

"A lot has happened in the past year."

"I could use some more of that bourbon." He drank silently, wiping an occasional tear and gazing vacantly toward the orchard where workers continued filling bushel baskets with apples.

"How'd you get mixed up with the Chinese?" Jeff asked.

"I was hungry; they took me in. Then there was a dispute with the Mexicans and this bunch, and I negotiated a peace, of sorts."

"How'd you communicate?"

"Wong and Ah Tye speak a bit of English, but they don't speak Spanish, and the Mexicans have no respect for them. They were willing to speak with me."

Randall screwed the top on the bottle that was now a quarter empty, and his features seemed to sag as a fresh realization of loss broke over him. "I'm very tired. I think I'll just lie down for a minute."

"Good idea."

"Just for a few minutes," Randall said, looking haggard. He walked back to his tent and collapsed on a cot.

Just after noon he burst out of the tent, looked wildly about, saw Jeff and stopped. His face fell with disappointment. "I thought I might've dreamt it. Your mom really is…"

"Gone, Pop."

Randall pressed a palm to his forehead. "Shit." He turned and kicked a tin coffee pot and sent it flying. "God damn it!" He kicked a coffee cup and kicked it again. Then, sudden fury spent, he calmly asked, "How long has the passage been open? We should get back before it closes again."

"No, we figured that part out. It closes when the dome light is switched off. Mom must've switched the light off, so you were caught."

"The dome light. That explains things. Of course. You haven't had any trouble getting past August?"

"Trouble? No, he's been helpful."

Randall laid a hand on Jeff's arm, looking concerned. "But he doesn't know."

"Of course he knows. Everybody knows."

"Jesus! Do you realize the danger we're in?"

"Yes, Pop, I get it. But...well, one thing followed another, and now our families know, and that's just one secret we're all going to have to live with."

"But we could just flip the switch and close it forever."

"If necessary."

"That's encouraging," Randall said.

"If we leave now, we could make Los Gatos by nightfall."

"I need to talk with Wong and Martini; we haven't finished the job yet. Anyway, you don't want to go through Los Gatos. You want to head east, out of the trees where the ground is flatter. I've walked it in two days; can you believe it?"

"Do you have a horse?"

"Horse? No. This bunch only has the two wagons, and those are for equipment and the sick."

"Can you ride?"

"I guess; it can't be that hard."

"We can make it all the way home in one go tomorrow."

Randall went to talk with Wong and Martini, while Jeff unsaddled the horses, led them to water, and hobbled them under the trees where they had plenty of fallen apples to eat. After an evening meal of bacon and fried rice, apples and tea, the men sat around the campfire passing the bourbon back and forth. Jeff thought he'd never seen so many stars.

When the fire began to die down they retired to the tent, Randall on a cot, Jeff in a mummy bag on the ground beside him. In the darkness they could hear the soughing of wind through the trees, the creak of branches, the hoot of an owl and the chittering of squirrels.

Jeff was thinking the worst part was over, and he wondered why he had worried so much about this day. Of all the scenarios he'd envisaged, none had come to pass. He'd found his father a changed man, older, weaker, less judgmental, even accommodating. He had not blamed Jeff for his mother's death, nor threatened to expel him from the house, nor gloated over the loss of his job. Jeff wondered if he'd ever really known his father at all, or if his impression was just the sum of his own misconceptions and insecurities.

Randall spoke from the darkness. "Are you working the ranch?"

Oh, here we go, Jeff thought. "I hired a couple of managers." He waited for the criticism or tone of disappointment.

Instead, Randall said, "That was smart." There was a pause, and then he asked, "Can we afford that?"

"The apricots were a wash, but there was a good profit on the Zinfandel. There's a demand for old vine fruit."

"Do you have any interest...?"

"No, Pop; I'm not a farmer." There was a long silence then as Jeff waited for a verbal jab that never came. Finally he said, "I found a drawer full of my articles."

"I have them all, I think. And photographs. You ought to do a book."

"I've been thinking about it." Conversations with his father were often punctuated with awkward silences, but here the silence was of his own making as he waited in vain for another compliment. "I didn't know you paid attention. You never asked about my work."

"Your work speaks for itself."

"You're not disappointed?"

"In you? No. I'm worried they don't pay you what you're worth. It's a precarious profession."

"No worse than farming."

"No, that's true."

"Anyway, we don't have to worry about money anymore."

"Why is that?"

"I'll tell you in the morning."

Jeff was just beginning to nod off when Randall said softly, "Jeffrey?"

"Hmm?"

"I'm proud of you."

"Thanks, Pop."

Chapter 59
Accidents Happen

Sat Sept 24, 1870 — Mon Oct 19, 2009

They broke camp shortly after sunrise. After breakfast Randall gave away his meager possessions, and Jeff distributed the supplies that Stormy had carried. Then they set off down the mountain at a walk. A horse could walk five miles an hour, and they were 20 miles from home, so it would take them about five hours once they got off the mountain.

Jeff felt overwhelming relief and smug satisfaction at having so quickly accomplished what he'd set out to do. The dreaded meeting had not unfolded as anticipated. His fears had been misplaced, and he struggled to reconcile his own memory of his father with the gaunt, aged character he'd found on the mountain. Randall was in a somber mood.

"What did you say Rosie's daughter's name was?"

"Sierra," Jeff said. "Rosie's going to be shocked to see you; she doesn't know about...about the time shift. We'll have to make up a plausible story about where you were."

Randall was silent, wondering how they could possibly explain his sudden reappearance after more than a year's absence. Eventually he asked, "Did you have a funeral? For your mom, I mean."

"No, you know Mom; she didn't want any fuss. We scattered her ashes under the laurel."

Randall waved to various pickers as they passed. Most were in the orchard now, the vines having already been picked.

Jeff asked, "What were you picking here? Carignane?"

"Probably. Martini has three varieties all planted together and calls the wine Chianti. How'd you know it was Carignane?"

"Shape of the leaf."

"You would've made a good farmer."

"We've been over all that before." Jeff said, a bit of annoyance creeping into his voice. "I'm not a farmer; I'm a journalist." Jeff left that statement hanging in the air for both of them to stew over for a minute.

"I just meant you know your subject."

"My subject? How is farming my subject? Did you ever actually read any of the articles you saved?"

"Of course. Think about it. Wine, food, travel. When you write about wine, you start out talking about the vineyards and how they're farmed. Your food articles and restaurant reviews are all about farm to table. Your travel articles always mention the regional cuisine. Maybe you don't see it, but to me you're like an art critic; he doesn't paint, but he knows art. You don't farm, but you appreciate the end result of proper farming — a good wine and a good meal. Of course I read your articles."

Jeff had thought he had nothing in common with his father, when in truth they simply came at the same subject from a different angle.

They followed the road down past the lake and into the cool of the trees beside Stevens Creek.

Randall broke the silence. "You said we don't have to worry about money. Have you found the goose that lays the golden egg?"

"Something like that," Jeff said, and explained.

Randall was amused. "What is it they say? One man's junk is another man's treasure."

At the base of the mountains they stopped to water the horses and eat a biscuit. Randall chewed slowly, staring at the creek.

"You all right, Pop?"

"It's funny how you can try to do the right thing, and it turns out all wrong. If I'd just confided in your mother...."

"I tried to hide it from Carolyn too, and I was caught out for a night. It would have been easier if I'd told the truth from the beginning."

"It won't be the same at home."

"No, but it's got to be easier than living in a tent."

"That's for sure," Randall admitted. "I'm looking forward to taking a warm shower every day, and opening the refrigerator any time I want." Then he uncharacteristically offered an observation. "You know, it's a more beautiful place without so many people in it. It's less complicated and there are fewer rules, but it's not easy getting by. You have to admire how self-reliant these people are. You have to admire their stamina." Then he muttered, "I wish your mother could have seen it."

They crossed numerous streams following the road southeast along the base of the mountains. At one point Honey became impatient and started to trot. Stormy followed suit and Randall cried out in panic as he bounced on the saddle. They went back to walking. About three hours out they came to a fork in the road. One road branched northeast to San Jose. Another bent southwest toward Pulgas. The road straight ahead continued southeast toward the bridge below Almaden winery.

"If we go through Pulgas we can stop for something to eat," Jeff said.

"No, let's keep straight; I want to get home."

A rider came quickly cantering down from Pulgas, turned toward Almaden and passed them without stopping. As he did he glanced back and did a double take. It was Nick Belfrage. Jeff waved and watched him enviously as he kicked his horse into a gallop, and soon disappeared into the distance. If his father could ride like that, they'd be home in half the time.

Bowman was waiting for them when they arrived at the bridge half an hour later. He sat on his dun mare at the near end of the bridge. How? Then he remembered Belfrage and silently cursed him. They stopped a hundred yards short. Jeff twisted in the saddle to look behind them and up the line of trees along Guadalupe Creek, gauging if there was another way over the creek. The problem was they couldn't do more than a fast walk, and Bowman would catch them no matter which way they turned.

"Crap," Jeff said.

"What's the problem?" Randall asked.

Jeff explained Bowman's obsession.

"We better talk to him," Randall said.

They plodded forward. When they were thirty feet from the bridge, Bowman called out. "Hey, old man, you cost me some money and it's time to settle accounts."

"I don't have any money," Randall called with annoyance, "and I don't owe you Jack. Now get out of the way."

Jeff squeezed his knees to set Honey in motion, but she didn't respond. Bowman turned his mare sideways, blocking the entrance to the bridge. He was a big man and accustomed to using his size to intimidate.

"You got your grapes picked," Jeff said. "What's your problem?"

"I had to pay more'n I oughta."

"Get the fuck out of our way, Bowman."

Bowman clucked his tongue. "Such language. This here is a toll bridge, and the toll is whatever you have in your pockets. And if that ain't enough, I'll take yer horses."

Jeff reached into his saddlebag and brought out the Smith & Wesson. "Move it."

Bowman didn't flinch; he sneered. "You ought not to play with guns, Junior." He began to withdraw a rifle from its scabbard.

Jeff had no wish to escalate the situation, but he didn't trust Bowman not to use the rifle. He thought a warning shot over Bowman's head might suffice, and squeezed off a shot. There was a sharp crack. The gun nearly kicked out of Jeff's hand. Bowman's horse half-reared, causing Bowman to let go of the rifle and grab at the pommel of his saddle. There was a whinny and a thud and hoof beats behind. Jeff turned to see Stormy running riderless in a circle, dragging Randall whose left foot was caught in the stirrup. Then she kicked to free herself of her burden. There was a sudden snap as one of her hooves connected with Randall's skull. His foot came out of the stirrup and Stormy bolted down the road. Randall lay motionless on the ground, his neck bent at an odd angle.

Jeff froze in disbelief.

"Ha!" Bowman crowed. "I couldn't o' done better if I pulled the trigger myself!"

In an instant Jeff was on the ground, his ear to his father's chest. Randall's heart was still beating, but he wasn't breathing. His eyes had rolled back behind half-closed lids. In a panic, Jeff pinched his father's nostrils and blew a breath into his lungs. The eyes fluttered briefly, and closed. Jeff blew another breath. He didn't hear the hoof beats until they hit the boards of the bridge. Bowman was leading Honey onto the bridge. In a moment, Jeff realized, they'd be stranded. He scrambled for the gun he'd dropped in the road and raised it in Bowman's direction. Just then Honey's head jerked up, and worried that he might hit the horse, Jeff raised the barrel, yelled, "Stop!" and simultaneously jerked off a shot. Bowman nearly fell out of his saddle from surprise. Dropping Honey's reins he gave his mare a vicious kick and the mare sprang forward like a thoroughbred out of the gate. Free and confused, Honey pranced first one way, then the other, blocking Jeff's aim until Bowman was too far away for an accurate shot. Jeff was astounded to hear Bowman cackling maniacally as he leaned low over his mare's neck on a tear down the road to the east. Then Jeff turned back to minister to his father.

Twenty minutes later a rider came from the north leading Stormy. He found Jeff in the dirt beside the body, head hung in despair, weeping like a child.

Less than an hour later Jeff rode past the Hermitage vineyard. Randall was slung over Stormy's saddle like a dead deer. His arms and legs hung loosely on either side, bound together by a rope under Stormy's belly to keep him from slipping off.

At the edge of the vineyard a long narrow dray was piled with grape-laden lug boxes. Owen recognized Honey and Stormy at a distance. It was only when they were closer that he made out Stormy's grim load. Then he rode out to meet Jeff, and quietly accompanied him back to the ranch.

August and Owen carried Randall to the parlor and laid him on the settee. The whole family soon gathered around like flies to carrion, drawn with solemn fascination to observe the husk of a man. Jeff, too, found it hard to believe that this body had been his father. Devoid of the soul that had animated it, Randall's body was now a strange and empty vessel outside of time. There was no future here. His hands would no longer grasp, his eyes no longer see. The light had gone out. *Elvis has left the building*, Jeff thought.

Middle school got out a half hour before high school. Jake found Jeff at the kitchen table.

"I thought you were on a trip?"

"It was cut short."

"You look terrible."

"I feel terrible."

Jake got some cookies and milk and paused before going upstairs. "Here, have a cookie, it'll make you feel better."

Abby was next to come home. She was both relieved and excited to see him. "Back so soon? Is Gramps…?"

"There was an accident," he said, and gave her the short version.

She hung on him, crying, until Carolyn arrived.

"Tell me," she said.

That evening after dinner, after commiserating with her husband, she laid out the facts. "If we bring him back, the coroner will declare him legally dead, which would free up the estate and make our lives a little easier. But it opens the door to inquiry, and I'm worried what they'll think. They'll start asking questions we can't answer. You can't say he fell off a horse, because we don't have one."

"We don't have to say anything. We can bring him back and leave him for someone else to find."

"And traumatize some poor child? Besides, you watch television. Don't they always figure out that the body was moved? They find some lint, or microscopic seed or something that leads right back to the perp."

"There is no perp."

"Well they don't know that. A blow to the head and a broken neck might look suspicious. I don't know. I just know we don't want police snooping around here."

She was probably overstating it, but it was true that if he suddenly showed up here dead, the authorities would want an explanation and they had none to give. It might look as though they had something to hide, even if the evidence suggested an accidental cause of death.

"What if we bury him in 1870," Jeff proposed, "and phone in an anonymous tip telling them where to find him?"

"Wouldn't it be obvious that the bones were too old?"

"Let them puzzle over it; the dental records will prove otherwise."

Chapter 60
A Question of Guilt

Sun, Sept 25, 1870 and Tues, Oct 20, 2009
through
Sun Oct 2, 1870 and Tues, Oct 27, 2009

There was only one place they could think to bury him that would remain both identifiable and unchanged for 139 years, and that was the churchyard in Pulgas. There was no longer a town by that name, and the church and clapboard buildings were long gone, but the old graveyard remained behind a strip mall. Carolyn took the day off and after she saw the kids off to school, she borrowed a dress and bonnet from Carrie, who was closest to her size. Dark blue was the best she could do, as Carrie had but one mourning dress. Jeff dressed in his black frock coat, hightop shoes and double-breasted vest.

They wrapped Randall (with his driver's license) in a plasticized tarp and a white sheet. Owen and Noah, given the solemn task of transporting the body, brought out Cider, a black Belgian, and hitched her to the dray. Jeff and August hitched the two mules to the buckboard. Then Jeff and Carolyn and the rest of the Kimball children climbed in the back and sat on the two benches facing each other.

"Sorry we don't have a buggy; seems like an extravagance on the ranch," August said.

"We don't go in for frills," Lydia said. There was a long pause during which she must have been thinking, for she then amended her statement. "Of course it's nice if you live near a town or a city. My father has a nice team and carriage."

"I've never seen the need for one out here," August added defensively.

They arrived early at the church to speak with Reverend Winters, who was sympathetic but disturbed. He had the Sunday service to perform and his gravedigger was gone for the day. In the end, Lydia and Carolyn took the girls and Charles to the German bakery and later to church, while August, Jeff, Owen and Noah borrowed picks and shovels and doffed their coats and collars and cravats to dig the grave. They'd hollowed out a three-foot deep space by the time the undertaker came calling, wondering what kind of casket they required.

"Simple pine box," Jeff said.

"Lined?" The undertaker asked hopefully.

"Just the box."

"You'll want the deceased embalmed, of course."

"No, no embalming." He'd taken another shovelful of dirt, before adding, "But we'll need a stone." He glanced around at nearby graves and pointed to a white marble headstone with a heavy base. "Something like that."

"What would you like carved on it?"

"Rand..." Jeff began to say and stopped. "Just put 'Joseph Rand. Died Before His Time.' That's all."

As soon as the undertaker had gone August said, "Joseph Rand?"

"I couldn't very well use his real name, now could I? How could my father end up in a century-old graveyard, under a stone with his name on it?"

"Good point."

The undertaker was soon replaced by the sheriff, who inquired about who was being buried, and the circumstances of his death.

"Just a simple accident, Monty," August said, lapsing into a lazy drawl. "Fella used to work for me. He was acomin' back from Saratoga, and his horse throwed him and broke his neck."

The sheriff frowned at the hole and nodded, seeming lost in thought. Then he looked directly at Jeff. "Ever find your pa?"

"No, not yet."

The sheriff watched them dig for a few minutes and left.

"He didn't even ask to see the body," Jeff observed incredulously.

"He knows me," August said, as though that explained everything.

The lack of bureaucracy was astonishing.

After services, they all gathered to hear Reverend Winters say a few words over the grave.

On the ride back from Pulgas the Kimballs were quiet and subdued, giving the Porters time to reflect and grieve. Jake was watching TV when they returned, and clueless as he was he picked up on the mood. "Why is everybody so mopey? Where were you?"

"It's been a long day," Carolyn said. "Just let it be."

He smirked and turned his attention back to the TV. "Be that way," he muttered. He had no patience for adult drama.

The next day, after everyone had left for school, Jeff bought a disposable phone with cash. He wrote a script, dialed the police, and handed the phone to Owen (for presumably the police recorded every call, and they could never mistake Owen's voice for his own). Owen read as instructed, "You have a missing person alert for Randall Porter. There was an accident. He was thrown from his horse and broke his neck. We buried him in the old Pulgas cemetery, under a stone that says Joseph Rand." After the call Jeff wiped the phone clean of prints and threw it in a dumpster behind a 7-11.

It wasn't until the following Monday that two San Jose police officers arrived to break the news. Lieutenant Hanes showed up a day later. He asked a lot of questions and seemed skeptical of Jeff's answers. "It's a very strange case. Did the officers explain how we found him?"

"Yes."

"The coroner's never seen anything like it. The dental records match, but he'd swear by the bones he's been dead for decades. Not only that — he was buried in someone else's grave, but there was no other body. It begs a number of questions, doesn't it? Like when did he actually die?"

"I'm sure I can't tell you. The last time I saw him was on his birthday last year."

"I hate loose ends," Hanes said in a tone that implied suspicion. He left unsatisfied, though unlikely to pursue the matter further; there were other more pressing cases.

Jake didn't understand the prevailing mood. He went to his mother one evening and asked, "Is there something wrong with Pop? Is he sick?"

"Your grampa has died," she answered, as though the source of his sorrow should be self-evident.

"But that was a year ago. Why is he upset *now*?"

Of course, she thought, Jake had long ago come to accept his grandfather's disappearance and presumed death, while to the rest of them it was fresh news.

"Maybe now that they found the body, it's hitting your father harder."

She searched her husband's placid face and worried that his calm demeanor hid inner turmoil. In truth he was more stunned than stoical.

"You did the best you could," she said.

"I know."

"It wasn't your fault."

"I know," he said again, and he did know.

He was reconciled to the immutable fact that in less than a year he'd played a tangential role in both of his parents' deaths. In his father's case he'd actually pulled the trigger, and though he might have been expected to feel guilt at his unwitting complicity, all he felt was sorrow. He couldn't turn back Time and change the course of events. Sometimes — often, it seemed — one thing lead to another in a way that was entirely random and unpredictable. The events kept playing through his mind in a continual loop. No one was to blame, or everyone was. If you could trace the trail parceling out blame along the way, they were all guilty. But feeling guilt for a lack of clairvoyance served no purpose. He could no more feel guilt for pulling the trigger, than he could blame his mother for turning off the light that had stranded his father in the first place. One might as well blame it on Fate for conspiring to put Nick Belfrage in their path. Fate: The past year had given him a window on the capricious nature of that fickle companion.

So much of life was determined by uncanny coincidence and unforeseen circumstance, one's destiny less a matter of will than of chance. You could be careful, but in the end something would get you, would get all of us — disease or accident, microbe or explosion. It was something we all knew and chose not to think about because there was nothing to be gained by it and no way to predict it. If August was right and there was a force directing the universe, its purpose and direction were lost on Jeffrey. Had he been religious, he might have blamed a deity, but he had no faith in any of the established gods. If there was a force that animated the universe, he thought, it seemed to have no moral purpose; it didn't care about good or evil, right or wrong, guilt or innocence. All it cared about was moving forward. Perhaps God was Time itself. Time was something to be grateful for, he thought, something he could worship.

Chapter 61
Ashes to Ashes

Mon Oct 17, 1870 and Wed, Nov 11, 2009
through
Fri Oct 21, 1870 and Sun, Nov 15, 2009

He was haunted not by guilt, but by the realization that he had never appreciated his parents as human beings in their own right, separate and apart from himself. All of their petty disagreements and daily annoyances were as insignificant as dust in the wake of their loss. His view of the world had suddenly shifted. In the stark vulnerability of grief, what he had once regarded as sentimental claptrap now seemed to reveal the true nature of what it was to be alive, and what gave life meaning: Love and connection, without which life would be unbearable, if not pointless. He awoke to a new appreciation for the gift of life and health, and felt full of love for the world, for the moment, and for the people with whom he shared this brief space of time on earth. It was an emotional, rather than logical response and was, perhaps, the closest he would ever come to understanding the religious frame of mind. It had taken the loss of his parents to open his eyes and heart.

His family, cognizant of his grief, allowed him extra hugs without complaint, and pretended not to notice when tears rolled down his cheeks, as they did at the most inappropriate moments.

Randall's ashes were delivered on a Wednesday. His will had specified that he wanted his ashes scattered in the ocean. Nonetheless, it seemed appropriate that at least a part of him should mingle with Virginia's ashes beneath the laurel, so Jeff privately tossed a handful at the roots and watered them down to a concrete-grey sludge. Then he wept silently, haunted by the memory of his father gasping his last breath, his slack mouth gaping open as though crying out a final, muted "No!" to the universe, his green eyes fixed and sightless beneath half-closed lids.

For years he'd felt in opposition to his father's expectations, only to learn at last that his father harbored no expectations, only concerns. And, Jeffrey acknowledged, his concerns were not unwarranted. He regretted now that he hadn't been mature enough to open a dialog years ago, but as his father was fond of saying, that was water under the bridge. He could only resolve to do better with his own children.

The following Saturday the Porters drove an hour south to Moss Landing at the mouth of the Salinas River on Monterey Bay. They ate lunch at Phil's Fish Market, then walked out on the nearly deserted beach where they mixed Randall's ashes with sand and built a sandcastle. When it was done, Carolyn took the kids to search for sand dollars. Jeff stayed to watch the tide wash the castle away. *Ashes to ashes, dust to dust*, he thought. *Bye, Pop; I wish I'd known you better.*

When they returned that evening Jeff crossed over and jingled the bell. Lydia opened the door.

"Is Gus around?"

"He's under the laurel, talking to Molly and Ivan." For a moment Jeff thought he'd misheard. Then she explained. "He goes out there sometimes when he's troubled. Sometimes he reads aloud from a book."

A neat, black, wrought iron fence enclosed the laurel. Two small, white marble headstones sprouted from the fallen leaves. August sat musing in the crotch of the tree.

"Hey, Gus. The check came from the auction house today."

"Do you know when we're all going to die?" August asked without preamble.

Jeff didn't answer immediately. He stuck his hands in his back pockets, stared at his feet and let out a deep sigh. "I don't think you really want to know. Besides, we can change the future if we know what's coming. Or try. We saved Carrie, didn't we?"

"That we did. That we did."

"You don't have to worry about anything for awhile yet."

"But you know when?"

"Yes," Jeff said, and then corrected himself. "Well not the exact time, but the year."

"A man shouldn't outlive his children," August said, gesturing toward the stones. "Ivan's birthday is coming up. He would have been Jake's age. You scattered the ashes today?"

"Yep."

"Our church doesn't allow cremation," August said.

"Times change. Speaking of which, starting November first we go off Daylight Savings Time. You'll only be 40 minutes earlier then."

"That's confusing," August grumbled. "They shouldn't play around with Time like that."

"It's all relative," Jeff said with a shrug.

"Don't it bother you? Knowing you'll never see your loved ones again?"

"Who says I won't?"

"But you don't believe in the Resurrection, for heaven's sake!"

"What's the Resurrection got to do with it? What comes after death is a great mystery. It could have nothing to do with religion. If there is an afterlife, it might be as natural as rain. I hope it is. It serves me to believe it is."

"But what if you're wrong? You've heard of Pascal's Wager? He said that since the existence of God is unknowable, it's only rational to bet that he exists, because if you bet against his existence and you're wrong, you have everything to lose and nothing to gain. But if you bet he does exist, you have everything to gain and very little to lose."

"That's assuming your god is the only one. There're plenty of gods to choose from. Anyway, it seems a Supreme Being ought to be smart enough to know when you're faking it. You can't will yourself to make a leap of faith. You either believe, or you don't."

"I look at the world around me and it's self evident." August slid off the branch and stepped out from under the tree. A quarter moon hung low over the western mountains, and unpolluted by electric light, millions of glistening stars studded the jet-black sky. "Just look at that."

"That's what I mean," Jeff said. "The problem with religion is it thinks too small. It's earth-centric. You want to see big? I'll show you big. Follow me."

Jeff led him back to his office where he flipped open a book of photos from the Hubble space telescope — galaxies galore.

August looked at the photos with a proper degree of awe and quoted Genesis: "In the beginning God created the heavens and the earth."

They could look at the same things, in the same way, and still come to different conclusions.

Chapter 62
Passing Time

It may be true that money can't buy happiness, but it can buy freedom (freedom from want, freedom from worry, freedom to pursue goals), and it can buy time. The time Jeff had spent in pursuit of money could now be spent with family and on projects of his own choosing. If his working life had once been shaped by the agendas and deadlines of others, now the trick was to find focus and discipline and pace on his own. He continued working on *Vineyard Seasons* and with Abby's assistance he began research for a book on old San Francisco.

As the holidays approached, he spent less time with the Kimballs, though he often found himself watching a second sunset from a rocking chair on their porch, and he sometimes stole up to the top of the cellar stairs to listen to the Kimballs sing around the piano in the evening. With the loss of Pop, there was no longer a pressing reason to go back, and the Kimballs were busy with the Harvest Dance, two barn-raisings, and putting up preserves.

Abby, whose new interest in History awakened an ambition to become a teacher, became a serious and diligent student, and spent her free time with Carrie learning to sew, knit, embroider, make candles and butter, preserve fruit, smoke meat, care for farm animals and cook from scratch. The experience profoundly altered her relationship to her contemporaries, whose view of the world began with their births, and ended with the meme of the day. When her aloof attitude naturally drew ridicule, she smiled mysteriously and turned away. She didn't mind. She had no interest in becoming popular, and no patience for her classmates whom, when she thought of them at all, she dismissed as vapid and lacking perspective.

She had an ongoing discussion with her mother about the way History should be taught. "In school all they teach us about is politics and war and memorizing dates. Who cares about that? I want to know how people lived." It also changed the way in which Carolyn taught her own classes.

Carolyn occasionally took Lydia to the supermarket to supply the Kimballs with paper products, deodorants, razors, pain relievers, toothbrushes and toothpaste, soap, cleaning products, spices, condiments, canned soups, pasta and tomato sauce. Soon encouraged by the abundance around her, Lydia asked if she might keep a few perishables in the refrigerator (cheese, meat, fish, milk and out-of-season frozen vegetables). It wasn't long before Jeff installed a small refrigerator in the root cellar that Lydia could access when the tunnel was open.

The Porters celebrated their Thanksgiving at Rosie's. "It would be too weird at the ranch without Mom and Pop," Rosie had pointed out, "and traveling with a baby is such a production." It seemed no less strange at Rosie's. She seemed to be trying too hard to fill the void left by their parents, and too distracted by her three children to relax, though Abby, much taken with Sierra, did an admirable job of helping out.

Twenty-five days later Jeff and Carolyn attended a second Thanksgiving at the Kimballs, a boisterous affair enjoyed by one and all.

Carolyn fretted about whether to invite the Kimballs to their Christmas celebration, but in the end it was decided that neither August nor Lydia would appreciate their profoundly secular version of the holiday, which was lavish by any standard. Nonetheless, when December 25th, 1870 finally arrived, they took great pleasure in presenting the Kimballs with an array of gaily wrapped gifts: zippered clothing, costume jewelry, a rifle with a telescopic site, binoculars, new boots, a magnifying mirror, books and various tools.

The years turned over to 2010 and 1871 respectively. Jeff began leaving the cellar light on during the day while his family was at school, to allow Lydia the use of the laundry and the luxury of an occasional shower.

On Presidents' Day in February, Carolyn and Jeff planned to take a long weekend to old San Francisco to gather more antiques, and to take photos that Jeff would render in black-and-white for a book of "newly discovered" historical pictures of the city.

Over dinner Carolyn announced to Jake, "Your father and I are going away for the weekend where we won't have cell phone coverage. If you need anything, ask your sister; she's in charge, so do what she tells you. She's agreed to cook dinners. For lunch I've stocked the fridge with frozen pizzas, and there's peanut butter and bread. Don't make a mess; clean up after yourself. I don't want any of your friends over while we're gone — which reminds me, Mrs. Kimball may come by to use the laundry. Don't bother her."

"I'll probably be at Teddy's most of the time."

"Be sure to tell your sister before you go out."

"I'm not a baby," Jake complained.

"Just do as I say, please."

Carolyn's worry notwithstanding, they had a good trip that she would ever afterwards refer to as their "Grand Adventure." Owen drove them to the train station. They left with one suitcase and a discreet point-and-shoot megapixel camera with a good telephoto lens. They returned with the suitcase, two hat boxes, a dress Carolyn couldn't resist, two trunks full of collectibles, and more than 400 photos of the doomed city. August and Charlie were waiting at the station when they returned at twilight. Back at the ranch, Lydia greeted them in the side yard, anxious to hear details. Carolyn was in a gay mood and full of stories to relate, but anxious to check on the children. "I'll tell you more later. Maybe you can come over after work tomorrow."

Jeff picked up the suitcase and hoisted the smaller of the two trunks onto his shoulder.

"I have so much to tell you," Carolyn continued, "so many questions. We..."

Jeff cleared his throat and nodded toward the house. "The door?"

"Oh, all right, just a minute," Carolyn said, gathering her hat boxes and the paper bundle that contained her new dress. "We'll talk later, Lydia."

August lit a lantern and led the way. "Leave the lantern on the barrel head," Jeff said; "I'll be back for the suitcase and the other trunk."

The passage behind the shelves was too small for the hat boxes, so Jeff put down the trunk and suitcase and muscled the shelves out from the rock until the opening was wide enough to accommodate the boxes. It was still too narrow for the trunk to fit through on his shoulder, so he boosted it onto his head and squeezed through.

"Help me out of this dress," Carolyn said, putting her purchases on the workbench. She changed back into a blouse and jeans and went upstairs. "I want to check on the kids, then I'm going to take a long shower."

Back at the Kimballs', Jeff struggled to heft the larger trunk to his shoulder. "Here," August said, "let me help you with that."

A little voice asked, "Are you goin' t' hell?"

"Charlie!" August admonished.

"Betsy said they was goin' t' hell."

"He's going home, Charlie."

Jeff smiled, amused. "Heaven and hell are all in your head, Charlie. Like Milton said."

"Just so," August said remembering the quote. "And didn't Jesus say, 'the Kingdom of Heaven is within you'?"

Together they lifted the trunk and carefully went down the stairs.

"I'll take it from here," Jeff said.

August helped him hoist the trunk to his shoulder. "Got it?"

"Yeah."

Jeff edged past the barrel, careful not to knock over the lantern, and with a mighty effort pushed upward while bending his knees to take the weight on top of his head. Then he ducked into the dimly lit chamber. The low frequency thrum filled his head. He straightened up and took a step forward. At that moment the top edge of the trunk struck the ceiling; he heard the sound of crystals bouncing off the floorboards; the load shifted backwards; the light flickered and the buzzing began to pulse like a beating heart. For a second he almost lost the load, then dropped to a knee to regain his balance. The light steadied and the buzz assumed a single low frequency hum again. He squeezed through the opening and dropped the trunk heavily onto the workbench, half convinced that he'd just destroyed the connection to the Kimballs' cellar. He re-entered the chamber and advanced cautiously along the floorboards, worried at what he might find. With his phone's flashlight he peered into the dark wine cellar. Everything was in its place as he remembered. Even so, in the back of his mind he sensed something was wrong; he just couldn't quite put his finger on it.

Upstairs he walked down the hall and found Abby and Jake watching a sitcom together. He called out to Abby, "Have you eaten?"

She looked up, distracted, and shook her head.

In the kitchen he rummaged through the refrigerator and cupboards, looking for inspiration. In the end he made a casserole of egg noodles, broccoli, cream of mushroom soup, tuna, and Parmesan cheese. When it was heated he called them all to the table.

That's when it struck him: The wine cellar had been pitch black. Had August taken the lantern? He was puzzling over this as they all gathered at the table. Carolyn prompted the kids for information about their respective studies. Then she turned to Jake and said, "Your father and I are going away for the weekend where we won't have cell phone coverage. If you need anything, ask your sister; she's in charge, so do what she tells you. She's agreed to cook dinners. For lunch I've stocked the fridge with frozen pizzas, and there's peanut butter and bread. Don't make a mess; clean up after yourself. I don't want any of your friends over while we're gone — which reminds me, Mrs. Kimball may come by to use the laundry. Don't bother her."

Jeff's mind reeled with deja vu.

"I'll probably be at Teddy's most of the time."

"Be sure to tell your sister before you go out."

"I'm not a baby," Jake complained.

"I'm not feeling well," Jeff said. He got up and went out the door to the side yard, where he leaned against the old oak, breathing the cold air and feeling his heart thumping against his rib cage. A small plane droned overhead, tracing a course toward San Jose International Airport. "Oh lord," he thought, "I've thrown us back."

The next morning Owen drove them to the train station.

As the train pulled out of the station Carolyn asked what was wrong.

"Nothing," Jeff said. "Really."

"You look worried."

"Just thinking."

"Think good thoughts. I want to have fun this weekend."

He did, and they did — again. It was a memorable and prosperous trip. But the thought kept playing through his mind: If he could send them back three days, might he be able to take them back farther?

Chapter 63
Managing Time

That only he was aware of the missing three days he chalked up to being inside the chamber when the shift occurred. On the train a second time, he found himself looking uneasily over his shoulder, glancing nervously across the street and across the hotel lobby, fearful of crossing paths with their doppelgängers, but it never happened.

Ever since he'd lopped off the branch that had crushed Carolyn's car, he'd been aware that they had the power to change the present by making changes to the past, just as saving Carrie's life had proved they had the power to change certain events in the past by actions they took in the present. But the real consequences were a complete mystery. Consider, for instance, the morning the limb fell on the Honda. He'd seen his family leave for school in the Subaru. The family that came back that afternoon in the Honda had no memory of the event. Did Time simply reset, or did it continue to flow and branch into other tributaries, other timelines? Did one timeline stop as another began, or did they run simultaneously? Could the family that left for school that morning still be out there in an alternate timeline? If so, was Jeff with them, or had they come home to find an empty house? The only thing he knew for certain was that his perception of reality bore him steadily forward on an unyielding current.

Up to now he'd had no qualms about the choices he'd made. He had done what he felt was right at the time, even when it hadn't always been the safest course. If safety were all he valued, he would have sealed the tunnel and left Pop to his fate. But he could no sooner have done that than he could have refused to drive Carrie to the hospital. It wasn't in him to refuse to. But things had become more complicated. The decision he now contemplated had murky ramifications. If he succeeded in disrupting the time continuum, in turning back Time (if the effect could even be replicated), how far might he be thrown back? Could he live with the consequences? The dangers were real and unpredictable and frightening. He felt like a cliff diver perched high on a ledge over black water, hoping against hope that the pool below was deep enough.

If knocking a few crystals awry had caused the Wheel of Time to slip a cog, what would it take to slip back three weeks, or three months? Could he relegate his parents to the past, when he had a chance to resurrect them? And what if he succeeded in bringing back the dead? Maybe he should leave well enough alone. It might save them from a future of debilitating illness and dementia. Or perhaps that was just a convenient excuse. He didn't want to believe that his reluctance to take the dive was the result of selfishness. Though he may have been deluding himself, he thought the events of the past seventeen months had made him a better person, a better husband, a better father. But what kind of son would he be if he abandoned his parents to oblivion?

At the end of the first day of that second trip to San Francisco, Jeff sat on the end of their bed in the Occidental Hotel and flipped through the photos he had surreptitiously taken with the little point-and-shoot camera. It was the same camera he'd taken on the first trip, and it had been in his pocket when he'd been thrown back in time. The photos from the first trip were still there. He thought about the months he'd tried to keep the tunnel a secret and the strain it had put on his marriage. "I need to show you something," he said.

When he'd finished with his story and the questions it brought up, Carolyn said, "If it comes down to a choice between your parents and our kids, the kids win hands down — they're the future. Your parents already had their time."

"You're right."

Still, losing his parents hadn't been a choice. Leaving them behind now, when he had a chance to save them, *was* a conscious choice. It felt like turning his back on floundering swimmers.

"Because anything could happen. Who's to say if you'd come back? I won't have our kids growing up without a father."

"Right."

"And I like where we're at now. I like where the kids are at. And you're happier, too."

He had to admit that he didn't really want to go back to the way things were, back in the employ of a failing magazine, scrabbling to make ends meet.

They were silent for a long while as he sorted through the photos. She peeled out of her dress and sat in bed with a book, but she couldn't read. She said, "We have a lot to be grateful for."

"Um-hum."

A minute more passed before she said, "Damn it."

"What?"

"I can't get over the feeling that we are where we are because of your parents' misfortune. We're living in their house, for heaven's sake. We have money in the bank because of them."

"I know."

"Then we have to try. But you're not going anywhere unless we all go together. If worse comes to worst, at least we'll be together."

At the train station Jeff urged August to hurry home. "We have some urgent business." So August urged the mules into a trot. When they came to a halt by the front porch, Jeff told August that he'd come back for the trunks later. In the dining room he turned on his flashlight and led Carolyn into the wine cellar. In the tunnel he paused to point out the spot on the ceiling where he'd knocked off the crystals. "See? If we were just reliving the same moment, this wouldn't have happened yet. This is in our present." They stepped into the root cellar. "Don't bother to change," he said, and they marched upstairs.

"We're home!" Carolyn called.

"Come join us in the kitchen!" Jeff added.

"Whoa!" Jake said, spying his father in a bowler and his mother in long dress and floral hat. "Where'd you get the costumes?"

Abby came in, book in hand.

"Jake, we've been keeping something from you," Jeff said.

"You're not going to tell him!" Abby protested.

Her mother patted her arm. "We have to, Sweetie."

"He's too young; it's too big a secret!"

"It's the biggest secret on the planet." Jeff went on. "We wanted to wait until you were older, but something's come up."

"This is a mistake," Abby said.

Jeff held up an index finger in the universal sign of *Patience*. "You know about the CIA, the NSA and black ops?"

Jake's eyes went wide. "You're spies?"

"No, listen. You've seen movies where Nazis drag people out of their homes and shoot them." Jake nodded. "You know what atrocities terrorists are capable of."

"Sure," Jake said.

"Now put all of that together and that's the danger we'd be in if anyone found out. Our lives depend on it. So the first rule is — you can't tell anyone about this, ever. Not even your best friend. The second rule is — this ranch is off-limits to anyone from the outside. You can tell your friends your grandmother is sick and needs quiet, or you have a looney uncle — whatever. Understood?"

Jake nodded solemnly.

"Keep quiet and we'll be safe."

"I will, I promise."

Then Jeff, with a few photos for illustration and a few asides from Carolyn, laid out the situation and their plans to knock off more crystals in an attempt to jump back in time. They had no idea what to expect. It might be a fruitless exercise. It was possible that nothing would happen. It was also possible that their world would be irrevocably changed.

Jake took the revelation in stride, of course he did; his world was already so filled with fantasy that he accepted it all as a matter of course. But Abby protested, "This is stupid. It's way too dangerous."

"What if it was you?" Carolyn asked. "If you died and we had the chance to bring you back, don't you think we'd try? Don't you think we owe your grandparents that much?"

"No, I'm sorry, I don't. They were old. Jake and I have our whole lives ahead of us. We have no idea where we might end up. It's too risky. They wouldn't want us to take that risk."

"Don't be so wussy," Jake said.

"Don't be a macho jerk!"

"Enough!" Carolyn cried. "No name calling. That's not helping."

"I agree it's a dangerous proposition," Jeff said, "but your mother and I have talked it over, and we think it's the right thing to do."

"As long as we go together," Carolyn added, "we can manage, no matter when we end up."

"I just don't think we should rush into anything," Abby said. "What makes you think you can just knock some crystals off and hope to get back to the right time? That's just crazy; who knows where we might end up?"

"She does have a point," Carolyn admitted.

"I'm open to solutions," Jeff said.

"We should be scientific about it," Jake said.

Monday after school Jeff and Carolyn took Jake to the Kimballs' side and sat down with August to explain their scheme. On the way back through the geode, Jeff showed the kids where he'd knocked the crystals off.

"So if it worked once, I was thinking it would be worth trying a second time."

"Maybe if you changed the voltage it might...." Jake suggested.

"I'm not an electrician," Jeff interrupted. "I wouldn't know how."

Abby gazed up at the ceiling. The copper wire had been stripped of its insulation a few inches before entering the back of the light fixture. The wire was affixed to the ceiling with hot glue and pressed tightly between protruding crystals where, she could now see, the bare wire might come into contact with a thread of gold that wove web-like throughout the crystal matrix.

"Gold conducts electricity, doesn't it?"

"It does."

"Could the wires be in contact with the gold?"

"Like a giant printed circuit," Jake said.

"There's one way to find out," Jeff said. "But the voltmeter is in *our* wine cellar, so we have to turn off the light."

They all filed into the root cellar. Jake went up the stairs and turned off the light. Then Jeff used his flashlight to cross to their own wine cellar and retrieve a voltmeter. Jake turned the dome light back on and they all stepped back into the geode.

The voltmeter had two probes which together measured electrical current. Jeff pressed one probe against a skein of gold near the dome light, another to a thin thread of gold four inches away. The dial on the voltmeter lay inert.

"Guess not," Jeff said.

"Try again," Jake said. "There could be other paths."

Jeff moved the second probe and the meter twitched. He tried once again with no result. On the fourth try the meter's dial came alive.

"Voilà!" Jeff said. "There's definitely an electrical current."

"So if that's what makes the time shift," Jake began, "and it takes us back 140 years…"

"…then theoretically, changing the circuitry should change the time interval," Jeff finished.

"But that still doesn't solve the problem," Carolyn said. "You still can't control it."

"Maybe I can."

Chapter 64
The End is the Beginning

It took more than a week to prepare. Jeff informed August what they were up to. As a precaution, Carolyn finagled some antibiotics from her doctor by saying they were traveling to the Amazon and wouldn't have access to healthcare. Jeff converted $500,000 into twenty-six pounds of gold bullion.

When the morning finally came, Jeff got up early only to find Abby already in the kitchen. She looked up from her History book and said, "I made coffee and bread. The bread's still warm."

He poured himself a mug and pulled up a chair.

"I don't know why they always teach History from a military point of view," she said. "The most powerful people in history aren't politicians or generals, they're the people who control transportation and communication."

Jake led Buster into the kitchen on a leash. "What smells good?"

"Your sister made bread."

"Sweet," he said, pulling off a hunk.

Carolyn came in — wearing a nondescript long skirt and white blouse, her hair still wet from the shower. "What a beautiful morning."

"I wonder," Abby continued, "what the next big technology will be. I mean, where do you go from planes and the internet?"

"Renewable resources," Carolyn said, opening the refrigerator. "Cheap energy."

"I'd invent a personal dirigible," Jake said. "It would be powered by solar cells, so it would be free to run, and it would be totally safe because, if you bumped into something, you'd just bounce off."

"Does everyone have their packs?" Jeff asked.

"Wait a minute," Abby said. "I've been thinking: What if we go back too far, to before the house was built. Won't we be trapped underground?"

Jeff shook his head. "I've considered that, and I don't think we could go back any further than the day Pop installed the dome light. Maybe a year and a half. Of course the interval between our time and the Kimballs' might change. We won't know until we try."

It had been decided that they would have to limit their packing to one daypack each, and one large duffle bag for the family.

In his backpack Jeff put the gold; printed photos; a collarless, white shirt; three boxer shorts; three pairs of socks; four double eagle gold pieces; four power bars; a turkey sandwich; a bottle of water; and the Smith & Wesson.

At 8:30 a.m. they descended the root cellar stairs and entered the geode — first Jake and Buster, then Abby, Carolyn, and Jeff standing an arm's length apart on the two 2X12 planks that now bowed under so much weight. The low frequency thrum filled their ears. A million crystals seemed to hold and amplify the dim dome light so that, in places, the walls of the chamber emanated a purple glow. He had no idea where to start.

"Okay," he said, "wish us luck; here goes." He held a three-foot-long length of copper wire, stripped of insulation on either end. He looked to his family, who all looked back at him in anticipation. He held one end of bare wire against a thread of gold close to the dome light and pressed it into place with putty. He did the same with the other end, then looked at the time and date displayed on his iPhone. "No change," he muttered.

"Maybe time doesn't change while we're in the geode," Carolyn suggested.

Jeff stepped into the root cellar and checked again. "Still no change."

He stepped back into the geode, pulled off one end of the wire, and moved it to another golden thread half way up the wall. Then he pressed it into place with the putty. For a millisecond the dome light blinked.

He stepped out and refreshed his phone's screen. "1:52 p.m., January 29th, six weeks ago. Let's check."

They filed out into the root cellar and went upstairs, fearful of meeting their doppelgängers, but the house was empty.

"Doesn't matter *when* it is," Jeff said. "We're *always* in our present."

"But we already lived this day," Abby said. "Shouldn't we be here?"

"It's creepy," Jake said.

"I think," Jeff said, "that when Time slips a cog, it simply erases everything forward of that moment. It's the ultimate do-over."

"It erased us?"

"In a manner of speaking. Imagine the geode is like a car and the odometer in that car counts off time instead of mileage. If we drive a mile up the road and stop, then back up a mile, the odometer turns right back to where it started, even though we remember the whole trip."

"We don't really know what we're doing, do we?" Abby said, more of a statement than a question.

"Not a clue," Jeff admitted. "But it seems like we're safe enough as long as the shifts occur when we're in the tunnel...in the car, so to speak. We just have to stay together."

Jeff led the way back to the cellar where they filed back into the chamber.

This time he picked a spot closer to the dome light. They all looked at him expectantly. "Ready?" he asked. They each nodded. He affixed one end of the wire to a patch of gold in the ceiling, and the other end to a thread on the wall. The light pulsed, a piercingly high pitch replaced the low thrum, and a ripple seemed to pass through the geode from the ceiling. It ran down the wall in front of them, passed beneath them, and rose up the wall behind them. As it reached the ceiling again, the dome light flickered and from its base crackled thin threads of electric blue light that ran outward along the skein of gold veins. There was a final sizzling sound. Then the dome light popped and they were thrown into utter darkness.

"Holy shit," Jake said in awe. Buster growled.

"You still think we're safe in here?" Abby asked doubtfully.

"I think we blew a fuse," Jeff said. "The cellar light is out, too."

"Turn the flashlight on," Carolyn said.

He fished the phone from his jeans and flicked on the flashlight. "Let's see where we are," he said. "Don't forget your packs." He slung his pack over his left shoulder and the duffle over his right, and stepped into the root cellar.

"Watch your step," he cautioned, shining the light at the floor as first Carolyn, then Abby exited the chamber.

When he turned to set the duffle on the workbench, he swung the flashlight away, momentarily blinding Jake who bumped into his sister who dropped her backpack on her toe. "Ow! Watch what you're doing, you klutz!"

"It's not like I did it on purpose!"

Buster barked. A moment later the door at the top of the stairs opened. They all looked up to see the silhouetted figure of a woman.

"Randall, are you down there? I heard a dog."

"Mom?"

"Gramma!" the kids yelled and rushed up the stairs.

"What are you all doing down there in the dark?" She flipped the switch off and on. "The light doesn't seem to be working. Why didn't you call? Is everything all right?"

"Oh, yeah," Jeff said, mounting the stairs behind Carolyn, "everything is just fine."

When they were all in the kitchen in the morning light, Virginia surveyed their faces — happiness, excitement, astonishment, glee and tears. "What has been going on? What were you doing in the dark?" Abby leaned over and kissed her cheek. "Look at you!" Virginia said, puzzled. "Are you wearing heels?"

"Look how different it all is," Jake said to Abby.

"What are you doing here in the middle of the week?" Virginia asked, looking thoroughly confused. "When did you get a dog?"

"I'll explain it all later, Mom," Jeff said. "First, where's Pop?"

A cloud passed over his mother's face and she pursed her lips. "Your father...," she began. "I don't know, exactly. He's taken to walking, lately. Or at least that's what he says he's been up to. I don't know," she sighed. "He's rarely home when I wake up."

Jeff smiled knowingly.

"Look at the floor!" Abby exclaimed to Jake. "I forgot what it looked like."

"What are you going on about?" Virginia scoffed. "It's the same as always."

Carolyn snatched the newspaper from the kitchen table and handed it to Jeff. The date read June 3rd, 2008.

"You want to tell me what's going on?" Virginia asked.

"All in good time," Jeff said, giving her a hug. "Love you, Mom. I gotta replace a fuse."

Abby, Jake and Buster went upstairs to see what their bedrooms looked like before the renovation.

The fuse box in the laundry room was the old fashioned kind that he'd had replaced during the remodel. There was, indeed, a burned-out fuse. He rummaged through the junk drawer for a replacement.

"I don't have anything for lunch," Virginia said, then reconsidered. "Maybe macaroni and cheese, or soup. I'll check the cellar," she said and opened the door — the wine cellar door, which was not yet sealed shut. Carolyn followed.

Jeff replaced the fuse and returned to the root cellar. The bulb that hung from the ceiling now illuminated the shelves and workbench. He hurried downstairs to check on the dome light. The tunnel was still in the dark. There was a light on the other side and he could see Virginia and Carolyn passing before the opening.

"I could use your help," he called to Carolyn. "We'll be up in a minute, Mom."

The glass dome that protected the bulb was hinged on one side and held in place by a single brass screw. She held the flashlight, while he backed out the brass screw and unscrewed the bulb. It was an ordinary 60-watt bulb. He found a replacement in the workbench.

"Okay, here goes nothing," Jeff said, reaching up to screw in the bulb.

Carolyn grabbed his arm. "Wait! We're in here. What happens when the light goes on? Are you sure we'll still be here, in this time?"

"Good point. We better get the kids."

He ran up to the kitchen, passed his mother and met the kids and Buster just coming down from upstairs. "Time for a family conference in the cellar." They all filed back through the kitchen.

Virginia sighed with resignation and said, "I wish you'd tell me what's going on. Lunch will be ready in ten minutes."

Back in the cellar Jeff said, "It occurs to me that when I screw in this bulb we're not really sure what'll happen. I don't want us to get separated, so we should all be in the tunnel when I do. There's also every possibility we'll just blow the fuse again, because with the current placement of the wire, it blew before."

They gathered up their packs and the duffle and re-entered the dark tunnel holding hands. "Ready?"

Jeff screwed the bulb into its socket. The dome light blinked on and the black curtain instantly appeared on the far side of the tunnel. For a moment the light dimmed, then came back steady, and the low thrum that once filled the chamber like an engine in the bowels of a ship, now changed to a higher pitch like the sound of a distant beehive.

He replaced the brass screw that held the glass dome in place, then stepped into the root cellar to check the date and time. "The same," he said. "Let's check the other side."

He had no idea if the interval between the times was the same or radically different. He only knew that the wine cellar they now filed into belonged to August. "Stay here," he said. At the top of the stairs he let himself into the dining room, crossed the room and let himself out the side door by the laurel.

August was sitting on the low branch above Ivan's marble headstone. "I was hoping you'd stop by before you left. I never got to tell you how much it's meant to me to see into the future. I still don't know what God meant by bringing us together, but I guess that's His business."

"It's meant a lot to me, too."

August slipped off the branch and the two men shook hands.

"Good luck," August said.

"Thanks, Gus. Good luck to you, too. Can you remember enough of what you read to stay out of trouble?"

"It's all up here," August said, tapping his temple.

Jeff thought about the names on the obelisk. If he weren't here to save them, Lydia and Emily would be gone before the close of 1872. "You might want to send Lydia and Emily on a long trip next year. Maybe you can all visit your folks in Pennsylvania." *It might be enough,* he thought.

Jeff turned and retraced his steps to the wine cellar. To his family he said, "Follow me," and led them all back through the tunnel to the root cellar. "Here in our root cellar we're back to 2008. Over there," he said, gesturing toward the wine cellar, "it's still 1871. Gus didn't even know we'd left."

"What happens if we pull off the wire?" Carolyn asked.

"My guess is we'd go back to 2010."

"We can't do that," Abby said. "Gramma and Grampa are both dead in 2010."

"I thought you were against taking the risk."

"That was before I saw Gramma again."

"If we leave it like it is, you'll have your gramma back. We still have the condo. You'll have your old friends back."

"I don't care about them anymore. And I'll bet Gramma would let us move in with her."

"Maybe. We'd still have to do a remodel, add a bath."

"What about Grampa?" Jake asked.

"It's complicated. When Pop left this morning, the time interval between here and the Kimballs was 139 years and 25 days. Now it's...I don't know. Carolyn, what date is it again?"

"June 3rd, 2008."

"So that makes it...about 140 years and nine months. Unless we can find a way to change the interval back to the same as it was before we...." Jeff stopped. "Before we...," he muttered again, as a solution presented itself. "There might be a way, but it means we'll never be able to get back to the 2010 we knew."

"It doesn't matter," Abby said, "as long as we're all together."

On the pegboard above the workbench Jeff found a coil of piano wire and a wire cutter. He cut a four-foot long piece and made a hook on one end. "Here goes," he said. He reached the piano wire into the tunnel, hooked the other wire and pulled it free. The dome light flared a little brighter, but otherwise nothing seemed to have changed.

Jeff reached out for Carolyn's hand and led them all through to the wine cellar again, and this time the low thrum was back. "Stay here while I check upstairs. I may be a few minutes."

Once again he let himself into the dining room and let himself out the side door by the laurel. Behind the house Lydia and Carrie were beating a rug that hung between two posts, with a younger Emily toddling at their heels. Betsy was sweeping the porch. Owen led Honey from the barn.

Jeff strolled nonchalantly forward and caught Lydia's eye. She startled easily, as usual.

"Excuse me, ma'am, I'm looking for my father — Randall Porter?"

She shaded her eyes with her free hand and said, "You mean Randall the handyman? He's 'round here somewheres."

Jeff found him in the barn loft, carpenter's belt bristling with tools, using a ratchet wrench to attach a large steel block to a stout beam. As Jeff came through the door Randall glanced down, did a double take, and nearly fell off his perch.

"What are *you* doing here?"

Jeff beamed — with happiness, with relief, with satisfaction. "I've come to take you home."

"Does your mother know?"

"Not yet."

"Let me finish up here."

A few minutes later they stood in front of the barn, out of earshot of the others. Randall asked, "How long have you known? How'd you find out? "

"That is a very long story."

"Give me the short version."

Jeff gave him the six-sentence version.

"Do you know the danger we'd be in if word got out?" Randall asked.

"I do. We've already had this conversation. Let's go home, Pop. I'll give you the whole story over a drink or two."

As they started across the side yard they heard the pounding of feet and turned in time to see a boy streak past with a dog at his heels. Far behind, August was sauntering out of the apricot orchard. The tow-headed, barefoot boy, whom Jeff knew only from a photo, stopped at the pump to draw water for the dog. Randall led Jeff to the pump to introduce them. Jeff shook Ivan's hand. "You look just like the son of a friend of mine. He used to go barefoot like you."

"I don't like shoes."

"Neither did he. They lost him to a rattlesnake. Good pair of boots would've saved him."

"I've told him as much," August said, coming up from behind.

Randall introduced the men.

With the pretense of washing his hands, Jeff surreptitiously pressed his boot into the mud beside one of Ivan's footprints and made a mental measurement.

They said their goodbyes and snuck back into the house by the side door.

"Why did you seal shut the wine cellar door?" Jeff asked.

"Seal the door? I haven't..."

"But you will. That is, you did."

"I've been thinking about it. I just found out about that."

"About what?"

Randall wiped a sleeve across his forehead, taking a moment to decide how much he wanted to tell. "You know when we go through the geode from our root cellar we end up in the Kimballs' wine cellar, right? And when we go from the Kimball's wine cellar to our root cellar, we go forward."

"Right."

"Well, a couple of weeks ago I was doing some work at the Kimballs', and I ran out of paint. I knew I had half a can in our wine cellar, so I came back and went down to get it. Then I remembered a tool I wanted from my workbench in our root cellar. I'd left the dome light on, so I just went through the geode. Only it wasn't *our* root cellar anymore. It turns out, we go forward too."

"Into the future?!"

"Yes."

"And?"

"Trust me; you don't want to go there. These are the good old days."

For just a moment after returning to his parents' kitchen, Jeff considered walking around to the wine cellar and stealing through to take a peek, but quickly dismissed the idea. The future would always be there beckoning, but it could wait. For now, he had a past to reclaim.

The next evening he carried a pair of boots up the wine cellar stairs to the Kimballs' dining room and set them on the sideboard. He could hear Owen and Carrie singing "I Dream of Jeanie with the Light Brown Hair" to the simple accompaniment of Lydia's piano. He listened until the song ended, then he tucked a note into the top of a boot: "For Ivan. Stay safe."

Author's Note

I've always been intrigued by the way technology affects how we live and how we perceive the world. Born in the 1880s, my grandparents grew up at the end of the horse-and-buggy era. But the world they came into was not the world they left. They saw the invention of the automobile and airplane, radio and refrigeration, motion pictures and television, antibiotics and the atom bomb, electronics and rockets. When my grandmother died in 1967 astronauts had orbited the earth and were aiming for the moon.

Of course technology isn't the only thing that defines an era. Politics, economics, changing mores, fashion, art and natural disasters all play their part in shaping an era. My grandparents also saw the end of the Victorian era, the Jazz Age, the Space Age, two World Wars, a Depression, the fall of European monarchies, the end of Colonialism, the right of women to vote and desegregation.

This book took 21 years to write. It stalled at about 150 pages. I started over several times, changing voice and point-of-view, and each time I stumbled into a blind alley. It began as Time Trials in 1994, and the protagonist, Peter Porter, was President of InfoCompression Systems. To present a contrast to the past, I wanted him to be at the cutting edge of technology. By the time I found my story, in 2011, the internet and the digital revolution made 1994 look as ancient as a phone booth. Times do change.

However, as fascinating as it is to compare and contrast different eras, that doesn't make a story. Some people are natural born storytellers. I'm not one of them. I am a writer with over 500 wine, food and travel articles to my credit, but that's a different discipline than being a storyteller. If given free rein, I'll blather on interminably until the reader loses interest. I've written other novels, but each one was a struggle wrestled out of multiple drafts. I was working on an early draft of *With Artistic License* when I came across *Story Engineering*, by Larry Brooks. Brooks gave me the tools to finish that novel, and a framework and method with which to create an engaging story in *Time Management*. I recommend his book to those of you who may be similarly afflicted.

ABOUT THE TYPE

The main body of text was set in Adobe Caslon Pro. Caslon is a typeface first designed in 1722 by William Caslon. It is a Transitional serif typeface, and is similar to its descendants, such as Cochin introduced in 1912, and Times New Roman introduced in 1931. The title and chapter headings are set in Goodfellow.

Cover photo: Scott Clemens
Front cover design: Scott Clemens
Back cover design: PerryElisabethDesign.com

49797460R00231

Made in the USA
San Bernardino, CA
05 June 2017